They risked their lives
to find a priceless book only to
discover treasure
most dangerous
in a
crossed
ve....

"Sweet God Above."

Somehow she was crushed against him, her heart lurching as he brought his mouth down against hers. Chessy forgot to breathe, forgot to think, forgot everything but how perfect it felt to touch him so. As a *woman*, not as a girl.

"God, Chessy—" The fingers buried in her hair tightened convulsively. *"More."*

The raw hunger in his voice was the sweetest joy of all. When he had kissed his laughing courtesan, his voice had held no such tremor, no loss of clarity or resolve. He had been in total control.

But he was not in control now. Far from it. One kiss had left him breathless, reeling, urgent.

Chessy was glad of that. Very, very glad.

From the rear stairwell came the scrape of boots. A moment later Swithin appeared. He stopped abruptly. His eyes narrowed as he studied the pair motionless by the wall.

"By God, if you've so much as laid a hand on her, I'll—"

Chessy silenced him with one trembling gesture. "Lord Morland is just leaving, Swithin."

Morland's face hardened. He looked like a man ready for a fight—maybe even *looking* for a fight. "Oh, Cricket," he whispered softly, "it's not going to be nearly that easy. Not this time. I'll be back."

"Come back and you'll find only more of the same!"

Morland's brow rose mockingly as he stared down at her flushed cheeks, at her dewy, well-kissed lips. "Is that a promise? If so, my sweet, it will be my keenest pleasure to return."

And then, with a perfect bow, the earl was gone.

THE BLACK ROSE

"As powerful, emotional, and sensual as *Defiant Captive*, *The Black Rose* will delight and enthrall Ms. Skye's fans . . . cleverly constructed, riveting, and breathtaking, *The Black Rose* ensures Ms. Skye's reputation as a writer of strong romances for . . . readers who like their heroes bold, their heroines daring, and their sex hot."

—*Romantic Times*

DEFIANT CAPTIVE

"Christina Skye's sure hand skillfully blends the delightful Regency period with searing sensuality. I highly recommend *Defiant Captive* to readers who like their heroes bold and dominant."

—Virginia Henley

"From page one, Ms. Skye captures the essence of London as it could only have been in 1816. . . . This book is an absolute must to tuck in with the suntan lotion for a steamy romantic holiday. 5 Stars!"

—*Affaire de Coeur*

"*Defiant Captive* is compelling, sensual, and impossible to put down . . . her fresh approach to an emotionally charged love story will quite simply thrill readers looking for a spellbinding read . . . Christina Skye holds you in her grasp until the very last word and you'll wish there were more. Don't miss *Defiant Captive*."

—*Romantic Times*

Also by Christina Skye

DEFIANT CAPTIVE
THE BLACK ROSE
THE RUBY

EAST OF FOREVER

Christina Skye

Published by
Dell Publishing
a division of
Bantam Doubleday Dell Publishing Group, Inc.
1540 Broadway
New York, New York 10036

ISBN: 0-440-20865-3

Printed in the United States of America

Published simultaneously in Canada

August 1993

10 9 8 7 6 5 4 3 2 1

This book is dedicated to four very
special booksellers:
Judy Spagnola, Ellen Fuscellaro, Kevin Beard,
and Thea Mileo

And to Kathryn Falk
Publisher, thinker, creator, and
catalyst *extraordinaire*

The reasons why would fill up this page,
So instead I'll just say thank you . . .

WITH DEEPEST THANKS:

to Helen Woolverton for tulips and windmills
and any number of fascinating
historical tidbits;

to Barbara Harkins for her unflagging aplomb
in the face of relentless deadlines;

and to Ronald Spangler, Deputy Executive
Director of the Mayor's Commission on Literacy
in Philadelphia, for graciously sharing his
expertise.

PART
ONE

North
of Night

1

London, England
May 1819

The woman in the black silk mask stood in the darkness, her breath checked, her hands trembling faintly. She looked neither right nor left, trying not to think of the sheer drop to the cobbled street sixty feet below.

Slowly her toes edged along the gutter. *Careful . . .*

Around her the wind howled and clawed. But she only tightened her focus, ignoring the twigs and gravel flung in her face.

Carefully she tested each tile, easing toe and cloth-covered sole forward.

One step, then another.

At the rear gutter she stopped, her slim shadow lost among the forest of black chimneys outlined beneath the moon. She crouched down, studying the next obstacle, blocking out a wave of fear.

Her violet eyes narrowed. It was six feet to the neighboring roof. Yes, it would be hard, very hard. For anyone else it would be *impossible*.

3

But not for her. Not for the woman called Midnight, who had studied with the monks of Shao-lin, living masters of the ancient Chinese art of *wu-shu*.

Slowly she came to her feet. She cast out her fear, replacing it with images of soaring cranes and gaily colored kites flapping over the Forbidden City.

From her pocket she tugged a silver star with an inch-thick strand of silk anchored at its center. With a graceful flourish, she tossed the disk.

Moonlight flashed off silver. Soft hissing filled the air. A second later, the star landed with a faint clatter.

She played out the silk, letting the weighted end fall until it wedged against the angled base of the chimney opposite.

Perfect!

Now came the hard part. She glanced swiftly down at the street. No one about.

Now. It had to be *now!*

She eased to a crouch, knees flexed, one foot braced on the slanting roof behind her. Gathering her breath as Abbot Tang had taught her that summer long ago, she sprang.

Her hand-stitched soles thrust at the tiles. She hurtled out into chill space, where she hung breathless for an instant high above the street.

Her arms craned forward. Her slender fingers dug at the air. Dear Lord, what if she'd miscalculated?

The next instant, her right foot struck home and her shoulder crashed into the steep tile slope. Immediately she drew herself as small as possible to avoid watchful eyes.

Safe! So far, at least . . .

Inching behind a chimney in the lee of the wind, the woman called Midnight focused her attention and listened for the sounds of alarm.

But the night was silent except for the rush of the wind and the distant click of a passing carriage. Beneath her the house was quiet. Faint squares of light pooled from the lower floors, casting dim rectangles against the cobblestones.

Carefully the slim, black-clad figure tugged at the

silken line and secured it around the chimney. Then
she began to climb, moving hand over hand along the
taut cord until she reached the ridge of the steeply
angled roof.

There she saw her goal.

Breathing a silent prayer of thanks, she made her
way to the second window from the left, eased open the
pane, and slipped inside.

As she'd expected, the house was empty.

Swiftly she crossed the hall, her cotton soles soundless on the thick Aubusson carpet. She was nearly at
her destination when a faint trill of laughter drifted up
the circular staircase at the far end of the corridor.

"Really, my lord, you are entirely too cynical. It
comes from being so cossetted and admired, I fear. And
you've drunk far too much brandy already tonight. Any
more, and you won't be able to—"

Here the husky female voice broke off with a high
squeal of laughter. The silence that followed was punc-
tuated by the rustle of silk and a low, breathy moan.

Midnight eased back against the wall. *This* was
something she hadn't planned for! The townhouse's
occupant, the voluptuous Germaine, was supposed to
be engaged at Vauxhall this night. Damn and blast,
what was the woman doing at home?

As if in answer, the breathless voice rose once more.
"You are a great deal too naughty, my lord. You pledged
to take me to Vauxhall, and I am not at all happy."

A man's voice came to Midnight then, a voice low
and smooth as silk. A voice rich with humor and yet
dark with command. She started slightly at the sound,
chill air pricking at her neck.

The Earl of Morland.

Midnight felt her breath catch. A queer pain invaded her heart.

Tony . . .

But she fought to sweep away painful memories.

And this was Germaine, the latest high-flyer under
his protection, so rumor had it.

The voices grew louder. Midnight's uneasiness

turned to positive panic. Dear Lord, they were coming *up*!

Swiftly she made for the first door to her left. She slipped inside and slid back against the wall.

Slippered feet scuffed up the stairs, soft against the thump of male boots.

No harm done, Midnight thought. She would simply wait here until the two finished their business. Easing the door closed, she stood motionless with her ear pressed to the wall. ·

"Really, my lord, what ideas you do take into your head! I vow, you put me to the blush!" A low giggle. "Monstrous naughty, it is!" Another giggle, rather more heated this time. Low male laughter rumbled up the stairwell, followed by the sharp *whoosh* of damask.

Sweat beaded up beneath the black mask hiding Midnight's face. Damn and blast, why didn't they just get *on* with it!

But it appeared that Germaine's companion was not to be hurried. Dark and commanding, his voice echoed upward, coming closer by the minute. "I absolutely insist, my sweet. The thought of you in pearls and lace garters is really too enticing to forgo."

"And what else shall I wear, my lord?" It was a sultry and quite calculated whisper.

"Why, absolutely nothing, of course."

Midnight's heart began to hammer. For the hundredth time this day she cursed the bad joss that had brought her to this chilly, foggy city on such a desperate mission.

Brought her *back*, she corrected herself. She had been born here, after all. But London held no place in her memories now. Soon after her birth her father had taken her off to Macao, the Portuguese colony bordering the mysterious Chinese empire.

It had been only months after her mother's death, in fact.

Midnight's eyes closed. *Don't think about that either. . . .*

Think of the waves studding Macao's outer harbor as you last stood in the Praia Grande, with the wind ruffling your hair. Think of the swallows sailing against the Peking sky, clay whistles singing as they soar over a sea of glazed tile.

Slowly her balance returned.

But the raw determination remained, for the Macao-bred beauty knew she must not fail. Not while her father's life hung suspended on the strength of her skill and concentration.

Satin whispered against broadcloth and wool. Germaine moaned. "Oh, yes. Please, my lord. L-like that!"

Fire and fiddle, they were right outside the door!

Midnight barely had time to slip behind a lingerie-covered screen before the door opened. Light swept through the dressing room, cast from a single candle. Germaine appeared, captive in the embrace of her well-born lover.

And then the Earl of Morland, too, came into view.

Midnight froze. Around her all time and movement seemed to slam to a halt.

So long. And yet not long enough to dim the pain, to ease the bittersweet memories.

He was still strikingly handsome, she thought. His hair was longer than was currently fashionable, falling thick and straight, the color of antique bronze. His lips were full and faintly cynical, and his smile was wickedness itself as he placed the candle on the mantel and turned to rummage through the gaudy waterfall of feminine apparel dangling over the ornate lacquer screen.

Tony Morland. The love of her life, who had wooed her and then betrayed her ten years before.

Only inches away, hidden behind the screen, Midnight waited, afraid to breathe, afraid to move.

Afraid to do anything except concentrate on being completely invisible.

A frothy length of sheer Valenciennes lace went flying over the carved black lacquer. "Yes, I rather like this one." Morland smiled darkly, holding a cloud-soft peignoir up to his mistress's lush form.

Dumb with embarrassment, Midnight closed her eyes, her ears, her every sense.

But nothing helped. Every illicit rustle struck her with the force of an earthquake. Every moan touched her skin with flame.

Silk pooled onto the floor with a soft hiss.

"Lovely. Now, I think, for the garters . . ."

Midnight tried to force her thoughts far away, tried to keep her heated gaze from the narrow crack between the panels of the screen. But she failed utterly.

Long, powerful fingers flexed and then inched skillfully over pink skin and heated thigh.

"Tony! Oh, p-please."

"Of course, pet. But first things first. . . ."

Midnight heard a high squeal of delight, saw the flash of eager, grasping fingers. "My lord! But these are from the matched set we saw at Rundell and Bridge's last week! Eliza will be *green* with envy!"

"I'm delighted to hear it," the earl said dryly.

Behind the screen the rustling reached a furious level. Whatever this matched set was, they were provoking a great deal of ardor, Midnight thought angrily. All this commotion for a few jewels! Why couldn't they just take themselves off to Vauxhall and their idle pleasures, as any ordinary couple would do?

But the Earl of Morland, she was about to discover, was anything but ordinary when it came to seduction, and he had a reputation for infinite patience—when it suited him, of course.

And just now it suited him very well.

"Ah, how wonderful is this thing called greed," the earl mused. "I adore how it spurs your passionate, conniving little heart, Germaine." Once again his voice held a hint of dryness.

"G-greed? It is no such thing! It is only—I am overcome. Yes, positively *overcome*. With your gift. And with you too, of course," Germaine added hastily.

As if to prove it, her pink fingers attacked the earl's exquisitely tied neckcloth. A moment later the pristine linen slid free and came flying over the edge of the screen. Midnight barely checked an instinct to duck out of range as the white linen fell against her shoulder, still warm with the heat of its owner's body.

Her breath caught at the contact.

She felt her cheeks flame red. Dear God, she could hear every sigh, every breath. And any minute they were going to—

She went completely still, summoning the image of a lotus opening in pristine silence amid a dawn garden. Petal by white petal, the perfect bud unfolded while green leaves spread like a carpet, rocked on cool waters.

Better. Yes, much better.

Low giggles filled the confined space, along with more rustling of cloth. Suddenly a jacket of blue superfine struck the screen, rocking the whole lacquer frame.

Midnight's fingers squeezed to fists. She caught her breath as the elegant panels swayed wildly, then finally righted themselves. Meanwhile the sounds behind the screen were making her restless. Each rustle and sigh made her tremble, made her think of hot, hungry skin and slow, searching kisses.

They made her remember how Morland's lips had felt on *hers*, one night ten years before. . . .

"Oh, T-Tony!"

"*Ummmmm*, have I told you lately that your skin is like silk? That your eyes are like—"

"Emeralds?" came the hopeful reply. "Very *large* emeralds? With matching diamonds?"

Dry laughter spilled through the small room. "What a greedy minx you are, to be sure." Abruptly the earl's voice trailed away.

Curious in spite of herself, Midnight inched closer to the crack in the screen. In taut silence she watched the tall Englishman, white shirt opened to midchest, ease back the sheer lace folds of his mistress's peignoir around a very fetching necklace of diamonds and a perfect, marquise-cut emerald.

The trespassing Midnight felt her face flush beet-red as Morland's strong fingers feathered over the taut peaks outlined beneath Germaine's sheer lace garment.

"T-Tony! You know how dizzy I become when—oh! *Tony*, you must not!"

But these breathless protests were ignored, as they were meant to be. The earl's head dropped. He parted the froth of ruffles with his mouth and eased one lush pink nipple between his teeth.

Stricken with embarrassment, Midnight jerked her head away. This was impossible! It *couldn't* be happening.

Eyes squeezed shut, she concentrated on repeating the opening lines of Sun Tzu's classic study on the art of war. But she got only as far as "All warfare is based on deception," before her concentration failed. The sensuous rasp of skin upon skin could no longer be ignored.

A raw cry tore from Germaine's lips. "Oh, Tony, yes! You know how I adore—" The next moment her limp body slid senseless down the wall into Morland's arms.

Only inches away, Midnight fought to ignore the strange pounding of her heart, the odd tremor in her legs. It was merely the logical resolution of opposites, she told herself sternly. Merely the male element of yang seeking its natural complement in the female element of yin.

Oh, absolutely! And you're the Queen of Sheba, a mocking voice answered.

"I believe we may now dispense with *this*." Wolfish laughter filled the room.

"My *lord*!"

"Exactly what I was thinking, Germaine. Shall we adjourn to—er, more comfortable quarters?"

About bloody time, Midnight thought irritably.

From the room next door came the rustling of bed linens. "I really must remember to give you emeralds more often," Tony murmured.

His partner answered with a soft moan. The bed creaked.

"Now, my sweet. Open your eyes!" Morland ordered hoarsely.

"T-Tony!" It was a cry of amazement, of shock, of wanton delight.

The sound made Midnight flush to the very ends of her toes. *But they were—*

A moment later Germaine's voice quavered off into

nothing, and her virile protector groaned out his own dark release.

Hidden and silent, Midnight fought to calm her pounding heart. After all, she had more *important* things to worry about than the sexual gymnastics of the depraved English aristocracy!

Only somehow she couldn't quite convince herself of that fact. . . .

The silence stretched on. Finally Midnight came to her feet, stretching like a cat. Carefully she inched from her hiding place. A velvet curtain was flapping idly in the breeze as she slipped into the neighboring room. And there she froze.

It was an elegant room with silk-covered walls, gilt-framed prints, and a pair of velvet armchairs.

But it was not the furniture that drew Midnight's eyes. It was certainly not the prints, which were of minimal artistic merit.

It was the two bodies sprawled amid rumpled sheets that held her fascinated gaze. The blond woman lay snoring slightly. Her companion slept with his back curved away, his pillow scrunched into a lump beneath his neck.

Spellbound, Midnight found her eyes tracing the muscled arms down to a bronze chest dense with darker bronze hair. His leg was bent, disappearing into the mound of white bed linens. His calves were lean but rope-hard.

He was utterly beautiful.

With a professional's keen eye, Midnight studied those hard inches, wondering what sort of exercise the earl pursued to keep his muscles so well toned. In her innocence, she did not consider that the activity she had just observed might provide a great deal of exercise.

A gust of wind tugged at the curtains. The man on the bed shifted slightly, dragging a hand across his forehead and then turning to his back.

Midnight's face filled with heat.

Dear Lord, he was completely—that is, the man had absolutely no—

Redfaced, she wrenched her gaze away. Somewhat unsteadily, she set about searching the room, from the cluttered dressing table to the half-opened armoire in one corner.

But she found nothing of interest, certainly not the priceless, jewel-laden book she had come in search of.

A raw sense of futility washed over her. One more wasted night; one more useless effort. Would she ever find the fabled Chinese pillow book, or was this whole search just a maniacal game devised by one of her father's enemies?

He had enough of them, Lord knew. There was that Portuguese merchant who had never forgiven her father for tricking him out of a cargo of stolen ginseng. Never mind that it hadn't been *his* to begin with. And of course there was the Frenchman who had tried to make off with the accumulated artifacts of a whole season's digging in the islands off the South China coast. She and her father had come close to losing a boatful of fine Yuan blue and white porcelain and some remarkable Han jades before they discovered the man's treachery.

The Frenchman had lost three teeth in the fight that ensued. His back would wear the mark of her father's lash even longer, she suspected.

Had one of *them* kidnapped her father for revenge?

She still had no answer, though she had thought of little else since the news of her father's kidnapping had reached her three months before. Hard on the heels of that had come the first in a series of anonymous notes directing her where to search for the sole object that would buy her father's freedom.

The price? One book. A book worth a man's weight in jewels. Diamond-encrusted and bound in gold, with illustrations designed to kindle the jaded appetites of an emperor who had tasted every pleasure and possessed every treasure known among the four seas.

A pillow book, said to be a thousand years old, each exquisite page detailing a different path to erotic pleasure. And that book was the one thing that would buy her father's release.

Midnight frowned. Misbegotten son of a turtle! *Where was the blasted book?*

At that moment the bed creaked, interrupting her musings. The earl muttered hoarsely and rolled to his side. A hard bronze thigh slid from the white linens. His long fingers flexed, cupping the pink-tipped breast only inches from his face.

Sighing, Germaine snuggled closer.

Dear Lord, not again! Had the two been taking Siberian ginseng?

Caught between fury and something far more painful, Midnight turned and slipped back along the wall toward the door. Her cloth-soled slippers moved in silence. She was halfway down the corridor when she heard a low curse.

"Damn it, Germaine, it's freezing in here! Did you leave another window open downstairs? You'll have every cutthroat and gallows-bird in London at the door."

Her heart pounding, Midnight darted to the window, eased up the pane and slid one foot onto the roof.

The curtains tossed about her head, blanketing her in silence.

Which was why she didn't hear the movement behind her sooner.

"Got you, you bloody little beggar!" Granite fingers seized her shoulders and hauled her back over the windowsill. "Thought it was all bob, did you?"

Midnight's breath flew out in a *whoosh*. The next second she was wrenched backward and crushed against a wall of muscle.

Hot, straining muscle.

Wildly she twisted, trying to fight free of the hard fingers digging into her wrists.

"Bring a candle, Germaine!"

Down the hall came the rustling of slippers. "I—I'm coming."

Midnight closed her eyes, trying to forget that her captor was wearing only the thinnest of dressing gowns. Dear God, she could not let him discover her identity!

Catching a long breath, she went completely slack, not resisting even when her captor's hard thighs pinned her to the wall.

"Give up, do you? Damned good idea, unless you want your arm broken. What did you take, you little thief? Silver? One of Germaine's bracelets?"

Deftly, impersonally, his hard fingers probed Midnight's silk-clad thighs and plunged beneath the waistband of her loose-fitting trousers. Her breath caught when one hand eased lower, tracing her flat, tense belly.

Catching a ragged breath, she struggled to remember some of the more pungent expressions she had learned at that little waterside tavern near the Macao wharfs. "Eee, what yer bloody doing?" she blustered, twisting wildly. "Take yer bleedin' 'ands off 'r me!"

"Cocky little bantam," her captor muttered. "But you'll find I'm no easy cull." His hands left her waist and tugged at the silk mask covering her face. Frowning, he searched for some knot to remove it.

"*Ooooow!* 'urt me, yer did!" She made herself go completely limp. Her breath wedged in her throat as she felt the heat of his thighs, all hard, corded muscle locked against her own. Dimly she was aware of a mingling of scents—of spicy soap, the floral odor of a woman's perfume, and the salty tang of sweat.

She had never been so close to a man wearing so little before, never felt every ridge of rib and thigh.

Tony . . .

Midnight's eyes filled with tears.

Her captor frowned. "Germaine! Bring the candle, damn it!"

No time, Midnight thought wildly. Fear slammed through her. *Forget him, unless you prefer to spend the next five years of your life dodging rats in a squalid English prison!*

At that moment her grim-faced captor eased the silk belt from his dressing gown.

Midnight saw his intention. "I ain't got nothin' of

yers, mister, 'onest I don't! Only a bleedin' 'andker-
chief." She schooled her voice to a low whine. "Just one
paltry bit o' silk. No call to truss a fellow up like a
bleedin' chicken for a bit o' nonsense like that!"

"Nonsense, is it? You'll spend five years at Newgate
for that nonsense, you beggar! Or maybe it'll be transportation for you."

Transportation? Dear Lord, what hope would her
father have then? With a gasp she let her body go
completely limp again.

"What the devil! Get up, damn it! You'll not escape
by—"

But the earl got no further. The next second his silk-
clad captive twisted desperately and darted between
his legs, kicking wildly. And then, with one well-aimed
thrust, Midnight drove him to his knees.

As he bent over in pain, Midnight exploded down
the hall, lunged through the open window, and slipped
out onto the roof.

Before her, the rising moon cast a silver nimbus
around the dome and dark spires of St. Paul's.

Beautiful, she thought dimly.

And unless she was very, very careful, it would also
be the last thing she ever saw.

Jacketless, hair disheveled, the usually immaculate
Earl of Morland raced down to the end of the yard.
Even as he watched, a slim figure eased past a chimney
and disappeared down the far slope of the roof.

Smothering a curse, Morland leaped the low
wooden fence and plunged down the narrow alley behind the townhouse. At the cross street he stopped,
watching spellbound as a small black smudge moved
toward the edge of the roof.

In silence the slender figure inched forward. His
toes rose gracefully, and his arms swayed like the slow,
graceful sweep of wings.

It was almost impossibly beautiful, Morland
thought dimly. Something tugged at the back of his
mind, some connection he knew he should be making.

But fear and brandy had numbed his usually acute senses, so that all he could think of was that small, dark shape perched so perilously at the ridge of the roof.

A gust of wind swept up from the street, tossing gravel and leaves in Morland's face.

Above in the darkness the slender arms floated outward, fingers carving elegant swirls against the smoky London sky.

By God, the whelp was well trained! Almost Asian, those movements were. And he might just make it, Morland thought, feeling a surge of reluctant admiration.

Without warning a clay tile tipped forward, then burst free, clattering down the roof and exploding to powder on the cobblestones sixty feet below.

Damn, the little fool would end up like that tile if he wasn't careful!

Atop the roof the slim shadow eased to a crouch. With one fluid movement he jumped.

Morland watched, his heart in his throat, as the small black smudge sailed over the street and plummeted onto a facing pediment. There the figure hung, fifty feet above the ground, while his slim legs dug into the stone face, vainly seeking a foothold.

"Hold on! There's a ledge to your left!" the earl shouted.

A moment later, the small feet began to kick, rocking back and forth until they gained enough height to snag the edge of the narrow stone shelf.

For the first time Morland breathed freely. He looked down, frowning at the scratches his nails had left on his palms.

What in the devil was the matter with him? Why did the struggles of one wretched little housebreaker bother *him*?

After all, it had been a long time since Anthony Langford, Lord Morland, second son of the now deceased sixth Duke of Morland, had felt any real concern for anyone or anything.

Even for himself.

And he wasn't about to start now, the azure-eyed peer thought grimly.

No, this was strictly business, for the little miscreant would be perfect for his plans. The devil was as nimble as a cat! Now all Morland had to do was track him back to his den.

But when the earl turned, it was too late.

Only shadows marked the rooftops, and nothing moved among the chimneys that rose in cold spikes against the moon.

Fighting down keen disappointment, Morland slowly walked back up the street.

He still couldn't believe he'd lost the boy. Deep in thought, he paced up the steps toward Germaine's townhouse.

His hands were on the polished brass knocker when he heard a low chuckle at his back.

"Can my eyes be right? Isn't that a friend of yours, my sweet?"

Frowning, Morland spun about. He broke into a smile as he saw his old friend, Viscount Ravenhurst, standing at the foot of the steps.

The ex-naval officer's dark brows rose in a questioning slant. "What, not going to ask us in?"

Morland made a great business of eyeing his friend, then turned his keen gaze on the slender lad in black breeches and cloak at Ravenhurst's side. "Perhaps. But not, I think, until I've met your friend."

With a tinkle of laughter, the viscount's companion doffed his tricorn hat and made Morland an elaborate bow. "What, have you forgotten me so soon, my lord?"

Morland's brow furrowed. There was definitely something familiar about that voice. . . .

"You *have* forgotten!"

Morland's eyes widened. "*Tess?* Is that you? Good Lord, Ravenhurst, what are you about to let her go careering off like this? She's—she's wearing breeches!"

The tall ex-naval officer merely smiled. "*Let* her? Since when have I had a say in anything the hoyden does? No, she's a rare and stubborn female, this wife of mine." His cool lapis eyes softened. "And I find I wouldn't have it any other way."

Morland dragged his fingers through his hair in exasperation. Damnation, he had *work* to do! Not that Ravenhurst would know that, of course, for Morland's latest mission was entirely secret. His most challenging to date, it involved a diplomatic mission to the Emperor of China himself.

Tess studied the house thoughtfully. "Is it true then? Do you truly house your mistress here, Tony?"

Morland went absolutely still. He seemed to be having trouble finding his next breath. "Well, er, that is to say—"

"Have you mirrors on the ceilings? I've always imagined that mirrors were de rigueur in a place like this."

Morland made a strangled sound that might have been curse or groan.

From the floor above them came the crack of a door and a muffled female voice. Morland felt sweat break out on his forehead. "Well, I wouldn't dream of keeping you. You both must be chilled through, after all."

The viscountess swept her auburn hair over her shoulder. "Bah! London life is deucedly confining! And I did give up running with the gentlemen, you know. A woman must have *some* pleasures, after all."

Her husband smiled faintly. "A woman *does* have some pleasures. And she enjoys them very much, as I recall."

The viscountess flushed slightly. "Besides *those*, my love."

Morland cleared his throat, feeling very much an eavesdropper. At that moment a querulous voice echoed down the staircase. "Tony? Are you there?"

Tess's eyes widened. "Oh, is that Germaine? Might I speak with her? Perhaps she could tell me—"

Ravenhurst bit down a laugh and caught his wife about the shoulders. "I'm afraid it is time we were going, my love."

"But—"

"We've plagued Tony long enough, I think." The viscount turned his wife about and steered her toward the street.

She sighed loudly. "Very well. I can see when I'm outgunned and outmaneuvered. But I still don't see why—"

"Then I shall have to explain it to you, shan't I?" The viscount's eyes darkened. He ran his finger gently across her cheek.

"*Hmmmmm.* Yes, I should like that, I think." Tess turned and smiled at Morland. "Give my regards to Germaine, won't you? And don't overtax yourself."

The earl frowned, feeling as if he'd just been knocked down by a runaway hackney.

Viscount Ravenhurst slanted his friend a sympathetic look. "Never mind, Tony. You'll get used to it. All of us do, I daresay."

As the pair walked off, arguing happily, Morland ran his hand through his disordered hair. What else could possibly go wrong this night? he wondered.

He soon found out.

Germaine met him at the stairway, elbows akimbo, green eyes glittering. "The little wretch got away, I see. Well, are you going to stand there daydreaming all night or come up to bed?"

Morland found himself thinking of the slim figure whom he'd pinned to the wall. Yes, there was definitely something odd about the little cutpurse, something he ought to have known.

"Tony?"

Morland studied Germaine's irate green eyes. "I rather think I must be off, my dear."

"At this time of night? You've another mistress, that's what it is! How dare you? How bloody *dare* you!"

A hail of angry words followed Morland to the foyer. A second later, he heard a thunderous crash.

It was the scandalous print of the pasha and the six harem girls, he decided stoically. Germaine had smashed the thing three times already.

He closed the door carefully behind him, savoring the cold, clean air that swept his face.

Yes, the luscious Germaine had *definitely* begun to cloy, he decided as he hailed a hackney and made for home.

Barely four blocks away, a nondescript carriage careened to a halt. A moment later, a small figure swathed in a black cloak darted across the cobblestones and jumped inside.

Immediately the carriage resumed its progress down the quiet street.

Closing her eyes, the carriage's sole occupant drew her first steady breath of the evening.

Too close. Dear God, each time it grew more dangerous.

Midnight's slim white fingers trembled, stripping away her silken mask to reveal creamy cheeks and high, arched brows the color of a raven's wing. Clear violet eyes assessed the line of blood trickling down her fingers. She must have done it when she'd jumped the street.

Yes, too bloody close by half, Midnight thought.

But what choice had she? Last night's note had been very specific, both as to where she must go and what she must look for.

And what would happen to her father if she refused.

Her high, proud brow creased. Where was it, this ancient book she had crisscrossed the roofs of London in search of? And why would men go to such desperate lengths to possess it?

But she knew the answer to *that* question, at least. It was the pictures that gave the pillow book its worth; exquisite hand-painted designs that glowed with jewellike clarity.

And the pictures all had one theme.

Pleasure. Pleasure in a thousand different shapes and guises. Pleasure in all the myriad ways that man and woman might share it.

Midnight's beautiful violet eyes darkened. She had actually seen the book once, long ago, when she and her father had visited a wealthy Chinese salt merchant during one of their secret trips to Yangchow. But she had been only twelve then, and the pictures had merely confused her.

Now, however, their purpose was crystal clear.

Midnight frowned as something warm and sticky trickled down her arm. Pain jabbed at her shoulder.

Outside, the dark streets rushed past in a blur.

One more night lost. . . .

She thought of her father, and her full lips began to tremble. Only her raw determination kept back the tears.

Damn and blast, she couldn't go all jelly-kneed now!

With a jerk, the carriage came to a halt. She realized they were home.

Home? She almost laughed at the idea. This smoky city would never be home.

Her eyes traveled over the narrow two-floor townhouse with the drab curtains at its unlit windows. No, this was no more than a stopping place while she carried out her covert mission to free her father.

Only then could she *really* go home, back to the white sand beaches of the South China Sea, back to the thousand little islands where the water ran azure and the sky seemed to go on forever.

From the front of the carriage came the creak of wood.

"You coming out o' there, Miss Chessy, or do I have to come fetch you out?" The carriage steps were let down with a bang. "Damned crazy schemes, the lot o' them! Don't know what you'd have done if that earl caught you. Aye, he's a knowing one."

Francesca Cameron, known to her English friends as Chessy and her Chinese friends as Midnight, managed a defiant sniff.

"Aye, and I don't care to think what your father's going to say when he finds out I let you do such a damned fool thing!"

"*Let* me?" Chessy stared at the groom and jack-of-all-trades who had been with her and her father as long as she could remember. "Why, you couldn't stop me if you wanted, Swithin. I'd have thrown you before you

took your first step. Besides, you love the old reprobate
as much as I do."

At that moment the moon slipped from behind a
cloud, revealing the silver tears that covered Chessy's
cheeks. With an angry sniff, she turned, brushing the
hot drops away.

Swithin frowned. "So I do, Miss Chessy. But it's a
damnable business just the same." The leathery-faced
servant shook his head. "And right now I can't shake
the feeling that things are only going to get worse."

Fifteen minutes later, Chessy stripped off her silk
jacket and smoothed an herbal paste on the jagged
wound across her elbow.

Grimly she slipped out of her black trousers and
attacked the thick twill that bound her chest. Round
and round the fabric came, then spilled onto the
threadbare carpet.

She stood for a moment, pale skin prickling in the
cold air. Suddenly she recalled the sounds of the man
and woman behind the screen.

The dark whisper of skin upon bare skin. Hot
sounds. Hungry sounds.

Love sounds.

Heat rushed to her face as she remembered how
Morland's strong bronze fingers had inched over Germaine's ivory skin, pushing her to pleasure.

Her own skin began to tingle, oddly flushed.

What would it feel like to be touched that way, to
be *wanted* in that way?

Enough!

Red-faced, she spun about, jerked her lawn nightgown from the bed, and yanked it over her head.

She had done no more than throw back the bedcov-
ers when she heard Swithin come pounding up the
stairs. Outside the door he paused. "Miss Chessy? You
awake still?" His voice was unnaturally tense.

Chessy ran to the door and threw it open.

"I just found this one." The old servant shoved a
piece of folded paper into her numb fingers.

Slowly she opened the note. It was written in the same spidery handwriting as all the others.

She pushed it back to Swithin. "Please—just read it. I—I can't—" Her voice caught.

The servant frowned. " 'Morland,' " he read. " 'Tomorrow.' "

Tall and silent, the man sat in the firelit darkness, toying with a silver-handled knife. His intelligent face was marred by a vast cynicism. "So you think you have information that might interest me?"

The woman's beauty was striking. "I am certain of it."

A glitter of something that might have been triumph or excitement lit his eyes as he contemplated the beautiful woman before him. "Why should I trust you? I hardly know you, after all."

"Because we are after the same thing, you and I. It is revenge that drives us both."

The man's eyes narrowed, catlike. He touched the cold muzzle of the pistol hidden in the pocket of his jacket and thought about killing her. She knew too much already, and he was not a man who took others into his confidence. Not *ever*.

But as he studied her lush curves, he decided there were better things he could do with a woman of her beauty than kill her. Perhaps she could even be forced to aid his own goal of revenge.

And in the meantime he might amuse himself with the ripe pleasures of her body.

He saw her head turn and knew where she was looking. He smiled coldly. "So my pictures amuse you, do they?"

He ran his finger slowly across the row of a dozen portrait miniatures. All were of the same man, captured at different ages and in different dress.

But all were of *Tony Morland*. The man who would soon die at his hand.

The woman laughed softly. "Yes, I enjoy them immensely. I didn't think—"

"Nor shall you start thinking now, my beautiful Louisa. I shall decide what is to be done to Lord Morland. And when and where. Do you understand me? I shall tolerate no interference in my plans."

Lady Louisa Landringham tossed her hair over her shoulders and shrugged. "As you will. As long as he suffers, it is enough for me. He has humiliated me, and no man may do *that* without punishment."

"I shall remember that, my dear." The man turned and studied the row of smiling portraits. "It is good to know the face of one's enemy, don't you think?" He chose one of the miniatures and pulled the canvas from its gilt frame.

Then with a harsh curse he tossed the painting into the fire.

Orange flames hissed up, enveloping Tony Morland's smiling face in smoke. Black splotches ate through the canvas as the fire took hold.

The man at the grate laughed as Morland's face was slowly consumed and then crumbled away to ash.

"It pleases you?" he asked the woman behind him.

"Vastly."

He released his knife and reached for his cravat. "Come here and show me how much."

2

"**A** pillow *what*?"

"A pillow book. Used all the time in Asia, so I'm told." The bushy-browed admiral scowled down from the head of a highly polished walnut table.

His tone was decidedly huffy. Even at the best of times he did not care to have his ideas attacked, but when the person doing the attacking was that brash upstart Atherton, then the whole thing was past tolerating!

At the far end of the table, the object of the admiral's anger sniffed contemptuously. "Bloody nonsense, if you ask me. Nothing but a lot of damned suggestive pictures."

"I don't believe I *did* ask you, Atherton. In fact, I distinctly remember the board deciding last month that *you* were not to be involved in any further decisions made in this chamber."

"Begging your pardon, but I rather think that recommendation was rescinded." The Earl of Morland stood at the opposite corner of the room. His eyes were sharp, in contrast to the studied casualness of his bear-

25

ing. "Surely you remember that message, Admiral.
Last week, I believe."

Oh, yes, the admiral did. Most precisely. He was not
likely to forget the moment when his own clear wishes
had been countermanded.

But he did not care to admit it in front of that snake
Atherton. "Message? What message?"

Lord Morland's sapphire eyes narrowed. He noted
the admiral's growing flush. "Ah, how remiss of me. I
fear you must have been at Carlton House at the time,"
he said smoothly.

"Last week, do you say?" The admiral sniffed.
"Wonder that I could have missed it." He slanted Atherton a disapproving glance, then turned back to the
earl. "But enough about that. I want to hear more about
this pillow book."

At the foot of the table, Atherton shifted about,
mumbling irritably.

Morland heard every word. "So you think it's a pack
of nonsense, Atherton? Nothing but suggestive rubbish?
Now there I really must disagree. Much more than
suggestive, I assure you. Such books leave very little to
the imagination. They are meant to be used as guides,
after all."

"Aye, guides to hellfire and damnation, by the
sound of it!" This salvo came from Lord Warburton,
whose views were notoriously rigid.

Lord Morland smiled faintly. "By our way of thinking, perhaps, Warburton. But there are those who say
physical union may be a technique to ecstasy—to religious salvation. When it's done properly, of course."

The other men around the table burst into sharp
guffaws.

"Never heard of such a thing!" Atherton barked,
tugging forcefully at his waistcoat, which had ridden
up over his protuberant stomach. "I'm beginning to
think you've had your head in those heathen books of
yours too long, Morland. The whole idea is bloody
preposterous!"

With a lazy smile Morland moved slowly across the
fine old Persian carpet, his limp only slightly visible.

He poured himself a drink from the rosewood side table and then for long minutes stood silent, staring out at the comfortable bustle of Great George Street and Westminster Bridge.

It was all so normal, he thought. So different from the noise and color and clutter of Macao or Cairo.

But it was no more true or correct, just for being British. Not that Morland could ever say as much to these men.

He twirled his drink for a moment. "Do you really think so, Atherton? For myself, I suspect I've read far too little. And on that I suppose we shall always disagree. But as it happens, I've brought a pillow book with me. Not in the grand style of the treasure I've been describing, of course. Mine lacks the pearls and jade and the master brushstrokes of that ancient masterpiece. Still, it will serve well enough to give you an idea of what we're talking about."

Carefully Morland reached down for the leather satchel by the table, then drew out a silk-bound volume.

If the committee was going to back out, he thought grimly, he wanted it to happen now and not later. Better to let them know *exactly* what they were getting into.

The men around the table leaned forward. Slowly Morland settled the silk-covered folio before them and slid open the ivory clasps, revealing the first page.

"B-but—" Atherton broke off in choked sputtering. "These—these are—"

"Bloody irregular," the admiral said flatly. "A damned good likeness, nevertheless. Religious salvation, you said?"

"Something like that." Morland moved to the next page, where two lovers were framed amid peony and hibiscus blooms.

"Never taught us anything like *that* when I was young." The admiral's bushy brows knit. "Mayhem if they had, believe me." He looked up at Morland. "So how is this priceless pillow book of yours supposed to help us with our diplomatic mission to the blasted Chinese emperor?"

Morland eased back down into his chair. "As you all know, the Emperor Chia-ch'ing has been firmly opposed to receiving our emissaries in Peking. But it seems that the emperor has a special fascination with pillow books—and with one such book in particular. For ten years the emperor has sent emissaries the length and breadth of China, searching for this fabled book called *The Yellow Emperor's Guide to Secret Arts*. Unfortunately, the book vanished ten years ago."

"And what makes you think *you* can find it?" Atherton sneered. "Even the heathen Chinese emperor himself can't."

Morland smoothed a painted page, his eyes distant. "Three years ago I had occasion to perform a certain favor for the captain of a Macao-bound brigantine. As a result, the man told me I would have his assistance whenever I required it. And, gentlemen, six months ago I called in that favor."

"Well?" Atherton's voice still held a sneer. "Pray, don't keep us in suspense."

"The captain responded to my query. He has finally located the book I have just described to you."

The admiral's jaw tensed. *"Where?"*

"In Macao—or at least it was in Macao until it disappeared once more. The captain says he has good reason to believe the book was taken aboard a ship that left Macao harbor in the dead of night, without papers or proper authorization."

Morland waited, letting the force of those words sink in.

"Well, man?" The admiral was curt. "Bound *where?"*

"For London, as it happens."

A low murmur swept the room.

Atherton's pale eyes narrowed. "How did this captain friend of yours happen to acquire this information, Morland?"

The earl swept a careless hand before him. "It hardly need concern you, I think. The important thing is that the book will soon be within our grasp. And we will at last have the key we need to open the Celestial Kingdom to British trade and diplomacy. Without any bloodshed or loss of life, I might point out."

The admiral drummed his fingers softly on the walnut table. "It has potential," he said at last. "A damned sight better than any of the *other* plans I've been hearing from the Foreign Office. Besiege Peking, sack the Summer Palace, and take the emperor hostage, indeed!" He shot a dark look at Atherton. The author of that inflammatory suggestion merely sniffed and tugged at his waistcoat.

The admiral turned back to Morland. "What is it going to take for us to obtain the book, Morland? Assuming that we do choose this course of action."

"You will understand if I prefer to keep the details to myself, Admiral." Morland's gaze hardened. "At least for the present. The captain tells me that five men have already died in mysterious circumstances while pursuing this ancient volume. If we wish to succeed, you will have to grant me carte blanche."

Atherton sat forward, sputtering, but the admiral cut him off with a sharp look.

At that moment the door leading to the next room opened. A tall black-haired man with an arrogant hooked nose and startling blue eyes strode into the room.

Instantly all the other men made to rise.

But the hero of Waterloo motioned them back into their seats.

The Duke of Wellington turned his hawklike gaze on the Earl of Morland. "Your plan has the advantage of originality, at least. But why should we entrust such a responsibility to you?" There was no rancor in the question, only the intensity of a seasoned military campaigner testing the weaknesses of his pawns.

Morland met the duke's gaze levelly. "Because I'm the only one with the knowledge to track down the book. Because I've the contacts here and in Asia to negotiate for it. And most of all, because I have the experience to recognize the real thing when I find it."

Wellington smiled faintly. "Quite impressive. But then, you always were a great one for plunging right into the thick of things, weren't you?"

Staring into that hard, proud face, Morland remembered too many times when he'd done just that. At Corunna. At Badajoz. At bloody Salamanca.

But he'd been running then, running wild and fast from a pain too deep to face. Oh, he'd buried it deep—no one had even suspected. Not even the keen-eyed Iron Duke.

And he was running still, Morland realized. The bloody war with France was over, Napoleon was exiled at St. Helena, and he was still running. . . .

Morland's blue eyes hardened. Maybe that was better than agonizing over the past. Better than wondering and worrying about what might have been—what *should* have been, if only . . .

Frowning, he dragged himself back to the discussion at hand. The men around the table were staring at him curiously.

"I see that you're buried in your schemes again," Wellington murmured. "In that case, I shall repeat myself. Where are we to find this book?" His voice took on a cynical edge. "And how much is it going to cost us when we *do* find it?"

"As to the first, I should have an answer before the week is out. And as to the second"—Morland stared at the duke—"twenty thousand pounds should do it, I believe."

The men around the table broke out in startled protests.

"My God, man, that will break us!" This from the admiral.

"Nonsense," Morland said briskly. "We would earn that much back in one week of trade."

The furor raged for ten minutes. Through it all the Duke of Wellington sat motionless in his chair, his fingers steepled before him as he listened to every argument. When the room quieted, he gave Morland a hard look. "Very well. But it had damned well better be worth every shilling," he said softly.

"But you're not—you cannot actually be *considering*—"

Atherton's sputtering was cut off by one cold glance from Wellington. "Do you have any better suggestions—Atherton, isn't it?"

"Well, er, not at this instant precisely. But I have been working on something—yes, something that will almost certainly—"

Wellington's face hardened. "Then we try it Morland's way. All in favor?" His chill blue eyes killed any protests before they could be formed. "Excellent. Morland, I believe the rest is up to you."

The earl bowed slightly. "I am honored, Your Grace. It will save hundreds, perhaps thousands of lives, I am convinced of that. And both countries will benefit from a regularized system of trade."

And for Morland that thought was of primary importance.

Some men he had been unable to save, choking men whom he'd held helplessly while blood gushed from their torn throats at Salamanca, or pooled from their chests at Badajoz. For those men, he had been able to do nothing.

Their ghosts would haunt him always.

But he would damned well see that he had no *new* ghosts on his conscience, spirits of sailors and soldiers far from home, dying unsung and unmourned on sandy beaches at the other side of the horizon.

And he could save the children, the sad-eyed waifs with young-old faces who were always hurt the most in war, left destitute and bereft in the wake of the killing. Morland had seen too many of those hopeless orphans, drifting like human debris in the wake of the war spilling across Spain and Portugal. And then when he'd come home from the war, he had seen his own niece and nephew devastated by a similar pain. Reckless once too often, Morland's brother had died in a coaching accident of his own causing. Morland could not mourn the brother for whom he had long ceased to feel any affection, but the children were different. Those children, too, Morland meant to see protected from any more trauma in their young lives.

No, he could not change the past, but he could bloody well do everything possible to change the *future.* . . .

At that moment Wellington pushed back from the table. "Very well. You have my support for your plan, Morland, unprecedented though it is. Let us pray to heaven that it succeeds."

In slow majesty the duke turned and strode to the door leading to the adjoining room. There he stopped, one hand on the polished wood frame.

His keen eyes scanned the room. "Come along, Morland. We've a few things yet to discuss, I believe. And you'd better come too, Blessington."

Few people in England would have dared to address the august admiral in such curt terms.

The Duke of Wellington was one of them.

As if on cue, the other men filed from the room. Atherton's face was suspiciously flushed as he shoved past Morland, mumbling something about "people who lose all sense of proper manners and morals in pursuit of heathen ways."

Morland ignored him. He had won, after all.

He wondered why the knowledge left him with so keen a sense of uneasiness.

3

White clouds sailed through a serene blue sky. A robin piped happily in its nest.

Two chubby dirt-streaked legs eased down over the edge of the sturdy wooden treehouse at the Earl of Morland's Suffolk estate.

"Where's Uncle Tony, Je'emy?" The speaker, a girl of five and a half, had a tangle of guinea-gold hair and dirt caking her chubby cheeks. By habit, she dispensed with the R in her brother's name.

Her brother, at the vastly mature age of nine years old, scowled down at her. "He's in London, of course, Elspeth. He told us he would be there till the end of the month." Slender and intense, the boy frowned, taking aim at a lightning-scarred beech tree. He picked up a stone from the pile beside him and hurled it.

It hit the trunk with a resounding *thwack*.

Jeremy Langford gave a yelp of delight, which he quickly concealed beneath a more sober veneer, as

befitted his dignity as the eighth duke of Morwood. He
was the master of the manor in his uncle's absence,
after all.

"How much longer is *that*?"

"We've two more weeks to go."

His sister clutched at the mangled doll in her lap.
"Miss him," she repeated softly, pulling the doll to her
chest.

Her brother sighed inwardly. Elspeth had been hit
hard by the tragedies of the last year. Within months,
their mother and father had both been taken from
them, the former in a boating mishap and the latter in
a coaching accident.

The news had been just as hard on Jeremy, of
course, but his extra years had given him more resources to conceal his pain.

His sister hadn't had that advantage.

What Elspeth did not know—and Jeremy could
never forget—was that their father had been driving
the coach when it had overturned, killing himself and
his four fellow travelers. And their father had been
roaring drunk at the time.

Jeremy sighed and hurled another stone. This one
went wide. Grunting in irritation, he stared down at
his sister. "Will you stop sucking your thumb, Elspeth?
It's terribly childish, you know. Uncle Tony doesn't
mention it, because he—well, *I'm* not so polite."

His sister's head slanted back. Her cornflower-blue
eyes widened. Her brother saw a gleam of moisture
well up in them.

"There now, don't cry, silly. You can suck your
thumb when we're alone, I suppose. Not so much harm
in that. Only—only don't do it otherwise, hear? It's—
it's just not fitting for the sister of the Duke of Morwood."

His sister promptly popped her grimy thumb back
into her mouth. " 'Y not?" she mumbled.

Jeremy gave her an exasperated look. "Because—
because it just *isn't*, hang it all!" Muttering, he flung
another stone across the path. This one struck home.

His frown lightened somewhat.

"Is our uncle Tony *ever* going to get married, Je'emy?"

The boy shrugged. "I suppose so. Most grown-ups do." He tossed a stone up and down, his expression thoughtful. "Why?"

" 'Cause I want a new mama." The little girl ran her fingers through her doll's tangled yarn hair. "Want someone to tuck me in at night—and listen to my prayers. Want someone nice and soft to hug me when I scrape my knee on that nasty ladder." A fresh wave of tears filled her wide eyes. "Nanny's nice, but she's not the same. And her apron is ever so scratchy." She gave a watery sniff. "Hurts my nose."

Her brother's fingers tightened on his stone. His thin features hardened. "Even if Uncle Tony *does* marry, the new countess won't be our mother, Elspeth. She'd be our"—his eyes narrowed with concentration—"our aunt, I think."

Privately Jeremy thought that the first thing the new countess would do was pack her unwanted niece and nephew off to some distant relative as far away from Sevenoaks as possible.

But the boy did not tell his little sister that.

Not when she'd had so much rootlessness in her life already. Instead, he waved a hand airily toward the west where the great city of London lay. "It makes no difference anyway. Uncle Tony is too busy enjoying the pleasures of London to think of marrying." Jeremy wasn't sure exactly what that last phrase meant, but it had sounded impressive when Cook had said it to the steward.

His sister studied him, her blue eyes disconcertingly direct. "Why not, Je'emy? Don't he like ladies?"

"Doesn't," her brother corrected absently. "And of course he likes ladies, Elspeth." Jeremy scowled down at his sister. "You saw him that day in the barn with that noisy widow lady from London, didn't you?"

Jeremy frowned, still not understanding the cause of the woman's breathless laughter—which had soon turned to low, panting moans. For a moment he had feared that the woman was sickening.

He had meant to sneak down for a closer look, but
something had held him back. And the pair's faces,
when they emerged from the barn some quarter of an
hour later, had been contented enough, even though
they did have hay scattered all over their backs.

Yes, he would definitely have to ask Uncle Tony
about that, Jeremy decided. It was time he knew about
such things. He was nearly *ten*, after all.

"So why won't he get married?"

"Hang it, Elspeth, how should *I* know?" The boy
scowled and reached for another stone. This one missed
its mark by at least three feet. "There, see what you
made me do! Now I'm almost out of artillery shells."

Elspeth's thumb slipped back to its perch. Her face
grew tense.

Instantly repentant, her brother leaned down and
hugged her clumsily. "No need to cry, silly. Grown-ups
are—well, just queer about such things, you know. They
spend hours mooning about, writing poetry and making calves' eyes at each other. Then the next thing you
know, they've gone and forgotten the whole business.
Damned waste of time, if you ask me."

Elspeth's eyes grew saucer-round at this unprecedented breach of what Nanny called "proper and gen-
tlemanlike deportment."

Her thumb popped from her astonished mouth.
"Oh, Je'emy! Nanny would surely cane you if she heard
that!"

"Well then, we'll just have to see that she doesn't
hear, won't we?" The boy shot his sister a conspiratorial glance, full of mischief and bravado.

The next moment, the two broke into wild laughter,
rolling about and hugging their sides until tears came
to their eyes, all their earlier differences forgotten.

When they finally settled back against the rough
wooden floor, Elspeth squinted up at the sky, her blue
eyes thoughtful. "But I *know* Uncle Tony likes ladies,"
she confided. "I think he likes them ever so much, in
fact."

Her brother frowned. "Not the same, you know."

"What?"

"Ladies."

Elspeth's thumb eased free. "Why not?"

"Because ladies aren't—well, they're not the same as *women*."

"But—"

"Hang it, Elspeth, don't ask me why! I know what I know, that's all. The second groom told me so. Ladies are for marrying, but women are for—" He frowned. "Well, they're for doing that noisy stuff Uncle Tony was doing in the barn with the widow from London. That sort of thing is *different*," he ended importantly.

Elspeth eyed him in round-eyed awe. "Golly, Je'emy! You know ever so much about men and ladies— er, women. How did you—"

But her brother had done enough explaining for one day. "Blast it, Elspeth, no more questions!" He fired off another of his dwindling supply of stones. The quartz missile spun through space, glittered for a moment in a bar of sunlight, then struck the beech tree with a satisfying *thwack*.

But Elspeth was not to be deterred, not even in the face of such impressive marksmanship. Her bare toes toyed with a trailing bough. "He lost his heart to Uncle Hawke's wife, you know."

A started sound broke from the young duke's lips. "Where did you hear that, you little devil?"

His sister merely smiled, kicking her feet back and forth in the warm air.

Jeremy elbowed her. "Come on, spill all or I'll tickle you until you scream."

"Will not."

"Will too."

"Will *not*!"

"*Will too!*" As if to prove it, Jeremy leaned close, his fingers curled in an elaborate gesture of menace.

"Stop! I'll tell! I'll tell!"

Jeremy's eyes softened. "Give over then, imp. Where did you hear it?"

Elspeth looked sheepish for a moment. "I heard it when—when I was in the linen closet."

"What in the blazes were you doing in *there*?"

The girl's chubby hands closed tightly over her dolly. "I was hiding. And then—then I was going to run away," she added defiantly.

"You were *what*?" Outrage tightened Jeremy's young face. "Without me?"

Elspeth sniffed. "It was last month. I was ever so lonely, and all you could think about was that ugly old tin soldier Uncle Tony brought you from London." Her fingers kneaded her dolly's hair. "You never sneak in to see me anymore after Nanny puts out the candle. You never come to take me fishing. And you never want to play knights and dragons. Not since you became d-duke." Her bottom lip began to quiver. "All you want to do is poke your head into some stuffy old book or loiter about with the grooms, or—"

Jeremy frowned, uncomfortably aware that there was more than a little truth to his sister's accusations. "I'm never too busy to talk with you, silly goose. And if you ever decide to run away again, you'd jolly well better take me with you, or I'll flay your hide! Understand?"

Elspeth nodded obediently at this stern admonition. A moment later her thumb slid from her lips. "Je'emy?"

"*Hmmmm*?"

"What's *flay* mean?"

Since the boy was not quite sure of this himself, he merely snorted scornfully. "Never you mind, imp. Just you count on the fact that I'd do it and it would be deuced painful."

They settled back against the planked floor. Elspeth's thumb slid back into her mouth. For a long time they sat that way, their eyes fixed dreamily on the passing clouds.

"Je'emy?"

"What *now*?"

"Uncle Tony was heels over head for Lady Ravenhurst, too." Elspeth's brow creased. "Or maybe it was head over heels. I couldn't hear so well when they tossed the sheets in."

Her brother gasped. "Lady Ravenhurst *too*?"

His sister nodded soberly. "The under-housemaid told the second parlormaid so. Cook smacked them both and told them they'd best stop carrying tales about their betters."

"I can just believe Cook would. Dash it, where were *you* all this time?"

"Hiding in the scullery, of course. What's *heels over head* mean, Je'emy?"

Her brother sighed. He had some notion of what this phrase meant, but decided not to tell his inquisitive sister. One question might lead to another, after all, and he was nearly out of his depth already. "Oh, it means that you like someone."

Elspeth smoothed her doll's skirts, humming. "I guess that means I'm heels over head with Uncle Tony," she said happily. "I wish *he* were our papa."

"He's our uncle, silly. He can't be our papa."

"Well, he *looks* just like our papa. And his name is almost the same. Besides, our papa wasn't good—all of the servants say so."

Jeremy had heard enough gossip of his own not to be surprised by this statement, but he didn't like the idea of his sister hearing it. "Just what have you heard the servants say, Elspeth?"

His sister shrugged. "That he cheated at cards. The third footman said he didn't pay his gambling debts, that he hadn't a—" Her dirt-smudged brow knit. "He hadn't a feather to fly with, I think. And he got one of the scullery maids with a bun in the oven. What does *that* mean, Je'emy?"

"Never you mind," her brother said in a choked voice.

Elspeth's voice dropped to a conspiratorial whisper. "Well, I suppose it doesn't matter. But Cook said that our papa was a man with a Great Vice. I wonder what she meant, Je'emy." Her small head cocked to one side. "Do you think that he stole scones from the stillroom like we did last month and got sent to bed without supper? Do you think that was what the third footman meant about getting a bun in the oven?"

Jeremy's eyes turned very chill. "I imagine it was something like that, Elspeth."

The lie came smoothly enough. After all, Jeremy had learned a great deal about lying in the last months.

He had also learned to bear the pain of cruel discoveries, but he deuced well wasn't going to see Elspeth suffering that same pain.

"Never mind." He ran a hand through his sister's tangled guinea curls. "You've got me to take care of you. We'll manage just fine."

Elspeth rewarded him with a sunny smile that reflected her endless faith in his talents.

And then a new thought struck her. "What if Uncle Tony never comes back? What if he goes back to that place he went before—China, wasn't it? Or to that nasty war with that mean old Frenchman? Boney, his name is—"

"He's Corsican, not French, Elspeth. And the war is over. Besides, Uncle Tony's never going back to fight. Don't you remember? He told us so the night he came here after—after . . ."

Jeremy's voice trailed away as he remembered the night Tony had arrived, mud-stained and exhausted, from Bath. He had gathered the children close, his hands tight about their shoulders.

And that was how they learned that their mama would not be coming home. Not ever again.

Their uncle had held them close several months later, when he'd told them the same thing about their papa.

Thank God for their uncle Tony, Jeremy thought. Without him, the months that followed would have been unbearable.

"I remember," Elspeth said softly. Her hand stole into Jeremy's. "Uncle Tony was ever so nice. I like him a great deal *more* than Papa, so there!" Her bottom lip began to tremble. "I wish *he* were our real papa."

"He can't be our papa." Jeremy's voice rose in exasperation. "They were twins, silly. Just because Jem coachman looks like the Prince Regent in his cups doesn't mean he can stroll into Carlton House and command the royal carriage to be brought around," he added scornfully.

Elspeth considered this for a moment. "What does *in his cups* mean?"

Her brother snorted. "Never you mind, imp! And give up this idea of having Uncle Tony for a father. He's our uncle. We'll just have to make do with *that*."

Elspeth gave a slow, thoughtful suck of her thumb. "But when will he come back?" she asked plaintively.

Jeremy shrugged. "In two weeks, just as he promised. He's never broken a promise before, has he?"

"Only that one time."

"He *had* to stay in London then, silly. It was Official Business, with the government and all. I thought you understood about that."

Elspeth merely sniffed. "You understood. I never said *I* did." Her answer held all the majesty her five years could summon. Suddenly a tear slid down her grubby cheek. Another followed.

With a low sound, her brother circled her trembling shoulders. For a long time they sat that way, black hair against gold, Elspeth's grubby rag doll crushed between them. The sharp pain of their memories was almost beyond bearing.

Finally the little girl began to squirm. Still sniffling, she pulled away and inched over to the ladder. "I w-want to go home."

"Be careful on those rungs," her brother cautioned, hovering close above her as she inched back down to safety.

But Jeremy took his time gathering the last of his stones into a battered canvas satchel. By then, his face carried tear tracks of its own.

The afternoon sun sank slowly, crimson and gold above the slender spires of St. Paul's.

Seated in a deep wing chair before a sunny window, the Duke of Wellington steepled his fingers and stared down his long, hooked nose at the two men opposite him.

"Damned bad business. Sometimes I think the whole country's going to rack and ruin. Riots and disorder. Disrespect of the grossest sort." The duke sighed. "The country's changing, mark my words. And something tells me I am not going to like the new country it becomes half so much. And then there's this whole bloody business with China." He dug into his pocket and pulled out a heavy parchment sheet, which he waved heatedly. "Have you *seen* this?"

Morland shook his head.

"It's a letter from the Celestial Son of Heaven himself, written direct to King George III. I've only just seen the thing today."

Scowling, Wellington hunched forward and began to read, his outrage growing with every word: " 'The Celestial Kingdom possesses all things. The Son of Heaven has no use for your odd or ingenious devices. Nor do we have any desire for your country's products.' "

Wellington's stern face took on a reddish tinge of fury. "And as if that weren't enough, the old autocrat adds this: 'Obedience is demanded. Only complete submission will ensure the harmony and prosperity you desire.' " Wellington slowly crushed the paper to a tight ball. "Has the fool any idea to whom he is speaking?"

Morland decided prudence lay in silence.

What good would it do to remind Wellington that the Chinese had ruled a vast, civilized empire centuries before the first Romans came to England and found themselves greeted by savages in blue paint? That Chinese armies had once controlled half of the world, while Chinese fleets had cruised the ocean all the way to Africa?

But Morland said none of those things. It would be wasted breath.

So he only waited.

After long moments the duke raised his glass in a toast. "Well, here's to your hair-raising scheme, Tony. Let us pray to God that it works. We've lost too many fine men already in Spain and Portugal. I don't care to lose any more."

The duke frowned down at his half-filled glass and topped it off. "England's changing, by God. All these infernal machines belching smoke and noise, turning out things people don't need for prices they can't pay. It didn't used to be that way. Northern nabobs, civil unrest. Damned if I know what to make of it. And more trouble yet to come, I fear."

The three men were silent, each recalling the horrors of war. And now, though the war had ended, the turmoil continued.

Blessington finished his drink and sat back. "What's to be done next?"

Morland stared at the cut-crystal decanter beside Wellington's fingers. It reminded him of cold passes and frigid Spanish dawns. Of promises made but not kept.

More memories. Each more bitter than the last . . .

When Morland looked up, his eyes were as clear and sharp as the crystal. "There are one or two points I did not mention to the others. You should hear them now. Even if I *can* get the book—and to you two gentlemen I must make it clear that it is still very much an *if*—we will have little time to accomplish our mission. As you know, the diplomat Amherst has just returned to England, having failed in his attempts to make our position on trade understood by the emperor. But representatives of the palace have indicated that the emperor might look upon us more favorably after presentation of the pillow book. In fact, they have given us three months to find the treasure and restore it to the emperor. So you see, if we are not swift . . ." He did not need to finish.

Wellington sat back slowly. His fingers trailed across a globe beside the window as he studied the vast blue oval marked *China*. "If it is lives to be saved, then we've got to try. One way or another, we *will* have open trade with China, but I'd rather it came about peaceably."

His finger rose slowly, tracing the curving coast and then sweeping inland to the imperial capital at Peking. "This plan of yours might just be a stroke of genius,

Tony, but how close are you to tracking the book down? And how will you be able to recognize it when you find it?" Wellington fingered the globe. "I gather His August Celestial Majesty wouldn't be half pleased if we tried to palm a forgery off on him."

Morland laughed grimly. "Not likely. I should think he'd execute the poor bastard who brought him anything less than the real thing."

Wellington sighed. "Damned complicated lot, aren't they? Once in India I watched a rajah order a whole village to—" He seemed about to launch into a tale but caught himself with a sniff. "But that is neither here nor there. I need an answer, man. One answer. Can you carry it off?"

Morland nodded. "I can. I'm going to have help, you see."

"Oh? Who is the lucky—or unlucky—fellow?"

"She," Morland said grimly.

Wellington's black brow rose. "Indeed? I can think of only one person who might help you, and that's James Cameron. He and his daughter are back in London, I've heard, but no one's seen hide nor hair of either of them. Cameron saved my life once in India, did you know?" The duke's eyes wandered over the globe, crossing the rugged expanse of the Himalayas and sweeping down through the dusty northwest passes to Delhi. "Five *dacoits* fell upon us one night as we slept. It was bloody chaos for a while, and then that great Scot swept out of the forest, dark as a heathen himself, beard and moustache bristling and a scimitar clenched between his teeth. I was more afraid of *him* than any of those damned *dacoits*, I can tell you! After he dispatched the bandits, he sat down and demanded to be given a bottle of our best whiskey." Wellington smiled faintly. "I don't mind telling you that I gave it to him— and two more besides—without the slightest protest."

Morland gave a low chuckle. "As damnable a knave as ever lived. Aye, that's James Cameron." His smile faded. "But Chessy—er, Miss Cameron—is *she* here in London too?"

"Living near Holborn. Twenty-seven Dorrington

Street. Not a wonderful area, I don't scruple to tell you. I've been around to call several times, but Cameron was not at home. Still, his daughter has a damned good head on her shoulders. Quite lovely too." Wellington frowned at Morland. "Don't tell me you mean to drag *her* into this."

"Why not? If she has even half her father's skill, she can verify the book for us without the slightest difficulty."

Wellington's forehead knit. "Not at all the thing, my boy. It's a *pillow* book, damn it. Nothing for a well-bred gentlewoman to look at. Most likely she'd be driven to a crippling attack of the vapors."

"Never. Not the Chessy I knew," Morland said softly. But his eyes darkened with the faintest hint of uncertainty.

Ten years was a long time, after all.

PART TWO

West of Morning

PART
TWO

West
of Morning

4

27 *Dorrington Street*. This was the place then.

Lord Morland frowned at the unprepossessing row of townhouses with their shabby, untended railings. Not in James Cameron's usual style, that was for certain. The flamboyant adventurer and Asian antiquarian would more likely have been found in Mayfair or St. James's, in a rented house complete with first-class staff.

But *here*? On the edge of Holborn?

Never, Morland thought as he pushed open a creaky iron gate and strode up a flight of unpolished marble steps.

At least, not the James Cameron he *used* to know.

But times change. *He* certainly had. Those idyllic months he'd spent in Macao and the outer islands belonged to another time and another place.

No, to another *man*, Morland thought grimly, brushing a fleck of grime from his immaculate doeskin morning gloves and studying the sheen of his polished Hessian boots.

And Dorrington Street was a universe away from the pristine white sand beaches of the South China Sea.

He'd gone there to recover from the trauma of Corunna; instead he'd discovered a greater kind of pain.

His face unnaturally hard, the earl hammered at the knocker. When no answer came he tried again, then retreated down the steps to the street.

Damn, what was that old reprobate Cameron playing at now?

Muttering harshly, Morland strode to the corner and followed a narrow alley to the mews at the back of the house. With every step he grew more irritated, and the catcalls of a passing pair of costermongers did nothing to relieve his ill humor.

When he came to the back of the townhouse he judged to be number 27, Morland heard the sound of angry voices. Shoving open the unpainted gate, he walked into the yard.

Two beefy workmen, shirt-sleeves rolled up over their bulging forearms, were hauling bags of coal out of a low wooden shed, while a thin man in a black coat issued sharp orders.

At that moment another figure emerged from the rear of the townhouse, wielding a broom as if it were a cat-o'-nine-tails. A battered straw hat rode cockily ajar on the girl's head, while the rest of her body was hidden beneath a baggy, soot-stained gown that was faded to a nondescript tan. Probably Cameron's scullery maid, Morland thought, settling back to watch.

"Take that, you scoundrel!" The girl's broom cracked soundly off one of the workmen's legs. "Thought to trick me, did you?" The fellow's companion received similar treatment. "Let me see what you think of that, you brute!"

The man in black darted past. With a sharp gesture, he sent his men staggering toward the street with their bundles.

"You *can't* do that! We had an agreement! Come back here!"

The tradesman merely smirked. "Agreement be-damned! Just see if I can't, wench! And tell that mistress of yers there'll be no more coal neither," he bellowed. "Not a single bleeding brick until she pays 'er last reckoning. I got a bleedin' business ter run, after all!"

Morland stepped forward, resplendent in buff breeches and crimson waistcoat, and blocked the path of the two brawny assistants.

The tradesman stiffened.

He tried to shove his way past, only to find his elbow caught in a tight grip. " 'Ere now! What's the bleedin' problem?"

"Why don't you tell me?" Morland asked lazily. His voice was low and soft—but more than one man who'd fought beside him at Badajoz would have known it meant trouble.

"Nothing yer need ter concern yerself with, guv. Now if ye'll kindly un'and me, I got ter—"

"I'll have an answer, man! Where are you taking that coal?"

"Back to the ware'ouse, o' course. 'Send around another load,' she says. 'I'll pay you tomorrow,' she says." The man's mouth twisted in a nasty sneer. "Well, she don't, and I hain't! So no more credit! And yer can just let go o' my bleedin' sleeve."

"This *is* number twenty-seven, I take it?"

"Bloody right it is!" the tradesman snapped.

"And your order was placed for a James Cameron?"

"For *Mistress* Cameron, it were," the small man corrected peevishly. He squirmed as Morland's fingers tightened. "But why would the likes o' yer lordship be—" Abruptly the tradesman's eyes narrowed. A look of cunning sharpened his features. "Oww, like *that*, is it?"

"Return the coal." Morland's voice was savage. "Send the bill to me. Lord Morland, number twelve, Half Moon Street."

At the same moment a gold guinea found its way into the man's grimy worsted pocket.

Suddenly the tradesman was all bows and good grace. Smiling unctuously, he motioned his men to redeposit their order.

At that moment the kitchenmaid came charging down the walkway. "About time you thought better of

your knavery! Thirty pounds, indeed! For two miserable bags of coal? And low-grade coal it was, at that! All
shale, if you ask me. Just what sort of a Sammy-soft do
you take me for?"

At Morland's discreet nod, the tradesman began to
back toward the open gate. "No offense meant, miss.
All a mistake, yer understand. Only too glad ter be of
assistance. I didn't understand the nature of things, ye
see. With yer mistress and all."

After a last knowing look at the earl, the tradesman
herded his men before him and disappeared into the
mews, slamming the gate soundly.

"Well, of all the ill-bred, self-important, *mutton-
headed*—" The girl spun about. Her broom fell slowly
to her shoulder. "And who in blazes asked *you* to—"

Suddenly she stopped. Her breath caught audibly.

Morland, well used to the effect his chiseled features
and startling azure eyes seemed to have on strangers,
merely smiled.

And then his smile widened.

Beneath the baggy skirts and bodice he made out
the soft curves of a rather nice female shape.

Immediately the day began to brighten.

The ankles were trim enough.

The neck was slender enough.

And the breasts looked sweetly rounded, with defi-
nite potential for further exploration. . . .

A muffled sound broke from the object of his scrutiny. The next moment, a broom handle prodded his
stomach. Before he could react, Morland found himself
being shoved through the gate into the mews.

"Now just one moment. I've come here to see—"

His words fell on empty air. The gate snapped shut
behind him, and the bolt slammed home.

Now how had the bloody female managed *that*? She
hardly seemed big enough to wrestle a dozen roses to
the ground, much less match horns with him.

But here he stood, smack in the middle of the mews,
staring down at a closed and bolted gate.

And he was growing angrier by the second. He'd

only been trying to help, after all. He'd even saved that coal delivery for her mistress.

Yes, who did the little fishwife think she was?

Morland banged loudly on the gate. "I've business with the master of the house, wench—James Cameron by name! Go tell him Lord Morland's here to see him, and be quick about it!"

That would do it, he thought smugly.

"Go bark up another tree, ye distempered cur! 'Tis no James Cameron who lives here, so I'll thank ye to go away an' leave a decent household in peace."

Morland frowned. "Then who—"

"Ha'n't time for any more o' yer nonsense. Go on about yer business, I say!"

Morland's eyes darkened. He stared at the flimsy gate.

The next minute, his boot crashed through the wood just below the latch. The gate exploded open, three planks splintering free of the crossbar.

"How *dare* you! That will cost a fortune to repair! You leave me absolutely no choice but to—"

"I mean to see Mr. Cameron, wench." His hands circled her wrists, which were surprisingly strong for a woman of her size. "Now, do you show me in, or do I find my own way?"

Her only answer was a sharp kick to his shins, followed by a punishing elbow to his ribs.

Cursing, Morland swung about and hauled her up against the fence.

Her chest drove into his shoulder. Her hips wedged against his thigh.

Soft. Surprisingly soft.

Frowning, the earl looked down.

They were only inches apart, her wriggling form caught between his thighs.

She squirmed sharply.

He inched closer.

Suddenly her belly drove against his groin.

Morland froze.

Supple. *Damnably* supple. Would she feel just as

supple beneath him? What would happen to all that fire and fight if she were in his bed?

Abruptly the blue-eyed earl scowled, wondering where that thought had come from.

"Lemme go, damn yer eyes! Lemme go before I—"

His fingers tightened unconsciously. She had the most curious manner of speech, this servant, using well-modulated tones one moment and gutter slang the next.

He scanned her face, shadowed beneath the floppy straw hat.

Her nose looked fine and straight, even streaked by soot as it was. Abruptly he caught a faint hint of fragrance, something rich and exotic.

It made him feel a sudden urge to see her eyes.

He shoved at her hat, yelping when her teeth bit into his wrist.

"Enough, you little savage!" With a dark curse he drove his knee between her legs and pinned her against the fence. Her hat slipped back on her head for a moment.

In that second Morland glimpsed her eyes.

They were dark and blazing. Death and dismemberment were the kindest thoughts reflected there.

But what else was it about those eyes?

Frowning, Morland studied his flushed, wiggling captive. Were they blue? Gray? Green, perhaps?

Frowning, he inched closer.

Sweet and delicate, her perfume filled his lungs. Her soft hips shoved at his thigh, her breasts at his shoulder.

He cursed long and harshly. His pulse hammered to a gallop.

Sweet Lord, the chit smelled good. And she *felt* even better. He inhaled slowly, trying to place her scent.

And then it did not matter, for somehow his hand was on her hip and she was crushed against his chest, the fence at her back.

The first thing he did was yank off that wretched straw hat. Gleaming ebony curls spilled free, falling over her shoulders and down past her waist.

Morland slid his fingers into the thick, blue-black strands. They reminded him of fine, polished mahogany.

For some reason he frowned. He felt a tugging at the back of his mind, something that urged caution, logic, sense . . .

But it was far too late for that. Smiling grimly, he tossed all reason to the wind and dug his fingers deeper.

Beneath the coal dust her face went sheet-white. Her eyes widened.

He still couldn't quite make out the color. . . .

No matter, for she felt *remarkable*! Her body was sleek, perfectly made to fill his fingers, cushion his thighs.

And yet those eyes. Something odd about those eyes of hers . . .

As Morland stared down, he felt madness grip him. He had to stop. He had to get a hold of himself. *Now.* Before he—

His aroused body paid absolutely no attention.

He eased her head back. He slid his mouth hungrily over hers and felt her hat slip free as his lips explored the soft arch of her mouth.

She tasted sleek. Wet. Rich with strawberries and mint.

He was still pondering that alluring blend of tastes when his captive came to full and furious life against him, her arms flailing, her feet kicking wildly.

"Bloody hell, woman! There's no need to—" Morland ducked as a slender fist smashed into his jaw. "*Ahhh!* Stop! I'm not going to—"

Her open palm cracked against his cheek. A moment later, her half-boot savaged his shin.

He jumped back, growling an oath.

But the little she-cat was ready for him. Her hair was a wild black mane about her face as she bunched her fists on her hips. All the while, those expressive eyes of hers were screaming for slow, painful annihilation.

Morland scowled. So the wench wanted a fight, did she? Well, he supposed he would give her one. He'd learned a few tricks in Spain that she wouldn't be expecting, in spite of the fact that she was obviously a seasoned fighter herself.

Probably James Cameron's latest stray cat. The old reprobate had a habit of collecting flotsam of every shape and size. Even the human sort.

Morland's eyes narrowed on the woman's slender hips, outlined for a moment as she jerked at her dusty skirts.

But maybe she and the Black Cameron had a more intimate association. Maybe she—

At that moment the woman began a furious advance. "You haven't changed a bit, have you? Still out to suit yourself! Still the same clever opportunist you always were!"

Once more her palm cracked down, this time against his shoulder.

Morland scowled down at the tangled curls, the sooty cheeks, the blazing eyes, trying to trace that low, throaty voice. "I beg your pardon."

"Pardon? You'll not have *that* from me, either, Tony Morland! There you'll find yourself sadly out, you bounder, because I know *all* your tricks. And if you have the slightest bit of sense—which I sincerely doubt— you'll take yourself off before—"

Bounder? Knowing his tricks? What was the little hellion talking about?

Morland feinted swiftly and seized her wrist as it whipped past his cheek. "What are you ranting about, woman?" But he got only a hissed oath for his trouble. Her slender fingers clenched and unclenched as he stared down at her.

A shudder lurched through her, from sooty face to slender, wiggling thighs.

And then, without a breath of warning, she simply crumpled, boneless as a stuffed doll in his arms.

Morland caught her barely a foot from the ground. Wrapping one arm around her waist, he swept her up against his chest. Damn, but the wench was light!

And soft.

And warm, especially at the lush inches where her breast nestled against his arm.

All that fight and fury, and the woman was nothing more than thistledown in his hands. . . .

Morland's jaw clenched as her cheek slid against his neck and her warm breath teased his bare skin. He felt an odd tightness in his throat.

Her black hair fanned out against her cheek. One strand slid over her shoulder and coiled like a dark ribbon against the crisp white linen of his shirtfront.

And at that moment Anthony Richard Langford, the fifth earl of Morland, knew desire, desire such as he had never known or even imagined before.

Gut-wrenching, it was. Blinding. Savage.

And yet infinitely tender of its object.

Not that he was in any position to do the slightest thing about assuaging that desire. Honor forbade taking advantage of a woman in such a state.

But, damn and blast, what was he to do with her until she woke up?

Scowling, Morland studied her pale cheeks and the dark lashes fanning out against her skin.

Abruptly his breath caught. He saw the small, star-shaped scar atop her right wrist.

"Chessy?" he whispered in disbelief. "*Little* Chessy Cameron? Good sweet Lord, when did you grow up on me?"

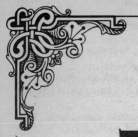

5

Seconds slid past, then minutes.

Chessy came to slowly.

She was rocking gently. Something hard shoved against her ribs. Her head ached, and there was an odd rasp in her throat.

Warily she opened her eyes.

Above her the sky danced a mad waltz for a moment. She blinked up at the sooty clouds flying overhead. Abruptly a storm of tiny white flakes rained down around her.

Funny, she hadn't expected snow. It *never* snowed in Macao. In fact, Chessy had only seen the chill white powder once before, while in China.

One of the flakes landed on her mouth. She tasted it with her tongue, frowning when it didn't melt. They were supposed to melt, weren't they?

Her brow wrinkled. It must be colder than she thought.

Something brushed the white flakes away. They hung in the air for a moment, then drifted slowly to the ground.

"Sorry about the hawthorn petals."

Petals?

She tried to sit up, but the movement sent new pain hammering into her head.

"Stop struggling. I'm carrying you inside. I don't expect you'd enjoy being dropped on the stairs."

Only then did Chessy notice the male arm clamped to her waist. The hard chest crushed against her ribs.

Her head flew back as she stared up into a pair of startling azure eyes.

"You!"

"I," Morland said slowly. "Apparently the last person you were hoping to see. Perhaps someday you'll tell me why, Chessy."

The woman in his arms squirmed against his chest, color flooding her cheeks. "L-let me go, you cabbage-head! I can walk perfectly well. Now put me d-down, or I'll—"

But the long legs did not slow their pace. In moments she found herself rocking up the rickety staircase at the rear of the house.

Around Chessy the world came back into focus. She heard the cries of street vendors, the shouts and clatter of a passing wagon. Slowly she grew aware of the pain at her wrist and ribs, where she had hurt herself in her perilous climb the night before. Most of all she felt the warmth of Anthony Morland's arm at her waist, the pressure of his taut thigh beneath her hip.

And like it or not, there was something damnably *comforting* about all that leashed animal strength.

Abruptly reason and realization returned. Chessy could have cried out with the instant, slashing torment of it.

Not Macao at all. Not even Asia. She was in London, and her father was a captive. And she had yet to find the book that would free him.

Sighing, Chessy struggled to move, but hard fingers clamped down upon her waist and pulled her motionless against taut male muscles that rippled with every step.

"Don't move, I said. We're almost there."

Sky-blue eyes probed hers, keen in a darkly tanned

face. "And then I believe you owe me some explanations, Miss Cameron."

The Earl of Morland's voice was low, but Chessy could hear the anger in it. The sound ignited her own fury. Who was *he* to storm into her house, disrupt her affairs, and interrogate her in this high-handed way?

Most of all, to kidnap her!

Grimly she jerked against his grip, but his hands only tightened.

Chessy fell back, white-faced. She closed her eyes as pain slammed through her head. Dear God, first last night's fiasco, now *this*!

Seeing him with his mistress had been bad enough. Hearing what he was doing had been worse. But last night, at least, Chessy had been occupied with her search, and that had kept her from bitter memories.

But now—now she had no such protection.

She swallowed.

Her voice, when she spoke, was taut with fury. "I owe you nothing, Lord Morland. Why should I? You see, I still remember the way you left us in Macao ten years ago. But you didn't make a formal departure, did you? You didn't so much as give a word of farewell. All you did was slink off like a dog in the night!"

Her eyes fixed on his, sharp as glass. "So you'll pardon me if I don't stand up and cheer at your arrival."

"I see." Morland's eyes narrowed.

"Now I suggest you put me down and leave, before one of us says—or does—something we shall both always regret."

"One of us already *has*, my dear. So since it's too late for caution, perhaps you'll tell me what you're doing here in London."

Chessy caught a steadying breath against the ache in her forehead. Her arm was on fire, and her head was throbbing.

Damn and blast! Why wouldn't the wretched man just take a hint and *leave*?

Too late, Chessy remembered the streak of stubbornness he'd always had. Blast it, goading him would only make it worse.

His face grim, the earl hammered up the last of the steps. "Where is the salon?"

Chessy's lips compressed to a hard line. Morland mumbled something under his breath and swung off down the hall to the right.

Blast the man, did he have to be able to read her mind too? Chessy's cheeks colored. If he really could read her mind, then he would know just what she was thinking.

And that was how solid he felt, how her skin tingled where his thigh brushed her hips.

How much she wanted to feel that warmth in other places . . .

With a ragged little sound somewhere between a sob and a curse, Chessy raised her chin and glared up at the man who was carrying her so carefully in his arms.

Sweet heaven, why did it have to be *him*? Didn't he know what he'd done to her when he'd left Macao ten years before without a word or a handshake?

No, she wasn't about to have old wounds reopened. She would have to make the man leave and leave now. Otherwise—

Morland's boots scraped against wood. "Here we are. The salon, I believe."

The next second, Chessy was lowered against the rather threadbare cushions of a shabby chintz settee in what her landlord had optimistically termed the Blue Salon.

She scowled up at the streaked, faded wallpaper. At one time it might have been a pale ultramarine. Now, it was the dismal color of a winter sky reflected in a muddy pool.

Back in Macao her walls had been hung with peach silk. The windows had been bordered with scenes of swaying bamboo and darting goldfish.

Chessy caught herself up short. *Don't think about it. If you don't find your father, you can't go back anyway.*

Suddenly Morland's thigh brushed her hip.

Instantly Chessy went rigid. With wary eyes she watched the tall peer reach over her for the blanket resting on the back of the settee.

Suddenly she was aware of heat—and sharpest cold. Of the vivid softness of the cushions—and the tense, corded strength of Morland's thigh.

Of the acute, heart-stopping *nearness* of the man.

Her mouth went dry as she watched him shake out the blanket, then settle it smoothly over her motionless form.

Then, oddly enough, he just looked at her. His jaw hard, he studied her body, every curve and hollow outlined beneath the light wool covering. Chessy could have sworn she saw his hand start to rise, only to clench and drop back to his side a moment later.

Could it be that he, too, held memories of that summer? That sometimes he felt a hint of regret for the way things had turned out?

Dreamer! Chessy cursed her stubborn, reckless imagination. She knew a great deal more of the world now than she had then.

She would not be fooled again.

Her eyes narrowed. She watched Morland settle his long frame lazily in the wing chair beside the settee. "I'm waiting, Chessy."

"And you can bloody well go *on* waiting, your lordship."

His booted foot swung idly. "My, my. One would almost think that London didn't agree with you."

"It doesn't."

"I shouldn't wonder at it, if you persist in going about dressed in that outlandish costume."

Chessy's cheeks flamed anew. "And what's wrong with this outfit? It's perfectly functional—and comfortable to boot. Which is a great deal more than the scandalous bits of gauze I've seen *your* society women wearing about on the street!"

Morland's brow arched. "Oh, not *my* women, certainly. I always see that they are properly dressed. In public, at least."

Chessy bit down an angry retort. The snake was just trying to goad her!

With that thought in mind, she lowered her eyelids and shot Morland a smile that would have made crème brûlée taste bland in comparison. "So sorry to offend your refined sensibilities, my lord. Of course I wouldn't *dream* of detaining you any longer. It must be excruciating to be in the presence of such a *boorish* rustic like myself."

Morland's boot continued to swing slowly.

"Leave, damn you!"

"Out of the question, my dear. Not before I have some answers."

"Very well, since you show absolutely no sign of behaving as a gentleman ought, I see I shall have to call—"

The next second, a knock came from the doorway. A ruddy red-haired manservant in outdated livery appeared in the doorway. "Feeling better, are you, miss? Right good thing the earl was on hand to catch you. Sheet-white, you was, and him lifting you like a bit of cotton fluff. Carried you straight up, he did, which was right civil-like, if you ask me."

"I did not ask you, Swithin," Chessy muttered. "Now throw the man out, if you please."

"Throw him—" The servant's eyes widened in dismay. "Now, why would I want to do a bird-brained thing like that, Miss Chessy?"

"Because I'm *ordering* you to, that's why! And don't be fooled by the man's smooth manner. He's a liar, a cheat, and the worst sort of deceiver!"

Swithin's broad brow furrowed. "Is that a fact? Never would have thought it to look at him. Dresses well enough. And that's one prime set of cattle waiting out in the street." He scratched his head. "I reckon you're sure about that, Miss Chessy? About him being a liar and a cheat and all?"

The object of this discussion merely continued to swing his foot, a lazy smile on his face.

"Of *course* I'm sure!"

Morland bent close, and his fingers curved around

her wrist. "Enough, Chessy," he said softly. "You're overwrought. You ought to be resting, not fuming on about some imagined offense that took place ten years ago."

Her violet eyes blazed. "*Imagined?* I suppose I imagined everything that happened while my father and I slept. Without a letter, without a single word, you slunk off in the middle of an important excavation, leaving us short-handed, with no way to finish before the monsoon set in. And now you try to tell me I'm *overwrought!*"

Swithin scratched his jaw. "Now, now, Miss Chessy. It don't pay to—"

Chessy ignored him, shoving at Morland's hands and trying to sit up.

But the azure-eyed earl was having none of it. "Hush, woman. We'll have plenty of time to argue about that after you rest." His fingers circled her trembling arms. They sketched soothing patterns against her skin.

And Chessy felt every touch, every hint of motion. They churned down to her toes, lanced deep into her stomach. *Damn the man! Did he think all it took was a caress or two and she would forget what he'd done? That she would turn into the same doting, moon-faced innocent she had been at fifteen?*

That thought made her blood burn white-hot. "*Rest?* With you within a hundred yards? I'd as soon turn my back on a Malacca Straits pirate! What did you plan to do *this* time, steal my boots? Strip the room clean?"

And then, to Chessy's utter horror and dismay, a tear worked free and crept down her cheek.

Quickly she thrust it away with a sooty fist.

But not before Morland had seen it.

His jaw went rock-hard, his eyes unreadable. "Chessy, don't."

"*Don't?* Don't remind you of the ugly truth? Don't tell you how you hurt my father when you left?" Her gaze slashed at Morland. "I'll never forget the look on his face when he found you'd cleared off while we were at our busiest time. He'd put so much of himself into

that excavation, such love and excitement! And you—
well, stupid as it was, he liked you immensely. Do you
know that afterward he totally changed? He never
laughed as he used to do, never sang those disgraceful
French shanties. He seemed to age years overnight, in
fact. That was all *your* doing. And now you stand there,
fine as fivepence, and tell me to *forget?* I can never
forget—nor forgive you!"

Abruptly she fell back against the settee. Her lips
trembled slightly as she rubbed her throbbing forehead. "Oh, go away—just go bloody *away!*"

Morland's lips thinned to a hard line. He turned to
the anxious servant. "Swithin, isn't it?"

"Aye, your lordship."

"Go and fetch us some brandy. And something to
eat. Biscuits or cakes."

The servant shuffled uncomfortably. "Don't reckon
I kin do that, your lordship."

"Why in blazes not, man?"

The servant continued to shuffle.

"Surely you don't suspect me of planning an assault
on her virtue? The woman's half insensible!"

"Aye, that she is," Swithin said unhappily.

"Well? Fetch the brandy and biscuits. That should
restore her."

"Most likely, your lordship. But I still can't oblige
you, for all that. We don't have neither, you see."

Morland began to wonder if he had stumbled headlong into Bedlam. "Then get something else, man.
Sherry will do, if need be. Or—"

Chessy uttered a ragged sound of protest.

Morland ignored her. "Don't tell me you haven't
any of that either!"

Swithin shrugged uncomfortably.

"What in thunder *do* you have?"

The rangy servant scratched his head. "Precious
little, truth be told. Few eggs. A bit o' flour. Some ham,
mebbe."

Chessy stiffened as she heard Morland mutter a
curse.

The kitchens *were* a shambles, but they'd only been

in London for a month, and she still hadn't gotten the hang of how business was managed here. She certainly couldn't afford the hiring of a staff to help her.

And that miserable, sneaking coal vendor this morning had been the last straw!

White-faced, Chessy massaged her left temple, trying to will the waves of pain away.

It didn't work.

Dimly she heard Morland rap out a volley of crisp instructions to Swithin. Next came the clink of coins.

At that sound her eyes flashed open, and she shot up. "You go too far! We don't need your money! What right have you—"

A large and very powerful palm planted itself flat on her chest and drove her back against the settee. "Stop ranting and let the poor man be about his work."

"He's not poor. And he's *my* man, not yours, so I'll thank you to—"

Behind her the door closed quietly.

"Swithin? Come back here, blast it all! Don't you dare—"

Morland's fingers tightened.

Suddenly Chessy felt—*really* felt—their hard contours against her collarbone. She remembered how those strong hands had slid over his mistress's bare skin, driving her to a breathless, cresting pleasure.

Chessy's face flushed hotly and she began to struggle. Anything was better than thinking about *that*! "Let go of me, you—you brute! *Swithin!* Come back here!"

Morland smothered a curse as her nails grazed his cheek. In taut silence he caught her wrists against the settee. "Swithin has infinitely more sense than *you* appear to have. Where is that wretched father of yours? I can't believe he's allowed matters to reach such a state. Sweet Lord, Chessy, how long have you been going on in this way?"

Chessy answered with a furious squirming.

The next second, Morland planted his thigh atop her legs.

Chessy felt the corded muscles bunch and ripple. Dear God, he was big. He was hot and hard and—

"Get off me!"

Morland's body went rigid. "What are you trying to hide, Chessy?"

"Hide?" Her heart lurched. "Why should I want to hide anything from *you*?"

"I was just asking myself that very question." Morland's elbow flexed slightly. His chest loomed inches closer. "Then where is he, Francesca? Off sermonizing at the British Museum? Sequestered with his cronies at the Royal Geographical Society? By God, when I find the man, I'll draw and quarter him!"

His face might have been carved out of granite, his eyes from Himalayan turquoise.

Chessy barely noticed.

Francesca . . .

How she hated that awkward name! She hadn't heard it in years. Certainly she hadn't heard it said the way he had.

He had used the name often that summer in Macao.

Sometimes it had been voiced in simple, blunt camaraderie, sometimes in irritation, and sometimes with an infuriating blend of hauteur and disapproval.

Just as he had a few moments before.

Suddenly Chessy remembered the other times he had spoken to her so. Times he had pulled her out of one scrape or other while her father had been busy with his maps and his exploration of the treacherous waters around the wrecked imperial Chinese treasure junk.

On one occasion a group of fishermen had been convinced that the foreign girl with violet eyes was an evil sea-devil stealing their fish. Morland had sauntered into their midst just as they were preparing to tie Chessy into a weighted sack and toss her overboard.

Chessy had been glad to see him *that* time.

Several weeks later, a powerful warlord from Canton, watching her swim near the wreck, had decided he must have her for his twelfth concubine. *He* was not so easily routed as the fishermen, since one of his advisers had suggested that union with the reckless violet-eyed virgin would give him the sexual stamina of a twenty-year-old.

It had taken Tony the better part of a day and a harrowing night to persuade the warlord that Francesca Cameron would not be at all good for his sexual health. Among the major reasons Tony listed were that she was no longer a virgin, and that Morland himself could attest to her insatiable demands in bed, demands that rendered a man old before his time.

Just look at himself, Tony had lied smoothly. Only fifteen he was, but the wench's unquenchable needs had left him looking like a man of nearly thirty in little less than a week.

At first the plan had appeared to backfire.

The warlord had studied Chessy's slim, budding body hungrily, fascinated by the tale Morland had spun.

Then there had come an even more harrowing moment when the warlord had demanded to verify these claims for himself. Morland had finally convinced him that with even one touch he would be damaged for life.

The warlord let them go ten minutes later, bestowing a gift of twenty taels of silver upon Tony in gratitude for the horror he had just escaped.

On the way back to their boat, Chessy had asked Tony how he had convinced the warlord she was not a virgin.

The tall Englishman hadn't answered.

Then Chessy asked him what a virgin *was*.

He'd given her only a low, raw groan in answer.

Later that day, by dint of questions directed to the girls in the local Chinese fishing village, Chessy had learned what a virgin was, in general terms if not in explicit detail.

She had avoided Tony for a week after that, as gut-wrenchingly embarrassed and ashamed as only an adolescent of fifteen could be.

Finally he had taken her aside and told her to forget the whole business. He assured her that he liked her far too much to sacrifice their friendship to a bunch of missish airs or misplaced modesty.

Besides, he would be leaving in a month, and he wanted to enjoy every moment of time they had until then.

Chessy had fallen prey to his charm then, just as she had again and again during that halcyon summer. The month had become two and then three. But she had never expected how it would end.

How precious were those memories. . . .

Then came the night Tony had stumbled across her while she lay on the smooth-planked foredeck, studying the constellations spread like winking jewels across the black sky. That night he had said her name with surprise, with gruff tenderness—and with something that might almost have been regret.

Then he had kissed her.

Just once. Softly and slowly. Almost as if the kiss were pulled from him against his will.

Even now, Chessy remembered how her heart had dived to her stomach, how her throat had turned hot and achy at his touch.

But most of all, she remembered how thoroughly *right* that intimate slide of lip and tongue had felt.

And how much more she had wanted from him.

Innocent that she was, she hadn't understood when the kiss had changed, when a simple gesture of friendship had exploded into something entirely different.

Something hot and reckless. Something as dark and potent and mysterious as the midnight currents streaming beneath their boat.

In that one unguarded moment, friendship had turned to savage passion. Morland had pulled her roughly against his urgent body. His fingers had dug deep into her hair while he held her still to meet the hot, seeking force of his tongue.

Somehow Chessy had responded. With an instinct as old as time. With a hunger that matched his own.

But the kiss had been over before it ever really began.

Cursing harshly, Morland had wrenched free of her trembling fingers and stood frozen in the soft starlight, in the warm tropical wind.

His face had been as hard and white as glass.

He had left the next day. Without a word of explanation or farewell.

And Chessy's heart had broken cleanly, irrevocably in two.

She had sworn she would never forgive him, and she had not.

Nor had she forgotten.

For ten long years she had carried the memories, not by design but because she had no choice. They were indelibly carved on her young heart.

And now here the man was again, with the same devil-may-care charm, with that same damnable ability to twist her up in knots inside.

Worst of all, he had the same knack for making her feel like a grubby and very clumsy fifteen-year-old.

Which was precisely what she *had* been, Chessy thought. But she was no longer!

Now she was a woman grown, with enough strength and skill to fell a man in seconds.

She straightened her spine and stared up at the Englishman, treating him to a full dose of the hauteur she had acquired in the last ten adventurous and sometimes hair-raising years. "No one calls me Francesca anymore, my lord. I would be pleased if you would remember that. It is *Miss Cameron* to you."

A hint of wickedness flashed in Morland's eyes. "Of course, *Miss Cameron*. I quite forgot. Perhaps it was the sight of all that soot on your cheeks. Or possibly it was the baggy gown. No, on second thought it was the memory of you brawling with that coal merchant."

"Brawling! I *never* brawl, you—"

Chessy broke into a liquid stream of volatile Chinese, which raised pointed questions about Morland's parentage and antecedents stretching back twenty-three generations.

Morland listened appreciatively. She had always known her way around a full-blooded curse, his Chessy. His lips curved in a smile. "Thank the Lord I never learned much Chinese during my stay in the Orient. I've a feeling what you just said would blister my ears."

But this time Chessy made no answer. It seemed her exertions had finally caught up with her. Her pulse came light and ragged, and she was finding it strangely hard to breathe.

Fire and fiddle! All she needed was to eat and then rest a little. Of course, it hadn't helped that she'd been up before dawn scrutinizing the outside of the next house she was to enter.

Lord Morland's house, in point of fact.

Then on her return there had been bills to discuss with Swithin and two local urchins to interview about the habits and peculiarities of Morland's household. After that she had had to pick out an elaborate ormolu clock and a length of fine wool worsted as a gift to be sent back to one of her father's antiquarian friends, who was a high government official in Canton.

Then had come the episode with that wretched tradesman. She had paid his last bill, of course, but the man had seen her vulnerability and pressed for an extra two months' payment besides.

Blast them all! She refused to be beholden to Morland for anything! Not even if it meant no fuel for cooking, no water for drinking, and no clothes to cover her hungry, trembling body. . . .

Chessy frowned. Now how had *that* thought crept in? Perhaps she was not entirely recovered after all.

Above her Morland's face seemed to blur. Chessy blinked as his hard, etched features seemed to streak away into streams of color.

Oh, this was *very* strange. . . .

A strong hand cradled her neck. "Come, Cricket, you're not going to faint on me again, are you?"

At the sound of that long-ago endearment, Chessy felt an odd tremor work through her throat. "Of—course I'm not, you—you wretched f-foreign devil! I'm only . . . I'm only—"

And with that last ragged protest she collapsed against the settee, lost to the world for a second time that day.

By all the saints, she had to be the most stubborn, the most impossible—the most *infuriating* female he had ever met!

Ten years hadn't changed *that*, Morland thought.

But other things about her had changed, and those things Morland was having to work *very* hard to ignore.

Carefully he lifted her cool hand and felt for a pulse. Light but steady.

He shook his head as he stared down at her white cheeks. The woman was beyond believing! He had saved her from the importunings of that rascally coal merchant, and her only response was to round on him like a mad bull!

And now *this*!

Now what? a quiet voice asked.

Why should she welcome you back into her life with open arms? You knew what you were doing when you left Macao. You knew exactly why you were doing it too.

You could have gone back at least once over the years. You could have found someone to carry a letter and see that it actually reached her.

Morland frowned.

He hadn't done *any* of those things, of course.

First there had come his father's illness. Then there had been the war and all the troubles with his brother and the estates. Somehow there had just never been time or opportunity for—

Liar.

This time Morland didn't fight that mocking voice. For that was true, too, of course. The fear had stopped him, fear that if he saw her again he wouldn't be able to leave . . .

He looked down and saw that his fingers were still holding the velvet underside of Chessy's wrist. All unconsciously they were tracing soft circles against her delicate skin.

Good sweet Lord, had he lost his bloody *mind*?

Was the madness happening all over again?

Muttering angrily, Morland shoved her hand back under the coverlet and jerked to his feet.

What was the matter with him? She was just

Chessy, after all. *Chessy*. The awkward, sunny, entirely unpredictable daughter of an old and charmingly ramshackle friend.

Only Morland found that he could not look away from her pale brow, from the dark half-circle of lashes brushing her cheeks.

From the gentle rise and fall of the breasts only hinted at by the shapeless gown she wore.

God, those breasts . . .

He still remembered that night on the deck when he had kissed her and felt their soft, budding curves.

The night when he had been on the verge of doing much, much more than simply kiss her . . .

With a harsh curse, Morland stalked to the door. Anything to put her out of his mind! Otherwise, the next thing he knew, he'd be kissing her again, unconscious or not.

And God only knew what he would do after *that*.

6

"**G**ood sweet heaven!"

The kitchen was every bit as hopeless as Morland had feared it would be. An old soot-covered open range dominated one wall of the basement room, while empty wooden crates filled most of the remaining floor space.

Morland kicked the crates away and jerked open the cupboard nearest to the range. A mouse went scurrying into the darkness.

So she had flour at least. Miraculously, it looked untouched by whatever other rodents and uninvited guests might be residing here.

Quickly Morland assessed the rest of the cupboards and the small stillroom next door.

Not good. But not so terrible either.

An odd smile played over his lips as he rolled his cuffs up over his bronzed forearms. Soon he had assembled a meager store of supplies and was beating milk into a chipped earthenware bowl full of flour.

It had been far worse at Badajoz, he thought grimly. But fighting wasn't all he'd learned on the Peninsula. Foraging had been nearly as important as the fighting.

Morland had vowed to see his men through, and so he had.

Up until Salamanca . . .

Suddenly, as he stood in the shadowed kitchen, his hands white with flour, Morland heard the distant rumble of French artillery. Once again he caught the pungent smell of sun-warmed wheat and the smoke of bread baking in Spanish cooking fires.

But most of all, he was remembering what it felt like to be hungry, so hungry one's stomach lurched and heaved in an agony of emptiness and pain. Until warmth and reality bled away and one's body simply gave out.

His hands froze on the chipped bowl.

It had been a long time since Salamanca. But apparently it hadn't been long enough.

Because there were still too many memories, too many things about those long, bitter weeks that Morland would rather have forgotten. But he knew he never could.

His jaw hardened. He had just turned back, frowning, to his preparations when Swithin staggered in, bent nearly double beneath a huge sack of provisions.

"Ah, excellent." Morland helped him maneuver the bundle onto a dusty sideboard. "Miss Cameron is still upstairs. If you would be so good as to scout me out a pan and start a fire in that lamentable excuse for a cooking range, I'll just go up and see how she's—"

At that moment, a low rustle brought both men about.

Pale and unsteady, Francesca stood framed in the rear staircase.

"*Chessy!*" the two men shouted together.

"You really needn't yell. I'm feeling much better. A dish of tea would not be unwelcome, however." She moved carefully toward the long wooden table opposite the range and eased into a rickety chair.

Neither man moved.

Chessy's brow furrowed. "Swithin, whatever have you got in that bag?" Her violet gaze shifted to the earl, whose forearms were dusty with flour. "And *you*—what are you doing there with the last of my precious flour?"

Morland gave her a look that promised retribution as he cracked a pair of eggs. His smooth, sharp motions spoke of great practice.

Without a word, he attacked the mixture with savage ferocity.

"I don't believe it!" Chessy gave a startled laugh. "*You?* It's—it's impossible—"

Morland cut her off with a look that was pure flashing sapphire. "I was under the impression that I was saving you from impending death by starvation. Clearly I was wrong, and my chivalry is wasted." Seeing that Swithin's efforts with flint and tinder had finally paid off in a tolerable flame, Morland slammed a heavy cast iron skillet down over the fire and tossed in a healthy lump of butter.

Scowling still, he tipped a bowlful of frothy yellow egg into the sizzling butter. "*Someone* has to look after you, since you clearly haven't the wit of a two-year-old."

"Now just one minute—"

Morland snorted and flipped the omelette deftly.

Chessy gave a faint gasp. "How did you do that? You're absolutely the *last* person I'd expect to see performing miracles in a kitchen."

"Which just goes to show how little *you* know about anything." Morland slammed a chipped but clean earthenware plate before her and proceeded to fill it with a steaming, golden omelette and a wedge of cheese that Swithin had produced from his bag.

"Eat!"

The raw command made Chessy blink. When her mouth began to tense for an answering volley, Morland shoved a fork into her hand and growled, "*Now*, woman! I won't have bloody good food going to waste!"

This time Chessy did as he ordered. In mere seconds every scrap of food had disappeared. And then as she watched, amazed, some sort of pale fried pancake, drenched in butter and dusted faintly with sugar, dropped lightly onto her plate.

Her stomach rumbled with embarrassing eagerness. Red-faced, Chessy bit into the cloud-soft cake.

Every bite was better than the last. Lord, it had been *months* since she'd eaten so well. She had never learned how to cook, living as she had, moving from place to place with her father. And Swithin was no better than she. As a result, their few efforts here in London had been appalling disasters. Since their arrival they had subsisted on a great deal of bread and whatever fruit Swithin had managed to procure.

Nothing like *this*.

With a small sigh, Chessy stared down at her empty plate. Carefully she set down her fork and sat back in her chair.

A rapturous smile lit her face. "That was nothing short of marvelous! One thing I'll say for you, barbarian, you certainly do know how to cook!"

Morland was saved from offering a reply by Swithin, who bustled past with two steaming cups of tea.

"Begging your pardon, your lordship, but I reckoned as how you might care fer something to drink. No whiskey at hand, more's the pity. But that there's grade-A Amoy black what Miss Chessy brung all the way from Macao. Goes down bloody fine, it does. Demned near as good as whiskey."

After settling the two cups, the rangy servant turned and busied himself opening a pair of faded curtains. A moment later, the room filled with sunlight. "Now if you don't mind, Miss Chessy, I'll just go and see to the rest of the provisions. Enough to feed a household fer a year out there, I shouldn't wonder. Only wish we had somebody to cook it fer us."

Without waiting for a reply he shouldered the unused flour and disappeared into the stillroom.

For a moment neither Morland nor Chessy moved. Their eyes locked, wary and intent.

Suddenly the room seemed very small. Very quiet. And blindingly intimate.

Morland was the first to break the spell. He grabbed up his tea and slid into the chair opposite Chessy. "Are you always so pig-headed?"

"Are you always so rude? So blasted high-handed?"

"Watch your tongue, woman. Your father might be a rogue and a vagabond, but I cannot believe he would tolerate such behavior in his daughter."

"You know nothing about him! And what possible concern is my speech or my behavior to you?"

"None, thank God. Not as a rule. But when you're with me, Francesca Cameron, you'll behave as a lady ought and keep a civil tongue in your head."

"Oh, forgive me! By all means, let me be proper and docile. Only you men may swagger about, curse, and carouse. Or prowl for shameless creatures who positively plead for your touch!"

Chessy caught herself up with a low gasp. What demon had made her blurt *that* out?"

Morland sat forward, his eyes narrowed. "What in the devil do you mean?"

"N-nothing."

"Come, come, my sweet. All that venom must have had some source."

Chessy glared at him. "I was simply speaking from general observation. All the English gentlemen I've seen here seem to carry on so."

"Indeed?" Morland settled back in his chair and sipped his tea. His eyes narrowed. "I suppose you've seen so many, of course."

"I've seen enough," came the grim reply.

Morland's sapphire eyes measured Chessy over the rim of his cup. "Now, my girl, I mean to know exactly what you're doing here in London."

Chessy met him, glare for glare. "That is absolutely none of your concern."

"Oh, but it is. Especially since we both know your father is nowhere within fifty miles of London."

Chessy's fingers tensed upon her teacup. "Of course he is! Well, perhaps not here in the house at the moment." Blast, why hadn't she prepared for such a question?

She gave an airy wave. "You know how my father is. He never cares to stop long in any one place. Right now he's—busy. Seeking funds for various new expeditions.

I daresay you wouldn't even recognize him, all stiff and respectable in a new frock coat and polished boots. Yes, out and about from dawn to dusk, he is. You know how restless he can be. He would be useless with the day-to-day details of running the house anyway."

Morland's eyes were chips of sapphire. "You're lying, Cricket. I always could see right through you." His voice was low, slightly husky. "And you know it too."

That soft, dark voice made Chessy shiver, as did the nickname that only *he* had ever used.

She stared down at her teacup. She saw that her fingers were trembling.

She made a discovery then, a very unpleasant one.

In fact, it was quite horrible.

She'd loved this man abjectly, utterly, blindly once, as a schoolgirl of fifteen. And it appeared that she hadn't gotten over him yet.

But damned if she'd let *him* see that!

Pushing away her cup, she came gracefully to her feet. "I thank you for your timely assistance, your lordship. The meal was . . . quite tolerable, actually. But now I really must—"

He was around the table in a second.

His hard hand gripped her waist, and he wedged her against the wall. "You're going *nowhere*, Chessy. Not until I have some answers. And this time, try giving me something besides witless prevarications. James Cameron would *never* come to London to fawn at some merchant king's coattails in the hope of raising funds for an expedition. Nor would he come to London without looking me up."

His fingers tightened on the soft skin at Chessy's wrist. Something dark and unreadable flashed in his eyes.

His jaw settled to a hard line. "So start talking, my dear. Unless you'd rather I worked the answers out of you in a different way."

7

Chessy went utterly still.

For a wild moment she considered giving him a quick chop to the collarbone. Fast and efficient, that. He would be howling on the floor in agony within seconds.

It would also leave him with residual pain and weakness for life.

Scowling, Chessy discarded the idea and focused on his legs. Yes, something swift and unexpected . . .

But the heat of his thigh kept getting in the way of her planning, leaving her strangely light-headed.

He's just a man, isn't he? Forget about anything but the danger!

But he wasn't just *any* man. He was Tony, the first man she had ever loved.

Suddenly all the wonder of those reckless, glorious weeks returned to her. Tony, bronze-maned and bare-chested, roaring with laughter as he tried to catch a fish with his bare hands.

The sun, glistening in a haze of gold as he dove into the water from the edge of their junk moored above a five-hundred-year-old Chinese treasure trove.

Days of laughter. Nights of churning agony, as the girl with violet eyes perched on the edge of the dark abyss known as womanhood.

With one kiss, with one searing touch, he had brought all those memories back to her, white-hot. And somehow Chessy found herself no more prepared now than she had been ten years earlier.

Morland's hands tightened. "Well?"

Chessy felt the hard outline of each finger, felt the edge of his boot imprinted against her shin, felt the terrible tension that gripped his whole body.

And with it she felt a strange wild heat that seemed to center in her chest and squeeze through her lungs, leaving her giddy, blind, dizzy.

And hungry. To feel all the rest of him pressed against her so completely.

With a hoarse cry she shoved her palms against his chest and tried to break free, only to find her hands caught at her sides. He edged nearer. Her arms went flush to the wall.

"Where is he, Cricket? Enough of this pretense. What sort of hot water is the old reprobate in now?"

Suddenly Chessy had to close her eyes to fight back tears.

It was too much. The sound of that old familiar nickname, coupled with the rough note of concern in Morland's voice, broke right through ten years of defenses.

It was no good, any of it. She had never been able to hide *anything* from this man. And if she didn't get him out of here soon, she'd disgrace herself with tears—or she'd reveal everything.

And that she could never let happen.

Dragging in a raw breath, she opened her eyes. Lord, she'd forgotten how tall he was. Her head eased back to meet his look, and the movement sent her midnight hair tumbling free. Like a cloud of black silk it spilled down her back and covered her hands where Morland held them against the wall.

Chessy saw a muscle flash at his jaw. As she struggled for some story to ward him off, her gaze fell to the bronzed skin at the collar of his shirt.

He had removed his jacket and cravat while he worked.

His shirt was open.

A fine white dusting of flour coated the crisp bronze hairs at his chest.

Chessy's breath caught oddly. Mesmerized, she studied the dense, springy hairs, the same color as his skin.

Her tongue swept her dry lips. Suddenly all she could think of was how it would feel to run her fingers through that hot, dense tangle where bronze hair met bronze skin. . . .

With a choked sound she jerked her face upward, feeling heat flood her cheeks.

Morland's eyes narrowed. His body went completely still.

"Bloody hell." Even his breath seemed to cease. "You really *have* grown up, haven't you, Cricket?"

Chessy's chest rose and fell jerkily. She was somewhere between flying and fainting, and she couldn't feel her feet.

Heavens, she couldn't feel *anything* but the hot, aching inches where their bodies met at thigh and wrist and finger.

It was the end and the beginning of a thousand schoolgirl's dreams.

Except that now it was real, and the man touching her was of keenest flesh and blood.

And *she* was a schoolgirl no longer.

"L-let me go." It was the merest whisper of sound.

Morland did not move. "Chessy," he murmured. "Sweet Lord above . . ." His fingers shifted, one hand moving to the thick, lustrous hair cascading over her shoulders. "You smell like sandalwood and orange blossoms. And your hair . . . so beautiful . . . It was *always* beautiful."

Her breath caught in a whimper. She closed her eyes against the desire she read in his face. For she knew all those things were in her own eyes, and she couldn't bear for him to see them.

"P-please, Tony. Let me go."

"Where have you been for the last ten years of my life, Cricket? What sweet, wild things have you been learning without me? Show me, Chessy. Show me now. . . ."

His hands slid through her thick hair and eased lower, where her hair fringed the softness of her hips. He inched closer, his thighs hard against her belly.

Chessy blinked as she felt the telltale hardness, felt the heat and hunger of the man. And deep inside she welcomed those things, because in spite of all the time passed this was *Tony*, the only man she'd ever loved, the laughing golden English stranger whom she'd adored with a schoolgirl's ferver that she'd never quite recovered from.

And then somehow her hands were curving over his shoulders. Her fingers slid through the textured bronze of his hair.

"God, Chessy. You can't—I'd be insane even to consider—"

Then Morland groaned as she finally did what she'd been longing to do and combed her fingers through the flour-strewn hair at the open neck of his shirt.

He was warm. He was hard. He was everything she'd ever dreamed he would feel like.

Ten years of forbidden fantasies had not prepared her for the reality of skin upon warm skin. A decade of dreams found their blazing culmination in that second, and Chessy felt a wild delirium sweep over her, freeing her from the past, parting her from her future, until there was nothing left but *now*, one sweet, trembling moment with a myriad dizzying textures of feeling.

"Flour . . . your chest . . ." Chessy swallowed, trying to marshal her chaotic thoughts. She raised her eyes and stared at Morland's mouth, which was locked in a taut line.

Even then her fantasy would not release her.

How would it feel if she—if he—

Her fingers slid deeper, tugging lightly through his

hair as she traced the hollow of his collarbone from
neck to shoulder. She shivered as she felt the tension in
his muscles, felt the hard ridge of his collarbone, the
subtle warmth of his skin.

Ten years?

It felt just like yesterday.

"Sweet God above."

And then somehow she was crushed against him,
her heart lurching as he anchored the back of her head
with endless care and brought his mouth down against
hers.

His first touch was soft, tentative, almost fearful.

He eased closer, mouth molded to hers, his breath a
soft, restless counterpoint to the sliding pressure of his
lips.

Chessy forgot to breathe, forgot to think, forgot
everything but how perfect it felt to touch him so.

As a *woman*, not as a girl.

Her fingers tensed. She held on for dear life, feeling
logic, habit, and the beliefs of a lifetime swept away
before the aching purity of his touch.

His hand splayed open against her hip. Groaning,
he urged her against his rigid thighs. At the same time
his mouth opened, moving with slow thoroughness
from one curve of her lip to the other.

His tongue teased the closed line of her mouth.
Chessy felt him shudder.

A wild curiosity seized her. With a gasp she opened
to his sleek, probing pressure, welcoming him inside
her, drinking in his heat and strength.

The change in him was instant and electric. He
pulled her closer, opening his legs to catch her between
the hardness of his thighs while his tongue found hers.

Ten years whirled past in a second. Chessy could
almost feel the deck pitch beneath her, hear the creak
of rigging tossed in a fresh tropical wind.

For years she had dreamed of reliving that moment
and finding out what would have happened next. Now
she was being given the chance.

Even while her mind screamed out for her to deny
him, to shove him away, Chessy realized she could not.

Not when he was everything she had ever dreamed of.

And damned if she'd let him think he was the *only* man she'd kissed in ten years.

Her fingers pulled him closer. Her lips closed sleekly around him.

"God, Chessy—" The fingers buried in her hair tightened convulsively. *"More."*

Chessy made a low, lost sound as he eased her lower lip between his teeth. It was a dark, exquisitely erotic slide of friction that made her dream of all the other exquisite textures of skin on skin that he could teach her.

"Cricket—I can't—"

But the raw hunger in his voice was the sweetest joy of all. Chessy realized that *he* was reeling from shock as much as she was.

When he had kissed his laughing courtesan, his voice had held no such tremor, no loss of clarity or resolve. He had been in total control, then and through all the intimacies that had followed.

But he was not in control now. Far from it. One kiss had left him breathless, reeling, urgent.

Chessy was glad of that. Very, very glad. Because it had left her the same way.

"Stop me, Cricket. I don't—we can't—"

He groaned. What he did next stripped Chessy of breath and reason. He caught her cheeks in his palms and drank in the richness of her mouth. He drank deep and long, as if he were waking from some long and thirsty sleep.

And then he brought his finger to her mouth. While they kissed, he traced the naked outline of their mating, of their wet, bonded lips.

Gently.

With infinite care.

Almost as if he were afraid that the union existed only in his mind.

The vulnerability of that gesture made Chessy's eyes blur with tears. She realized then how deeply she had fallen, how vulnerable she still was to his rakehell charm.

And that thought made her think of other things—bleak, unbending things like honor and pride and the duty she owed her father.

It was only those cold realities that dragged her back from danger at the very last moment. One second she was pliant and breathless against him, infinitely vulnerable, and the next she was shoving, her fingers splayed tensely against his chest.

For a moment he didn't move.

His jaw could have been carved of fine granite, and he seemed to be having trouble breathing.

And in those breathless seconds when reality came lurching back, Chessy saw that he had been no more careful or cogent or calculating than she had.

So it was true. *His* need had been as fierce and unexpected as hers.

And it was driving him still.

From the rear stairwell came the scrape of boots. A moment later, Swithin appeared, mopping his sweaty brow with his cuff. "Food's all stowed, Miss Chessy. Reckon you can—"

He stopped abruptly. His eyes narrowed as he studied the pair motionless by the wall.

And then he registered the pallor of Chessy's face, the redness of her lips.

"By God, if you've so much as laid a hand on her, I'll—"

Chessy silenced him with one trembling gesture. "Lord Morland is just leaving, Swithin. We wouldn't w-want to detain him."

Morland's face hardened. He looked like a man ready for a fight—maybe even *looking* for a fight. "Just like that?"

Chessy didn't pretend to misunderstand him. Her unsteady fingers clenched at her waist. "Just like that," she said flatly.

"Oh, Cricket," he whispered softly, "it's not going to be nearly that easy. Not this time."

And then, before Chessy could shout or swear or

deny the tears that were threatening to spill free any second, he turned and slowly shrugged on his bottle-green jacket, which he'd slung over a chair when he'd begun his cooking.

But his sapphire gaze never left Chessy's face.

It told her that he was harder, more determined than ever. That *he* had changed, too, in ten years.

"Oh, yes, I'll be back, Francesca Cameron. And when I come back, I am definitely going to have some answers."

Chessy groped blindly for the table at her back, struggling to support herself against the sudden weakness in her legs.

For she could never let him see the power he held over her! He had fooled her once, long ago when she was a green girl of fifteen. He must never do so again.

"Come back and you'll only find more of the same!"

Morland's brow rose mockingly as he stared down at her flushed cheeks, at her dewy, well-kissed lips. "Is that a promise? If so, my sweet, it will be my keenest pleasure to return."

And then, with a perfect bow embellished by the flourish of his immaculate doeskin gloves, the earl was gone.

*W*retched, witless fool!

Chessy gripped her sooty muslin skirt, listening to the drum of Morland's feet as he pounded up the stairs and crossed the front foyer.

Fool! How could you let him turn you inside out this way?

Tears pricked at her eyes. Her throat felt raw and scratchy.

How had it happened? She could have overwhelmed him in a matter of seconds. She should have had him bound and insensible in mere minutes.

How had all that training and discipline melted away beneath the heat of one soft, stunning kiss?

Chessy swallowed a sob as she heard the front door

slam. The sound crashed through her, echoing cold and hollow right through to the bone.

Dear God, what had she done? What had *he* done to her? How had he managed to destroy all her careful control, all her poise, all her defenses in one brief encounter?

Behind her Swithin coughed discreetly.

Abruptly Chessy remembered that she was not alone.

"You're—all right, miss? Nothing you need to tell me, is there?"

Chessy heard the gruff concern in that dear, familiar voice. The sound made her brush furtively at her eyes.

No, now was not the time for tears.

When she turned around, her bright smile was firmly in place. "Oh, I'm feeling much more the thing, Swithin. Amazing how a decent meal can restore a person's spirits. Although I don't know how I'm going to pay our visitor back for all that lovely food."

Swithin's eyes narrowed. Chessy had the sudden feeling she wasn't fooling him in the slightest.

Meanwhile, her net worth was precisely fifty-one pounds, and the lease on this house would set her back twenty-one of those pounds.

She sighed. It made little difference, really. It would be enough.

She had very little time left to find that wretched book, so the last anonymous note had said. Otherwise, her father . . .

She forced down the thought, her eyes dark with pain. "We are going to find that book, Swithin. We *have* to. Then we are going to leave this horrid, barbaric city forever."

For some reason her throat tightened at the thought. Swiftly she spun about, fighting back tears.

"And now I'm g-going upstairs. If anyone else calls—*anyone at all*—I am *not* at home!"

*F*ool. *Bloody, bloody fool!*
How could you let her twist you around her finger that away again?

The words pounded through Morland's head as he stalked down the steps and signaled to a passing hackney.

Just as the driver creaked to a halt and waited for Morland to ascend, the earl changed his mind and waved the vehicle on.

What he needed now was to walk. Maybe exercise and fresh air would clear his head.

Not bloody likely.

Nothing could make him forget the way Chessy's soft hands had felt pressed to his neck. The full breasts crushed so sweetly to his chest.

And then, sweet Lord, when she had run her fingers over his skin, beneath his shirt . . .

Morland growled a curse and ran his hand through his hair, trying to fight down the heat that blazed back to life at the mere thought of the unforgivable thing that had occurred in the stillness of the kitchen.

Was he *mad*? She was little Chessy, the innocent daughter of one of his closest friends! And so James Cameron was, in spite of all Morland's carping. The man had even saved his life on two occasions!

And this is how you repay him? By trying to seduce his daughter?

Morland scowled, sending two passing matrons into agitated titters. But he noticed neither their reaction nor the cheerful, everyday chaos of the street around him.

All he could think of was how sweet Chessy Cameron's lips had felt in their first tentative response.

How her cheeks had taken on a lovely flush as she ran her fingers gently across his chest . . .

Enough, fool! Put her out of your mind! There must be several thousand eligible females in London. Don't complicate your life by dreaming about the only one you can't have!

But as Morland stalked blind and restless through the noonday crowds, his leg aching keenly, he had the nagging suspicion that it wasn't going to be nearly that simple.

8

When Morland left his magnificent house on Half Moon Street that evening, it was with one grim resolve: to be bloody roaring drunk by midnight. And by the time the charming little ormolu clock in Brooks's struck the hour of ten, he was halfway there.

Around the Great Subscription Room, with its floor-to-ceiling windows and gleaming central chandelier, elegant men sat at ease, losing ten or a thousand pounds with the same careless grace. The company was a little thin this night, but at least one royal duke was present, huddled in a corner with his cronies, losing rather heavily at faro.

Morland nodded to several old acquaintances as he finished his fifth brandy.

He was feeling a decidedly pleasant little glow when Atherton walked by, encased in a violet waistcoat that emphasized the protuberance of his stomach.

Somehow the dark silk also reminded Morland of Chessy's eyes.

With a low curse, the earl sat forward, signaling for a waiter to refill his glass.

She was the last thing he was going to think about tonight!

At a nearby table he heard a low groan and the sound of a hand being tossed in. "Count me out. No more high play for me. In dun street already. Ho, Morland! Care to take my play?"

Morland turned to see a slender red-haired man motioning to him.

Why not? he thought grimly. A few hands of loo might take his thoughts off a violet-eyed hellcat with lips like warm silk. . . .

He took his seat amid the usual idle banter and studied his playing companions. On his left were two dandyish fellows he had known slightly during his years at Oxford, both dressed in remarkably ugly shades of puce. To his right sat a morose baronet from Somerset.

And of course he could not forget Atherton, watching everything with that cold, glittering gaze of his.

Warm with the glow of his fifth brandy, Morland decided simply to ignore Atherton's existence.

Soon the play settled into a comfortable rhythm. Morland lost fifty pounds in the first few minutes, then gained twice that sum back.

The baronet studied Tony morosely. "What do you make of this string of robberies about town, Morland?"

"Wretched business." *And not only the robberies,* Tony thought. *It was everything to do with James Cameron, his irritating daughter, and that cursed pillow book!*

"Broke into my townhouse last week," the baronet continued. "Took a fine bottle of port I'd been saving for a special occasion." He tossed down a card, then settled back with an even gloomier look.

"Broke into Alvanley's three nights ago, I hear. Odd, but they didn't take anything." This from the vision in puce and scarlet across the table. Morland could only blink at the fellow's waistcoat; the sight made him decide that he hadn't drunk nearly enough.

As Morland signaled to a vigilant waiter for a refill, the man in puce continued. "Did you know that the ruffians had the utter brass to invade the Royal Asiatic

Society?" He gave a shudder. "One can hardly guess what the devils will be about next."

Atherton smiled tightly. "Just let the bastards try to pass *my* walls. They'll find themselves regretting it quick enough." His voice had grown slurred.

Morland's eyes narrowed. He could well imagine what pleasure it would give Atherton to corner the burglars that had been eluding every magistrate in London for the last month.

Suddenly the earl recalled the lithe fellow who had danced across his roof and disappeared into the night. Could there possibly be a connection?

But the brandy was taking effect, and Morland found his thoughts beginning to unravel at the edges.

"What about you, Morland?" Atherton fixed the earl with a cool stare. "Have *you* been robbed?"

Tony frowned. The curtness of Atherton's question irritated him, almost as if it were a challenge—perhaps even a warning.

He tossed down a card and gave a negligent wave of his fingers. "Not yet, I'm happy to report."

"Not that you have much to steal, of course." Atherton finished his drink and set the glass unsteadily on the table. "From all I hear, that brother of yours pretty well cleaned out the estate before he had the grace to take himself off in that coaching accident."

The gentleman from Somerset choked on his sherry. A stunned silence settled over the table.

Morland stared down at the gleaming crystal in his fingers. He refused to be baited, least of all by someone of Atherton's crudeness. "I am delighted to inform you that the rumors are vastly exaggerated, Atherton. My brother, the duke, was impetuous but not grossly reckless," he lied smoothly. "Although I'm certain that the *truth* of the matter does not interest you in the slightest. After all, it is so much more pleasant to carry gossip when it bears no connection to reality."

Atherton sneered. "A sore point, is it, old boy? No need to turn snappish."

Morland stared coolly at Atherton. After a moment he flicked a nonexistent speck of lint from the immac-

ulate sleeve of his superfine coat. "I hadn't realized that
my fortune—or lack of it—was such a source of interest,
Atherton. Shall I send my man of business around to
keep you personally informed?"

Atherton's face took on a slight flush. His fingers
clenched for a moment, then he tossed back his drink
and tugged irritably at his waistcoat. "It's a matter of
complete indifference to me *what* you do. One hears
things, that's all." His eyes glittered. "About you and
Louisa Landringham, for example. Are you still plowing her? She always was greedy for anything in pants,
as I recall."

Morland's eyes hardened. "If I were, Atherton, do
you think I would boast of it here? To *you?*"

"Why not? You must have had most of the females
in London by now, Louisa included."

Morland knew Atherton was purposely trying to
provoke him, angry at having been overruled in the
day's decision about the pillow book. He suspected the
drunken peer had had his eye on Germaine for some
time now too. Perhaps it was just as well. Morland had
already decided to give his mistress her *congé*.

But Atherton, flushed with drink, was just beginning
his attack. "And of course there's the fair Germaine.
That mistress of yours is a hot-blooded little bitch. Did
you share her with Andrew the way you shared Louisa
between you?"

For a moment Morland thought of calling him out.
It would be pleasant to send a bullet straight between
the man's eyes. But not over Germaine, he decided.
Certainly not over a jade like Louisa Landringham.

So instead of the challenge Atherton expected, he
received only a mocking smile. "First my finances, and
now my bed partners. Really, Atherton, one must assume that you lead an exceedingly dull life to be so
interested in mine."

Atherton's face flushed crimson. "By God, I'll—"

Still smiling, Morland tossed in his hand and
pushed away from the table. "I'm afraid that does it for
me, gentlemen. My luck's out. and the company grows
rather insipid tonight, anyway."

Muted protests came from the other players at the table, but Morland paid no attention. Loath to hear more of Atherton's crudity, he rose to his feet and sauntered off through the saloon, nodding to an acquaintance here and there.

Only the narrowing of his eyes betrayed his inner fury.

Andrew again. Even now he couldn't escape the sly looks, the barbed reminders of his twin brother's profligacy and extravagance. Blast it, when would he finally be free of his brother's black reputation?

But Morland's face was impassive when he strode past the porter at the front of the club. "Ah, Sommerby, good to see you looking so fit."

The head porter, a pasty-faced man of indeterminate age, hastened to provide Morland with hat, cane, and gloves. Then he gave a discreet cough. "I shouldn't go out there if I were you, my lord."

"Indeed? You intrigue me, Sommerby."

"There is a carriage waiting in the street. I believe it has been waiting there for some time, my lord."

"I see. And no doubt you can supply the identity of the carriage's owner?"

Another cough, equally discreet. "Lady Landringham, I believe."

Morland stiffened. So the woman had resorted to following him. She had been pursuing him for months now and had even had the temerity to conceal herself in his carriage on one occasion. She had been quite naked except for garters and stockings under her cloak, as Morland had discovered.

But Louisa Landringham's venality was too sharp to be offset by her beauty, Morland found.

So he was especially appreciative of Sommerby's intervention. "Do you have a back stairs? Something through the kitchens, perhaps?"

The porter smiled conspiratorially. "I believe the thing might be arranged, my lord." A gold sovereign passed discreetly into the porter's fingers.

At the rear staircase the two men parted without

another word, each well satisfied with the evening's work.

Outside, Morland drew a deep breath as a damp wind lashed his cheeks. He was feeling faintly reckless, the result of the quantity of brandy he had consumed, no doubt. But he was enjoying that recklessness, enjoying a pleasant sense of invulnerability.

Perhaps brandy had its uses. At least his leg did not bother him as much as it usually did.

Morland started for the rear alley that led to the side of Brooks's, secure in the knowledge that Louisa would never dream of looking for him there. As he started down the cobbled alley, he wavered a little.

Careful, old man. More than a little bosky tonight.

But Morland decided he didn't give a damn if he was. Maybe tonight he would be able to sleep without the ghosts of Salamanca hovering at his shoulder.

A dim bar of moonlight drifted through a slit in the velvet curtains. The faint light filtered in a soft halo around a slender figure tugging on a jacket of black padded silk. Loose silk trousers followed, and then cloth-soled slippers.

Last of all came the black hood, dropped in place and anchored firmly about the neck.

Then, fully dressed in the black that made her blend into the night, Francesca Cameron turned to the east and bowed respectfully to a teacher ten thousand miles away in the heart of China.

She cleared her mind with the movement, focusing on nothing beyond the respect owed by student to teacher. And as old Abbot Tang had taught her long ago at Shao-lin, with that first careful movement she carried herself beyond fear, beyond uncertainty.

Beyond preparation even.

For the best preparation, Abbot Tang had shown her, was *no* preparation at all. It was a life lived in full awareness of the moment, a life of careful harmony enhanced by sharpest instincts.

Only that way could one be balanced enough to respond instantly to any threat.

And there were many kinds of threats, Chessy knew. The most dangerous of all were those that lived inside one's own head.

But she did not think of that now. Now was for the old ways, the ways of silence and softness, the ways of centuries-old skills that gave one a strength beyond iron or gunpowder.

First with mind, then with breath, and then with body she called up the balance and harmony that were always the beginning of each exercise. Dreamlike, she slid her hands before her, her mind clear, pure and empty as a mountain stream.

Her cloth soles made no sound as she slid through the familiar movements. Slow and fluid she circled, cutting across the beam of moonlight with the same silent grace that had made the old abbot marvel all those summers ago.

And Midnight was still graceful, still swift. Only she was no longer a girl, but a woman.

Without warning foot and palm flashed from the darkness in a blur of black silk. She twisted, then rolled to her feet with no loss of balance or excess motion. Had an enemy stood on that spot, he would be choking right now, she knew.

She was glad it had never come to that. To allow an enemy to force one to fight was to lose.

But she knew that tonight she would need all her skill and all her control, since balance and calm would not come easily to her.

For where Lord Morland was concerned, Francesca Cameron had discovered that her heart was anything but calm.

9

Morland's head was throbbing by the time he rounded Half Moon Street. Scowling, he hunched his shoulders against a slashing wind that promised rain before morning.

As usual his knee was troubling him. When the weather was about to change, it bothered him most of all.

The earl smiled grimly. Surely *trouble* was too kind a word for the pain gnawing through his injured joint now.

His jaw hardened as he covered the last block, trying to blot out the ache that seemed to eat out from the very center of his joint.

It had been this way ever since Salamanca, of course. He had gone back to the Peninsula immediately after his return from the Orient, driven by anger and bitterness at a happiness he could never have. He had been running hard, trying to forget a pair of haunting violet eyes . . .

He had taken a ball from behind during the final assault on the city. The French voltigeur had been swift but very efficient.

Mercifully, the impact had not shattered his knee. The ball had lodged in the tissue behind the bone and had to be gouged out under conditions that could only be described as barbaric.

After that Morland had been packed off to England for recovery. For three months he been unable to walk—and unable to walk comfortably for ten.

Not that he was *ever* really comfortable.

But by habit he ignored the pain. He had learned that it was always best to ignore what could not be changed.

He tried to do that now. Tried—and failed.

For even with the brandy fumes clouding his brain, he could feel every excruciating movement, every subtle jarring of bone against tendon.

And yet as he climbed the steps to the elegant colonnaded townhouse that had been his family's London residence for nearly two hundred years, Morland's pace was steady and his back straight.

Only at the top step did he falter slightly, misjudging the distance in the darkness. His boot skipped, and his knee jammed into the wall.

He smothered a curse, grabbing at the iron rail. Pain slammed white-hot through his knee.

But by the time his butler answered his knock, his color was even, and his features once again composed. "Ah, Whitby, a fine night for a walk. Rain before morning, I shouldn't wonder."

"Quite likely, my lord." Only by firm force of will did the butler avoid glancing into the street.

Not that it mattered.

The coach would be there waiting, just as it always was. The coachman would have followed the earl home from his club—or wherever else he had been—close enough to be hailed but never so close as to intrude.

And just like every other night, the coachman would be ignored, while the earl forced himself to walk, no matter how great the pain.

Whitby suppressed a raw curse.

Bloody war, he thought.

Bloody French.

Bloody Salamanca.

He still remembered how Morland had looked when he'd returned from that last grisly Peninsular campaign. Gaunt, pale, his skin stretched over his high cheekbones, he'd looked more dead than alive.

Even then he'd said little and complained not at all.

But everyone in the house had heard him moan in the night, struggling with pain and unknown demons. The months had passed, and his leg had healed, but Whitby knew that the pain had persisted.

And then Andrew had died. Tony had stepped in to oversee the estate's dwindling resources and, of course, to comfort Andrew's children. Anthony's recovery, Whitby knew, had owed a great deal to those two children who'd come to rely upon him completely.

"Uncle Tony" soon became the world for them, and sometimes Whitby wondered if the reverse wasn't equally true.

The servant sighed. He watched the tall, stubborn ex-soldier strip off gloves and hat and stride not quite steadily toward the staircase.

As usual, all Whitby could do was follow, knowing full well that Morland would accept no help from him or anyone else.

Morland scowled at the polished marble stairs leading to his bedroom. They seemed to smile back at him, smooth and chill as a row of giant teeth.

Not quite up to that yet, old man, he thought grimly. *Better have one last drink before attempting the ascent.*

"No need to wait up, Whitby. I'll be up for a while yet."

"Very well, your lordship." If the old retainer who had been butler to three generations of Langfords had any doubts about this explanation, he did not show it. "Good night, then, your lordship."

Morland smiled grimly. At least he had dispensed with an audience for tonight's performance. And he knew it wasn't the brandy that would make him stumble on the marble steps.

Slowly he crossed the polished marble floor and entered the rear room that he'd converted into a study. Books lined two walls from floor to ceiling, while the third wall was covered with an eclectic assortment of botanical prints, naval scenes, and a pair of matched Chinese vertical scrolls in bold black calligraphy.

God bless Whitby for seeing that a fire was laid, Morland thought, sinking into a worn velvet settee and raising his leg onto a footstool before the fire.

For a moment the pain was blinding. His face paled as he dug his fingers into the taut, knotted muscles that were his legacy of Salamanca.

Finally the agony began to ease. With a sigh Morland lay back, too tired to fix himself the drink he knew he didn't need anyway. For a moment his eyes settled on the book-covered desk, where a pile of papers awaited his attention. But work was beyond him tonight. Instead he stared into the flames, watching the colors flicker and dance together.

When his eyes finally drifted shut, he was dreaming.

Dreaming of a balmy tropical night and a starstrewn sky. Of violet eyes. Of blue-black hair lush with the scent of sandalwood and orange blossoms.

A damp wind growled up Half Moon Street, ripping at the first spring bluebells, scattering soft petals to the hard earth.

But the slim figure hidden among the twisting chimneys paid no attention to wind or chill. Her eyes were focused on the lights being gradually extinguished in the adjoining wing.

Not very long now.

Chessy shivered as a gust of wind whipped at her face. She would allow him a little under an hour before she made her way around to the empty attic room at the rear of the house. She knew its location perfectly.

And until then . . .

Curling into a ball, she slid back against the sloping roof. There, hidden between two overhanging gables, she let her mind wander. . . .

*T*he hills had been green and fragrant with cedar and pine that summer when her father had delivered her into the care of a Chinese merchant who was to see her safe to Shao-lin.

Boylike, her long hair tugged harshly into the requisite braid, Chessy had blinked back tears as the time for parting came.

Her father had hugged her close. "So you've gotten your wish at last, little one. It won't be easy, you know. You've had good teachers here in Macao, but none like you'll find there at Shao-lin. You'll all train in secret, of course. The emperor is still afraid of plots to overthrow him. And if anyone except the abbot learns that you are not the mixed-blood Kirghiz boy from Turkestan that you claim to be, then your life will be in grave danger."

Her father's hands had clenched on hers for a moment. Chessy knew he was fighting an urge to tell her to give it up and return home with him to Macao.

But he had not. James Cameron of all people understood her restless urge to do something no one else had done before, to accomplish something that had been a burning dream ever since she was old enough to mimic the Chinese village boys playing emperor and rebel in the market square.

They had parted in silence then, she a slender fifteen-year-old in rough black trousers and padded jacket, with a face that showed wisdom and determination far beyond its years.

Her father, gaunt and imposing with jade green eyes and a shock of prematurely white hair, had squeezed her fingers tightly, then stepped back, watching expressionlessly as she was handed up into a curtained palanquin to begin the long trip north.

If his tears had flowed, it had only been much later in the privacy of his own room.

The year that had followed had been miraculous, grueling, and wonderful beyond Chessy's wildest dreams. There had been only one other foreigner there, a broad-shouldered warrior of French, Scots, and Manchu parentage. Every morning, she had risen with keen excitement for what marvels the day would bring. And every night she *had gone to sleep bruised and exhausted, with split knuckles and bleeding hands.*

But she had learned.

When at last the abbot had summoned her to his private chamber, she had gone with mixed emotions. For she had learned too well, it seemed. A certain Manchu princess, passing through the village one day, had been intrigued by the slender young Kirghiz boy of mixed blood. Chessy's talents had been noted, as had the strange amethyst shade of her eyes.

So she could stay no longer. The abbot was sorrowful but adamant about that. He had also been relieved, Chessy noticed. Her masquerade had brought danger upon the whole village, and she could only guess at the vast favor he must have owed to her father for him to agree to her year of training there.

They had had one last bout then. It had been exquisite with ritual since each one knew this would be their last. The old master warrior had reserved none of his power or skill this time, yet Chessy had parried him easily, sustaining only one blow to the shoulder instead of the dozens she once would have borne.

The abbot had been very pleased. "You have learned well, young one. But now you must go, before Precious Pearl returns with her roving eye. She is insatiable, that one, and goes through men as quickly as she does slippers. Ah, the stories I could tell you. . . ."

He had held Chessy's shoulder a moment, gazing deep into her eyes—even deeper into her heart. "Seek far, English one with the midnight hair. To seek is part of the great game of life. But do not forget the greatest wisdom, Midnight: What seems most distant is often the closest at hand."

High on the rooftop in the dark of the London night, Chessy shivered slightly and reached inside her collar. Her ribs were still aching from her leap across the rooftop the night before, so she had not worn her usual tight binding at her chest.

Her cold fingers ran over the jagged outline of the

jade dragon that hung at her throat. Perfectly carved
from one piece of apple-green Burmese jadeite, the
dragon had been her teacher's last gift. The old abbot
had retained the second half for himself.

Chessy traced the broken line where the dragon was
cut in two above its tail. She could still hear her old
teacher's voice, not quite steady: "With this, English
one, my spirit will follow you. Remember that, Midnight. Remember, too, that one day, should you require
my help, you will find it through my dragon."

As the damp, smoky London wind howled over the
rooftops, Chessy stroked the dragon and remembered.
Suddenly she felt lost, adrift, and very far from home.

And then she crouched forward. Had something
moved there among the chimneys?

Tensely, she watched the darting shadows cast by
the cloud-swept three-quarter moon.

Nothing.

With a sigh she sank back against the eaves. Of
course there was no one, she told herself sternly. Who
else would be foolish enough to huddle up here among
the chimneys on such a night?

But as she settled down to wait, a faint prickle of
tension gathered at the top of her spine and did not
leave.

Precisely one hour later Chessy slid from her hiding
place. Carefully she inched past a singularly ugly gar-
goyle, then crept on toward the main wing of the house.

It was an imposing sight, even with windows darkened. On three sides granite wings rose before a high
stone wall surmounted by griffin heads.

But Chessy had no time to admire the architecture
of Lord Morland's London residence. Already she could
feel the air growing chill, dense with moisture. In a
matter of hours there would be rain. Even she, agile as
she was, could not move safely on wet tiles.

Which meant it was now or never.

Quickly she crossed the high, slanting roof and
made her way to the main wing. An ornate stone railing

ran along the entire front face, mirrored two flights
below by a row of balconies overlooking the courtyard.
Chessy's eyes narrowed as she calculated the distance
from railing to porch. Just in case . . .

Her cloth soles made no noise as she inched to the
top of the roof and crossed to the back slope. Carefully
she made her way down to the darkened window at the
far end.

The window was unlocked, just as this morning's
note had promised it would be.

Slowly Chessy raised the pane and listened. Hearing
no sound, she slid cautiously inside. She had already
memorized the plans of Morland's house and had no
trouble finding her way down the corridor to the huge
circular staircase that dominated the heart of the
house.

She did not take the servants' stairs, where she
would be more likely to encounter some late-working
steward or kitchen scullion. No, best to take the main
staircase and slip out of sight before anyone noticed.

A lone pair of candles flickered by the columned
entrance as Chessy darted from the stairs and took
refuge in a shadowed recess next to a marble Greek
nymph.

She studied the arrangement of the grand columns
and small mirrors flanking the front door. Bad *feng-
shui* there. Oh, yes, very bad. The mirrors should be
moved to cast their light upon all who entered, spread-
ing good fortune and energy throughout the household.
And two was an inauspicious number. Three would be
better, nine best of all.

She frowned. Great misfortune might stem from
such an arrangement, especially when it occurred at
the front door, where the *feng-shui*, or energies of the
whole household were collected and stabilized.

Chessy was still frowning when she heard footsteps
approach from the corridor to her left. She shrank back
into the recess as a black-clad servant with a lone
candle crossed the foyer and disappeared down the
facing corridor.

Chessy waited. She knew precisely where to look.

This morning's note from her father's captors had been very specific.

A few moments later the servant returned the way he had come, his face grave. Chessy slipped down the corridor toward Morland's study.

The room was lovely, with one wall covered with beautiful artwork and a very fine pair of calligraphic scrolls. A silver candelabrum burned on a rosewood side table, casting a mellow glow as Chessy slipped inside.

She skirted the lacquer screen flanking the fireplace and made for her goal, a mahogany campaign desk whose surface was nearly hidden beneath papers, journals, and well-marked books.

It was a room made to be used and enjoyed, a room that reflected the energy and eclectic tastes of its owner, right down to the matched imperial jade carvings on the edge of the desk.

But where was the bloody book?

Abruptly Chessy froze. From the corner of the screen, where a pair of settees faced the fire, there came a faint creaking. Her eyes widened as she saw the motionless figure stretched atop the nearer settee.

A figure with broad shoulders and tousled blond hair.

Sweet heavens, what was *Morland* doing down here? He ought to have been in his room hours ago!

Chessy shrank back into the shadows. Her heart hammered as she studied the even rise and fall of the earl's chest. When she was finally satisfied that he was asleep, she crept from her hiding place.

The witless man hadn't even removed his boots. Chessy sniffed the air. Alcohol—and a great deal of it, unless she was mistaken. So he had been drinking.

But somehow Chessy could not look away from the broad brow and sculpted features, deeply bronzed in the flickering firelight. Yes, he was still every bit as handsome as he had been ten years earlier, she admitted reluctantly. It was fortunate that she was on to his tricks now and would know how to defend herself against that lazy charm he used so well!

The same way you defended yourself this morning? a mocking voice asked. *The way you melted into his kiss and moaned at his touch?*

Flushing at the memory, Chessy scowled down at the desk's secret drawer. There was the lion, just as the note had said. As she twisted the animal's tail, a hidden latch was freed and an inner compartment sprang open.

From inside Chessy drew out a handful of rolled vellum sheets. Frustration seized her. She stared down blankly at column after column of ornate script. *Son of a turtle*, she could make nothing of it!

Perhaps they were some sort of code, mementos of his days at war.

Another noise came from the settee. Quickly she stuffed the documents back into their hiding place, then twisted the lion's tail to reseal the compartment.

Her breath checked as Morland shifted restlessly and threw one arm over the edge of the settee.

And then she saw it. Beneath his arm, half concealed by the white linen of his sleeve, lay a silk-covered Chinese book.

Chessy's breath caught. She stared at the hand-sewn fabric cover. *Could it possibly be the book that would buy her father's freedom?*

Silently she crept to the head of the settee. The binding was right. The silk was very fine. And the title read—

Frowning, she tried to make out the Chinese characters in the candlelight, but failed.

Her heart pounding, she bent closer. Only inches away, Morland twisted in his sleep. Muttering, he rolled to his side, leaving a little more of the book revealed.

With trembling fingers Chessy tried to ease the volume free.

Just a few more inches . . .

At that moment the sleeping earl tossed out an arm, which swept across Chessy's silk-clad breast.

She froze.

His strong fingers opened, cupping the soft curve he had discovered. A muscle flashed at his jaw.

Chessy stood rigid, her breath a hot, wild thing trapped behind her teeth as Morland's experienced fingers made a slow but thorough exploration of this virgin territory.

Heat leaped through her, but she still did not move, afraid to pull away, afraid even to breathe for fear of waking him.

His hard fingers slid back and forth. The movement sent bright tongues of flame to each contact point. Chessy bit back a whimper as he found the taut bud that bloomed beneath his skillful caress.

Morland felt it too. He groaned and rolled the tight, pouting nub between his fingers.

Desire, hot and reckless. It crackled between them, sweet and lush as a tropical night.

Morland stiffened. Frowning, he twisted over onto his side, mumbling low.

"Enough! Go away, damn it. . . ."

Even then Chessy could not move. Somehow her knees had turned to sponge cake, and the strange melting sensation that began in her throat and ended in the unnamable place between her thighs didn't even bear thinking about.

She was just inching back toward the recessed windows when Morland gave a low, harsh cry. She waited, her heart hammering.

Morland clutched at his leg, tossing from side to side. His nails dug into the velvet cushions. "Get down over there, Simms! Snipers coming over the hill, man! Simms? Dear God—" His voice shook. "Give me a hand here, sergeant. Quickly, he's hit! Hurry or he'll—God, they're coming over! No bloody time. Tighten that line, sergeant. Move, man! Do it now, or it'll be too late!"

Chessy listened in terrible silence, watching Morland toss restlessly. His long fingers gripped the pale cushions. A strange burning pain filled her throat.

She felt a wild urge to seize his hand and offer words of comfort, to wake him and free him from his dark dreams.

But Chessy knew she could never allow Lord Morland to discover her here. All she could do was watch,

cold with horror, while the earl tossed back and forth
on the velvet settee, his mind hundreds of miles away,
trapped amid the bleak, rocky passes of Portugal or
Spain.

Could she ever understand what demons haunted
him? And even if she could, what difference would it
make? There was nothing between them now, nothing
but a few brief golden memories followed by a vast
black sea of regret.

*What happened to you, Tony? What happened to both
of us? And why, oh why can't life ever work out the way it
does in dreams?*

Somewhere in the darkness a clock chimed four
o'clock. With a soft sigh Chessy made for the corridor.
Soon the servants would be rising, laying fires and
fetching water. She could do no more here tonight.

Without warning the tall figure on the settee jerked
upright. "Who's there?" He dragged trembling fingers
through his tousled, flame-bronzed hair. "Whitby? Is
that you?"

Chessy shrank back amid the curtains, white-faced.

Morland gave a low, harsh laugh as he stared into
the darkness. For long moments he did not move, but
simply sat staring into the fire. One hand slid down to
massage his right knee. Chessy saw him grimace as he
worked his way slowly up the other side.

Then with a sigh the earl lifted his leg between his
hands and awkwardly maneuvered it down until his
boot was flat upon the floor. Clenching his fingers upon
the arm of the settee, he pushed to his feet and began a
slow, stiff-legged progress across the room.

Again and again, his right leg scraped the polished
floor. Twice he had to reach out to support himself
against the wall.

With every step, Chessy felt a cruel pain gnaw deep
into her heart. By the time Morland reached the door,
her cheeks were wet with tears.

10

The knocking began on Chessy's rear door the next morning promptly at the first stroke of eight.

Two servants stood at the back staircase, looking stiff and proper and extremely out of place. Even Swithin, who ushered them inside, pronounced them to be a vastly impressive pair of superior London domestics.

"But there must be some mistake," Chessy told Swithin when he brought her the news. "I hired no new staff. You know as well as I that we cannot afford the extra expense."

"No mistake, miss. Said as how they was to explain it to you direct."

Chessy sighed. "Oh, very well, Swithin. Where have you put them?"

"In the yellow room, Miss Chessy."

A few minutes later, Chessy opened the door to the little room off the front foyer. As always, her eyes narrowed in distaste at the jaundiced walls that had long since ceased to resemble anything so attractive as yellow.

And there at the threshold she halted, amazed.

The butler was impeccably clad and looked to be an utter martinet. The housekeeper was immaculate in black bombazine and crisp white linen. Chessy could only stare in growing confusion as the housekeeper ran a white-gloved finger along the dusty windowsill, then shook her head in disapproval.

"But there must be some mistake. I'm afraid I did not—"

The butler bowed. "There is no mistake, Miss Cameron. His lordship's orders were quite explicit. Number twenty-seven Dorrington Street. Duration of service to be six weeks."

The butler's iron-gray eyes fixed impersonally on a faded patch of wallpaper above Chessy's right shoulder. "All wages are to be paid by his lordship, of course."

Chessy felt a strange, not quite unpleasant hysteria snake through her. "His lordship?" she repeated faintly.

The Earl of Morland. He has discovered that Morwood House is adequately staffed without our presence. He thought you might find our services—er, useful."

Chessy watched in amazement as the housekeeper summoned a groom from the rear yard. Out in the mews a parade of men in thick leather aprons began to convey a load of heavy crates toward the house.

"Oh, but I couldn't! It would be quite out of the question for me to—"

Swithin bent low and whispered in her ear. "What's all the argle-bargle fer, Miss Chessy? Don't look this gift horse in the mouth, that's what I'm advising."

"But it's not right," Chessy said. "And I can never hope to—"

"No need to fret yourself. You heard the man—paid fer all right and proper, they are. And as yourself is knowing just as well as I am, we're sorely short of help right now."

"Yes, of course, but—"

"Besides, if this earl sees fit to send over several of his people to help out, who are you to cut up stiff? Knowing your father as he does, why, mebbe the man just feels in a manner of a relative. Sommat like—like your uncle, say."

Chessy frowned, watching in dismay as the windows were thrown open and a trio of crisp young women attacked the house, mops and brooms in hand, all under the militant eye of the housekeeper.

Uncle? Tony Morland? Is that what he considered her, an awkward, gawky niece?

Pain darkened Chessy's eyes for a moment. "I can't hope to repay him, Swithin. You know how things stand. At the very least I must make my financial situation clear to him. And then—well, if he still persists in this outlandish generosity, I suppose . . . I suppose I must accept it."

Swithin smiled faintly as Chessy walked upstairs. He liked the earl, so he did. And the old servant had decided that it was time Miss Chessy had someone taking care of *her* for a change!

Less than a quarter of an hour later, a terse note reached Half Moon Street. The script was awkward and hastily written.

> *I am honored by your assistance, of course, but I cannot hope to pay the wages of such superior servants.*
>
> *F.C.*

Ten minutes later a liveried groom brought back an equally terse reply.

Chessy fingered the unopened note that Swithin had brought her. Outside the door a liveried groom waited impassively.

Chessy gnawed her lip. "Perhaps you would—care for some refreshment? While I frame a reply, that is."

Only when the groom had gone below to the kitchen did she hand the unopened missive to Swithin. She gave a ragged, rather desperate laugh. "What an utter dunce I am! More letters to be read." Then she sighed and her eyes misted with tears. "How ever would I manage without you, Swithin?"

"Damned fine is how you'd manage, Miss Chessy! I've not the slightest doubt of it." The servant's voice was gruff. "But there's no reason that you can't learn to read. After all, I did it."

Chessy's chin rose proudly. "No lectures, Swithin. Not now, please. We've been through this all before. The language is hopeless, and I'll have to manage without it. I've tried and I've failed. So will you please just read me the message?"

The servant's brow creased as he smoothed the velum sheet and studied its elegant script. Haltingly he began to read.

> *My dearest Miss Cameron,*
>
> *The honor is all mine in your accepting this trifling gift. As for payment, if you would consent to receive me later this morning, then I shall be glad to discuss some manner of remuneration that will be acceptable to us both.*
>
> *Yours, etc.*
> *M.*

Swithin looked up, his eyes keen. "Will you be wishing to send a reply, miss?"

For a moment Chessy's violet eyes glistened with unshed tears. She stared down at the indecipherable script, at the line of English letters that formed words she had never learned how to read. She who could read Chinese verse eight centuries old, she who could write lines of poetry of her own with exquisite brushwork.

But Chinese was not English, and to Chessy these vowels and consonants might just as well have been arcane Egyptian pictographs.

It had all begun as she had drifted from one part of Asia to another with her ever-restless father. She had detested the stiff, disapproving governesses he engaged, preferring to spend her time in the dirt beside him, digging for antiquities.

Through the years she had learned everything there was to learn about prehistoric arrowheads and primitive cutting tools—but nothing about reading or writing in English.

And what her father's restless, unstructured life had begun, pride now kept her from rectifying. There it was again, she thought. That deadly Cameron pride. But Chessy found she was too old to change.

No, she would never again seek the services of some prosy pedant. She had tried that once, only to suffer the humiliation of having the fellow tell her not to bother. The giddy female mind was incapable of accomplishing such a task at the advanced age of twenty-one, he had pronounced decisively.

That had been her last effort.

But what did it matter if she couldn't read English? Soon her father would be free, and she would be on her way back to Macao. She would never visit this chill, fog-infested country again!

Chessy walked to the window. Out in the bustling street, a short man in a rumpled coat stood leaning against the fence of the house opposite. A shiver worked down her spine as he stared insolently up at her window.

Was he working with her father's captors? He was not the *first* man to study her house over the last few weeks, Chessy knew.

Forget it, my girl. It's just nerves. Nerves and an overactive imagination. A few weeks more, and this will be no more than a brief and very bad dream.

Chessy only wished she could believe that. . . .

She heard a rustling sound and looked down to see the vellum sheet crumbled to a misshapen lump in her hand.

When she looked back out the window, her mysterious lurker had gone. If only all her *other* problems would disappear so fast, Chessy thought bitterly.

11

"**Y**ou are *impossible!* I can't imagine *what* lunacy convinced me to consent to this, you know."

The white-haired Duchess of Cranford sat stiffly, her eyes keen on Lord Morland's face as his carriage sprang into motion.

"What, you didn't do it because you fell victim to my extraordinary rakehell charm?" The Earl of Morland gave his elderly companion a self-mocking smile. "Don't tell me you mean to dash my pretensions, Your Grace?"

The duchess studied her companion with a look that mingled exasperation and fondness. "You really are the worst sort of scoundrel, Tony Morland. Don't think you fool me for a second."

"*I?* I wouldn't dream of trying."

The duchess's blue eyes sharpened. "And now, since I have so unwisely committed to this rash course of action, you had better tell me about this female we are to visit. Cameron, did you say her name was?"

Morland nodded, wisely holding back a smile.

"Cameron . . . I knew an Arthur Cameron once. Ages, it's been. The man was quite smitten with me, as a

114

matter of fact." The duchess's lips curved up at some secret memory. "Of course, he was an out-and-out rascal, without a feather to fly with. A match was quite out of the question. I heard he upped and sailed to America to make his fortune, leaving behind a string of broken hearts from Southampton to Scarborough. I wonder if he could be any relation."

Almost certainly, Morland thought.

"Speak up, boy."

"Er—quite unlikely, Your Grace. The Camerons are an old and respected family. Holdings to the north, I believe." The lie came very smoothly.

The duchess stared intently at Morland. He was looking remarkably handsome this morning. His frock coat of dark blue superfine had the superb fit that pronounced it the work of Weston, while his waistcoat of gold damask added the ideal hint of color. His cream-colored pantaloons were perfection itself.

Of course, the duchess did not tell him this. "Humph. One thing I'll say for you, my boy, you always could tie a neckcloth to perfection. Nothing hamhanded about you. Even my poor departed Bartholomew, bless his soul, never could aspire to the Oriental."

Her head angled forward as she studied the exquisite folds of Morland's crisp linen. "Or is that the Mathematical?" Her eyesight was not as good as it once was, but she refused to make any concession to her advancing age.

"It's a design of my own creation, actually," came the lazy reply. "It has been dubbed 'the Langford,' I believe."

"Humph. And a Corinthian to boot. What if I said it was time you put those talents of yours to better use? Like setting up a household, perhaps." She shook her silver-handled cane for emphasis. "And a nursery, while you're at it, young man. It's high time, after all."

Morland raised one lazy blond brow. "Your Grace had someone particular in mind? Or is this duty of mine to be exercised upon a nameless abstraction?"

The duchess planted her cane and gave way to reluctant laughter. "Oh, I could name you half a dozen

eligible females who would have you in a second. And
there must be a hundred more giddy but entirely ineli-
gible females who've set their caps on you even as we
speak. But no, you exasperating boy, I have no *particular* candidates in mind right now."

"If you did, I would most certainly know it," Morland said dryly.

"The problem with you, Tony Morland, is that
you've had too *many* giddy females with more hair
than wit trotted out for your inspection in the last five
years. It's hardened you, changed you. When you look
out at Almack's now, you might as well be eyeing the
horseflesh at Tattersalls."

Morland gave a faint shrug. "But my dear, I never
go to Almack's anymore. Too endlessly fatiguing."

"You see? There it is. The whole business has gone
to your head, that's what it's done." The duchess's cane
struck the carriage floor for emphasis. "But let me tell
you this, young man, if I ever *do* find the right woman,
never doubt that I'll set her at you like a cat to cream.
Aye, and I'll not stop until I see you anvil-bound and
leg-shackled, you young jackanapes!"

"You deprive me of speech, Your Grace."

"Rubbish! You were *never in your life* speechless."
Abruptly the duchess chuckled. "So what's the female
like? An out-and-out harridan, no doubt? Totally un-
manageable, I should imagine. And why are you taking
such an interest in the gel?"

Morland smoothed a tiny wrinkle in his immaculate
buff doeskin morning gloves. "Which question would
you like answered first, my dear? I believe that makes
three."

The duchess's blue eyes glittered. "The *last* one."

"My interest in Miss Cameron is in the nature of a
debt of honor. As I believe I informed you earlier, Miss
Cameron is the daughter of an old and very dear friend.
After her father saved my life—for the second time, I
might add—in a fit of weakness I promised him whatever assistance I could in securing his daughter's entrance into London Society."

His voice was all bland sincerity.

You can use that story to great effect in Society, Tony Morland, but it won't hold water with me, the duchess thought.

At that moment their carriage drew up before a narrow townhouse on a street that was far from fashionable.

"I am sure you will find Miss Cameron delightful. You of all people should understand the, er—charms of someone quite out of the ordinary way."

The duchess gave a snort. "Don't try to turn me up soft, boy. I learned the art when your scamp of a father was still in leading strings!"

"I have no doubt of it, Your Grace." The earl restrained a smile as he handed the fragile old woman down the steps.

"Impertinent whelp."

But the duchess's eyes, Morland noted, were sparkling with an excitement he had not seen there in months. And though her step was not quite steady as she leaned on his arm in ascending the marble stairs, her chin was high.

No one would ever think to look at her that she lived in continuing agony, he thought. Right now she looked quite the dragon, in fact. To all but Morland, who knew too well the cost of holding a smile in the face of constant pain.

But she was not thinking of her infirm joints now. She was caught up in her matrimonial speculations. Yes, Tony decided, the next few minutes should prove thoroughly amusing. *Almost* enough to compensate for the damnable discomfort of having given the two finest servants in London into Chessy's employ.

The earl gave a faint shudder, trying to forget the sight of the burned toast and congealed eggs that had awaited him in the breakfast room that morning. He only hoped that Miss Cameron realized *exactly* what a paragon she had in her new housekeeper.

When the door opened, Whitby's aquiline profile was revealed. "Your Grace. Your lordship," the butler intoned. "If you will follow me."

They passed down freshly polished corridors heady

with the scent of lemon oil and beeswax. Morland nodded approvingly. Mrs. Harris was as efficient as ever.

He sighed, recalling the chaos he had left behind him at Half Moon Street, where the parlormaid had been busy quarreling with the valet, and the groom had been quarreling with both of them.

Yes, he truly hoped that Miss Cameron enjoyed her treasure. . . .

Whitby turned and held open the door to a small, sunlit rear parlor. "Miss Cameron will attend you shortly. Would you care for refreshment while you wait?"

Morland glanced at the duchess, who shook her head. At the moment she appeared too interested in the room's contents to think of eating.

And Morland couldn't blame her. The room's wooden shelves boasted a row of striking curiosities. Idly Morland ran his fingers across a ceramic teapot worked in the shape of a peach, complete with leaves for a lid and a twisting stem for a handle.

Beside the teapot stood an exquisite goddess in rare lavender-colored jadeite. That single statue alone, Morland estimated, would have netted Chessy the cost of hiring a whole army of servants and all the coal she could use in a lifetime.

He could only respect her good taste in refusing to part with such a treasure.

Beneath the sculpture stood two very elegant blue and white bowls decorated with peonies. Morland guessed them to be early thirteenth century. They were the finest he had ever seen.

The salon door opened. Beside him the Duchess of Cranford stiffened. One hand tightened on her silver cane, and the other clutched at the lacquer table for support.

Morland frowned. Perhaps the climb from the carriage had been a greater strain than he had realized. Quickly he moved to take the old woman's fragile fingers and tuck them into the crook of his arm. Only then did he turn back.

His eyes widened. Chessy stood on the threshold, luminous in a gown of lavender muslin with darker violet ribbons. The silk perfectly matched her eyes, Morland thought dimly.

And her hair . . .

Something tightened in his throat. Something quite disturbing.

Instead of curling and frizzing her hair into the ringlets so favored by *ton* beauties, Chessy had pulled back her hair in a violet bow that allowed the dark, glossy mass to cascade straight down her back.

She should have looked juvenile and countrified. She should have looked awkward and harsh.

But she did not. Far from it.

At that moment she looked to Morland like Beauty incarnate, with all the exquisite grace of a Grecian goddess.

Morland felt his body tighten from chest to groin, stabbed by a blaze of white-hot desire.

A pressure on his arm called his attention back to reality. He bowed smoothly. "Ah, Miss Cameron. You are looking utterly ravishing today. I trust you will forgive my impertinence in bringing by a good friend to meet you. May I present the Duchess of Cranford."

He looked down at his companion, frowning when she did not move. Could it be that she was in greater pain than he thought?

"I—I rather think I must sit down," the duchess said faintly. Morland started to move toward an armchair beside the door.

But Chessy was before him. "Of course you must sit. How very rag-mannered you must think us!" With a cool grace that Morland found remarkable, Chessy took the duchess's hand and led her to a cut-velvet wing chair beneath a sunny window. "Whitby will be up with tea directly, but if you'd prefer something stronger . . ."

The duchess seemed to be slowly regaining her color. "No need to fuss, my dear. It's just—you have the look of someone I met many years ago, and it's taken me quite by surprise. Strange how time and memory play tricks on us. Twenty years gone."

The duchess closed her eyes for a moment, patting Chessy's wrist. "But how I'm running on. You'd be quite right to think me a hen-witted old fool. I don't usually behave this way. Morland will vouch for that."

The earl propped one broad shoulder against a newly polished mantel crowned with a vase of freshly cut daffodils. "Oh, she's right about that, Miss Cameron. The Duchess of Cranford is a terrible dragon. The whole *ton* lives in dread of her slightest setdown."

Chessy's eyes crinkled. "Indeed? Then I must remember to be on my best behavior."

"What nonsense the boy speaks." The duchess shot Tony a quelling look. "Just ignore him, my dear. I'm not half so black a figure as he paints me."

Chessy smiled. "I rather think I shall ignore him."

Morland was saved from a response by the arrival of the imperious Whitby bearing a silver tray.

"Thank you, Whitby. On the lacquer table, I think."

Morland watched appreciatively as Chessy sat down and began pouring tea. Every movement had an innate grace, he thought, watching the exquisite care with which she shifted each saucer, centered each cup, and then tendered them to her guests.

For some reason the sight made him think of her performing the same service for him.

In his home.

In his parlor.

As his wife.

When Chessy held out a fine, gold-rimmed teacup, some devil made Morland brush her fingers lightly with his own. He felt her instant tremor, saw her lovely eyes widen.

Now they were darkest purple, the earl thought dimly, nearly forgetting the teacup clutched in his fingers.

Like spring lavender.

Like richest amethyst.

Like violet damask, which was exactly what he would wish her to wear when she served tea from thin-walled porcelain cups in his sunny parlor facing Half Moon Street.

As his *wife*.

He shook his head, fighting the pull of that seductive image.

"Do you plan to meditate over your tea or to drink it, young man?" The duchess was staring at Tony with narrowed eyes.

Somehow Morland managed to wrench himself from his daydream. He smiled rather crookedly at Chessy. "You see what I mean, Miss Cameron. A regular dragon, she is." He seated himself and sampled his tea, but all the while his mind was fixed on the vision of beauty before him.

Chessy worked to hide a smile at these skirmishes, which both people clearly took great pleasure in.

"Jackanapes," the duchess muttered. "Lovely tea, by the way, Miss Cameron. I'm afraid I don't recognize the blend. Hyson? Gunpowder?"

"It's first-grade Imperial Crimson Robe. I couldn't resist the indulgence of bringing some with me from Macao. The tea comes from bushes limited to the emperor's personal use. The bushes are said to be more than four thousand years old. It was—that is, my father always—" She put her saucer down with a faint clink. "It was his favorite, you see."

Chessy cleared her throat. "But how remiss of me. I—I've neglected to offer you any of these lovely lemon tarts that Mrs. Harris has been busy at all morning."

She spoke in a rush, her face still pale, and Morland watched her with growing tension. What was it she was struggling so to conceal? "None for me, thank you," he said. "I wouldn't want anything to interfere with this superb tea."

The duchess studied Chessy as she sampled the housekeeper's work. "Quite tolerable," she pronounced when she had finished the crumbly sweet. "Good cooks are hard to find, especially when one is new to London. You must be very resourceful, Miss Cameron."

Chessy's eyes flashed to Morland's face. "Simply a bit of, er—luck, Your Grace."

At that moment, her "luck" slanted her a dark smile, which Chessy resolutely ignored. "Would you care for another?"

The duchess declined, then sat back to study her hostess. The old woman's brow knit as she fingered the silver cane propped beside her chair. "Not related to the Kinross Camerons, are you?" she demanded abruptly. "Not at all the thing, I'm bound to tell you."

"I believe not, Your Grace, but I cannot honestly say for certain. My father has been many years in the East, you see, and I have never had occasion to meet any of my relations, Highland or otherwise. In fact, I'm afraid my knowledge of the family tree is quite sketchy."

The duchess looked thoughtful for a moment, then sat forward, her cane caught tightly between her gnarled fingers. "I'm having a party two days hence, Miss Cameron. Nothing special. Just a small affair—old friends and such. But I'd be most pleased if you would attend."

Francesca looked slowly from the duchess to Lord Morland. "That is very kind, of course, but . . . I believe I must not impose on such short acquaintance."

The duchess's chin rose imperiously. "My dear girl, if *I* do not choose to feel imposed upon, then how can *you* find anything to dislike in the scheme?"

Chessy looked helplessly at Morland. "But I have not—that is, I am quite unprepared for—" She caught a breath. "I had not planned upon attending any fashionable events while in London." She ran her hand absently over her serviceable muslin dress, her eyes grave and very determined. "No, I'm afraid it's quite out of the question, though I thank you for the honor you do me in asking."

The duchess barely contained a snort as she studied the slim, self-possessed female beside her.

"Honor? All mine, I assure you. You could take London by storm, child. Ah, with those eyes and that figure. Yes, and I've half a mind to watch you do it."

Chessy blinked.

She felt the force of the old woman's will. Even worse, when she looked up Morland's eyes were upon her. Something about the intensity of his look made warmth shoot through the pit of her stomach.

She watched his long fingers cradle the fine porcelain teacup, bronze against pale blue. Somehow the sight reminded her of all the other things those strong fingers had cradled.

His mistress's naked breasts and white thighs, for a start.

Or Chessy's own silk-clad body, as he'd pulled her struggling from the window . . .

Abruptly Chessy's cheeks flushed with color. Why couldn't she put those shameful memories out of her head once and for all? The man was obviously the worst sort of libertine! It was absolutely unthinkable for her to let her thoughts run on this way!

But somehow her eyes were on his lips, and she was remembering the wild burst of heat she had felt when he had kissed her yesterday in the kitchen.

The way he had shuddered when he had touched their joined mouths.

Chessy jerked her gaze from his face and looked down, making a great business of refilling the duchess's teacup. When she looked up, the duchess was studying her keenly.

"You've not given your heart away already, have you, my dear?"

"H-heart?" Chessy stiffened.

"Warned you she was a dragon, didn't I, Miss Cameron? Nothing for it but to answer her, you know. When she's on to a thing, she's like a dog with a bone." Morland's eyes darkened. "Have you? Formed an attachment already?" he asked softly.

Chessy felt a strange pressure in her chest. Her fingers curved over the edge of the table as she fought for composure. "My heart is quite my own, though I don't know what business it is of *yours*, my lord. Actually, I've yet to meet any man who could tempt me to give up the pleasures of independence."

Morland's brow rose. "A bruising setdown, my dear. Observe how I bleed." His eyes were smoldering with an emotion Chessy could not read. "But you might find that the men of London are a different breed from those you've known in the East. Perhaps if you were brave enough to look, you might even find someone who would make you glad to set aside your precious independence."

"Do you think so?" Chessy managed a saucy little shrug. "For my part, I doubt it. And my visit here is strictly in the nature of business. Once my father and I complete that business, we shall return home. As swiftly as possible." She rose to her feet, her eyes glittering. "And bravery has absolutely *nothing* to do with it," she snapped.

The duchess rose also, an odd smile on her face. "Yes, you are the very much the image of her."

"Her?"

"A friend of mine. A very dear friend. But I fear we have provoked you quite enough for one day, my dear." The duchess pressed a small vellum card into Chessy's fingers. "Just in case you change your mind, my dear." She chuckled, shaking her head. "Demned if I wouldn't relish seeing Louisa Landringham's face when you came in, though. She's reigned over the *ton* long enough, if you ask me. Now come along, Tony." She moved imperiously toward the door. "I cannot abide laggards!"

Morland studied Chessy for a moment, his eyes strangely intent. "Are you truly recovered, Cricket?"

Chessy nodded, her fingers clenched at her waist. She was feeling strangely dizzy. She watched his hand rise to her chin.

Her heart began to pound as his warm fingers brushed her cheek. The pad of his thumb skimmed the full curve of her lower lip.

Heat. Dear God, the heat . . .

"Of—of course, I'm all right."

He gave her a tight, unreadable smile. "You are quite wrong, you know. It *is* a question of bravery, my dear. Sometimes to feel, to *really* feel, is the most terrifying thing in all the world."

And then, before Chessy could recover her breath for a scathing retort, the azure-eyed earl was gone.

"Unusual gel." The duchess's face was thoughtful as she settled back against the leather squabs. "Don't believe I've seen eyes like that in years. Not since—"

She twisted her cane idly. The likeness was remarkable! But she decided not to reveal her suspicions to Morland. Not until she was absolutely certain. Heavens, what if she was right!

"Since?"

"Oh, nothing. Do you think she'll come?"

"Impossible to say. She's a mind of her own, as you've seen." Morland's face was shuttered, unreadable in the shadows.

"What is that father of hers about to let her go racketing about by herself? The man ought to be horse-whipped."

Morland said nothing, but the hardness in his eyes suggested he saw a great deal of merit in the idea.

"She really could take the *ton* by storm." The duchess's voice grew wistful. "In a week she'd be knee-deep in suitors and positively flooded with offers. How vastly amusing it would be to—" She straightened, her face settling into its usual formality. "But talking won't pay toll. What's to be will be. If the gel chooses to be headstrong, there's nothing more to be done."

Morland smiled faintly, remembering the fire in Chessy's eyes when he had accused her of being afraid. "Don't give up hope, my dear. Miss Cameron may come around yet."

The duchess studied him sharply. "I suppose you mean to say no more than that."

"Afraid not, Your Grace."

"I remember now why I felt the need to issue your father, the duke, a slashing setdown upon our first meeting."

"I can't imagine him taking it well."

"Oh, the rogue didn't. Not in the least. But we soon found how to go on. Actually we became fast friends. I miss him greatly, you know," she added softly.

Morland caught her hand gently for a moment. "So do I. More than I ever imagined."

The duchess cleared her throat. "I only wish that I could see Louisa Landringham's face when she realizes that her throne has been toppled."

12

For long minutes Chessy did not move.

Her heart was pounding, and she could still feel the warm imprint of Morland's hands at her chin, the gentle slide of his thumb across her lip.

And the *hunger*, the unimaginable *wanting* . . .

What does that make you, little fool? Just another one of his lightskirts, that's what!

She walked to the window and stared out at the narrow square, where a border of spring bluebells trembled in the wind.

Her fingers tightened on the starched curtains. She simply had to forget the wretched man. He was nothing but a distraction, and right now *any* sort of distraction was dangerous.

But her gaze lingered on the carriage that was just rounding the corner. Her finger slid softly against her lip as she remembered the pressure of Morland's hand, the faint brush of his breath at her cheek.

What if she had her chance? What if for just one night she could be like all the other carefree, laughing ladies with nothing more important on their mind than

who would partner them at dinner and whether their
dance cards would be filled?

Chessy's vision blurred for a moment. She had been
snubbed all too often by the supercilious sons and
daughters of English merchants and government offi-
cials in Macao, Calcutta, and Madras. How they had
delighted in cutting the daughter of a ramshackle adventurer notorious across half of Asia.

Are you afraid? a goading voice asked.

*Maybe I am. If so, I have good reason to be. Those
wounds cut deep.*

But just once, what would it feel like to be escorted
by a woman who could guide and advise her? To feel
the warmth of a man's eyes in appreciation, rather
than the hard, speculative leers she was used to receiving?

*And where better to hear information than at a ton
ball?* a sly voice whispered. *Where else do the wealthy
and elite of London gather to gossip but at such an
evening's entertainment?*

Yes, at such a event she might hear all sorts of useful
gossip, even news about who might recently have acquired a precious Chinese book with fittings of pearl
and solid gold.

Chessy's chin rose. Yes, by heaven, she *would* go!
The information she acquired would be invaluable. She
might even gain an introduction to several well-known
collectors. Any one of them might have received word
that the stolen book was now being offered for sale—no
questions asked, of course.

She turned and crossed the corridor to the opposite
room. Carefully she probed the bricks above the empty
fireplace. After a moment one sprang free.

Chessy pried a long green box from the recess and
opened it.

A necklace, bracelet, and earrings lay nestled on a
bed of crimson satin. The glittering set had been a gift
from her father on her twenty-first birthday. A double
strand of perfectly matched pink pearls circled a gold
medallion worked with dragons and phoenixes. And

scattered over the golden face was a fortune in cabochon rubies and emeralds.

It was jewelry fit for an empress, her father had told her, and later Chessy learned that the set actually *had* belonged to a Chinese empress. But five centuries ago the junk carrying the precious cargo had been blown off course in a typhoon and had sunk with all hands.

James Cameron had discovered the wreck by studying old Chinese shipping documents. The blue-green waters of the South China Sea had revealed many treasures that day, but this set was the very finest.

And now Chessy meant to pawn part of it to a stranger.

Her heart rebelled for a moment. Her fingers gently stroked the delicate golden medallion.

Swiftly, before she could change her mind, she snapped the case shut. There was no choice. Even one tiny bit of information might provide the key to save her father's life.

Clutching the box in unsteady fingers, Chessy went to summon Swithin. The rout was set for Thursday, two days hence, so the duchess had said.

That would leave her very little time.

Two hours later, at a very discreet establishment on Curzon Street, a white-haired jeweler sat studying one of the finest bracelets he had ever seen in all his forty years of providing gems and fashionable ornaments to the *ton*.

The bracelet was of an Oriental style, its large unfaceted emeralds and rubies fitted with hammered gold. Clearly, the piece was old and very rare. What was even more curious, the jeweler decided, was that the piece was vaguely familiar.

Quickly he consulted a row of small wooden boxes that contained his notes on a lifetime spent buying, selling, and repairing the finest jewels in Europe.

Finally he found what he was seeking. He sat back with an audible hiss of shock.

Sweet Lord above, if this was true . . .

A moment later his pen scratched back and forth across a crisp sheet of vellum, which he folded and sealed with not-quite-steady fingers. Immediately he dispatched the missive.

But for long moments after the runner left, he simply sat, staring at the gems that lay before him, glittering in the sunlight.

He was unable to believe the amazing good fortune that had just come into his path. The Duchess of Cranford had been searching for just such a piece for five years.

And she had made it very clear that she would pay well for any information that came her way.

13

"There you are, miss, done at last. And quite fine you look too."

The very superior lady's maid whom Whitby had secured for Chessy stepped back from the mirror, smiling triumphantly.

Chessy could not speak. She could only stare in wonder at the elegant woman who looked back at her from the cheval glass.

It was impossible. It could *not* be *her* there. And yet . . .

Her cheeks were flushed, not from human device but from the heat of excitement. Her long hair was upswept with a few dark strands left to coil artlessly about her face and neck.

But it was the dress that glimmered and shone like a living thing, holding her awed gaze. As she turned back and forth, the candlelight flashed off rich folds of violet damask. At each movement woven cranes and phoenixes seemed to dart and dive across a sky of richest amethyst.

"Magnificent," the dresser said softly, and with this Chessy could only agree. Indeed the modiste whom the

Duchess of Cranford had suggested had outdone herself.

Chessy had sent around a note of acceptance the afternoon of the duchess's visit, and an answer had come back instantly. She was to wait upon the duchess that very evening to discuss details of her gown. It was, further, to be kept an express secret, the duchess added, for she meant to teach Lord Morland a lesson.

To that much Chessy had happily assented. And now, staring in wonder at the reflection in the glass, she could only be thankful that she had put herself so completely in the duchess's hands. Even the use of this unusual damask had been the duchess's idea. Chessy had to admit that against her glowing skin and dark hair the effect was remarkable. Of course, the silk also drew attention to the rare hue of her eyes.

She touched the rich damask gently, feeling a pang of regret that she had been forced to part with the precious bracelet that had been her father's gift to her. But there had been no choice. She had a staff to feed, and now she had to cover the cost of fashionable apparel.

For the gown had been only the start, of course. There also had to be satin slippers and embroidered gloves of silk and finest doeskin. Then came an ivory fan and an evening cloak of black velvet lined with matching violet silk. And since Chessy had only a few gowns that were more than threadbare, she had consented to have several new morning dresses made up, along with a walking costume and matching velvet pelisse and muff.

Chessy turned from the mirror. "Yes, Madame Grès has indeed outdone herself. I can hardly believe that person in the mirror is me."

"Of course, it's you, miss. And a more elegant carriage and graceful deportment I've yet to see," the servant said crisply, well pleased. Not one girl in a thousand would make the entrance that *this* one would tonight, the dresser thought smugly.

But Chessy could feel only a flutter as she thought of the evening ahead of her and the sea of strange faces.

Her only comfort was the thought that the duchess
would be present and had expressed a keen pleasure in
her company.

"Shall I add the flowers now, miss?" The dresser
lifted a pair of creamy hothouse gardenias. At Chessy's
rather distracted nod, the maidservant slid the pale
blooms into the lustrous depths of Chessy's blue-black
hair. "Oh, miss, you look the very picture of beauty.
Like spring come to life, I'm thinking." The woman
flushed, afraid of what must appear an impertinence.

But Chessy merely laughed. "Do you think so, Miss
Henderson? As for myself, I feel more like winter than
spring, I assure you. But thank you for the lovely compliment."

The maidservant blushed becomingly. "And now for
the necklace?"

Chessy nodded. In the flickering candlelight the
necklace seemed to glow with an unearthly light.
Across the face of the repoussé golden plaque at the
center of the necklace, two imperial dragons seemed to
spin and fly, vying for the cabochon rubies, emeralds,
and amethysts studding the exquisite golden medallion.

She had parted with the bracelet, but Chessy knew
she could never, never part with this.

"Oh, miss, it's—it's ever so beautiful. Fit for an
empress, it is." The dresser watched in awe as Chessy
slid the priceless necklace into place. A matching pair
of earrings followed.

The jewels felt cold against Chessy's skin, but the
effect was striking. The gold and pearls made her skin
glow, while the cabochon gems added just the right
touch of color to her gown.

There came a tap at the door. Outside, Swithin
stood motionless, his weathered face stiff. "The carriage is below, miss. If you're ready?"

Chessy felt her heart lurch. Carriage? And then
what? A sea of malicious faces? A host of *ton* beauties
just waiting to cut her to shreds?

The realization of exactly what she was doing hit
her then. It was no longer a game, a prank between her

and the duchess to floor Tony Morland. And as she stood frozen before the cheval glass, Chessy had a wild urge to send around a note to the duchess with apologies due to illness.

Sweet Lord, what if she had to *read* something? A menu or even a dance card? Chessy shivered. What fun the haughty English misses would find in *that*!

What if she were simply ignored as the awkward, backwater colonial that she was?

Then Chessy straightened her shoulders. She was every inch James Cameron's daughter. She hadn't come this far just to turn mush-kneed now! Not when her father needed her so desperately . . .

"Thank you, Miss Henderson. You have worked magic."

After the maidservant left, Chessy stood staring at Swithin. "Well, old friend?" she said softly. "Do I pass muster? I feel dreadfully out of place, you know, and am longing for my digging costume of buckskins and battered straw hat. I certainly never aspired to anything so fine as *this*." As she spoke, she smoothed a lustrous fold of damask.

Light shot off the silk. A phoenix seemed to tremble and then disappear into violet waters.

Chessy's old servant shook his head wonderingly. "I reckon I'll never be able to think of you as a hoyden again, Miss Chessy. Not after seeing you rigged out like that. You do your father mightily proud. If only he could be here to see you."

Chessy felt pain tighten her throat. "Do you think so, Swithin? I suppose I must take heart in that then." She gave the servant a crooked smile. "Perhaps it will help me forget how my knees are trembling and my slippers are pinching my toes."

After taking a long breath, she drew on her gloves and laid her hand on Swithin's crooked arm. "I—I believe I am ready."

Liar, a mocking voice whispered as she swept up her skirts and descended the stairs.

Oh, father, where are you when I need you?

King's Reach
The Thames

The room was damp, pungent with the smell of sea salt and the cargo of fish that slapped in the ship's hold. Water gurgled and sucked against the wooden hull.

A man lay sleeping in the darkness, but his sleep was not peaceful. Again and again he twisted, muttering darkly and clutching at the threadbare blanket his jailers had thrown over him.

Damp. Always damp. And so bloody cold.

He began to cough, and this time it was worse than the others. He could not seem to stop. He felt blood well up in his throat.

He stumbled to his feet and made his way to the door in the darkness. It must be almost time for them to bring that wretched gruel that passed for his food. Maybe this time, if he was waiting just beside the door . . .

He heard the clang of boots in the companionway. He slid back against the wall, trying to fight back a cough.

If only it weren't so cold. If only he weren't so tired. . . .

A key grated in the lock. He raised his fist, waiting for a glimpse of his captors. A shadow formed, moved closer in the darkness. He heard the rattle of tin.

Now!

His foot cracked against bone and muscle, and he heard a sharp curse. But that was the last thing James Cameron heard. The next minute, a fist slammed into his head and he pitched forward onto the floor with a groan.

"Get him back to bed." A stocky man stood in the doorway. A jagged scar ran the length of his cheek. He gestured sharply to his burly companion, then shoved Cameron over with his foot. "He won't give you any more trouble now."

He smiled and the smile made the jagged scar on

his cheek pucker obscenely. "Be sure to put more laudanum in his food. And cover him too. He's been coughing the night through. Damn, who'd a thought the old
bleater had gamey lungs?"

His eyes narrowed as his confederate tossed the
dingy blanket over James Cameron's motionless form.
"Aye, treat him careful, we will." He laughed coldly.
"After all, we wouldn't want our brave English friend
to die before we get paid, would we?"

"**B**last. It looks like an infernal crush." Morland muttered irritably, surveying the long line of vehicles reduced to motionlessness.

He had planned to be no more than half an hour
late. According to *ton* notions of time, that would have
been unfashionably early. But he hadn't counted on the
mob before him.

Frowning, he recalled the duchess's words to
Chessy: *"Nothing special. Just a small affair."*

Morland laughed grimly, surveying the throng before him. A few old friends, indeed! There had to be
fifty carriages there! If he arrived under an hour late,
he could consider himself lucky!

Then it came to him. Wellington was to attend
tonight, in one of his first social evenings since his
return to England from the Peninsula.

Leave it to the Duchess of Cranford to secure *that*
triumph.

With a sigh Morland sat back and prepared to wait.
For a moment his lips twitched in black humor. He
could always throw open the door and walk. He would
be at the duchess's steps in a little over five minutes.

But the man who had daily walked twenty miles on
the Peninsula and had survived an agonizing trek
through icy mountain passes at Corunna knew that
walking was out of the question tonight.

London had its own unassailable rules, after all.
And in their own way, Morland knew, they were every
bit as rigid and merciless as the rules of war he'd
encountered in Spain.

"**A**h, Morland, there you are. Damnable squeeze, ain't it?"

Clad in claret silk and a vast amount of gold braid, Sir Reginald Fortesque surveyed the dazzling company through a silver quizzing glass. "Everyone's turned out, I vow. Even Ravenhurst and his incomparable wife are on hand." The dandy dropped his quizzing glass. "I believe I shall pay my respects. The viscountess set me on to a wonderful old inn as I was passing through Rye. The Angel, it is called. Ever heard of it?"

Morland gave the foppish fellow a rather inscrutable smile. "The name occasions a memory or two."

"An excellent place. And that steward—Hobhouse, his name was. The most complete hand! The fellow had some of the finest damned brandy I've tasted outside Paris. Well, I must be off and thank the dear lady, you know. Just pray that husband of hers ain't hanging about. Blast, it don't do to monopolize one's own *wife*, after all!"

With a great fluttering of lace, Sir Fortesque vanished into the sea of satin and damask.

Morland could not help a bittersweet smile.

Well did he remember the quaint fourteenth-century inn on Mermaid Street. Before she had become the viscountess, Tess Leighton had run the old inn with an expert hand. There, too, she had overseen an audacious smuggling operation with France, an operation so successful that Lord Ravenhurst had been sent down to squelch it. Morland supposed, in a way, that he had lost his heart there, to the brave woman whose laughter had never quite managed to conceal a vast, consuming sadness.

And sadness was something Anthony Morland understood very well.

At that moment a light hand fell upon his wrist.

"Woolgathering, are you? At the social triumph of the year?"

Morland turned to see the Duchess of Cranford surveying him with narrowed eyes. He cursed mentally, praying his momentary melancholy had not shown upon his face.

His voice was light as he patted the duchess's frail fingers. "Not precisely, Your Grace. I was rather trying to calculate where you would possibly find an inch of spare space to cram in any more unfortunate latecomers."

The duchess studied the glittering assembly with a look of satisfaction. "Quite a squeeze, isn't it? Poor Bartholomew would have hated it. But things should grow calm now that everyone has had a chance to ogle the Duke of Wellington."

"So the Great Man is truly here? You've finally done the impossible and lured the Iron Duke from his lair?"

The duchess nodded. Only her fine eyes betrayed her triumph in carrying off what would surely be the social event of the season. "Although I cannot say for how much longer he will remain. I overheard him mutter that if another gimlet-eyed mama set her Friday-faced daughter on him, he'd find the nearest window and jump." Her voice grew thoughtful. "I fancy all is not as it should be between him and that meek creature he took to wife. A great shame, really. But she is such a shy, dutiful thing, and he is so very forceful. One can only wonder . . ."

Morland frowned. "One does far better *not* to wonder, I assure you." He hesitated over whether to drop a word of warning in the duchess's ear to scotch her meddling.

Any interference in that quarter would be looked upon with hearty contempt by Wellington. The uneasy state of affairs between him and his wife had escaped none of his young officers on the Peninsula. Although Morland had the highest respect for the fierce determination and steely will that had made Wellington a successful campaigner, privately the earl could not help but think those same qualities must make him a very difficult sort of husband.

But loveless marriages were hardly an exception among the *ton*. Morland could name any number of couples among his acquaintance who smiled dimly at one another over the breakfast table while they planned an illicit rendezvous with a lover that night.

It was quite the done thing, actually. The only requisite was that such *affaires* be conducted with discretion and without any messy excess of emotion.

Morland should have known. He had been a partner in a fair number of such liaisons himself.

And what about his brother? His twin's marriage had been just such a one, the two partners affable enough while both pursued their diverse and rather cold-blooded pleasures with different—and numerous—partners.

But Morland had drawn the line when his sister-in-law had invited him to share her bed not a fortnight after her wedding ceremony to his brother.

Even now, he felt a moment of revulsion as he remembered how her crimson nails had trailed down his chest to stroke his manhood.

In a way it had been a blessing when a storm had carried away the yacht she had been traveling in during a summer excursion to Scotland. Then only a few months later his twin brother, the seventh duke, had also died and the title had devolved to young Jeremy.

Morland sighed. His twin brother, he was honor bound to admit, had been even more dissolute than his wife. In five years Andrew Morland had whored and gamed his way from one end of England to the other. In another three or four more years he would have run through all the Langford fortune, losing Sevenoaks, the beautiful sixteenth-century manor house in Suffolk, and the larger holdings in Somerset in the process.

Luckily, Morland had not been home to observe these excesses. But even in Spain snippets of gossip had reached him, enough to make him gnash his teeth and curse the brother he had never liked, much less respected, for a complete and utter fool.

His *twin* brother.

Even now, Morland caught an occasional stare, as if he were being measured against some memory of his twin.

But Andrew was dead now. And if Tony had a certain cynicism about women and the staying power of that vaunted emotion called love, then he supposed it was only to be expected, considering the things he had seen.

All these bitter recollections took place in the span of a half-dozen seconds. When he turned, the Duchess of Cranford was studying him.

"You're quite the only moth among the butterflies tonight, young man. But that severe style you affect becomes you. Black breeches. Black waistcoat. Very elegant. And that embroidery is impeccable. French, I suppose?"

Morland nodded absently, searching the room. He realized belatedly that he was searching for a slender pair of shoulders and a cascade of blue-black hair. For a pair of violet eyes that could shift from sadness to fury in a matter of seconds.

He shrugged. "Paris still has its uses, I find."

The duchess was in no way deceived by the earl's casual rejoinder. She had seen the bleakness sweep Morland's face, the tension that gripped his jaw as he drifted in dark recollections.

Yes, she had seen. And it had wrung her heart.

Knowing the *ton* as she did, she guessed it had something to do with that repulsive twin of Morland's. Or his equally odious wife.

But her face, as she stared at Tony, was perfectly impassive. There was just a hint of mischief in her keen blue eyes. "And now I have a charge for you. Here's Palmerston, red-faced and irritable, looking like a cannon about to explode. He's searching for Wellington, so I'm told. Some odious bit of consular business, no doubt. You might as well go and fetch the Great Man."

Her air of careful nonchalance did not reach her eyes, which were intent on Morland's face.

Blast, but he'd have to step carefully around the duchess, Morland realized. She was still as needle-witted as they came! "I'd be delighted to. But surely Palmerston will sight the duke himself."

"I'm afraid Palmerston will have no luck, for the Great Man has fled the field. He'd had quite enough of being ogled by the mob. Said Waterloo was *nothing* compared to one of my routs." She chuckled softly.

"Yes, I believe you must fetch him. Palmerston is beginning to look quite apoplectic."

Morland bowed and turned to leave. As he did so, the duchess touched his hand. "Did I forget to mention that Miss Cameron has arrived? She is with the duke, I believe."

"You quite astound me, Your Grace." He offered her a second elegant bow. "My compliments. I begin to think you have accomplished the impossible *twice* tonight," he added softly.

The duchess merely smiled, remembering her involvement in furthering the attachment between Lord Ravenhurst and his lovely wife. It had been a near thing, however, and certain parts of the affair did not reflect to her credit.

She did not mean to inform Lord Morland of that fact, however, for she still had a few tricks up her sleeve. "You have quite a dangerous charm, you know. In fact with every passing day you remind me more and more of your father."

Morland smiled at what could only be construed as a monumental compliment.

"Now off with you. I must attend to my guests. That odious man Atherton has just arrived. Louisa Landringham, meanwhile, has not yet glimpsed her rival. She is simpering at two matrons by the punch table. You will find Wellington and Miss Cameron in the conservatory, unless I miss my guess. They can be quite alone there." She frowned slightly. "Except, of course, if Louisa Landringham finds out where they've gone."

"I shall endeavor to be before her, Your Grace." With an elegant bow, Morland disappeared beneath an arch covered with braid and trailing silk.

A faint smile played about the duchess's lips as Tony disappeared into the jeweled throng. It was her sincerest wish that she *would* work a miracle this night. The two young people were obviously in love, after all.

And what better way to occupy her time than to see them thrown together until they acknowledged that affection?

14

Ten minutes and any number of silent curses later, Lord Morland had finally maneuvered a course around the card room, through the ballroom, and along the corridor that led to the narrow conservatory that ran the length of the duchess's commodious London townhouse.

The duchess enjoyed having flowers about her, and the conservatory had been designed to supply her with fresh flowers year round.

It was at any time a lovely room, warm and fragrant with the scent of peat, orange blossoms, and the variety of flowering plants that she treasured. But now it was especially lovely, as the newest batch of peonies had just come into bloom.

Morland had a sudden thought of a dewy-eyed Chessy Cameron sequestered in a candlelit corner, while the famous general held forth about one of his more hair-raising episodes during the late Peninsular campaign.

His jaw hardened, and his pace increased abruptly.

He didn't like the idea—he didn't bloody like it by half!

And when Morland opened the door to the glass-walled room at the back of the house, his worst fears were confirmed.

Wreathed in a halo of lamplight, the duke stood between two potted palms and a flowering hibiscus, gesturing animatedly to his slender companion, who was wearing the most remarkable necklace Morland had ever seen.

His breath caught. His eyes ran hungrily along the slender line of Chessy's neck, where blue-black hair was caught low and adorned with two creamy gardenias.

Even from where he stood, Morland fancied he could catch their scent, as sweetly seductive, as rich and elusive as the woman who wore them.

And her gown—good Lord, it clung to every soft curve and hollow, shimmering in a dark flow of purest violet.

Just like her luminous, unforgettable eyes . . .

He watched, stiff-lipped, as Chessy laughed at some witticism made by Wellington, then began an earnest recitation of her own, to which the general listened with equal seriousness.

Then the duke moved closer, his aquiline face intent as he nodded at something his partner said.

At that moment Morland was feeling anything but charitable toward the hero of Waterloo. In fact he discovered he was feeling downright furious.

His fingers tensed on an overhanging plant. If the man so much as touched her, by God he'd—

Hearing a snap, Morland looked down to see that he'd broken a twig of flowering orange cleanly in two.

At the sound the pair looked up, but Morland was hidden by the surrounding greenery, and they soon returned to their conversation.

And then, while Morland watched in savage, churning silence, the duke took Chessy's hand and raised it to his lips for a kiss.

Damn the man! Weren't there enough hardened flirts and keen-eyed widows about? Did he have to go campaigning after a woman but newly arrived in London, a woman who had no idea of the rules by which such games of seduction were played?

Watching Chessy's slender white hand tremble beneath Wellington's lips, Morland felt a burst of raw, blinding rage such as he had never felt in his life. Fortunately, he curbed the impluse to charge from the shadows and call the duke out summarily.

After all, *he* had not been deputed Miss Francesca Cameron's protector. And judging by the look on her face when they were together, he was the *last* person she might have chosen for such a role.

Morland's jaw tensed as Chessy looked up at Wellington. He felt a sudden, burning bitterness that she had never angled her head and studied *him* with such a look of admiration.

Perhaps the chit had a preference for older men, he thought grimly.

As he watched, the duke bowed over her hand, then turned away, no doubt to fetch some refreshment. Still hidden, Morland saw Chessy turn.

For the first time he saw her face in the full glow of the score of wax candles gleaming on the wall. His breath caught.

She was impossibly beautiful, her violet gown subtly complemented by gold and violet braiding at sleeves and hem. Her cheeks were delicately flushed as she bent to smell a potted orange tree in full bloom.

Beautiful, he thought, feeling his blood grow hot. And at her neck hung a double strand of pearls that caught a beaten gold plaque of dragons and precious stones.

As Chessy straightened, the candlelight struck the hammered gold, casting soft light around her in a warm nimbus.

Sweet Lord above, she was exquisite! How could she ever have considered herself plain, even as a shy, coltish fifteen-year-old?

Driven by a need he could not name, Morland stepped from the shadows.

Chessy started. Her fingers locked at her sides. "Y-you!"

"I'm sorry to startle you."

Chessy's color fluctuated wildly. "Were you eavesdropping? Did you expect to hear military secrets betrayed by my clever probing? Or were you simply hoping to see me disgrace myself?"

The gardenias in her hair trembled with every angry word. The dragons on her golden medallion seemed to quiver and fly. Her cheeks took on a positive riot of color.

Morland thought that he had never seen her look lovelier.

He was on the verge of demanding where she'd gotten such a bloody ramshackle notion of his character, when he realized that she'd gotten it from *him*. From his importunities in her backyard. From his inexcusable conduct in the kitchen after that.

Sweet heaven, how had he managed to bungle everything so badly within mere days of meeting her again?

He bit back an angry reply and moved into the candlelight. The crisp white linen at his neck shone in striking contrast to his immaculate black evening attire.

Chessy stiffened as he moved closer. "G-go away! I am just beginning to enjoy myself, and I don't care to be lectured at or interrogated right now." And then, as she saw the determination on his face: "The duke will be back any second, you know. He's only gone to fetch me some ratafia."

Morland's eyes were unreadable as he looked down at her. "Do you think so? I'm afraid you will be sadly disappointed, my dear. My godmother, the duchess, will have him cornered any second. That's why she sent me in here, in fact. Although I begin to suspect. . ." He did not finish.

He took a step closer and watched Chessy withdraw the same distance.

One blond brow rose. "Never say you're afraid, my dear."

Chessy scowled at him between two dwarf potted palms. "*Afraid?* Of *you?* What would give you such a sap-headed notion as *that*?"

Morland skirted a wicker settee and two porcelain planters, cornering Chessy neatly against the bank of windows edging the conservatory. "Because you are trembling, my dear. And a pulse in pounding at the curve of your throat." His eyes darkened. "But perhaps you flee in boredom. I have not the duke's great presence and reputation, after all. I am desolated to inform you that he is a married man, however lax he might appear in those vows."

Chessy's cheeks flooded crimson. "How—how *dare* you! Who are *you* to censure me, you who—" She stopped abruptly, her hands clenched at her sides.

The little ivory fan in her fingers snapped cleanly in two.

"You appear to have broken your fan, my dear." Morland's voice was low, as soft as a caress.

"I'm *not* your dear. I am *nothing* to you! You lost the right to use those words to me ten years ago! Now please go." Her chest rose and fell sharply as she struggled for control.

Morland was fascinated by that wild rise and fall. He watched the phoenix and dragons tremble against the sweet curves pressed against the purple damask.

And suddenly it was there again, the desire pulsing hot and wild through his veins. A blind recklessness seized him. "How do you know *what* you are to me, stubborn one? In ten years many things might change, after all." His lips twisted in a bitter smile. "For me they most certainly have."

Chessy inched sideways, only to feel the thorns of a potted rose bite into her shoulder.

Morland smiled darkly. She was well and truly cornered now, and she knew it.

"Go *away*! How much more plain must I make myself? I do *not* desire your presence. I do *not* desire your conversation. And I most certainly do *not* desire your attentions!"

Her breath was growing more ragged by the second, Morland noted. Her color was deliciously high, and at a most fascinating spot at her neck a muscle flashed whenever she spoke.

He wondered what it would feel like to tongue that satin inch of skin. Yes, she was a woman of incredible passion. Just looking at her told him she would be hot and reckless and wonderful in his bed.

He ran his fingers idly over a blushing rose petal, wishing it were her he was stroking so intimately.

Chessy's eyes followed each slow, suggestive movement. Her tongue inched out and touched the underside of her top lip.

Morland felt an ache build in his groin. He was going to die if he didn't stop this. And he was going to die if he did!

"Oh, you'll have to make yourself *very* plain with me, Cricket. Subtle snubs and indirect setdowns just won't work, I'm afraid." He watched with interest as her fingers locked against her chest, driving the ivory curves above the gown's tight bodice, where the golden medallion rose and fell upon her naked skin.

The pounding in Morland's blood became a roar. Dimly he realized that he was not quite rational at that moment, that he was about to commit an indiscretion that he would seriously regret in the morning.

But as he stood inches away from her, with the rich scent of her gardenias intoxicating his senses, Morland found he didn't give a bloody damn what might happen on the morrow.

Because there was only now, only this night. Only this moment of reckless, blinding magic that he had waited ten years for.

And he meant to find out just how sweet she would taste, how soft she would feel, when he—

His eyes narrowed on the full lip that she was savaging between her teeth.

"My lord—Tony—"

It was the breathy, restless way she said his name that finally did him in.

Suddenly he had to hear her say it again, only this time while she was crushed against him and he explored the warm silk of her mouth.

And neck.

And the scented hollow of those maddeningly lush breasts—

He caught her locked fingers and brought them to his chest. "You're trembling, Cricket. I would have thought it very warm in here."

His eyes probed her face. Suddenly Chessy's color seemed to bleed away. "Tony—my lord—don't! I don't want this, not any of it."

"Too late, Chessy. I've waited ten years to do *just* this." The earl circled her wrists with exquisite gentleness and pinned them against the glass. "For I *do* want this. To a quite astonishing degree, in fact." One hard hand rose to trace the tense curve of her jaw. "And suddenly I find myself immeasurably hungry. For one thing only . . ."

Gently he touched the gardenia anchored at her ear, then bent forward to inhale its exquisite fragrance. "For you," he whispered against her skin.

His body was only inches from hers. Through the haze of his passion he saw the muscle flash at her neck, saw the unnatural tension that locked her slender shoulders. "Yes, I want it. I *need* it. And I think you want it too, Cricket."

"*Don't*. Don't call me that, not ever." There was an edge of raw desperation to her voice.

"Why not?"

"Because—because it's not fair!"

"Are such things ever fair, my love?" He ran his fingers along the curve of her ear, then anchored her chin in his palm. "I might lodge the same complaint against *you*."

Trapped in the shadows, in a world turned upside down, Chessy could only stare up at him blindly. What had happened? What had changed her?

For she *was* changed. Her blood was on fire, and her body seemed to belong to a stranger.

A reckless stranger.

She shivered as the earl detached one gardenia and carried it to his lips. His eyes never left her face as he kissed the creamy petals.

"It suits you, Cricket," he said huskily.

Caught against the cool bank of windows, Chessy shivered. Her breath caught as he worked the flower into the buttonhole nearest his heart.

Suddenly she was too hot. Too cold. Too *close*.

She shoved at Morland's hand. "I don't—we can't—"

"Yes," he said huskily. "Oh God, yes. Right now, Cricket."

And then, as her pulse beat a wild, churning path through her chest and her heart missed a score of beats in a row, Chessy swayed. He caught her with his arm, with the bulwark of his chest, with the hungry line of his taut thigh.

She, too, hungered. She, too, ached. And in that moment she *needed*, just as much as he did. Logic and common sense could do nothing against the blinding need she felt.

Dimly she realized that his head was descending. Dear God, his eyes were dark with an intensity that she found terrifying. That she found irresistible.

She shuddered. Her eyes fluttered shut. "*Nooooo.*"

"Yes, Chessy." He brushed the arch of her lip with aching gentleness. "Yes, my sweet." His lips found the soft curve of her eyelid. "Here." Slowly he nibbled his way down her cheek and across to the corner of her mouth. "Oh, God, *here*."

Chessy caught a ragged breath; wild anticipation seized her. Her mouth trembled. She wanted to feel his against it.

What if he did?

Dear God, what if he *didn't*?

Then nothing. Only warm, scented air. Only aching, hungry skin that raged for more.

Her eyes flashed open.

He was standing immobile, the lines at his mouth and forehead very marked. His hair glowed with hints of fire in the light of the dancing candles. Chessy was mesmerized by the dangerous gleam in his eyes, by the sensual curl of his hard lips.

She swallowed audibly, unable to speak, unable to breathe. Unable to string two clear thoughts together.

"Just once," the man she'd loved forever whispered. "Just *once*. For—the past. For all the sweet dawns we spent picking up shells along the beach. For the lazy afternoons we swam alongside your father's boat." A muscle flashed at his jaw. "And for the nights. For all those raw, aching nights when I sat awake wondering how it would feel if I—"

His hot gaze swept her face. "If I touched you, if I tasted you everywhere, the way I was dying to do. . . ." He waited, searching for an answer Chessy found herself powerless to give.

She had to deny him, had to pull away. She should be thinking of her father, not *this*.

But first she had to find out if what she'd felt in the kitchen had been just another dream, like the others she'd lived on for ten years.

She swallowed. Her fingers splayed apart against his chest, no longer tensed in protest. Her wide eyes rose to his mouth.

Her lips parted, ever so slightly.

A raw curse tore from Morland's throat. His hands closed over her shoulders, holding her captive as he closed the heated space between them. "Chessy—"

At that moment a shrill falsetto of laughter burst upon the peace of the conservatory. Instantly Morland pulled Chessy back into the shadows behind a dwarf palm.

Bloody hell! Louisa Landringham! Now they were well and truly sunk, Morland thought sourly. No one in London had a more vicious and unrelenting tongue than Louisa's.

His fingers tensed warningly on Chessy's back. He was relieved that she did not try to pull free.

"You say they came in here? The Duke of Wellington and that—that *creature* in purple. The one wearing that outlandish necklace." The *ton*'s reigning beauty gave a rather brittle laugh. "If so, unless my eyes fail me, they have also managed to disappear, my dear Reginald."

Lady Landringham peered intently into the shadows along the rear windows, a hardness about her green eyes that had not been there before. "Just as the

Earl of Morland seems to have disappeared," she said slowly.

Morland's fingers tightened. Behind him came a faint scratching. A moment later two shadows exploded from the greenery and skittered across the floor.

Louisa's eyes widened in horror. She opened her mouth to scream, but her companion cut her off deftly with a palm to her heavily rouged lips as a mouse dashed through the open doorway with a ginger-striped cat in hot pursuit.

Louisa's wild squeal ended as a muffled croak.

Her face turned a quite unattractive shade of russet as she tore at Fortesque's blocking fingers.

Finally he let her go. "A thousand apologies, m'dear, but it wouldn't do to have you screaming. Bring the whole *ton* down upon us. Next thing I'd have to offer marriage. Quite a beauty and all that, m'dear, but marriage ain't in my line." Sir Reginald watched with interest as Louisa's crimson mouth opened and closed several times while she struggled with her fury. "Glad that's all settled. Shall we go now?"

"*Go?*" his companion yelled. "With *you*? I wouldn't go *anywhere* with you, you idiotic, sap-skulled—"

But Sir Reginald was spared any further vitriol by the arrival of the Duke of Wellington, two glasses in hand. The general's aquiline features took on an even harsher cast when he saw the pair staring at him from the conservatory entrance.

He offered a curt nod, oblivious to Louisa Landringham's furtive efforts to straighten the feathers upon her forehead, twitch down her skirts, and clamp a dazzling smile on her face. But his attention was all for the woman he had left standing beside a dwarf palm.

The woman who seemed somehow to have disappeared.

15

Chessy was just on the verge of moving toward the duke when Morland's low curse came at her ear.

A current of warm air brushed her shoulder. She felt him move closer. "Wouldn't advise it," he whispered. "It would make the devil of a scandal if we were seen. Like *this*."

Suddenly Chessy was very conscious of the hard hands cupping her shoulders, of the iron wall of muscle at her back. Breathless, trembling, she tried to pull away, only to feel Morland's fingers tighten.

Uncertainly, she stared at the trio in the doorway. She was too new to London ways to know if what Morland said was true.

Louisa Landringham, meanwhile, had inched closer to Wellington. Soon the three were engaged in conversation and showed no sign of leaving.

The devil take all of them! What was she to do now?

She caught her lip in her teeth, tugging irritably. Surely there must be some other way of escape. A door at the far side of the conservatory, perhaps?

She froze as she felt Morland's breath sweep her

neck. His head fell as he inhaled the scent of the
gardenia in her hair.

Of all the cheek! Did the rogue really think he could
sway her by—

And then her breath caught. She felt the slow, hot
glide of his lips along her neck. A moment later he
caught the lobe of her ear between his teeth.

Waves of sensation chased through Chessy's stomach, hot and chill in turn. She blinked dizzily.

Morland's teeth gently scored her earlobe.

Chessy swallowed. She had to reach out to balance
herself by clutching the potted palm at her side. "Just
what do you think you're—" But her low cry was cut
short by the rough-soft slide of his tongue inching into
the tender heart of her ear.

She caught back a moan. Suddenly she was breathless and the night was hot—hot and sweet with passion.

Blindly her eyes fixed on the three people chatting
amiably in the doorway while she felt her world fall
away into ashes around her.

And all that was left was the exquisite sweep of
Morland's tongue feathering over her hungry skin. The
tantalizing rhythm of his fingers as they slid down her
bare arms and anchored her waist.

She fought for sanity, fought to ignore the pleasure
that burned to life with each knowing movement of his
fingers. But caught in the darkness against him, unable
to move, Chessy could feel the hard wall of her defenses
crumble brick by brick.

Choking back a low moan of protest, she tried desperately to jerk free. In the process a twig of the palm
she was clutching snapped in two.

Instantly the trio at the door turned, peering into
the shadows.

"Never thought to worry about snipers at a London
fete." Though the duke smiled, his eyes were sharp.

"Oh, it can be naught but mice, Your Grace," Louisa
tittered. "The place is positively littered with them."
She smiled up at him. "But you were describing Waterloo." She gave an exquisite shiver. "It sounds quite

frightful. How lucky we were to have such a strong, decisive man as yourself in charge."

The beautiful Louisa knew perfectly well the value of a quarter-hour seen in the Great Man's company, after all. Her social prestige, already significant, would soar higher with every minute.

And when they left the conservatory, she meant to be sure that the Iron Duke had her arm in his, and that everyone saw it.

Nor did she discount the possibility of a discreet *affaire* with the harsh-faced hero of Waterloo. Yes, it might prove vastly amusing. After all, he had been away campaigning for months. Denied the pleasures of a woman's body, he would be deliciously *potent* in her bed. . .

She licked her lips delicately and offered the duke a fawning smile. At the same time she contrived to brush her hips ever so gently against his thigh.

Chessy, however, noticed none of this. Her world was reduced to the heated texture of Morland's strong hands, the granite power of his thighs at her back.

So this is what it feels like, she thought dimly. *To want and be wanted.* Sweet heaven, she was dying.

Slowly. Irrevocably.

And it was the most glorious feeling she had ever known. . . .

Morland's lips closed over the pulse point at her neck.

All unconsciously Chessy shuddered. Her head fell back against his shoulder as magic enfolded her.

Morland made a low sound that might have been groan or curse. His hands climbed upward, slid beneath her heavy gold necklace, and then gently cupped her breasts.

"Chessy . . . God . . ." He drew a ragged breath as he felt her shudder. That slight movement inflamed him as nothing else had. She was exquisite, passionate, utterly breathtaking.

And she was *his*, only his!

He gazed hotly at her shimmering hair, at the delicate flush that crept over cheeks. At the sweet rise and fall of her breasts.

Then he frowned. Damn, but that gown revealed too much of her by half! He wouldn't have Fortesque and Atherton and a hundred other libertines leering at her beautiful, nearly naked breasts!

In that moment Morland felt a raw wave of possessiveness such as he had never felt for a woman before. By God, he wanted her. He hungered to feel her hair slide like black silk through his fingers. He yearned to see her shiver when he eased that infuriating dress down and bared every creamy inch of her.

For *him*, only him . . .

Had Morland been even halfway sane then, the depth of his possessiveness would have sobered him instantly. But in that moment, as the warm, sweet air enfolded them, rich with the scent of gardenia, orange blossom, and evergreen, Anthony Morland found that touching Francesca Cameron was the only thing left in the whole bloody world that made the slightest bit of sense.

His eyes were dark with passion when he eased her back against him, shuddering as the soft curve of her bottom goaded the hard barrier of his thighs. And then, almost unaware of what he was doing, Morland slid his fingers inside her bodice.

"N-no—" Chessy stiffened. A whimper escaped her lips.

Morland nibbled at her mouth, extracting another exquisite whimper. It fed his desire, seared his blood. God, she was sweet! And far more passionate than she knew.

Something blocked his fingers. He swore silently. But heated nights in many beds—*too* many? Morland wondered dimly—had given him a sensual expertise second to none. By his third try, he'd freed the offending obstacle.

The next moment Chessy's warm breasts spilled lush and full into his hands, freed from her loosened gown.

Morland shivered at the weight of her, at the soft thrust of her nipples against his fingers.

Stunned, he gazed down. But the rich curves were hidden by shadows.

Maybe that was just as well, he thought. If he had *seen* those silken curves as well as felt them . . .

Morland's hands trembled ever so slightly. He struggled against a blinding impulse to shove her against the wall and impale her. He knew she wanted him. He could feel it in her racing pulse, in the nipples that hardened against his fingers.

All it would take was one hot, driving thrust of his thighs, and he'd be inside her.

Already he could hear the sound of her moans, feel the hot, wet pull of her around his throbbing sex. He wanted her that way, too, moaning and frenzied while she wrapped her white thighs around him and took him all the way inside her.

"T-Tony. Oh, please . . ."

It was the break in her voice that finally stopped him. He felt the confusion, the wild uncertainty that underlaid her passion.

Damn it, what was he doing?

He looked down at his hands. They were shaking visibly. Beneath them her nipples rose, faintly visible, puckered and tight like dusky buds against her ivory skin.

As he watched, her dress slipped a fraction lower.

Good, sweet God, what was he doing?

His breath came raw and jerky. He felt the curve of her back against his chest. He felt the warmth of her head, where it rested against his shoulder. He felt the softness of her hips, an unspeakable torment against the raw heat of his aroused sex.

Morland cursed, low and long and very graphically. And then he did the only thing he could do.

The same thing he had done ten years before.

He let her go.

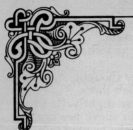

16

Chessy heard the raw curse and tensed.

Slowly her head lifted from his shoulder. With a little shudder she opened her eyes, registering the potted plants around her, the dusky scent of flowers and damp earth. And the fact that his hands were no longer touching her.

The fashionable trio still blocked the conservatory doorway. Somewhere from the far wing came the distant strains of a waltz.

The world labored on.

Only *she*, it seemed, had been halted in her tracks, frozen in another place and time.

She pressed her eyes shut, fighting back tears. Behind her Morland's thighs locked. He tensed. "Chessy, we can't just—" He caught a ragged breath and gripped her shoulders. "Damn it, I don't want to hurt you."

White-faced, Chessy looked down. Her bodice was pooled, revealing hot, aroused skin. She caught back a sob.

Fool! You've fallen right back into his arms. With a sigh and a smile you let him do whatever he wanted with you!

Pain and bitter betrayal slammed into her like a fist. "Take your hands from me," she demanded. "Otherwise you will shortly find them broken."

The man at her back frowned. His hands did not leave the silken skin that ached for his continued mastery.

"I shall give you until the count of five," she said icily.

"Chessy, don't. Not this way. Let me ex—"

"One. T-two. Three . . ."

Smothering a curse, Morland pulled her around to face him. "This solves nothing," he said. "You're angry, of course. *Rightly* so. But we can't just—"

"Four," Chessy snapped. *"Five."* Her hands captured his forearm. Morland didn't know about her martial arts training, of course. All that had begun later that summer after he had left.

Sometimes she suspected that her father had encouraged that training as a means to distract her from the pain of her first experience of falling in love. She had never been able to hide her feelings from her father, of course, though she had put a vast amount of effort into the attempt.

Now the thought of all the tears she'd shed and all the innocent, girlish dreams she'd spun only made Chessy more furious.

Morland's forearm was strong, well muscled. From the illicit glimpse of him that she'd had in Germaine's bedroom, Chessy knew that he was in flawless physical condition.

Even at that he would be no match for her. One quick twist, and his bone would be dislocated.

Not that she would actually go so far.

Dimly Chessy registered that Wellington and his two admirers had finally quit the room. She spun about, her eyes a violet haze of fury. "Are you *quite* finished?"

Morland's mouth set in a hard, thin line. "Not nearly, my dear." His eyes narrowed to azure slits as he watched her tug furiously at her dress. "Stop twitching, damn it! Let me do that."

The next moment he spun her around, jerked the damask up over her shoulders, and shoved the buttons closed at her back.

"My, my! What experienced f-fingers you have, my lord."

Morland's face was an icy mask, but he said nothing. He deserved that much, he supposed. Hell, he deserved a whole lot *worse*! He had nearly swept up her skirts and taken her right there in the middle of the Duchess of Cranford's bloody conservatory!

What was *wrong* with him?

Morland restored her dress to order, then turned Chessy around. When she tried to pull away, his fingers clamped down upon her shoulder. "My deepest apologies, Miss Cameron. What I did was entirely inexcusable. I cannot imagine what—"

For the first time his steely veneer wavered. He raked his fingers through his long hair. "I—I don't know what on earth came over me, Cricket. I never meant to—"

Chessy stared at him with frigid hauteur. So now he meant to imply that what had happened was simply a moment of madness! A lapse of sanity! After all, no man could desire thin, awkward Chessy Cameron! Hadn't that point been driven home to her often enough back in Macao?

She concealed the swift, agonizing pain of that thought beneath a vast hauteur. She would show him that she was no longer an innocent and inept little schoolgirl! "No apologies are necessary or expected, I assure you. Now if you will kindly move out of my way . . ."

Morland frowned at her. Legs apart, hands on her shoulders, he continued to block her exit.

Chessy glared back. Rot the man if he thought she was going to dash around him like a terrified rabbit! No, he would move away properly, or he'd soon find himself flat on the floor with a broken leg!

Abruptly Morland's hand closed over her upper arm. Chessy stiffened instinctively, her muscles bunched for an attack.

Morland felt the movement perfectly. He also felt her strength and preparedness. It was hardly the sort of thing one expected to encounter in an English gentlewoman.

Morland's eyes narrowed. He caught her wrist and turned her palm up for his scrutiny. Chessy tried to pull away, knowing exactly what he would find there.

The skin was ridged at the outer edge of the palm. There were dozens of old scars along the base of her palm, all mementos of Shao-lin.

"By God, I don't believe it! Never tell me that your father actually let you—"

White-faced, Chessy jerked away from him. The last thing she wanted was for the earl to know about her training. She managed a bitter laugh. "Let me what? Toughen my fingers packing and unpacking our artifact crates? Scrubbing the deck of that Chinese junk we called home? I'm afraid he did, my lord. I'm sorry it offends your nobility."

She pulled her hands from his suddenly slack grip and squared her shoulders. Her eyes glittered dangerously. "And now good night, your lordship. No, make that *good-bye!*"

Morland felt as if he had just been kicked by a rabid hunter.

It couldn't be! Chessy, a trained warrior? His Chessy?

A pulse hammered at Morland's brow. He could see from her furious features that she was in no mood to discuss anything logically right now. And a *ton* ball was no place for a scene, unless one wanted every tongue in London wagging about it.

"Are you going to move or not, lout?"

"If you insist."

"I do!"

"Very well. But first—" Without waiting for an answer, he bent forward and anchored the drooping gardenia more securely in the midnight sweep of her hair.

Chessy stood rigid, unbreathing, while his light, expert hands moved in her hair. She fought to ignore him but failed.

A moment later, Morland stepped back, his face

shuttered. "There. You are, as always, perfection itself. I suggest, however, that you allow me to precede you by several minutes. The London tabbies thrive on gossip, you know, and this would make prodigious gossip, I fear."

He offered her a lazy bow. "And of course the lapsed time might help to rid you of that lovely but quite unmistakable flush that stains your cheeks, your neck, and your exquisite—"

His sapphire gaze dropped to the creamy expanse of her chest. Even now, Chessy could feel a telltale flicker of heat tighten her nipples.

"*Other* places," Morland finished softly. "I hereby bid you good night, Miss Cameron. But most certainly *not* good-bye."

And with that soft, half-mocking rejoinder he was gone.

Standing beneath an elegant arrangement of silk gauze and sprays of flowering cherry, Viscount Ravenhurst watched his friend make his way through the Duchess of Cranford's crowded ballroom.

Few others would have seen the tension behind Morland's lazy smile or drawled pleasantries, but Ravenhurst had known his friend too long to be easily fooled.

"He's upset about something, isn't he?" The viscount's auburn-haired wife was also following Lord Morland's progress, it seemed.

Ravenhurst smiled inwardly. Nothing escaped Tess's keen eye. He should have known that well by now.

He patted her hand. "I rather think so, my love. He's been tense as a drawn bow all evening." He stared thoughtfully at Morland's retreating back, then turned back to the conservatory.

At that moment a slender figure in violet damask appeared in the same doorway where Morland had emerged moments before. Her hair shimmered like polished lacquer beneath the chandeliers.

Ravenhurst gave a soundless whistle. So *this* was the Macao-bred beauty that the Duchess of Cranford had been telling him about.

The woman stood for a moment. Feeling herself unobserved, she gave a furtive twitch to her skirts and a tug at her bodice.

One hand checked the gardenia in her hair.

Ravenhurst's lips curved in a faint smile. *Ho! Blows the wind from that quarter, Morland, my boy?*

"Whoever is that fascinating creature who just emerged from the conservatory? Dane, isn't that where Tony just—"

Ravenhurst caught his wife's fingers and gave them a warning squeeze as a pair of keen-eyed dowagers moved past. Tess offered the women a careful smile, then instantly turned back to her husband. "But who—"

"Let's walk, shall we, my heart? The conservatory, perhaps." Ravenhurst smiled down at his wife. "I rather think we'll be unobserved there." He studied the stiff back of the woman in violet who was now threading through the crowd. "Yes, the night has turned out to be quite fascinating after all, wouldn't you agree, my love?"

"**A**h, Morland, just the man I've been wishing to see."

As the earl crossed the crowded salon, he was cornered by the Duke of Wellington, who was surrounded by a host of admiring females. Seeing Morland, the duke made a cursory bow to the group. "My deepest apologies, ladies. Business calls, I'm afraid."

The next moment, Morland was maneuvered toward a curtained alcove that gave onto an isolated corridor.

"Lord, Waterloo was nothing next to that encounter! It always pays to know the terrain, Morland. Remember that. Never enter an engagement without surveying all avenues of escape in advance."

The duke brushed aside the curtain and stalked to a shadowed seat. "We can speak privately here."

But even there, Morland found he could not relax.

All he could think of was how Chessy had felt in his arms, how she had shivered when he kissed her.

By God, I'm losing my mind. And she is responsible!

His jaw tensed as he fought to forget the sweet warmth of her satin skin. God, those husky little cries she'd made as he'd freed her breasts and—

". . . feeling poorly, Morland? I don't believe you've heard a single thing I've said."

Morland started, realizing the duke was addressing him. "Too much of this unrelenting peace, Your Grace. Routs one night and balls the next. If this keeps up, I'll have to buy back my commission just to find a little peace and quiet."

The Duke of Wellington frowned. This answer did not fool him for a moment. He, too, had noticed the woman in violet damask who had emerged from the conservatory only moments after Tony.

But that was pleasure, and this was business. He sat forward, lowering his voice. "Amherst says the situation in China appears to be even worse than we'd thought. Graft is rampant, and the court grows daily more unstable. We'll have to work as swiftly as possible. So tell me what sort of progress you've been making with that damned book."

Morland steepled his fingers and began to speak, his voice tense.

In their concentration neither man noticed the beautiful Louisa Landringham, who had slipped into the shadows just beyond the doorway.

17

An hour later Chessy Cameron stood on the far side of the room, slanting a gay and utterly false smile at a young officer in a scarlet regimental uniform.

Soon she was surrounded by four, then six, then eight more adoring swains.

Her light laughter floated in the air as she was besieged with offers to dance, to accept proffered cups of ratafia.

Across the room the Earl of Morland saw every gesture, heard every lilting laugh.

And each one was like a knife thrust into his gut.

Suddenly he could stand no more. His face a hard mask, he turned and stalked through the glittering crowd, oblivious to man and woman alike.

Chessy's soft laughter followed him all the way to the door.

". . . Lovely party."
    ". . . wonderful crush, my dear."
    ". . . always manage to outdo yourself?"
The Duchess of Cranford smiled and moved among

her guests, catching snippets of conversation, offering
a word here, a compliment there, making deft introduc-
tions with the part of her mind that always knew who
was best suited for whom.

But it was all a mere facade.

Her real attention was locked on the graceful beauty
surrounded by a clamoring throng of suitors, whose
numbers swelled with every moment.

And of course, on the grim-faced earl who watched
every movement while trying hard to look as if he were
not.

Ah, to be young again, the duchess thought wistfully. To feel the reckless joy, the first wild rush of
passion . . .

And the pain. There was always that, too, of course.

She fought down a wave of loneliness, remembering
a spring night of her own forty years before, when the
air had been thick with the scent of roses . . .

". . . share a box . . . dinner at ten . . ." Absently she
smiled at old friends, not quite hearing the words.

No need to hear. She had heard them all before.

Now all her attention was on Miss Cameron, who
had just removed the gardenia from her hair and surrendered it with a laugh to a swain who waited on bent
knee before her. The man refused to rise until she'd
offered him a token of her regard.

The duchess heard a faint crack and looked across
to see Tony Morland snap a fragile and rather ugly
porcelain figurine between his long fingers. She realized that he didn't even register what he had done. And
his expression was nothing short of murderous.

The duchess sighed.

Ah, to be five and twenty and in love again.

As she watched Morland stalk from the room her
eyes began to twinkle and a secret smile played over
her lips.

At least one other person had noticed the earl's abrupt
departure, and she had taken her own leave soon after.

Now Louisa Landringham's beautiful face was set

in a petulant sneer as she smoothed her silken skirts. She had been ignored quite unforgivably tonight! *She*, who was the reigning beauty of three seasons, who had broken hearts by the score since her elderly and very gouty husband had done her the great courtesy of expiring in his sleep after a hard day of hunting—and an even harder night of exertion in her bed.

All of which left Louisa a free—and *very* rich— woman.

She had used that money discreetly and imaginatively. It had bought her many things, from satins to mold her creamy skin to rarest perfumes from India and unguents from China.

Then had come the reckless weeks of blindness, of raw drugging lust, during which she'd found a different partner for her passion every night. Sometimes more than one at a time, in fact.

Yes, all that had amused her very well. For a while, at least.

But she wanted more.

She wanted what she had *always* wanted, and that was Tony Morland, the only peer who had ever openly scorned her advances. The man who had publicly humiliated her in doing so.

Her eyes narrowed to glittering slits as she slipped her mask more securely about her face and bent forward in the shadows of her luxurious traveling coach.

The man before her was young, muscular, and superbly ready.

She ran her jeweled fingers along his naked chest and down to his thighs, which tensed at her touch.

It would have amused her more to have the great Wellington, of course. He would have been a pleasant diversion while she pursued her revenge against Morland. But the Great Man had been preoccupied and oblivious to her lures tonight.

A wave of fury swept her.

But no matter. There were other men. And there were many different kinds of pleasure. They would suffice until she had Morland where she wanted him.

She gave a low, breathy laugh. "You like that." It

wasn't a question. The hard muscle that throbbed against her clever fingers was answer enough.

She eased the buttons on his breeches free. Slowly. Tantalizingly.

His breath was coming raw and jerky now. And *she* controlled every touch, every bit of his pleasure.

"Shall I find out just how much you like that? Adam, wasn't it?" The name did not matter, of course. It was probably as false as the name she had given him. And she would never see him again after this night.

Her companion groaned thickly as his manhood spilled free and lay pulsing in her smooth, skilled fingers. "Do you like this too?" Louisa's eyes glittered, as cold as the diamonds at her throat. Slowly she slid her fingers around him, milking him with expert skill. "Or this, perhaps?"

He was quivering against her palms. His face twisted in a mask of utter pain and cruel pleasure.

It almost made her laugh to see how vulnerable he was—how vulnerable they *all* were.

And one day soon, it would be Morland standing next to her. He would not be so cool and mocking when she had her hands around him like this!

Louisa's expert fingers tightened with the keenness of that image. Her heart began to pound. *Yes, Morland . . .*

She bent lower, her lips wet and seeking.

Her companion was hot and swollen and very ready. Just as she was.

"Tell me," she ordered hoarsely. "Tell me if you like what I'm doing. Tell me what it makes you think of."

Her voice was hoarse as her lips closed around him.

She didn't even hear his answer.

18

It was nearly three o'clock before the Duchess of Cranford's carriage returned Chessy to Dorrington Street. Her feet were aching and her eyes were prickling from the cloying perfumes, pomades, and the press of bodies.

But worst of all was the way she felt inside.

She had tried to ignore him, had tried to block him right out of her consciousness. Yet when Morland had strode from the room, she had known it without even looking.

Because she had *felt* it deep in the pit of her stomach, in the coldness that mumbled her neck and shoulders.

Chessy shivered, fighting the tide of longing that swept over her, driving her back in time, back to the innocent schoolgirl she had once been.

And then her chin rose. She was a girl no more, and her father needed her. She must never allow herself to be weak or distracted. Lord Morland had simply become some sort of a dream figure, played up out of all proportion. And Chessy had no room for a man in her life—especially not a man like the arrogant, womanizing earl.

She looked down at her dresser, where a carved bamboo comb nestled against a small silver brush and hand mirror. There were no cheek colors or lip tints, no jewel cases or perfume bottles.

Nor was there any new letter from her father's kidnappers.

For a moment weariness overtook her. She sank down onto her bed and eased off her slippers. Outside, she heard a faint crack against the window, and then another.

Rain . . .

Funny, but that was Chessy's only real memory of England. Her father had explained that he'd taken her east when she was very young, soon after her mother's death.

It had rained, day after day. Week after week. In fine mistlike sprays and heavy, sullen sheets.

Yes, Chessy remembered that English rain, but very little else.

Idly she picked up a lumpy figure from her bed, a grubby rag doll dressed in muslin skirts and a white apron.

One eye was missing and her yarn hair was nearly gone, but the figure brought back poignant memories.

Keenest of all was the night she'd come down with cholera. At six years old, she'd been terrified to see sickness sweep through Macao, felling servants and friends.

And then she, too, had been gripped by the terrible fever, the dry, racking coughs.

But her father had held her and rocked her for nearly three days until the danger had finally passed.

He had been her world, then and ever since. If sometimes she had missed having a mother to advise and comfort her, to tell her the things girls sometimes needed to hear, she never showed it, for fear of hurting the man who had worked so hard to be both father and mother to her.

Nor did Chessy tell him the names the other girls had called her at the missionary school she attended, names like "mixed-blood" and "slant-eye" and things far worse, things that it had taken her many years to understand completely.

But even then the general meaning had been clear enough, along with the hatred and envy that had spewed out with those epithets.

She was as English as they were, of course, as *innocent* as they were, but that did not matter. She and her father were *different*. They spoke the heathen tongue. They studied the heathen culture. At times they even adopted heathen dress.

Yes, James Cameron and his daughter were very different, and in that narrow, closed little colonial society anything different was a threat.

So Chessy had been mocked and shunned. And she, with her stubborn Cameron pride, had told her father nothing about it. She had been especially careful not to tell him how the English boys stared at her with lazy, knowing grins and found reasons to be nearby so they could drop their books and brush against her with their hot, groping fingers.

And the names *they* whispered were even worse than the names that their sisters used.

Clutching the threadbare doll, Chessy threw her hands over her ears, trying to block out the memory of those rough words and the hollow, mocking laughter.

But she never quite succeeded. Even now she felt as if the laughter hung close by, waiting to mock her. Only at her exercises did she manage to hold the jeers at bay, or when she was deep in some excavation with her father, the more demanding the better.

But ever since her father's capture, Chessy had begun to feel that the laughing voices were winning. As every day passed, they grew louder, warning her that her father's time was growing short and that she could never succeed.

Carefully Chessy straightened the old doll and placed it back upon the bed.

Outside, the rain grew harder, smashing and hammering at the window. The sound pulled her back, back to her earliest memories, which were as bleak and cold as the London streets right now.

She made her decision at that moment. In truth, she had known what she had to do for three nights now.

She must go back to Morland's and get another look at that book in his study. Then she must search the bedroom, as her father's captors had ordered.

And it must be soon.

19

Whitby's face held just the right blend of recognition and impassivity when he held open the door to Lord Morland early the next afternoon.

"Miss Cameron is receiving in the, er—green salon," the butler intoned, taking the earl's gloves and hat.

"Thank you, Whitby." Morland caught a trill of laughter from the end of the hall. "A busy morning?"

With a mere lift of his white brows and a pessimistic sigh, Whitby managed to convey a world of information.

Morland frowned. "Gentlemen callers too?" He'd expected her to take, of course, but not *this* soon.

"In droves, your lordship," the butler said lugubriously. "Lounging about the steps, flooding the alcove with flowers, and rattling on about 'the divine poetry of Miss Cameron's eyes.' Shouldn't wonder if there weren't a dozen of them in the salon right now, in fact." The butler turned resignedly. "If you would care to follow me, your lordship."

A chorus of booming male laughter assaulted Morland, leaving him in no doubt of Whitby's assessment.

Blast, what did the woman think she was about? It

was the height of impropriety to entertain male callers without a chaperon present. When word of the business made its way through the *ton*, Chessy's reputation would be ruined. Had the woman cloth for brains?

His face hardened as he came to the end of the hall and stood surveying the room where Whitby had led him.

Dear Lord, it was even worse than he'd thought! Ten or twelve men thronged the room, laughing and chatting or examining the Oriental rarities displayed against one wall.

And in the center of the melee, cool in a peach muslin morning dress, stood the woman Morland was fast coming to believe would be the destruction of his peace, his sanity, and his very life.

He strode inside, ignoring the exaggerated groans of several young sprigs.

His eyes were only for Francesca.

He saw her instant stiffening and the faint tremor that swept her shoulders. Even then, she kept her back turned, and that defiant gesture infuriated him. So *he* was not to be allowed into the inner sanctum, was he?

By God, it would serve the little fool right if he simply washed his hands of her! Yes, give her free rein for a week and let her break every social rule. Soon every matron in London would be down upon her.

Then she'd come running to him quick enough.

But in spite of his anger, Morland did not really wish to see Francesca Cameron snubbed and jeered at. The thought of her affecting the simpering mannerisms of most of his female acquaintances made him shudder.

After all, it amused him to spar with her. It was a pleasure to discover a female who stood up for her own ideas—no matter how outrageous they happened to be.

Morland fought down a wave of fury as a gangling youth in emerald velvet dropped to one knee before her.

By God, the woman was actually *encouraging* them!

Only then did Morland notice the flowers covering every available surface in the room.

Belatedly he realized he had brought no offering of

his own. The knowledge made him feel awkward and slightly angry.

So she had been a success. He had expected it, of course, but . . .

Morland felt a strange tension grip his chest as he watched Chessy raise her swain from bended knee. For a moment he had a wild urge to sweep the whole noisy lot of them out into the street.

But that would be sheer madness, of course, and would only give rise to the very sort of scandal he was trying to avoid. Besides, she was obviously enjoying her first taste of acclaim. What sort of callous cad would he be to deny her that?

A muscle flashed at Morland's jaw as he waited in silence for Chessy's notice.

It did not come.

It appeared that he had caused more harm than he had realized last night in the duchess's conservatory.

Which was only fair, Morland thought bitterly. *She* had done the same to him.

He gave up waiting. "Miss Cameron. A word, if you please." His mouth tightened when she still did not turn. "If your company can spare you, that is," he added grimly.

A hail of protests met this request, but Morland barely noticed. His attention was trained on the woman turning toward him while sunlight poured through the window.

His first thought was that she looked remarkably fresh and clear-eyed after a night that must have gone on nearly until dawn.

His second thought was that she looked wrenchingly, impossibly beautiful. That much had not changed.

Morland's fingers clenched behind his back as he watched a faint wave of color stain her cheeks. Unspeaking, she lifted a full-petaled rose from a vase that must have contained some three dozen.

For a moment she twirled the crimson bud, as if considering Morland's request. "Ah, but you do not state your business, my lord. I must be wary of such requests. I have no one to protect me here in London, you see."

Behind her the bevy of swains took instant issue with this assessment, all swearing loud vows to protect Miss Cameron unto death.

At any other time Morland might have found the scene amusing and quite harmless.

But now it only made his pulse hammer.

Was the woman purposely orchestrating this display to annoy him? "I believe it would be preferable for us to speak outside, Miss Cameron."

"Do you, indeed?" Her eyes glittered. "Lord Morland, isn't it?" She laughed recklessly. "But I hardly know you. And I, on the other hand, cannot see that we have the slightest thing to discuss." She slanted him a tight smile. "In private or otherwise."

"Chess—" Morland caught himself with a silent curse. "Miss Cameron—I am certain that your guests would not begrudge me a few moments of your time."

Another chorus of protests met Morland's pronouncement. With every word his sapphire eyes grew icier.

Chessy surveyed him through half-lowered lids. "What do you think, gentlemen? I am afraid it is really quite improper of him to ask."

More voices rose in protest.

Chessy stared at Morland and shrugged gracefully. "I'm afraid the majority must carry the day, my lord. Perhaps some other time."

Something snapped in Morland then. With a harsh oath, he strode across the room and caught her wrist. "Outside, my girl," he hissed, so low that only she could hear.

Instantly six men blocked his path. Hard faces glared at him.

Morland ignored them all.

Chessy's face bled white. "Oh, very well. Since you are so tedious as to insist. If you will excuse us for a moment, gentlemen?"

She swept from the room, chin held high.

Once outside, she spun around and glared at Morland. "Well, my lord? What was so vastly urgent that it required this uncouth invasion of my house?"

For a moment Morland could not speak. He had not envisioned seeing her again like *this*, with fury in her face.

By heaven, nothing was going as it should!

Scowling, he stared down at the exquisite beauty in peach muslin. "I—damn it, Chessy, what happened last night was a grave mistake! I never *meant* it to happen. And I give you my vow it will never happen again."

At his words Chessy's cheeks blazed. "A *mistake?* Is that what it was? Are you so sure it will never occur again?" Her eyes seemed very bright for a moment. Then she lowered her gaze, toying with the rose between her fingers.

"I don't ask you to forgive me. It would be more than I could expect. But I hope you will accept my apologies."

Chessy's fingers tightened on the rose. "It is as well that you do not ask my forgiveness, my lord, for I shall never give it. Nor shall I accept your apologies."

A cluster of petals fell to the polished wooden floor. Chessy's lips tightened. "But do not distress yourself. You have only done what any man would have done, given the same opportunity."

"Damn it, Chessy, don't—"

Chessy's smile was very brittle. "Don't what? I hardly see what all the fuss is about. It was just the usual male amusement, was it not?"

Morland's hand shot out and caught Chessy's arm. *"Don't, damn it!* Not to me. I know you too well to believe this charade."

"Do you? I think you do not know the *slightest* thing about me, Lord Morland. And now you will please release your hold on my arm."

Morland's face was harsh. "It started—oh, I don't know, in friendship. And somehow it changed, became something vastly different."

"Friendship? It has been a long time since I counted you my friend. Ten years, to be precise."

Morland's jaw locked as fury whipped through him.

"So you refuse to accept my apology? I can only wonder why."

Chessy gave a raw laugh. "Because no apology is required. You were only acting as you must always act. The incident is entirely done and forgotten. It holds absolutely no importance for me, I assure you."

Morland's frown darkened to a scowl. For some reason this last reply goaded him most of all. "Your memory is very flexible, my dear." His azure eyes narrowed. "*If* I believed you, of course. Which, my dear Chessy, I do *not*." His voice dropped. "In spite of the fact that you're a masterful little liar."

Chessy pulled at his hand. "I do *not* lie. The episode might never have occurred as far as I am concerned."

"Indeed." Morland's eyes took on a reckless gleam. "Do you care to wager on that, my dear?"

"I only wager among my friends."

"You give me a very clear notion of your opinion of me. Very well, since I'm already damned in your eyes—" With a low curse he backed her against the wall and buried his fingers in her gleaming hair. His other hand slid around her back.

Her waist was a pliant curve beneath his hand. Sweet Lord, she was small and soft and—

Perfect. Achingly perfect.

He inhaled the scent of her skin. Sandalwood, wasn't it?

Then she twisted. Fire snaked through Morland's groin as he felt the brush of her thighs.

But she did not fight him. Something told him she was too proud to give way to a struggle.

Good . . .

He raised her chin slowly. "Forgotten, is it? Then prove it, witch. Show me just how indifferent you are to me."

Before she could move, before she could even frame a protest, his lips were on hers. Light and warm, they skimmed her stunned mouth.

Teasing. Goading.

Reminding her of the fire that she claimed she had forgotten.

But it had been a lie, of course.

For Chessy Cameron remembered every blinding minute of pleasure she had found in this man's arms. Every sweet second of discovery she had learned from his strong fingers.

She remembered the slow, effortless mastery of his mouth. The wild, sweet yearning that began somewhere in her chest and melted out into a thousand silken pleasure points.

Until her heart churned like a junk in choppy seas. Until her knees grew strangely weak and her hands seemed to acquire a mind and will of their own.

To comb through his thick hair.

To skim the taut line of his neck.

To tease the hardness of his mouth.

And suddenly it was all there again, the wild, breathless discovery. The exquisite, melting pleasure.

But most dangerous of all was the sense of *belonging*. Of coming home at last, after years of rootless wandering.

With that realization, Chessy understood just how much danger she was in and how vastly she had underrated the power of this man.

With a moan she stiffened and tried to pull away, only to realize that her own fingers were wrapped around his neckcloth and her lips were open to the satin slide of his tongue.

Sweet, unforgettably sweet . . .

And God forgive her, she wanted more, wanted to feel his hands in places no man had ever seen or touched. And she longed to do all the same to him in turn, exploring the faint indentation in his cheek, the fair hair that curved slightly above his brow.

Until she knew what would make him smile and groan with a hunger of his own.

But she never would—never *could*. Not after the way he had turned his back on her.

And then, with her blood pounding like a typhoon-driven sea, Chessy released Morland's tumbled neckcloth and shoved wildly at his chest.

For a moment he did not move. Chessy felt the

tension grip him, felt the thunder of his heart beneath
her taut fingers.

Most of all she saw the undeniable flame of desire
that darkened his eyes as he stared down at her.

And she felt the unmistakable heat of his arousal at
the curve of her belly.

Chessy tried to tell herself he would have felt the
same for a score of women, that this was just one more
example of his utter profligacy.

But she couldn't quite believe it.

Because there was just the faintest tremor in the
hands that held her neck through the silken cloud of
her hair. And because his breath wasn't the slightest
bit steadier than her own.

How easy it would have been to let her wanting rule
her then, to give in to the hot rush of exquisite sensations.

But the world came surging back, as it always
would. Moaning, Chessy shoved at Morland's chest,
jerking her head away from the overpowering pleasure
of his kiss.

"God—" Morland's voice was dark, raw. Lost.

Chessy knew the same sense of shiftlessness, of bewilderment. And her own heart answered the silent
plea she heard in his voice.

But there was no time for sighs or sweetness for her.
No time for anything that would make her soft. Not
while her father's life hung fragile in the balance.

"Sweet God, Chessy—" Morland shuddered and
drew a hoarse breath. "You can't forget *that*."

"L-let me go!"

All emotion swept from his face.

Chessy had a sudden sense that she did not know
this man at all, that there were things about him that
no one understood.

Perhaps himself least of all.

Her breath came fast and ragged as she wrenched
against his body. But every motion drove her into his
heat, his unimaginable hardness.

And her body shuddered in response to that hardness.

For long seconds they stood frozen, his hands braced beside her head, their bodies tensed.

Morland's eyes darkened. He stared down at Chessy's flushed cheeks, at her red lips, swollen with the force of his kisses.

No, not that way. Not with pain or bitterness . . .

His hand slid slowly from her hair. "Talk to me, Chessy. Tell me what you want—"

But Chessy hardened her heart and willed down the hand that yearned to smooth and comfort the crease between his eyes.

Better this way, she thought. Better with all hope severed and only the pain and the anger left between them. Yes, this was the only *safe* way. . . .

She forced her face to icy impassivity. "You—disgust me, my lord." Her voice was flat, even though her skin trembled and her heart drummed madly against his. "I shall thank you to leave this house now and n-never return."

To her fury Chessy felt the sharp prick of tears. Dear God, she must make him leave! She couldn't hold out much longer.

"And should we have the misfortune to meet again, I shall give no sign that I have ever known you. For the Tony Morland I once knew is gone. Dead." Her voice caught. "Perhaps the Chessy Cameron he knew back in Macao is dead also."

Morland's face went pale. A muscle flashed at his jaw.

Chessy thought—*feared*—that he meant to speak, but he only stared down at her in terrible, harsh silence.

And then in one swift movement he pulled away and offered her a perfect, heartbreaking bow. "In that case—there's nothing more to say, is there? You've made your wishes perfectly clear." His mouth set in a bitter smile. "As for myself, I shall remain—your servant, Miss Cameron. For now and forever."

And then he was gone.

For a long time Chessy did not move. Her back slid down, supported against the wall. Her knees threatened to cave in any second.

He was gone. She had done it at last. Her insults had driven him away.

And she would never see him again.

Without warning a burning ache filled her, wrapping itself about her throat and choking her.

Down the hall she heard Swithin's questioning voice, followed by Morland's curt answer, then the sharp crack of a door.

Done. Finished. Forever.

A single tear slid down her cheek as Chessy stared blindly at a circle of damp rot on the far wall. She touched her cheek softly, wanting to save this memory of him. Even if it was only a tear, it was all she would have to hold on to through the long, empty days. The chill, haunting nights . . .

She caught back a sob and forced her attention on that spot on the wall. Yes, she would have to cover the stain. It looked remarkably ugly. She must mention it to Swithin.

Or perhaps to that fellow Whitby, who always seemed so efficient.

She scrubbed at her cheek, surprised to find it so cold.

A light footstep sounded behind her. "I say, Miss Cameron, I was wondering if—" There was a brief hesitation. "Oh, has Morland left? But I thought—"

Suddenly it was more than she could bear. Chessy's fingers twisted against her chest as she fought to keep her voice even. "Pray—pray forgive me, Lord Grantham. I—I must go out. Would you please convey my apologies to—the others?"

"Of course. But is there nothing I can—"

Chessy didn't hear any more. She merely walked past him up the stairs, her face as white as polished marble.

She didn't go out, of course.

She only tugged on her black silk suit and climbed

blindly up the back stairs to the attic room she'd reserved for her exercises.

To lose herself. To stop the pain in the only way she knew how.

First came the cleansing breath. Still and strong. Effortless precision.

Legs firm, she moved, knees soft as water.

Gradually the room faded and she was there again, safe amid the centuries, among red tile roofs and flying white scrolls where a stern old man observed each movement in impassive silence.

"Not so, Midnight." His head shook in that swift, curt way of his. "More knees—all from the knees, as I am one hundred times telling you."

Without another word he swept into a bent-knee stance with arms outstretched. "Think of earth and sky. Think of a mountain stream in high spring. Think *here*," he ordered, tapping his lean stomach just above his navel. "Above all, think without thinking. Think with the part of you beyond words and without mind. Only then will you move in perfect grace, with heart and body one."

Chessy had tried, and slowly she had learned to do all those things.

There had been another foreigner with her at Shaolin, tall and amber-eyed. Sometimes Chessy had sparred with him under the abbot's watchful eye. She wondered what had happened to him since she'd left.

Long, so long ago . . .

Suddenly it was only yesterday: the darting kites, the rich dark earth. The emerald rice thrusting up through silver pools.

Slide. Push. *Feel.*

Her hands cut through the air, carving space into smooth, flawless curves.

"Move like water through sand, Midnight. Move like wind in the grass."

She did. Just as always, each movement calmed her, delighted her, empowered her.

Renewed her. Even when she thought there was nothing left to renew.

Finally the pain shivered and moved apart from her like a black shadow.

And there it stayed.

Never touched. But never quite forgotten.

20

"What in the name of heaven are you doing?" Swithin's face was tense with worry and disbelief as he faced Chessy that evening.

"I'm going to Morland's, of course. To find that wretched book!" Chessy concentrated on securing her mask.

"Are you *mad*? It's been raining through the day. The tiles will be like ice tonight. If you don't fall on your head and break your neck, my girl, it will be nothing short of a miracle!"

Chessy gave a reckless laugh. "Perhaps it would be just as well if I did!"

"You're talking rubbish, girl! What your father would say if he knew—"

"But he doesn't know, does he? And he *won't* know unless I can find that cursed book." She turned then, her eyes huge and wild. "Oh, Swithin, don't fight me tonight. You know as well as I that time is growing short. My father's health has never been robust, not since he was felled with malaria five years ago. Every day I worry about how he is being cared for—and whether the fevers have returned."

183

Swithin gave her shoulder a swift, brusque squeeze. "Don't plague yourself on James's account. The man has the constitution of an ox. He'll be fine, just fine. It's *you* I'm worried about."

Chessy reached for her black cloak. "Whatever for?"

"Because you're in a strange taking tonight, my girl, and I don't like it by half."

"The book must be found. Can you deny that?"

Swithin's lips tightened, but he did not answer.

"Quite. And the sooner the better. So there it is." She turned then, her form swathed in black. "Now please fetch the carriage, Swithin"—her voice faltered for a second—"before I lose my nerve."

The old servant raised a hand as if he meant to protest. But Chessy spun about and disappeared down the rear stairs before he could speak.

The ascent was far worse than she'd expected. Twice she'd slipped, dangling inches from destruction. But both times, she'd forced herself back up, clinging desperately until she'd found a toehold.

By the time she made her way to the rear window, Chessy was pale and trembling and wishing for nothing more than that the night were over.

But the night—and all its dangers—was just beginning.

As before, she made her way to the first-floor study. The room was empty tonight, a single candle burning on the mantel. Chessy searched the room quickly, under the settee and behind the curtains, even inside the desk.

But the book was gone.

With a growing sense of urgency, she crept back into the hallway and started for Morland's bedroom on the second floor. *Try the false panel beside the bookcase,* the note had ordered.

Her heart was hammering when she slid open the door at the far end of the upper corridor. A single branch of candles burned on a marquetry card table.

In the flickering light Chessy made out amethyst damask curtains and snow-white sheets.

Sheets that just now were mounded high about a broad-shouldered form that lay fast asleep.

At least this time he'd taken off his boots. She frowned down at a tangle of clothes tossed carelessly on the floor between door and bed.

Chessy's throat tightened as she watched for any sign of movement from the bed. None came.

Now or never, she thought grimly.

She crept to the bookshelf opposite the bed and ran her hands along the wooden shelves. Nothing moved.

The secret panel had to be here somewhere!

Carefully she probed the rear wall, searching for indentations or hidden levers.

Again, nothing. No sign of latch or closings.

She searched the shelves, then slid to her knees to test the wainscoting along the floor.

But the effort was fruitless.

She was just about to rise when she spied the small stucco design that ran waist-high on both sides of the bookshelf. Frowning, she bent closer. That was odd. The patterns were not quite symmetrical.

She traced the outline of a spray of flowers that was two inches larger than its mate. A second later Chessy sprang back with a cry as the wall began to inch open.

She'd found it!

Carefully she reached inside the darkened recess, feeling her way along dusty shelves.

Then she felt something bulky at her fingers, something covered in silk and secured with ivory closings.

With her pulse thundering in her ears she eased the bulky shape up into the candlelight.

The jewel-encrusted binding fell away. A thick mass of hand-sewn pages lay in her hands.

Her heart in her mouth, she inched back against the wall and stared down.

Surely her luck was about to change . . .

Carefully she opened to the first page. And then her heart sank.

Oh, the painting was skillful enough. In jewellike

colors it showed a pair of lovers reclining amid a garden of lotus and peonies.

But it was not the work of a master, not the priceless art object she had glimpsed long ago in the studio of a rich Chinese merchant.

Chessy swayed. So close. This time she had been so sure. . . .

She blinked, fighting back tears. *Dear God, when would it be over?*

Behind her came a low burst of muttering.

Whirling about, Chessy stared at the motionless figure on the bed. She must leave now, before he awoke as he had done the last time she was here!

Quickly she moved back to the bookshelf, the book clenched in her trembling hands.

And then she gasped. Iron fingers caught her right wrist and pulled it upward. Scowling, Tony Morland studied the scarred palm and callused fingers.

"Going somewhere, little felon?" His voice hardened. "Or should I say *friend*?"

The book in Chessy's other hand fell to the floor with a crack.

"Yes, I thought the book would lure you back, my dear."

Hard fingers pulled at her headcovering. Chessy gasped and wrenched backward, out of reach. "But you—"

"The bed? An old trick I learned in the Peninsula." In the candlelight the earl's face looked carved from stone. "And now I think we can dispense with the mask, since I know your identity well enough."

Chessy heard the hiss of tearing silk. The mask slid from her face. "How did you know?"

"That it was you?" Morland laughed grimly. "I couldn't seem to shake the image of a black-clad urchin inching across the roof. And then when I saw your hands, when I felt all those calluses—" His eyes hardened. "Oh, I don't claim that it came immediately. I still thought there were two of you, working together. But when I felt your palms just now, and there were those same calluses—" He dropped her hand abruptly, as if it hurt him. "Why, Chessy? That's what I want to know. And then I want to know *how*."

Chessy inched sideways, her hands against the wall. Four steps to the door, maybe five. *Distract him somehow. . . .*

"Why? Very simple." She edged slowly to the left. "Because it was a challenge, my lord. You know I've never been able to resist a challenge." *Two steps left.* "As for how, let's just say that there are many things I've learned since you left Macao."

"Obviously. You've studied with a master. That explains the calluses on your hands, the surprising strength in your arms. But where did you learn such things?" And then Morland's brow furrowed as the answer came to him. "Not in *China!* Not even your ramshackle father would be fool enough to—"

Chessy gave him a tight smile. *Almost there.* "Very observant of you, my lord. And yes, in China." Abruptly she bolted to the side, keeping her body low and tucked.

But she wasn't low or fast enough.

Morland's foot slammed into her knee. A moment later, she went flying face-down onto the Persian carpet.

"Damn you! L-let me go!"

A rigid knee anchored her to the carpet as Morland captured her flailing hands. "Stop fighting me, Chessy! You're going nowhere until I have some answers!"

She felt a brisk yank and found herself flat on her back beneath him, staring up into a blaze of sapphire eyes.

"Now *talk*."

"I won't! I hate you! You're arrogant, abominable, insolent—"

"I'm waiting, Chessy. Was it for money? Because of some scrape your father got you into?"

She wrenched wildly, but his granite frame did not budge.

"You—you'll be sorry for this!" She wrestled one hand free and slammed it down callused edge first, right against his collarbone.

Morland cursed. His grip wavered for the slightest moment.

It was all the opportunity Chessy needed. She yanked her other hand free and twisted sideways. The next second, her right hand flashed through the air and slammed against his knee.

His right knee.

Morland's face went utterly white. His lips locked.

"Dear God, I—" Horrified, Chessy realized where she had hit him.

But the blaze in his eyes recalled her to her danger. The next second, she was on her feet and hurtling toward the window.

She made the sill and shoved the pane open. Her leg went through. She heard a dark curse behind her, but shut her mind to the pain she had just dealt.

It had been necessary. Like so many other things she'd done, this had been neither right nor wrong, only necessary.

But the thought brought her no comfort as she heard Morland's grunt of pain and his shuffling gait.

And then she pushed out into the darkness, out into the night and freedom. Only halfway out, she felt the grip of callused fingers. They circled her knee and held on relentlessly.

Before she could blink, she was wrenched backward and caught against Morland's chest.

She told herself to strike him. She raged at her hands to slash at neck or collarbone.

But she could not.

And then it was too late.

His eyes were icy, relentless. He didn't ever spare his breath to speak this time, only jerked her up into his arms and toppled her backward onto the bed.

His mouth was a flat line. "First the book, Chessy. Why did you take such risks for it?"

Chessy glared back at him and inched toward the side of the bed nearest the window.

His eyes narrowed. "You'll never make it. And you're not leaving this room until you give me some answers."

"I'll tell you nothing!"

Morland shrugged. "I imagine it will be a long night in that case." He shrugged off his shirt of fine blue cloth and moved around the bed, never taking his eyes from hers. "Was it for money? Are you that badly dipped?"

Chessy edged farther away.

"Is it some fantastic new project of your father's?"

No answer.

Carefully Chessy maneuvered her hand along the bed, looking for any weapon to resist him. She found nothing. Nothing but crisp linen sheets and a damask dressing gown.

"I'll tell you *nothing*. No matter how you threaten me!" She arched her back suddenly and delivered a blow to his side.

Had she tried, that blow could have incapacitated an enemy. As it was, Chessy planned only to force Morland to keep his distance.

Grimacing, he jumped back, then moved in from the side.

Her second kick caught him across the thigh, and the shock exploded all the way down his leg.

She saw him stiffen, then slowly straighten.

His eyes darkened with fury. "You'll have to do better than that, my dear. I am quite prepared to stay here all night, you know."

But Chessy saw the ridge of tension at his locked jaw, the strain about his eyes.

The way his fingers surreptitiously pressed his knee.

She felt a sick ache in the pit of her stomach, imagining the pain he must be feeling. Damn it, why wouldn't the man just give in?

"It's your father. They've got him, haven't they?"

For once Chessy was speechless. She could only stare, too stunned to utter a denial.

"Well?"

"How—how did you know?"

"I have my spies, my dear." He gave a bitter laugh. "In this case, at least, they were right. How long has he been missing?"

Chessy swallowed. "Three—three months now."

"Good Lord! And *that's* why you've come to London? To find him?"

Chessy frowned, her lips taut.

"Tell me, damn it!"

"Why? What difference does it make to you?"

"Because I want to help him, you little fool. But I won't know where to begin unless you tell me what's happened."

"There's nothing you can do," Chessy said bitterly. "They kidnapped him in Macao three months ago. And it will go far worse for him if you try to interfere. These are dangerous people. They'll not balk at one more death to achieve their ends."

"*Who?* What people would do such a thing?"

"Triads, I think. Any one of a dozen secret societies that litter China and every part of Asia. Yes, almost certainly it is the Triads. The scourge of the East—and now it appears that they've moved to London."

Instantly it made perfect sense to Morland. The Black Dragons and Red Tigers or any one of the fanatically loyal outlaw societies would have the means and the opportunity to kidnap James Cameron. He had tangled with them before, when they'd tried to rob him of some freshly excavated treasure.

He'd won then, Morland thought. But it seemed that this time he'd failed. "What is the price for your father's release?"

Chessy stiffened. Something held her back from answering.

"Something very precious, no doubt." In a lightning movement he grabbed her wrist and turned it up. "Sweet God, Chessy, what things you must have seen and done since I last saw you!" His eyes darkened. "You were good up there on the rooftop. Damned good." He gave a grim laugh. "By God, I thought my heart would drop through my chest when you jumped the street."

Chessy swallowed. "So did I."

Morland's fingers tightened on her hand. "You're a bloody fool, that's what you are, Chessy Cameron! You could have died up there. And if not then, it could have happened a hundred other times that night. Damn it, I might have shot you *myself* if I'd had a pistol about me."

Chessy shrugged, feigning a nonchalance she didn't feel. "A necessary danger. One gets used to them."

Suddenly Morland went very still. "You were there, weren't you? While Germaine and I . . ." He did not finish.

Chessy nodded, glad he said no more to describe that evening.

"You saw—heard?"

Again she nodded. She could not have spoken even if the Emperor Chia-ch'ing himself had stood in the doorway.

Morland did not move. "Bloody everlasting hell! Of all the times for you to—"

While his brain was still whirling, Chessy tried to tug free. "Let me go. You've got your answers. There's n-nothing more for me to—"

Morland's face hardened. He cursed as Chessy's leg jammed into his knee. "Not yet, my dear. You haven't told me the price for your father's release."

Chessy twisted, but this time he was ready. He shifted so that his right leg was out of reach and shoved her beneath him. His hard thighs pinned her flat to the bed. And his hands—

Dear Lord, they were like iron. As hard as anything she had faced in Shao-lin.

"You may as well tell me. I'll have it out of you soon enough."

She thought of driving her foot against his knee. She could see that it was paining him even now. But decency would not allow it. Instead she twisted and shoved, straining to move her leg free to aim a punishing blow at his manhood.

He gave her a grim smile. "Don't even think about it. You wouldn't like the results, I assure you."

Chessy flushed faintly, suddenly aware of the intimate press of their bodies, of the crisp blond hair dusting his neck just behind his ear.

Of the rising heat of his arousal against her belly.

Morland uttered a low, savage curse. His grip tightened.

"Their price—it was the book, wasn't it?"

Chessy's breath caught. She'd hoped to have more time than this. But she knew that her instant stiffening had betrayed her.

She nodded reluctantly.

"By God, I should have known!"

"Let me go. You—you have all your answers now." Chessy twisted sharply. A shudder ran through the man pressed against her.

She should have fought free then. She should have struck in the hundred different places of vulnerability that she had been trained to strike.

But she didn't. She *couldn't*.

She only lay beneath him, remembering how he had tossed in his nightmares. How he had struggled to conceal his pain.

And Chessy found herself wishing she could pull him closer and drive away that pain forever.

But she didn't have forever. She didn't have *any* time at all, not with her father captive of the Triads. "Let me go. I—I can see you're in pain. Don't make me do anything m-more to hurt you," she said raggedly.

At that moment a curl slid free of its binding at her neck. Shimmering like blue-black satin, it cascaded across her cheek.

Morland's jaw tensed. Slowly he reached out and smoothed the strand back above her ear.

That movement—so singular, so gentle, so utterly unexpected—made Chessy gasp. Heat rushed to the pit of her stomach.

"What do you know about my pain? Unless—" A muscle flashed at his jaw. "So that was *you* that night in the study. I had thought it was Whitby."

Chessy nodded.

"Did you enjoy your visit?" Morland's face was grim. "Did I put on a good performance?"

"Had you gone to bed when you should have, I would never have disturbed you!"

"My sincerest apologies. I found I wasn't quite equal to the ascent." His voice hardened. "As no doubt you noticed."

Chessy considered denying what she had seen that

night. Somehow that seemed the coward's way out. "I saw. How—how long has it been?"

"Since I've been like this?" He shrugged. "Long enough."

"And it always bothers you? Like it did then?"

Morland shrugged. "Let's just say I always feel it. But I don't want your pity, Chessy. Nor your tears. All I want are answers."

He was lying. He wanted anything she had to give him. He wanted *everything*. And the hard muscle cushioned against her straining belly proved that he did.

He knew she felt it too. Why else had a wave of heat flushed her face?

Morland bit back a curse. *Think, fool! Forget how beautiful she is, how perfect she feels lying beneath you. Remember what you have to do—and why.*

"So the Triads have your father, and they want the pillow book. Then we'll just have to find it and give it to them," he said grimly.

"You—you don't have it? Oh, God, I was hoping—"

"I'm afraid not. I was even planning to track down that skulking little urchin who seemed to know his way around the roofs of London. I hoped that *he* might be able to help me. I suppose it *was* you behind those break-ins?"

Chessy nodded, her expression defiant.

"Even at the Royal Asiatic Society?"

Another nod.

"By God, you're *mad*! You might have been killed! And what if you had been caught?"

"I—there was no choice. The notes were most precise. They said—"

"Notes?" Morland gripped her hand. *"What* notes?"

"The ones that directed me here—and to all the other places."

Morland's voice took on an edge of urgency. "Do you still have them?"

"Of course. But they're useless. There was no name, no sign at all of where they came from." Chessy squirmed to pull free.

Morland ignored her. "How were they delivered?"

"Sometimes by link boys, other times by hackney drivers. Always a different person. Always someone who had no idea who sent them."

"Only to be expected, I suppose. And the last note told you to look here for the book?"

Chessy nodded. "It's almost funny. *They* must be as much in the dark as we are."

"I wonder," Morland said slowly. His eyes narrowed.

And then he froze.

"Tony? What were you—"

"*Hush.*"

The next moment Chessy heard it, a low tapping somewhere outside the window. The scrape of twigs, perhaps?

Or shoes inching across a tile roof?

The sound grew closer, soft and furtive and quick.

"Get behind the screen," Morland whispered.

"But—"

"*Now, damn it!*"

21

The harshness in his voice made Chessy obey. A moment later, she slid behind a lacquer screen overhung with a rich satin dressing gown and a flowing shirt of finest linen.

Even now his smell hung about them, a faint blend of spicy soap, leather and—*gardenias*?

Chessy stiffened as she saw her white flower sticking through the third buttonhole of Morland's shirt. But why—

Then there was no more time for thought.

The room was plunged into darkness as Morland blew out the candle. "And whatever you do, don't move from behind that screen," he ordered. "I don't care to go stumbling over *you* in the dark."

Chessy waited, her heart pounding. A queer dizziness attacked her blood as the sound on the rooftop grew closer.

A scraping came at the window.

Close, so close . . .

Automatically she took a slow breath, made her knees soften, relax.

Ready, always ready. As she had trained herself to

be in Shao-lin. No matter what she'd promised Morland.

As she stood motionless in the darkness, Chessy caught the faint, sweet scent of gardenias. Light. Fine. Inexpressibly sensual.

Hysteria licked at her senses. They were in gravest danger. They both might have their throats slit any moment, and all she could think of was the fact that he'd saved her gardenia—had thrust it into his shirt just above his heart.

The windowpane rattled slightly. The next minute, Chessy felt a current of cold wind sweep through the room.

The pane squeaked as it rose. And then came the rustle of cloth.

Chessy locked her lips, unable to endure the waiting, captive behind the screen while all her senses screamed for her to launch into an attack.

Cloth slippers brushed the carpet, heading for the bed.

And then a gasp. A low grunt. *Morland's?*

She held her breath, focusing desperately on the muted sounds of struggle coming near the window.

Muscle smashed against muscle. Breaths checked, the enemies clashed, each movement muffled, desperate in the darkness.

And though it was one of the hardest things she'd ever done, Chessy waited motionless.

A table crashed to the floor. She heard the shrill sound of ripping silk.

And then a low curse. Morland's curse.

Her fingers locked.

Another curse. This one high, sharp.

A Chinese oath.

So it *was* the Triads. They must have followed her here!

An armchair thudded onto its side as the two bodies made a phantom progress in the darkness, closer and closer to the screen where Chessy waited. And then came the explosive sound of shattering glass, followed by Morland's raw curse.

A moment later, a heavy body struck the screen, sent it swaying, and finally knocked it backward.

Morland's grunt of pain was the last sound Chessy waited to hear. The next second, she darted from the path of the falling screen and listened for signs of the intruder.

She heard only Morland's rasping breath.

And then it came. The faintest scrape of cloth against cloth. A hiss of silk at the far side of the bed.

Chessy followed, careful to avoid the side table that had fallen to her right. The intruder was equally careful, making no further sound. But she caught the whisper of air and knew he was beside the bookshelf, searching the same panel she had searched earlier.

If she could capture him, they might find out where her father was being held.

Soundlessly, she inched closer. And then her cloth slipper crunched as it met shattered glass.

Instantly she jumped sideways, away from the betraying noise. But not fast enough.

A hard hand slashed downward, catching just the edge of her elbow. Gritting her teeth, she dipped low, then swung about, trying to elude the blow that would come from the darkness.

Her foot flashed out. She met silk and human skin. She kicked, once and again, meeting muscle each time. Instantly she leaped backward, out of reach. She heard the low rasp of breath, and a muffled curse.

Blindly she inched in a wide circle, making for her attacker's back.

And then she sent a slashing chop to the point where she estimated the back of his neck would be.

She struck muscle—a sinewy forearm.

Gasping, she spun about and kicked high.

This time she caught the man flush in the unprotected stomach. The force of the blow sent him staggering backward.

"Aiyeeaa!" He spoke fast and shrill in Cantonese dialect. "You fight well, shadow. For a stinking foreign dog, that is!"

Chessy did not speak. She knew the taunt for what

it was—a ploy to force her to speak and betray her location. Silently she circled back toward the window.

There she waited. She knew he was hit and that now he must think of leaving.

The blow came without warning, callused palm straight to her neck. Only a handful of warriors could accomplish that maneuver. Chessy had hoped to study it, but the abbot had never agreed, saying it was all flash and no substance and not for such a one as she.

But a Triad would have known that sort of move.

Chessy staggered forward, then spun about, reaching wildly for her opponent.

Too late, she caught the whoosh of wind, felt the damask curtains sweep about her face.

The window!

She shot forward and peered into emptiness.

She was too late. Across the roof a dim figure slipped behind a chimney. As she watched, Chessy imagined that he turned and bowed mockingly.

She was halfway outside, intent on pursuit, when she heard the raw groan at her back. A moment later, another chair toppled to the ground.

This time Morland made no sound at all. And that, Chessy decided, was worse than any number of curses.

Grimly she turned, ignoring the shadow melting back into the night, knowing that Morland needed her most now. She made for his prone form and found a pulse, low but steady. Gasping against the pain in her arm, she felt for blood.

Instead of blood, she found two lumps, one rising just behind his ear and the other over his right brow. No doubt those were what had toppled him. Grimacing with strain, she maneuvered him to a sitting posture and touched his cheek.

"Tony? Wake up!"

A shudder ran through him. "What—" He smothered a curse. "Chessy? Is that—"

"Right here. Unfortunately our intruder got away. He was a man of great skill, I think."

Hard fingers reached out and captured her wrist in

the darkness. "Feel strange." He smothered a curse. "Are you—did he—"

She laughed bleakly. "Oh, I'm fine, other than a few bruises. But I lost him, blast it."

The fingers flinched for a moment. "Next time we'll fare better."

Suddenly light filtered beneath the bedroom door. Muffled voices echoed through the corridor. A moment later the door was thrown open.

"My lord, are you there?" The unseen arrival cursed as his foot struck wood. "Go and fetch a lantern, Alice! And bring along the groom!" Heavy feet crunched over shattered glass.

"Here—Skelton. Mind the bloody glass." Morland released Chessy and eased away from her.

Light flickered up the corridor, then swept the room as the servant entered, bearing a branch of candles.

"My God! Whatever—"

The room was a scene of chaos.

Chairs and tables were pitched sideways, and the screen lay overturned in a crazy sprawl, clothing scattered all about it. Glass fragments glittered beside the window, where the goblets and decanter had gone flying in the scuffle.

The servant gasped. His gaze fell upon Chessy, who was wedged against an overturned armchair. "Who—"

He never finished. Stunned, he watched Morland push to his feet, moving hand over hand along the back of the armchair. The earl swayed and began to move toward the door. " 'Fraid the blackguard spoiled the brandy. Better—ahhhh—fetch more, Skelton."

"Don't!" White-faced, Chessy watched Morland make an awkward progress across the glass-strewn floor. "You mustn't!"

But her warning came too late. The next moment, Morland grimaced and caught at his thigh.

Then, before Chessy's stricken face, he began to totter.

"Help me!" Before the valet could react, Chessy was at Morland's side. Swiftly she caught his waist, staggering beneath his weight.

And then the servant was beside her, struggling to hold the earl upright.

"What in the name of heaven? And who are *you*?" The man's eyes widened, taking in the blue-black cascade of hair that had until then been hidden behind Chessy's back. "But—you're a woman!"

"Of course I am, blast it! Now help me get the earl to the bed before he does himself any further damage."

Between the two of them, they half carried, half dragged the unconscious Morland to the bed and settled him on his back. There was a gash across his breeches, and she could see blood darkening the fabric.

Chessy frowned as she saw another gash on his arm.

She gnawed on her lower lip, staring at the fresh, pooling blood. From a Triad dagger, no doubt. But why should it have rendered Morland unconscious?

She bent close, studying the clean line of the wound. Not deep, not a great deal of blood lost. So why—

Abruptly she stiffened. It was the odd, sour scent that gave her the first hint of warning. Swiftly she bent forward and brushed the edge of Morland's forehead, then his arm.

"Now see here, miss—whoever you are! What's been going on here, that's what I want to know! And what are you—"

Chessy paid him no heed, intent on the faintly metallic scent on her fingers.

Somewhere she had smelled that before.

And then she froze, as the memory returned.

Twelve years earlier, it was, at a village banquet. She had smelled that scent and then watched a man lapse into white-faced terror and die.

Dear God, don't let me be too late!

She was already issuing orders as she tugged off her padded outer jacket, then ripped at the sleeve. "I'll need hot water and a knife—freshly boiled. Send someone around to fetch Whitby and Mrs. Harris from my home."

Hearing silence behind her, she spun about, furious. "Well, don't stand there gawking, you fool! Twenty-seven Dorrington Street. Tell them to bring Swithin and my kit. Hurry, man, or he'll die!"

At that, the valet closed his gaping mouth and lunged from the room, calling for the groom.

Chessy watched Morland's pallid face and uttered a desperate prayer for the man who lay motionless on the bed.

Fugu, the Japanese called it. Pufferfish. The source of the deadliest toxin known to man. It paralyzed a man in seconds, choking him with relentless efficiency.

She had little time. Right now, with every surge of Morland's pulse, the relentless poison was inching closer and closer to his heart.

His legs were totally numb.

It was pleasant at first to feel the ache at his knee subside into blessed painlessness.

He tried to tell Chessy, but his thoughts were sluggish. Somehow it felt better to lie against the crisp white sheets and float on dark currents.

Then the coldness began, inching up his legs. Soon he felt nothing beyond a heaviness where bone and muscle had once throbbed.

He tried to speak. "Chess—"

No sound emerged. His mouth felt swollen and strange, as if it belonged to someone else.

With a savage effort of will, he raised his finger.

But Chessy did not see. Her head was turned while she issued rapid-fire orders to his frightened valet, who turned and ran from the room.

Morland tried to move, tried to speak, mesmerized by the fear in Chessy's eyes.

He could do neither. Now even his finger was frozen, and the slow, creeping death was everywhere, in everything, part of every slow, painful breath.

"Chess—"

Then even his eyes closed. He did not move again.

He was no longer moving. His color was nearly gone. Already he had the look of death about him.

Chessy ripped at his clothes, recognizing all the signs of the deadly poison's progress. First the numbness, then the chill. And then the total paralysis as the body's organs simply shut down, one by one.

Her fingers trembled as she ripped another length of silk and tied it in a second tourniquet just above the first. That might delay the poison's progress. And with any luck Swithin should be here soon with her supplies.

But until then . . .

Swiftly she bent over the bed and jerked at Morland's neckcloth. She tried to avoid looking into his locked face, all too aware of the nightmare realm he was caught in.

His shirt buttons came free. She wrenched the linen from his taut shoulders. The wound on his arm was fiery red now, laced with angry slashes of yellow. Chessy caught back a sob as she tightened the top tourniquet.

Just then, the earl's valet returned with a knife and a pan of boiling water. Outside in the hall several more anxious servants gathered, peering into the room.

Chessy paid no attention, dousing a fresh piece of linen in the steaming liquid. Quickly she sponged out the wound, careful to scrub away any lingering traces of poison.

Whispering nervously, the servants dispersed.

All the while Morland lay motionless, lips locked, body tense beneath her.

Sweet Lord, she only hoped that Swithin hurried.

The incense drifted, slow and mesmerizing. The old Triad leader steepled his hands, seated behind an exquisite rosewood table. "Well, Ah-fang? Did you kill him?"

"The cut was deep. The poison of the pufferfish will soon do its work."

"You used enough?"

"Most certainly, honorable lord."

"Tell me what happened."

The warrior in black bowed. "I did not harm the

woman. The secret panel was open when I arrived. The woman was before me, looking for the book."

"Did she find it?"

"I cannot say, lord. She did not have it when we fought."

The Triad leader drew a hissing breath. "You *fought* her? Fool! She might have been harmed. We must keep her safe until the book is found. Only then may we turn the emperor more favorable to our society."

"But she was not hurt, lord. She is very skilled."

"And the *yang-kuei*? The Englishman?"

"He, too, fought well, but not well enough." A low laugh. "He will die, lord. Just as you ordered."

"Excellent, Ah-fang. He is a distraction to the woman, and we must not allow that. Not until we have the book back."

The warrior's eyes narrowed. "And then? After she has given us the book?"

"Then you may kill her father—and do whatever you wish with her."

The warrior smiled. It was just what he had hoped to hear.

22

He was floating in a place of absolute darkness.

It was not uncomfortable, at least not at first. At first it was like swimming at night, as he had done often as a boy, in the clear, cool pond at Sevenoaks.

Then the weight came. It was shapeless, without beginning or end—and soon it was relentless, like a boulder crashing down upon his chest.

He tried to rise, to shove the rock away.

He tried to speak.

He tried to live—and realized he was failing.

Chessy ran to the door as she heard Swithin's familiar gruff voice echo up the stairwell of Morwood House.

"Swithin, is that you?"

"Just so, miss. And I brung your bag of needles, all right and tight." He held out the precious bag. "How is his lordship faring?"

Chessy snapped open the leather case and began rooting inside it. "Bad—oh God, very bad. And there's so little time." With a glad cry she found what she was looking for. She held a packet of herbs out to Swithin.

"Have this made into a paste with boiling water, and bring it back the instant it is finished."

She did not turn as Swithin bounded from the room.

Already she was slitting Morland's breeches with a fine silver-handled knife. She studied the lean, muscular thighs beneath. Her fingers ran along the scarred knee. She winced at the savage lines of silver radiating like a starburst from the joint.

The horror. The agony he must have felt.

But Chessy did not allow herself to think of that, not now, when his present danger loomed so great. She used *hao-chin* needles, fine and long. She slid the first into place just above his knee and twirled it firmly. The second she inserted at the center of his thigh, and the third four inches below his groin.

Had she been totally rational at that point, she would have blanched in the face of such an excruciatingly intimate task, but now she thought only of Morland's advancing chill, his growing pallor.

Dear God, let her not be too late. Let her fingers be strong and skillful and absolutely accurate as she practiced the needling techniques she had learned long before from old Abbot Tang . . .

Retrieving three more needles from her bag, she inserted them at the same points along Morland's opposite leg, watching for any sign of motion or sensation.

Nothing.

Just then Swithin returned, bearing a cup of steaming brew.

Chessy dabbed some on a piece of linen and applied it to the wound, then stood back, gnawing her lip desperately.

"Keep adding more of the paste, Swithin. I—I must concentrate." She closed her eyes, willing away the racking fear, concentrating on the points she had learned long years before in the abbot's tree-shaded study.

"The *tai-mai* meridian controls internal sicknesses. Needle its master points, and you can promote great healing."

Chessy frowned. Nothing was *working*! Not the needles, not the herbal blend. There had to be something else, something she was not thinking of!

She clenched her fingers, struggling to remember. If she had known how important those lessons would be, she would have paid more attention.

Then with a wild cry she turned and dragged out a box with white powder from her bag. It was dangerous, of course. Too much, and he would die.

But if she did nothing, he would die anyway.

Forcing her fingers to steadiness, Chessy lifted a tiny amount of powder on a silver spoon and scattered it over the wound.

She watched Morland's face for any return of color.

Nothing. His lips were blue-tinged, and his breathing had nearly ceased.

She clasped her hands to her chest, willing and praying that Morland recover. "Don't give up now. Not yet. Not when there are so many things I have yet to make you pay for!"

Desperately, she applied a touch more *ma-huang* powder. The stimulant was made from a native Chinese herb that charged the body, making the heart pump furiously and the blood vessels expand.

It would speed up the transit of the poison through the body. If he made it through the next few minutes, he might survive.

Tears were streaming down Chessy's cheeks, but she paid no attention. Her fingers shifted the delicate needles, spinning them just as she had seen old Tang do.

"Try, do you hear me? Fight it!"

But if Morland heard, he gave no sign. His breathing continued, slow and shallow and nearly nonexistent.

Chessy bit her lip. There was nothing more for her to do now. Nothing to do but wait.

And remember . . .

It had been one of those perfect blue and white days in early spring, the kind found rarely in the tropics. All day the sun had poured from a flawless sapphire sky, turning the water to crystal.

They had swum and explored the reefs, then climbed to a tiny island and eaten berries and fish roasted over a fire Tony had built. Chessy had laughed at his first awkward attempts to kindle a flame, then had finally taken pity on him and done the job properly herself.

He had answered by boning the fish and laying the fillets out on rocks, where they had sizzled noisily. While her stomach rumbled, Chessy added a handful of savory herbs. A rich cloud of wood smoke had billowed around them, imparting a sense of magic to everything they did.

Chessy had spun about in a little dance, thrown back her head, and laughed.

Just for the pleasure of it. Just for the sheer joy of being alive on such a perfect day in spring. Just because the sky was clear as sapphire and the sea ran on like glass all the way to the horizon.

Because the wind was fresh and they were alone in their tiny island kingdom, away from anyone who would censure or disapprove or scold.

Because this moment in this day was heaven, or as close as Chessy ever expected to get to heaven.

At that moment Morland had let out a rumble of laughter, spinning her about and throwing her up into the air.

He had caught her, still laughing, still the amused, half-mocking older brother she had always wanted but never had. It had been an embrace of simple camaraderie. Of pure animal delight.

And then it had changed. Somewhere between breaths everything had changed, no longer simple, no longer uncomplicated but now intense. Breath-stopping.

And dangerously personal.

He had put her down slowly, very careful that their bodies should barely touch. His face had changed, its simple exuberance darkened by a racing blend of emotions, shock and denial key among them.

Chessy had stared at him, wide-eyed, as he'd raised his hand to her cheek. The wind had blown a strand of hair around his arm, binding them as if in some primitive pagan ritual.

She gasped, watching the unnatural tension in his jaw, the sudden darkening of his eyes.

Tony caught her shoulder. Unmoving, he had stared down at her, his eyes full of an unspoken question—a question that Chessy was still too young and innocent to understand.

Slowly he had bent his head. His breath had swept her cheek. His mouth had followed.

Then, oh then, he had touched her, lip to open lip, mouth to trembling mouth. It had been wonderful, awful. White-hot and icy cold. She had put up her hands to push him away, to draw him close. She had shivered, feeling his tongue push between her lips.

Oh, God, his tongue . . .

And then, just as swiftly as it had begun, it was over.

"I—I'm sorry, Cricket," he had said, jerking back, releasing her awkwardly. "I can't imagine what—why—" He raked his fingers through his sunlit hair. "Forgive me."

Chessy had only stared at him, bewildered. She didn't understand, not him, not this. Especially not the things she was feeling.

She'd only shrugged, trying to shake off the strange fluttering in her stomach, the lightness of her skipping pulse.

What had happened to her? Why was her skin quivering? It was only a kiss, after all.

But it was a kiss that had lasted far too long—and ended far too soon. Even now she could remember every texture of it, every agonizing heartbeat of it.

And all she could find to regret was his apology, which had hurt her far more than any liberties he had taken.

Yes, it had all begun there on that windswept, cypress-ringed hill surrounded by the silver water of the South China Sea.

But it certainly hadn't ended there. . . .

A hint of sound teased her ear.

Chessy scrubbed at her cheek and turned to the other side.

"Chess—"

The sound jerked her up from the chair where she had dozed off.

"Tony? Can you hear me?" Anxiously she studied his face, looking for signs of recovery. Was his color slightly deeper? And there, at his jaw, were the lines of tension lessened?

Quickly she dug for a clean strip of linen and applied more herbal paste to the wound.

This time she definitely saw a muscle flex at his forearm.

"Just once, Tony. Oh, please, prove to me that we've done it."

As if in answer she saw a faint twitch of his eyelid. The fingers of his right hand curled ever so slightly. And then she heard the faint breath of sound.

"D-didn't know . . . Should have guessed . . ."

Slowly, with a superhuman effort, his eyes opened. His startling sapphire eyes blazed over Chessy, dark with a desperation she had never seen there before.

Awkwardly his fingers circled her wrist.

"Need to tell . . ." He swallowed, grimacing. "Never meant . . . to put you in danger."

Chessy caught back a sob and stroked the gaunt line of his cheek. "Don't try to talk. It will be fine now. Just rest."

". . . hear . . ."

Beads of moisture trembled in the bronze hair dusting his powerful chest. He was hot now, as hot as he had been cold only seconds before.

She wanted to run her fingers deep, to tug at those crisp bronze strands and feel him groan with pleasure.

She gave herself a shake. "There's no need to talk," she whispered. "All that can wait until tomorrow."

"Chess—" He swallowed, then took a jerky breath. "Must . . . stay." His eyes were bright, fierce with fever. "Not . . . safe."

Chessy shivered as she made out his ragged words. "Don't talk, my love." The words slipped out without her awareness. "We'll have all the time in the world to talk tomorrow, after you're well."

He closed his eyes. A shudder shook him. "Must s-stay . . ."

And then, with his fingers still wrapped around her wrist, he fell back against his pillow.

Chessy sat frozen for long minutes. His color was better, and his breathing stronger. He was going to *live*!

She touched his damp forehead. His temperature was normal now, and his muscles had lost their frightening rigidity.

Dazed still, Chessy watched the steady rise and fall of Morland's chest. Even then, she could not control an urge to touch his face, to smooth back his hair, to run a trembling hand to smooth his blankets.

When Whitby pushed open the door a moment later, he found her that way, with Tony's hand cradled in hers and hot tears coursing down her cheeks.

"Dear God, miss, he isn't—"

She turned a blinding smile on the old butler. "He's safe, Whitby! God willing, he's g-going to be fine." She swayed to her feet and then threw her arms around the old servant, giving him a fierce hug.

After a moment of shock, the butler returned the hug, stifling a sniff of his own.

Chessy released him and scrubbed at her eyes, half laughing, half crying. "He'll be angry as a bear in spring when he wakes, I fear. The *ma-huang* I gave him will leave him with the very devil of a temper."

Whitby smiled faintly. "In that case I'd better go prepare the others, I expect." He studied her for a moment, his eyes measuring. "He owes you a great deal, Miss Cameron. He won't like that. Sometimes I think he's afraid of owing anybody anything."

Chessy stared down at the gaunt face against the pillow. "Why—?"

But she would have no answer. Behind her the door closed quietly.

Carefully Chessy bent down and brushed back a bronze strand waving over Morland's brow. His face was relaxed now in a natural sleep. "Wretch," she whispered. "Impossible, arrogant rake. You're going to live, do you hear me? To *live*, Tony Morland."

It was a dream, the same dream as all the others.

It was a girl, the same one he always saw. Sable-haired with eyes like purple damask.

She burst from the silver waters of the cove and caught him like the magnificent sea-creature she favored, spilling her laughter around them like circles of bright sunlight.

Morland shut his mind to the exquisite power of that vision, to the heat that swept through his body at the touch of her hot, slick thighs.

Dear God, how he wanted her! Even when it had been forbidden, he had wanted her, naked and urgent like this. . . .

Only leaving had kept him from having her.

So he'd done the sole thing he could. He'd snuck off in the night like the miserable dog she said he was, without a handshake or a word of farewell.

Yes, he'd been a fine gentleman, to be sure. He'd saved her body that night, managed to keep her pristine and pure for the husband who would one day be hers.

But in the process, it seemed, he'd broken her innocent young heart.

Morland flung his hand up to sweep away the gnawing memories. It grazed softness, female softness. He stiffened, searching for the source of that velvet warmth.

And then he felt skin. Sleek skin. Skin that trembled, then peaked beneath his touch.

His breath caught. He opened his eyes. A lantern flickered upon the side table.

And there was Chessy, black silk jacket discarded in favor of his flowing white linen shirt.

Sweet God, white linen.

White shoulders.

Whiter thighs . . .

No dream. White, so white. So damned soft. He had

only to move, to slide them apart and shove full into
their forbidden heat—

He couldn't. She was the daughter of his best friend.
She was innocent, fresh, with her whole life in front of
her, while he had been in too many beds with too many
women he hadn't even liked. No, by God, she deserved
far better than a cripple like him, a hardened rake like
him. And he was going to see that she got it. But first
he had to learn to forget her fire, ignore her beauty.

He wrenched his hungry eyes away.

And found worse torture. The top three buttons of
her shirt were opened. Her hair spilled like dancing
shadows over the white linen, the white bedclothes, the
white, soft shoulders and creamy thighs.

Heat again. Gnawing, relentless.

He blinked and tried to sit up, dizzy with pain. And
his arm—

Frowning, Morland looked down at the gauze strip
wrapped around his forearm. Six silver needles dotted
his shoulder and naked thighs.

What in the devil?

Realization hit. Piece by piece, the jagged memories
fell together. An intruder—the slash of a blade. *Poison?*

How else to explain the bleeding away of sense and
sensation, the numbness that had squeezed through his
body and made him claw for every breath?

Morland looked down in stunned understanding.
She had caught him, pulled him back from that ghastly
creeping paralysis and certain death.

Morland touched his chest. A bead of moisture glistened in the bronze hair. Not sweat. No, in that nightmare place he had known only icy cold. It was tears—
her tears, small and silver. They had fallen like soft,
forgiving rain, while he tottered on the very edge of
death.

Sweet, spring tears, releasing the clutch of winter,
of death.

His jaw locked. Maybe she still felt something for
him after all. Maybe even after long years of separation,
after the cruel way he had left her . . .

In that instant Tony Morland glimpsed exactly what

he had been missing for the last ten years, exactly what he had been chasing through the mountain passes of Spain and in all those shadowed, scented bedrooms that followed.

Through all the lonely, driven years after he'd left Macao . . .

Just *this*. This tangle of dark hair on his pillow. These soft hands upon his face.

He thought of a spring day long before when a girl trembling on the edge of womanhood had fed him fish with her fingers and danced barefoot beside the silver waves of the South China Sea. Her laughter had rung out and caught him.

They'd pledged their vows of loyalty then, with blood pricked and mingled. With solemn oaths.

"I'll be your friend, your forever friend," he'd said. "I'll be your heart and your bravest warrior, against all foes. Until . . ." He'd frowned then, his imagination giving out.

Chessy had smiled up at him, a blinding smile of endless admiration and total trust. "Until—until north of night," she'd said solemnly, pressing their bleeding fingers together. "Until south of the sun. Until somewhere . . . east of—of forever."

East of forever.

God, how could he have forgotten those days and how much she had trusted him, adored him?

Yes, he'd see her laugh that way again. He swore it, even now, while he shook with dizziness and his vision ran in a dark blur.

It did not matter what it took or how many tears her laughter cost him. He would do all those things.

He searched for the warm curve of her and found it. His fingers worked that softness, not content until they had savored and measured all of it. Until the softness budded, sweet with sleepy arousal.

Yes, tears or laughter, there would still be this.

That was Morland's last thought as he sank back against her. And he was touching her still when the drowsiness won out and his eyelids finally closed.

Seated before a crackling fire in a charming little bedroom overlooking Bedford Square, the Duchess of Cranford studied the pearl- and amethyst-studded bracelet that had recently come into her possession.

It was amazing, she thought. Its design was exactly a match for a ring she had had in her safekeeping for some years now.

It *also* matched the necklace Chessy Cameron had worn to the ball.

The duchess frowned, twisting the bracelet so that firelight shot off its gold and jeweled surfaces. This might be the key to many things, she knew, to secrets she had been unable to unravel no matter how hard her efforts. She would have to make her plans carefully this time.

As she frowned over the magnificent piece of jewelry, a knock came at the door. "I have your hot milk, Your Grace. If you are ready."

Quickly the duchess shoved the bracelet back into its leather case, which then went under her pillow. "Yes, Lizzie, I'm quite ready." She smiled as her companion entered carrying a silver tray with the duchess's habitual late-night glass of milk. "You are far too good to me, you know."

"Nonsense," her dark-haired companion said. "Quite the opposite, and well you know it."

"Indeed? Sometimes I forget who's giving the orders here," the duchess mumbled as she took the warm drink.

To her dismay, she saw that her hands were not quite steady.

Yes, she would have to be *very* careful. It would be deadly if the gossip escaped too early, carried by one of the servants.

23

"Almost done," Chessy whispered to herself. Her needles glittered in the candlelight. Her fingers ached as she pulled the last piece of metal free and cleaned it, then slid it carefully back into its velvet case.

She reached up, massaging her neck, then sank onto the day bed that Whitby had set up beside Morland's.

She blew out all but one candle, then eased onto her back and studied the intricate plaster designs on the ceiling. It would be three hours until the needles needed to be reapplied. Four hours until the bandages had to be changed.

And twelve until she could be certain he was out of danger.

Chessy closed her eyes. Sighing, she went over her calculations about meridian lines and needle sizes one more time.

"Won't have any damned laudanum." Morland's voice was thick, slurred from sleep. "Won't bloody take it, I tell you!"

"Of course you won't have any laudanum," Chessy

215

said soothingly. "There's not a trace of laudanum in this."

It was a lie, of course, but he needed to rest.

Morland glared at her. "No? Then, b'God, *you* have the bloody stuff."

He'd woken just as surly as Chessy had predicted. For the last ten minutes he had been twisting restlessly, refusing the herbal drink she'd offered.

"Tongue's . . . on fire. Skin feels like . . . ahhh . . . it's going to leap up and do a bloody dance. What the devil d'you give me?"

"Something that saved your life, you ungrateful barbarian. And you'll drink this too!" Seeing that he was still unconvinced, Chessy gave an angry sigh and downed half of the drink herself, then held the rest out to Morland.

He studied it warily. "You . . . promise? No laudanum?"

Despite the nudging of her conscience, Chessy nodded firmly.

Morland took the glass and drained it.

"You see? That wasn't so bad."

The Englishman merely scowled. "Take me for a bloody fool? Think I don't know laudanum when I taste it?" But his voice was growing more slurred. "Bloody little . . . liar." His eyes closed. "Beautiful, treashr'ous liar." He reached out and slid his fingers deep into her hair. "Kiss me, liar. Now while I'm too damned weak to do anything about it . . ."

Chessy laughed at the sheer outrageousness of the order. It was the sulkiness, the low, slurred timbre of his voice and the pain it concealed that finally made her comply.

She brushed his collarbone with her lips.

When he sighed and moved his fingers idly in her hair, she bent closer, tracing his jaw and tasting her way lightly up to his mouth.

By the time she got there she was hot—and shivering with cold. She was restless and more than a little drugged herself.

Drugged with the taste of him. With the urge to taste him all over his hard, bronze body.

"Why di'n't you . . . answer?" It was a slurred whisper.

"Answer?"

"My letters. Wrote you. Why . . . no answers?"

Chessy paled. "We'll . . . discuss it tomorrow."

"Now," he said sulkily.

"You have to rest. That . . . well, that can wait."

"T'morrow? Promise?"

"Yes. Now go to sleep."

"T'morrow," Morland repeated. His hand slid beneath her jacket. Sighing, he explored her warmth until he found her satiny breast. He cupped it, flicking the already hardening nub between his thumb and forefinger. "Cert'n?"

"A-absolutely." The word came out high and squeaky. She swallowed. "Now just—just go to s-sleep, my lord."

Morland's long fingers tightened. Protectively. Hungrily. "Sleepy . . ."

Chessy heard his breath slow, felt his body relax. Carefully she reached out and slid his hand from her breast. She couldn't leave it there, of course. That would be out of the question. It was utterly wrong.

It was blissfully right.

It made her uncomfortable.

It made her sigh with pleasure.

Besides, she didn't want him to touch her.

She wanted him to do nothing else.

Chessy scowled, wishing she hadn't drunk quite so much of that drug-laced tea to make her point to Morland. With a sigh she curled up on the day bed. Dimly she realized her vision was blurring.

She closed her eyes and dreamed then, vivid dreams of silver seas, of fish that jumped into her open hands. Of treasure ships and pine-dark isles. Of blood oaths and shared vows.

Of all the beautiful things that might have been.

Sunlight framed the curtained window when Chessy opened her eyes next. Disoriented, she clutched at the crisp, lavender-scented bed linens.

Tony . . .

She knelt beside him and listened. His breathing was low and rhythmic. She touched his forehead, sighing with relief when she was certain that the fevers were gone.

Without warning his eye cracked open. "C'm'ere." He patted the bed. "With me. Bloody day bed can't be comf'able."

It wasn't. Chessy's back was aching with the strain of holding the needles and rotating them for long intervals.

In spite of that she shook her head and tried to pull free when he caught her wrist.

"Sit . . . here."

Seeing that he was growing agitated, Chessy finally complied.

"Is it t'morrow yet?"

"No," Chessy lied.

"Then I'll wait for my answers, Cricket. But until then . . ." His hands tightened, tugging her closer until she sprawled across his warm, naked chest.

At the movement her black silk jacket gaped open. One creamy breast spilled free, the nipple already rosy and furled.

Chessy gasped and moved to tug the garment closed.

But Morland caught her wrist and held her still. His eyes smoldered darkly as he stared at the lush ivory curve. "No—don't," he said hoarsely. "Let me . . . look at you." His voice was growing ragged. "Only look . . . while you kiss me."

His fingers trembled against the pulse that danced at her wrist. A haze of sweat dotted his brow. Chessy realized she'd have to comply, just until he settled back into sleep. She couldn't risk a relapse.

"Insufferable man," she said softly, feeling her cheeks burn as his eyes roamed over her, shot with fever and a dark male hunger. Already he was recovering. And it was far too fast for her safety.

Her skin grew flushed, tingling beneath his heated scrutiny.

"Kiss me, Chessy."

"No," she said weakly.

"Otherwise, I'll get up. Got . . . work to do after all . . ."

"You can't! You nearly died!" Seeing the feverish determination in his eyes, she sighed.

"Oh, very well, you insufferable man." Closing her eyes, she bent forward to give him the kiss he'd demanded.

Her lips skimmed his brow.

"Call that . . . bloody kiss?"

Muttering darkly, Chessy planted another kiss just at the edge of his mouth.

But he twisted and pulled her down until her hair spilled over them like a shining black cascade. Like a soft satin canopy that blocked out the rest of the world.

Morland sighed, opening his lips to taste her. Letting her taste him in turn.

He tasted good. He *felt* even better, all sleek, effortless power and fluid friction.

And then his hard fingers closed over the aching point of her breast.

Chessy shuddered and tried to pull free. "S-stop that, you—you reprobate! I never said—"

He shuddered.

Frowning, she stared down, realizing that his grip had loosened. In fact there was no resistance at all in his fingers now.

And no wonder. The wretched man was sound asleep!

Chessy had just finished her next needling when she heard Whitby's low cough at the door. "Begging your pardon, miss, but I've brought you some dinner."

She hadn't even thought about eating. But at his words, her stomach gave a lurch.

A moment later Whitby entered with a tray emitting a mouth-watering array of aromas. "Mrs. Harris insisted you eat. She's made you pigeon pie and asparagus in lime sauce." The butler put down the tray and turned to stare worriedly at the earl. "Lord! He's so pale."

"He'll be fine, Whitby. If only I can keep him still so that he rests."

The old servant shook his head. "He was never one for coddling. Even when he was a child he wouldn't—" The butler broke off and turned to straighten Chessy's dinner tray. "Well, miss, if that will be all—"

Chessy frowned at Whitby. "Even as a child he wouldn't do what?"

Whitby sighed. "Many is the time I saw him dig in his heels for a fight. And all too often it was over some bit of mischief that hellion twin of his had devised. Not that young Tony would ever pass the blame. Oh, yes, his brother Andrew was always very good at seeing that someone else took the blame for his deviltry."

"Twin?"

"He died last year." Whitby shook his head again. "Bad bloody business—if you'll excuse my saying so, miss. And there was his lordship, barely recovered from . . ."

"From?" Chessy prompted.

"From the wound he took over in Spain." Whitby's face turned hard. "You wouldn't have recognized him, miss. He'd lost half his weight, it seemed. And pale, so pale."

Chessy went white.

"I beg your pardon, miss. I would never have spoken of it, except . . . well, it was just seeing him there like that, you know. It brought back all the memories. He was months getting well, you see. Not that he ever *did* get well. No, I'm of the belief that his leg never set right. And the sawbones who tended to him—" Whitby snorted. "Ah, well, I suppose they did what they could. It was a battlefield, after all."

Chessy's fingers dug into the velvet hangings along the bedpost. "The pain—I never knew."

"No one knew. He never spoke of it. Even now, he refuses anything that hints at coddling. Bloody stubborn he is." Whitby's voice fell. "Lord bless him."

He turned them, his face returning to its usual impassive lines. "You will be staying, won't you?"

Chessy couldn't mistake the hopeful note in his voice.

She told herself she had to go, that Whitby could take care of Tony now. She told herself that she didn't want to be here, that it wasn't *safe* for her to be here.

But somehow that didn't change her answer. She gave a long sigh and nodded. "Yes, I expect I shall, Whitby. I'll need more boiled water. And some tea, too, if you could manage it. I'm—I'm afraid it's going to be a long night."

24

As Chessy had feared, the Earl of Morland slept neither long nor well. Barely an hour later, he began to mutter and twist restlessly in his sleep.

"Damn it, not there, Wilkins! Too close—can't you see them?"

Chessy started at the hoarse cry. "Tony?"

He didn't seem to hear her. His legs twisted, caught in the sheets. "Must—stop 'em. Third battalion's too damned close."

Suddenly Chessy felt him stiffen. He groaned and threw his arm to one side, catching her across the waist.

The dreams. Dear heaven, she'd forgotten all about his nightmares.

The hands at her waist tightened. His breathing quickened and turned harsh.

Chessy shoved at his chest, trying to push him back down, but he fought her, cursing, his hands like iron. Breathless, she fell back, trapped by his fever-driven fingers.

In the struggle her jacket billowed open. Taut tendon met supple, curving breast.

Morland froze. "Chessy?" His voice was low, slurred. She wondered if he was even aware that he spoke.

"I'm here." She stroked the hair from his face. "Trying to sleep. But you make a wretched sort of patient, I'm afraid.

He caught her hips. His hard fingers moved in search of warmth and softness.

He found both.

Chessy gasped.

Not that it meant anything, she told herself. The man was half asleep, after all. It was only a muscular response, an animal urge to seek solace and warmth in a time of stress.

But none of those explanations made Chessy feel those strong fingers any less. None of them made her breath come easier or held the spiraling heat from her stomach—or lower, where it pooled in maddening waves.

Her pulse began to pound. She had to go! She couldn't let him—

Why not? Why not this once? Sweet heaven, just once before she left!

It was wrong, she knew. He wasn't even conscious of what he was doing. To let it go on would be totally shameless.

But no matter how reason protested, her body told her it was right—right to feel this way, right to want this from him before their paths split again forever.

Yes, just once.

His thumb rose and found her nipple. He gave a dark rasp.

"Chessy." It was a ragged sound—a statement of recognition, of delayed discovery. Of raw desire. "Am I dreaming or—is that really . . . you?"

"Not unless we're both dreaming. Both mad—which maybe we are."

"You saved my bloody carcass. Can't think—ahh—why." His head fell, nestled in the hollow of her shoulder.

Pain-pleasure flared to instant life beneath his lips.

Chessy made a choked sound. No more! She couldn't bear it!

She tried to shove away, but he caught the folds of her jacket and held her still. "Sorry—such a damned fool."

Instinct made her flippant. "Which time? There have been so many times you've been a damned fool, after all."

And then flippancy fled. His head turned, seeking more of her heat and softness. Chessy's mind closed to conscience and logic. Down she sank, aware only of the utter rightness of the sensations driving through her.

He ran his stubbled cheek against her breast. The rough stroke of friction made her shiver, made her toes curl. And then came the question she'd been fearing.

"It's—t'morrow. Tell me . . . about the letters."

She didn't move. She didn't want to remember that, not now. All she wanted was to drift along the dark currents and feel him safe and warm beside her. "Later," she whispered.

"Now."

In desperation she slid her fingers through the amber hair matting his chest. "Later," she murmured as she tugged lightly.

He groaned. "L-later . . ."

He began to whisper, openmouthed against her sensitized skin. Hot words, broken words, dark words, they poured over her like whiskey and silk.

Her jacket gaped wider. The unbound velvet of her breast spilled into his fingers. Chessy bit back a moan as he palmed the lush curve and then eased his mouth around its dusky, raised center.

"No, Tony—"

But she barely heard herself. Somehow her hands slid up to knead his neck. "Please—oh, please don't—" Her breath hissed free. "I have to go—I can't—"

He paid no attention. His nail scored the other hot, thrusting peak he'd uncovered. She bit back a sob of pleasure when he rolled the budded crest between his fingers.

Each new touch left her burning, hungry for much

more. She had to end it now, while she still could! "Stop, Tony. You c-can't. You're not—well!"

"Not well . . . damned true enough. Dying—for you. Kiss me, Chessy." His voice was thick. "Kiss me all over, until I burn up. Until we both burn up." He tongued a hot, slick path across her breast. "Love me, Chessy. Dear God, how I need to feel you wrapped all around me in love."

Chessy closed her eyes against a hot press of tears. *Love him? How could she help it?*

She'd loved this man for ten years, ever since the day he had strode onto her father's boat and demanded to see the little wretch who had been stealing all his fish.

That wretch had been her, of course. And once she'd thrown off her battered hat, Morland had realized she was a female.

He'd threatened to take her over his knee and flay her hide. Instead he had tossed her overboard, then jumped in to join her.

There the golden days had begun. The laughter had started.

And it had all ended the day he had left, without even a farewell.

Oh, yes, I do love you, Tony Morland. Far more than I should. Far more than you'll ever know. And that's the only reason on earth that this is happening between us.

"Chessy." He closed his eyes and made a ragged sound, somewhere between a laugh and curse. "No laudanum in those witch's brews of yours? Like hell there wasn't!" He shuddered as he felt the curve of her against his cheek. Slowly he flicked his tongue across her breast. "God, you taste—so bloody good."

Chessy whimpered. How would *he* taste? How would he feel if she touched him where his hair clung dense and bronze across his chest and along his taut waist? At his lean, muscular thighs?

Dear God, was she losing her *mind*?

She tried to pull free, but Morland's fingers flattened, driving her down against the bed. He twisted and found the first pouting bud to plunder.

At the scrape of stubbled cheek and searching

tongue, Chessy drove her heels into the quilt to keep from crying out with pleasure.

"Sweet . . . like tight little berries . . ." He tasted his way around the crested flesh, slow and reverent, missing nothing.

Blindly Chessy shoved at his hand, trying to marshal what was left of her reason. But reason fled when he shoved one muscled thigh atop her legs and stretched his big body over hers.

Dear God, like this he dwarfed her. Like this, he made her feel tiny and fragile, a soft, beautiful thing caught beneath his hardness. And there, at the curve of her belly where he rose hot and hard in arousal, he made her feel aching and empty.

Almost without knowing it, Chessy shivered and pressed up against that daunting length of blade-hard muscle.

He groaned and adjusted himself to her. Hardness coaxed softness. Softness answered with a heated challenge of its own.

"Sweet—little thief. Beautiful enchantress. Tonight—I must finally have you."

The oath was velvet against her, a promise of fire and life. Her head fell back. Her hands dug into his muscled shoulders.

Without thinking she drew him closer. In the darkness around them every ragged breath, every rustle of fabric became intimate and endlessly erotic.

His knee inched between her legs. Chessy shuddered and opened to him, to the blind pleasure he offered.

Without regret or reservation.

Just like in her dreams, in all those hot, forbidden fantasies she had lived on for the last ten years . . .

Murmuring thickly, Tony caught her breast and grazed it with his teeth. Chessy arched blindly, flung headlong into a pleasure as hot and dark as a South China night. In some part of her mind she trembled, afraid of the unthinkable power of what she was feeling. But her body, lithe and taut and well honed from years of discipline, had ideas of its own. It moved to its own rhythms now, drunk with a dark power that urged her to take every pleasure this man had to give her.

He groaned and kneed her legs apart wider, then pressed into her. Only his breeches separated them now, along with her jacket. Wildly Chessy shoved at the wadded folds of silk, sighing when they slid free. She wished that his breeches were gone and he would sink down upon her with nothing but heat and naked skin.

"Chessy, I can't—stop. Not this time." He gripped her thigh. Open-handed, he moved slowly upward until he could climb no more. Until he met heat and a tangle of black curls.

He groaned when he found what he'd been searching for. The softest part of her, where her heat drove him wild.

Dream-driven, love-blind, Chessy arched against him.

How long she'd wanted, waited, dreamed . . .

He caught her hips and held her, open to his fevered gaze.

"I'm going to please you now, enchantress. Right now—and then again."

Low, choked sounds filled the night. Chessy gasped at his lazy foray of teeth and tongue at the aching heart of her sensation. One minute he was slow, the next he was urgent. One minute he was gentle, the next he was blindingly thorough.

His strong fingers tightened, curving over her hips to hold her steady beneath his sensual invasion.

Dimly, so dimly Chessy heard ragged sounds of passion echo around her. His? Hers?

Or were they one now, one reckless being forged of fire, blind with hungers too long denied?

Pleasure broke over her in a quicksilver rush. Her closed eyes watched color kindle, rising like imperial firewords above the Forbidden City.

And the sounds. She heard his hot, whispered vows. Love sounds, dark sounds, they reached out and trapped her.

Chessy shuddered, wanting all those words, wanting

everything that Tony had to give. Wanting *him*, reckless with desire, groaning as he buried himself deep and hard inside her.

But he didn't give it.

"Tony—I don't—"

His breath was an exquisite torment on her love-sleek skin. "Too late. Too—damned sweet. Can't—stop."

His tongue slid over her, velvet on endless velvet. With each movement he gave her blinding pleasure. He gave her all the dark, tortured fantasies she'd had to live upon for the last ten years.

They were the very same fantasies he had lived on.

He gripped her pale thighs and covered her, missing nothing with his tongue. He gave her light dancing over her trembling skin; he gave her color, spun up in bright, soaring tendrils.

He gave her pleasure. Vast, blinding pleasure that caught her close and wrenched her inside out. Chessy dug her feet into the damask quilt, arching with the dark violence of her pleasure.

There she hung—mindless, shivering, utterly stripped in body and soul before the blond lord she'd always loved.

And then the world exploded into color and texture. Into driving sensation. Until every pore held the smell and taste and touch of him. Until her blood screamed for dark, sweet things she couldn't even begin to name.

"Tony! Oh, God, I didn't know—"

"Yes, my beauty. Feel all I have to give you. Take it from me now—" He shuddered as his beard-rough cheek grazed her inner thigh. "Chessy. Sweet Chessy— how much I've always loved you . . . always wanted to give you . . . *this*."

Roughness and heat. Softest yin and piercing yang.

Chessy shivered as ageless man met endless woman. She cried out at the textures of her body as it grew, changed, shaped itself to his.

In love. Endless love.

And suddenly she was there, in that place where their hearts had been and always would be one, in that place where love once given never fades or ebbs. Where time knows no beginning or end.

There she sailed, in senses blindingly real, not by dream or fantasy this time but by the touch of his loving hands and lips.

And Tony followed her. Giving without greed. Sailing the same quicksilver sea, where dreams took wing and hopes turned real. Somewhere beyond living and just this side of dying.

Somewhere . . . infinitely beautiful.

Somewhere north of night, it was. Somewhere west of morning and south of the sun.

Somewhere—*east of forever.*

25

When she could move, when her blood stopped singing and her brain crept back to sluggish life, Chessy raised her lids and stared at the man who had just loved her to the very edge of delirium.

A wave of color swept her cheeks.

The earl laughed, low and husky. His eyes glittered. "You look like a cat. A sated, spoiled, and very clever little cat."

"No—don't. How could I—it's wrong, terribly wrong."

"You didn't dream of that, back on board that ship in the hot tropical night? You didn't think about me doing all those sweet, wet, forbidden things to you?"

Chessy swallowed. The color in her cheeks flared higher.

An answer in itself.

Morland smiled darkly, though desire rode him still. "Tell me you did."

Chessy nodded, unable to forget all those heated dreams.

He caught a shining strand of blue-black hair and carried it to his lips. "There'll be no right and wrong in this big white bed of mine, my beautiful little thief. Not tonight. Tonight there's only what is and what can be. Only what we want or don't want. What we *need* or don't *need*."

His eyes blazed over her sleek body as desire racked him, raw and unassuaged. "And what I want now— what I *need* now—is you. All the ways I've ever dreamed of having you. For you were always the beginning and end of every fantasy I ever had. Even then."

He clenched his jaw, fighting back the driving urge to take her fast and endless beneath him. Instead he focused on the pain. Only that would keep him sane now, immune to the dazed desire in her glorious violet eyes.

"Do you know how many times I've dreamed of loving you, of having you beneath me like this? Time and again I thought of how you would feel against me, how you would moan when I touched you. I used to walk outside your cabin on that junk, did you know that? Night after night I stood outside your door, listening to you breathe, hearing those hot whispered sounds of rustling bedclothes. And while I stood there, I imagined it was me making those sounds, me touching you and making you moan while I spread you beneath me."

He smiled bitterly, watching surprise flash through Chessy's desire-glazed eyes. "You didn't know that, did you?" He gave a bitter laugh. "I was careful to conceal my hunger, you see. Damnably careful. But now there's no need to conceal or deny what we both want. So make those sounds for me now, Chessy. Those dark, rustling sounds. And this time let's find out if it's all we imagined it would be."

Slowly, bone by bone, he moved up her body. "I can feel you, Chessy. Hot and trembling. You are hot, aren't you? And this does make you tremble, doesn't it, my sweet?"

Chessy arched as he slid his breeches away and brought his straining skin against her. "God, I'll never forget the sight of your breasts that night. It was dark and quiet. You had just come up from the water." He heard her gasp and laughed. "You never knew I was there, did you? The heat and silence affected me, too, and I'd gone on deck planning to do the very same thing. But you were already in the water when I got there. And then all I could do was slip back into the shadows, watching you cut through the moon-silvered waves. God, you were so beautiful."

He thumbed her dusky areola, feeling it swell. "You looked like a mermaid that night, your white thighs gleaming in the moonlight, your hair a curve of shadow against your naked skin. And your breasts, oh God, your breasts—" He froze for a moment, his hands tense. "So full. Gleaming and silver where the water clung just here, then slowly ran free."

He acted out the words with his finger. Slowly. Exquisitely. Until she twisted with pleasure, remembering too.

"Your nipples were hard. Tight and dark, swollen from the cool water. God, how I wanted to touch them. To take you in my mouth and suck every drop of water away. I came damned close to taking you that night, Chessy, whether you wished it or not—whether it was *right* or not. With my best friend, your father, sleeping only a few feet away."

His voice dropped, bitter with self-mockery. His fingers curved over her hips. He let her feel his heat and the unleashed force of his arousal.

Chessy gave a low, choked moan. "Please—oh, God, Tony—I want—"

He laughed darkly. "Want what?" He was moving now, easing apart her sleek petals.

"Y-you. Oh—*this.*"

Morland grimaced as her nails scored his back. His arm was throbbing, and his knee felt like hell itself.

But he didn't think of that. He thought only of her.

His head fell. His hard mouth molded the dusky bud already distended with need. He gave her drenching heat. He gave her fire. Tugging on and on, without release.

Chessy whimpered and twisted beneath him, wanting him inside her. Wanting him as reckless and love-drunk as *she* was.

But he refused to be hurried. With leisurely thoroughness he tongued his way to her budded twin and offered it the same excruciating pleasure.

"Tony—*now*—"

"You're sure, Chessy? Ah, God, I—"

"Yes. Oh, yes, I've never been so sure." In the candlelight her skin glistened golden, tinged with a hectic flush of arousal.

"Ah, God, Cricket. You're all gold and silk. You're the most beautiful woman I've ever seen. And I don't think I can wait much—"

"Don't—please. *Don't* wait!"

"Lord, Chessy, how long I've dreamed . . ." His voice was harsh, strained. "About you like this. All pink and ivory, warm with honey and thinking of nothing but me."

His fingers slid into clinging silk. Into forbidden heat. Into infinite pleasure.

Chessy gasped. "No, not again, I—oh, God!"

"You see, I always have loved you, Cricket. I always have wanted you this way—even when it was a mortal sin to do so. Even when I disgraced my best friend to lust after his daughter in such a way. But now—now you're a woman, and I mean to have you. To drink your moans against my lips. To watch you shudder and catch fire when you I take you straight up into starlight."

To Chessy it seemed that she was a creature of sea and night, caught in webs of silver, anchored by tides of desire. And with will and reason shattered, she could not find the strength to swim free.

Morland's eyes never wavered as he palmed her, edging deeper. "A thousand forbidden dreams—a thousand nights of torment. But maybe they were worth it for me to feel what I'm feeling now. To touch you like this."

And then deep, so deep. Heat on heat and never enough.

Body on fire, Chessy twisted, seeking all he had to give and all that she could give in return. Tiny, choked sounds hung in the air as passion exploded through her anew.

She cried out, lost to anything but him and this blinding new world of sensation. His strong fingers moved like velvet, parting fold upon liquid fold until he found the throbbing pearl where sensation flooded.

Chessy cried out at his touch. Her eyes flew open as passion crested through her.

Tony had to close his eyes then, denying himself the sight of her wild beauty. He shifted, trying to ease the ache where his manhood rose in jutting, painful arousal.

Closing his eyes didn't help, of course. He still saw her. He still *felt* her. God, he could feel every hot, wet tremor deep inside her.

And then he could wait no longer.

He pushed her thigh high. His eyes darkened as he studied the shadowed delta of her curls. His breath came hoarse and heavy as he pushed down into that hot, wet haven.

She arched beneath him, her foot driving against his rigid buttocks as she fought for a deeper release.

But Morland had waited too long to end it yet. On and on he teased her, holding her on the edge, letting her hunger build. But the struggle cost him more and more. Her breathy little whimpers were driving him mad, making him shudder with an urge to pound deep and pour his hot seed inside her.

Just a little more. God, she was tight, so tight. And she was nearly there . . .

Her nails curved and sank into his hips. *"Tony!* You must—I can't—"

Morland shuddered. Sweat dotted his brow.

Now. Oh, yes, now . . .

Deep, he fell, then deeper still. In a long slide of purest velvet he drove through the wet, swollen petals of her sex.

Ah, God, she was tight. She was hot and wet and—

And then the barrier. The threshold that she still had to cross to leave behind her maidenhood.

His jaw locked. So there had been no others. He was truly her first.

Morland stiffened, feeling guilt cut coldly through

him. She ought to have more. She ought to have someone much better, much younger and less cynical than
he to—

"T-Tony?"

He groaned. Guilt and regret fell away forgotten as
he felt her tighten around him. "It's—it's going to hurt,
Chessy. Just a little. Just—at first."

She twisted. He wondered if she even heard him.
Her fingers were clinging, urgent.

"But not for long, I swear it." Carefully he moved,
feeling the barrier beneath him. He eased deeper, giving her time to grow accustomed to his size. "As little
as I possibly can."

And then he rose up and plunged swiftly, driving
through the thin membrane in one smooth thrust. Despite his care he felt her go rigid beneath him, her nails
driven hard against his back.

Morland froze, cursing the dark tides of pleasure
that screamed for him to move, to shove, to take and
take and take until he drowned. God, she was tight. He
thought he'd die of the hot, sleek way she gripped him.

But Morland didn't move. He didn't do any of the
things his blood screamed for him to do. One thing he
did know: What he needed right now was not to *take*
but to *share*.

Finally the tumult passed.

He heard Chessy draw a shaky breath. Her voice
was low, unsteady, but full of forced optimism. "So . . .
that was it. It was not . . . not precisely what I thought
it would be. Still—that is . . . perhaps I'm not—"

Tony laughed hoarsely and cut her off with a swift,
hard kiss upon her trembling lips. "Oh, God, Chessy.
You sweet, idiotic fool, how much you delight me! And
you very much *are*, as you're going to see right now!"

As he smiled down at her he began to move once
more—slowly, easily this time, now that the barrier
was gone. Now all that was left was heat and shimmering friction. Restless, lapping desire.

"Oh!" She squirmed, suddenly breathless. "But I
thought—"

"No, it's not over, my foolish one. Not *nearly* over.

Did you think I would leave you like that, my wonderful, innocent, stubborn beauty?"

With a moan she arched upward. This time Morland sank down to meet her. He had to move carefully, for she was small and so utterly tight that he wanted to scream with the pleasure of it.

And the way she clutched him, dear God, deep inside her, where he rode her deep.

"Tony! You're so—it's too—"

He shuddered to hear the husky catch of pleasure in her voice. He concentrated on the rich contralto of it, holding his own need at bay even now, close, so close to what he'd always wanted.

Every hot glide of friction left him shuddering. Every husky gasp from her throat left him aflame.

And then he felt her tremors begin, there where she sheathed him so tightly. Her heels dug into the sheets, and her back arched.

"I'll be your heart," he whispered as the passion took her high and free and soaring. "I'll be your friend, Chessy. Your forever friend."

He locked his jaw and fought his own desire, watching the beauty of her passion, feeling it break over him like a long-forgotten promise. "I'll be—ahhh—right hand. L-left eye. Your heart. Your—bravest warrior. Against . . . all foes."

Even against myself. Because I'll be the man who loved you first and best, my sweet Chessy. And you'll never even know it.

Only then did he begin to move again, while her woman's flesh still clung sweet and liquid. While her eyes still shimmered, blind with passion.

Shock, joy, awe flashed over her face. "T-Tony?"

"Here, beauty. No dreams, this time. No—ahhh—fantasy. Just me. Just you. Just *this*."

She wrapped her legs around him. Her head slid back and her hair spilled against the lavender-sweet sheets in a wild, smoky tangle. "I choose . . . oh, I choose—"

As she spoke, she tensed. The passion rode him now,

vast and blind and rocking, so he almost didn't hear her.

Then perception came—not with his ears, but with his heart.

"I choose—*you*." She sheathed him in sweetness, her body rigid in its crest. "Oh, God—*this*. With you. For—always."

And always was where he fell, captive in her sweetness, warrior to her sultry Eve.

Hero in her adoring eyes.

It was the worst thing he'd ever done. The Englishman knew that already.

But at that moment, with Chessy's soft cries ringing in his ears, with her legs locked around him and release slamming through him like a giant velvet fist, the Earl of Morland found that he didn't even care.

He was dressed when she awoke, standing before the window and staring out at the night.

"Tony? Are you—"

"I'm fine." He turned and gave her a crooked smile. "Well, perhaps not quite *fine*, but at least I'm no longer feeling as if I've just died—or I'm just about to."

"Why are you dressed?"

He sighed. "A runner came around from the Foreign Office. Whitby came up to tell me. I tried not to disturb you."

"You didn't." Chessy yawned and stretched. "I had absolutely no idea, I confess. I must have been beyond hearing."

"You've had a busy two nights."

"Yes, I quite have, haven't I?" Her voice was low, husky.

It made the fine hairs on Morland's neck prickle. It made every muscle in his body tighten. But he tried valiantly to ignore it. "Did I say thank you? I hope so."

"You did, my lord. Only fifty times already."

But he did not smile, not even at her teasing. Chessy saw the grimness in his eyes, and it frightened her. "What is this all about?"

"That's the question, isn't it? It's about pride, I suppose. And honor. Long ago I made you a vow, Chessy. I said I'd be your warrior, your heart. Against all foes. But this—this thing between us just won't seem to go away. Though I'm too jaded, too battered to be any good for you. And right now you should be running from me as hard and fast as you can."

"Would that help?"

"I don't know. I'm not sure I could give you up now even if you wanted me to."

Chessy sat up slowly. Lithe muscle rippled at calf and shoulder with a sleek beauty that made Morland's groin twist with sudden pain.

"I'm glad to hear that, Yang-Kuei." She moved closer and ran her fingers over his cheek, stiff with a faint edge of stubble. "My father always said destiny is made in men's hearts, not in the stars. If so, then I would have *you* be my destiny."

Morland scowled. "Unfortunately, your father is often a fool."

Chessy smiled, lightly tracing his hard, stubborn mouth. "No, he's a genius. It is *you* who are the fool, Tony Morland, in spite of all your experience." Her gaze fell, riveted to his full lips. "My foolish friend. My forever friend." Her voice turned deep and husky. "My dearest love."

She slid open the first button on his shirt. She felt him shudder.

"Don't, Chessy. Don't make it any easier for me. Not while I'm trying to tell myself all the reasons this is wrong. The way your father would tear out my heart if he knew what I've been doing to you in this bed of mine tonight."

Chessy's lashes dropped, black silk over shining amethyst. Her voice turned hushed, wistful. "Are you sorry?"

"Good God, no."

"Then . . . you do want me? Just a little?"

"A little? Sweet God, I could keep you here for years and never get enough of you. *Want* isn't nearly the word for what I feel for you."

Chessy's gaze fell to the straining cloth at his thighs.

Slowly her untutored mind put two and two together. She frowned, starting to ask questions of why and how and when.

But then she decided words would tell her nothing.

Instead she circled Morland's neck. Two more buttons slid free. Smiling, she pushed him down beneath her onto the bed.

"What are you—"

"Be quiet, barbarian."

"Chessy, you can't—I'm absolutely the worst—"

And then his jaw locked. He shuddered as her mouth explored the warm tangle of bronze hair at his neck and trailed lower.

Chessy blinked, staring at the turgid male nipple. Wondering . . .

No right or wrong, he'd said. *Only what we want or don't want.*

And what she wanted now was to taste him. Everywhere.

She started to do just that. He was salt and citrus, smoke and shadow, with just a tinge of medicinal ginger.

"Chessy—" His voice was raw, slurred. "Chessy, help me. God, don't—"

Only what we choose or don't choose . . .

She chose him. She chose feeling all of this. And if tomorrow brought tears, then so be it. Life was too short for regretting. The swift, unexpected violence of two nights before had taught her that.

She pulled off his shirt and brushed his chest gently with her tongue, thrilled when she felt him shudder, felt his big hands slip around her shoulders.

"Do you . . . was that. . . ?"

He gave a dark sound that was part laugh and part purest pain. "Was it what, my little thief? Was it paradise? Was it torture? Was it the best damned thing I've ever felt? The answer is yes—yes to all of those things."

Emboldened, Chessy tangled her fingers in the bronze hair and brought her head lower, down where the dark pelt narrowed. Where his breeches lay taut, stretched over throbbing muscle.

Her hair lay against his chest, blue-black upon bronze, a cloud of softness upon unalloyed hardness.

At that moment Lord Morland gave up fighting. He slid his fingers deep into that dark cloud, afraid to believe that this was really happening to him, afraid that this dream would vanish, the way all his others had done.

But maybe if he believed hard enough, maybe if he wanted badly enough . . .

Her fingers danced over him, whisper-soft. She searched awkwardly for the buttons that restrained him.

And he felt each unsure flutter all the way to his toes. He marveled at her courage. Dear God, how could he love her any more than he already did? But it seemed that with each passing minute he managed it.

And then—

Then she found the first button of his breeches. Slowly she slid it free.

He threw back his head, shuddering as another button followed.

But by now he was huge, so swollen that the cloth clung tight. He smothered a curse as he felt her warm breath play over his waist, leaving him in torment.

He yearned to pull away and rip the offending cloth free so that nothing came between them.

But he didn't. Because this was her fantasy now, just as much as it was his.

Only what we choose and don't choose . . .

He groaned as she eased down a taut corner of cloth. And then her breath fell hot upon him.

"Am I—does this—"

"God, it does. If you choose it, take it. That's all I've ever wanted for you. *From* you."

Her lips curved up. He could feel the smile, light and fragile where her mouth brushed his straining skin.

And then her fingers were at the cloth, moving at a pace that was nothing short of agony.

Or paradise.

Finally the swollen length of his sex sprang free. He locked his mouth against the fury of it, aching to shove her over and drive inside her.

But he didn't. His fantasy . . . her fantasy.

Theirs, blending together with flawless sweetness.

He heard her give a ragged laugh and gritted his teeth as he felt her touch him. "You're so—big. So . . . swollen. Are you always—that way?"

Her fingers traced him lightly, teaching him new meaning for words like *heaven* and *hell*.

He gave a raw laugh. "No, thank God, I'm not. But all this talk, these unbelievable things you're doing— it's making me *very* . . . swollen. Did they teach you torture at that monastery of yours? I hear the Chinese are masters at it."

Instantly she released him. "Oh! Did I—am I . . . *hurting* . . . you? Is that why—"

"Sweet God, you're hurting me! And if you even *think* of stopping, I'll murder you, my beautiful little witch."

"Oh." Slow, nearly audible comprehension. "Then . . ."

She smiled slowly, moving just like the clever, sated cat he said she resembled. Morland felt that smile as it settled over his turgid, hungry flesh, carried by her lips.

His fantasy . . . her fantasy. Catching at his heart, wrapping its heat around him, pulling him down ever deeper into mystery. Until he came close, so close to losing every shred of his control.

With a groan, he stiffened. Not quite gently he caught her cheeks and pulled her up against his chest.

"But why—"

"Because I want you, Chessy. *Now*. With nothing held back and nothing left to give. With your long legs clinging tight while we find forever. That forever we swore to all those years ago in the middle of a silver Chinese sea."

He moved over her before she could protest, his body big and hot. He slid his hands along her belly, delighting in her instant shudder, delighting in the sweet heat that told him she was ready, more than ready for him.

Her eyes, as she stared up from his pillow, were huge. "Tony? Do you want—"

"Yes. Oh, God, yes. Though I'm a fool and a perfect bastard even to—"

"No, you're perfect," Chessy whispered recklessly. "Just perfect." Her bare sole stroked his tensed calf.

And then she smiled up at him tremulously and he was lost.

"It won't—hurt this time. I'll be careful. You'll probably be a little sore, of course, but nothing more. And if I do anything that you don't like, Chessy, anything at all, just—"

"Tony?"

"Yes, my heart?"

"Be quiet."

He was. And he gave her what she wanted then. He gave her now—and forever, easing deep into that place he'd always wanted to be and groaning when he felt her stretch softly to take him.

God, the heat of it. The utter, sweet *pain* of it . . .

Deep, then deeper. The faintest tugging as those sweet petals fell away and heat met clinging heat.

Soon the rich dark rustle of bed linens was the only sound left in the room.

At length the great, ferocious beast called London began to awaken.

The first light spilled dim through narrow, smoky streets. Flower vendors called their wares and link boys trotted gray-faced and exhausted toward home. And the great city shook and growled and shuddered back to life.

But in the second-floor room at the front of Number 12 Half Moon Street, the light of dawn was soft and caressing. The air was heavy, slow, and very sweet.

And somewhere in that soft, dreaming dawn the Earl of Morland coaxed the woman he'd always loved beneath him again, while her eyes were still full of sleep and her body full of sweetness and glorious surfeit.

Her cries were soft and husky. There were no words between them this time, nothing but a dark slide of flawless friction. He made it slow and endless for her, just as he knew the rest of their time together could not be.

But this at least he meant to make last. This, he wanted Chessy to remember.

Always, just as he would.

Even after she left, which he knew she surely would.

And as he pulled her close against him, the Earl of Morland tried to tell himself the future didn't count. That *now* was all that mattered, the now of thigh against thigh, of wrist pressed close to wrist.

Of heart to reckless heart.

Oh, yes, he tried—and the wonder is that he almost succeeded.

26

"It's time, Chessy. Time to talk."

Rain drummed softly on the window. The candle had guttered out hours ago, and dawn was nothing but a memory now.

Morland was braced against the headboard, staring down at her. In the dim light his face was a study in bronze and amber, his hair alive with a dozen shades of gold. "About tomorrow. About yesterday—and about those letters you never answered."

"L-letters?"

"Letters. The ones I wrote to you for months. I think you owe me an answer."

Chessy thought for a moment of denying she'd ever received those thick vellum sheets. It was a miracle they had ever found her at all, crumbled and tattered, stained with the dirt of a dozen outposts at the edge of the British Empire.

Calcutta. Cairo. The Punjab. All the places Tony had gone after leaving Macao. Much later had come the other names.

Badajoz. Ciudad Rodrigo. Salamanca. A string of other dusty, war-torn towns in Portugal and Spain.

Like a strange foreign song, the names still echoed in Chessy's mind.

She'd opened the first letters with infinite care, crying as she studied every line of flowing script. She hadn't been able to read them, of course, but she'd engaged a tutor in the vain hope that she could learn fast enough to manage it.

But she'd failed. Only two weeks after Tony's departure, she and James had moved yet again, and a thousand responsibilities had fallen on Chessy's young shoulders. But the letters had kept coming. Finally, in desperation, she'd asked a Eurasian friend to read them to her.

How ironic, Chessy thought. Wu Mei had never set foot in England, and yet her reading ability was flawless. Chessy felt tears gather in her eyes, remembering how mortified she'd been at her ignorance. It had been excruciating to hear Tony's words coming from someone else's lips. But Chessy had hung on to every one of those words.

And then she'd tied the letters up tightly, locked them away in a rosewood box, and never glanced at them again. It would have been too painful.

He had been goading and bland, mocking and angry by turns. All his keen wit had been there, along with his sharp eye for detail and human nature. They had left her feeling she walked beside him as he toured the chaos of marketplace and shipyard and raced under tight canvas on scudding seas. . . .

But the hurt had shone through in every line, even in his lightest moods.

Chessy knew that hurt well, for she felt it too. But her hurt was keener, since it had been her first taste of love and she had had no other experiences to soften it.

She had cried each night after Wu Mei had read her a new letter, cried and rocked, holding the sheets tight to her chest as she thought about some hair-raising adventure Tony had had. Through those dark days Morland's letters had been bitter pain and sweetest pleasure, a constant reminder of all she had lost when he'd left. But they had also taught her a bittersweet lesson. Life went on—for her just as it did for him. Even when they were half the globe apart. In the end that knowledge had saved her sanity, perhaps even her life.

Chessy had never wavered about answering them. That would only have opened her to more pain. By then, she knew that she'd reached her limit.

So she had gone off to Shao-lin. Her father had suddenly turned favorable to the idea after two years of strident refusals. Chessy knew he was worried about her, seriously worried. Only that had brought him to such a desperate course of action.

At least at Shao-lin there were no letters to weep over. At Shao-lin she had other things to think of, secret training and physical challenges that had kept her too exhausted to worry about anything else.

That, too, had saved her. And Chessy had not returned until she was whole enough to face Tony's letters again.

Now as she looked at him, she remembered those bitter months and fought to keep the pain of that remembering from her face. "I—I received them." Her voice was flat, expressionless.

Morland's fingers tightened on her shoulder. " 'I received them'? That's all you have to say? Just like that—no explanation?" He gave a hollow laugh. "I wrote you more than forty letters, Chessy, but I never had a single reply."

She stiffened and tried to pull away.

"No, stay. Talk to me, damn it. There had to be a reason."

"Would it have mattered? You were gone. There was nothing more to say."

"It mattered to *me*."

She sighed. "I was—busy. You know how James can be when he gets a new scheme into his head. We moved twice that fall, and—"

"I was busy too. Fighting a war." His voice hardened. "Burying my best friends in rocky passes in Portugal and Spain. Trying to keep the rest of my men alive."

"I'm—sorry. So sorry."

"I don't want your apology, Chessy! I want the truth. Why didn't you answer?"

"I . . . couldn't." Tears were stinging her throat.

"There you go again. There were ways. Even then ships crossed the ocean every week. You could have found some way to—"

"*No.* I couldn't answer. Not then and not now. Because"—she swallowed, feeling shame wash through her—"because I can't—I can't—"

Dear God, she couldn't say it! Even now the humiliation was too great.

Tony went very still. "Because you can't read." His voice was stunned.

Chessy could only nod. She tried to pull away, but he held her fast. "Even now?"

She shook her head and scrubbed furtively at her eyes.

"God, Chessy, why didn't that ramshackle father of yours arrange a tutor or see that you—"

"He tried. But we were always pulling up stakes, always on the move, searching for some new treasure he'd heard about." Her eyes were huge, seas of amethyst and shining silver. "And it would have changed nothing, don't you see? You were—knee-deep in your own problems. And I . . ." She laughed bitterly. "I was nowhere that mattered. Somewhere digging in the dirt on a hillside in Nepal. Or perhaps on an island in the South China Sea. What difference would *my* letters have made?"

Morland frowned. "You could have left me something to say about that." He saw that Chessy's face was red where he had abraded it with his beard-rough cheek. He stroked the skin gently, cursing himself for his haste.

In so many things.

He remembered her hair, framing her cheeks, her eyes dancing like starlight as she tossed him a piece of fish, still hot from the cooking fire. . . .

He remembered the bawdy songs he'd taught her as they worked at the rigging, songs that she'd instantly mastered and sung back to him in a clear, delighted soprano.

God, how she'd made him laugh all those summers ago! How *young* she'd been. And how he'd yearned to stay and watch her grow up into a woman!

Bloody hell. How wrong he'd been about so many things.

Chessy saw the darkness slide into his eyes. "No, don't." She ran her hand over his. "I want you to know that—whatever happens—I'll never regret this. *Us.*"

He pulled her back against him on the bed, his eyes smoky, the fire kindled anew. "I'm very glad to hear it, beauty. Because I mean to exact my payment for those forty letters. In fact. I know *precisely* what sort of retribution I'll demand."

Chessy ran her tongue along the crease of her lips. "Retribution? Surely not—forty?"

His eyes filled with heat. "At the very least, my sweet."

A knock sounded at the door.

"Go away, Whitby!" Morland pulled Chessy down onto his chest and buried his fingers deep in her midnight hair. "Come back tomorrow." As he stared at her parted lips, he groaned. "Next month."

Whitby's voice rose, stiff and embarrassed. "My apologies, your lordship, but—" He cleared his throat. "That is, I require a word."

"Next month, Whitby. Maybe next year."

"But—five messages have come already, your lordship." Whitby's voice was agonized. "This last one makes the sixth."

"Let 'em wait! Tradesmen or matrons, I've nothing to say." Morland bent and nuzzled the already pouting crest of Chessy's breast. "Oh, God—next year. Definitely, next year."

Footsteps approached the door. Low whispers came from the corridor. A moment later, Whitby's voice rose, more strained than ever. "But it's from *him*! The *duke*, your lordship! From Wellington himself. The groom says His Grace is fit to be tied and has sworn to come around in person if he doesn't hear from you within the hour."

Morland sighed. *Wellington.*

Suddenly that other world seemed so dim, so unimportant. All that mattered was being here with Chessy, caught up in wonder and discovery.

Bloody hell. Bloody, bloody hell.

Whitby cleared his throat carefully. "And there is the duchess. She has sent around several messages of her own. Er, eight to be exact, my lord. Somehow she learned of your, er—accident, and she is extremely worried."

Morland cursed softly.

"You—you'd better go." Chessy stared wistfully at his mouth. Her fingers toyed with the crisp hair matting his chest.

"Damned if I'll make it anywhere with you looking at me like *that*!"

"Like what?"

"Like you want to do exactly what I want to do. Right now. Hard and deep and fast. And then slow. Gloriously slow and thorough."

Chessy bit her lip and tried to pull away, but Morland caught her fingers and brought them slowly to his lips. His burning turquoise eyes never left her face as his teeth nipped at the soft mound of her palm.

"I'm sorry, Chessy. It looks as if I really must—"

Chessy swallowed. *Not yet—not so soon . . .*

But she smiled brightly. "Of course I don't mind. You must have a great deal of business to attend to."

"If it were anything else, anyone other than Wellington—"

"I understand. Of course it's all right." *No, stay! Don't go. If you go, I'll have to think of what I've done, face the changes that this day must bring.*

But Chessy said none of those things. Though her eyes gleamed with a suspicious brightness, her smile was steady. "Be gone with you then. Sooner gone, sooner returned." She gave his jaw a final touch, memorizing its faintly rough texture, the power of bone and muscle beneath warm skin.

The muscles flashed at her touch. "Give me—fifteen minutes? I shan't be longer. Not if the Regent himself comes pounding at my door."

Chessy drew her hand away. Her smile wavered for just a second. "Twenty. After that I'll begin to think that—that you're sorry."

"Sorry? *Never.*"

Chessy swallowed hard and wriggled from beneath him, then propped her back against the headboard and tugged the sheet up to her chest. "I'll be counting, I warn you. Your dressing gown is there by the screen, on the floor. Mind the broken glass."

Go now. Make it swiftly, before I lose the last shreds of my composure.

Morland still did not move, and Chessy forced a vexed look. "Out with you, barbarian! A woman needs *some* time alone, after all! I must look an utter fright."

"You look a spectacle, to be sure." His eyes darkened. "An utter spectacle of beauty."

Chessy closed her eyes and drew a sharp breath. "Do not try to flatter me, English barbarian." She struggled to make her voice light and teasing. "Twenty minutes is my absolute limit, and I won't be budged."

After a final, swift kiss, Morland slid to his feet and strode to the door, his body an awesome line of broad chest and naked, rippling thigh.

Afterward, Chessy was very proud of herself.

She didn't cry until he'd tossed on his dressing gown and padded out into the hall.

27

"**I** am most sorry to bother you, your lordship."

Whitby hurried to match the earl's long strides.

"Quite all right, Whitby." Morland tried to hide the impatience he felt. "Of course you had to fetch me."

No, you didn't. Why in the hell did the message have to come now? Why won't the world just go away? "Where is it?"

"Right here, your lordship." Whitby held out a wafer-sealed letter.

Morland felt a sense of misgiving as his fingers brushed the thin sheet sealed with a dark stain of crimson wax.

Bloodred, the wafer was. Just the color of a wound beginning to thicken.

He shoved away his foolish sense of uneasiness and ripped open the seal.

So they had done it. They had finally run down one of the Triad members. Morland's jaw hardened. Now all they had to do was make the man talk. Given the fanaticism of the Triads, it would be no easy task.

Morland turned slowly. One hand rose, braced

against the window while he stared out into the late
afternoon rain.

*Rain again. Funny, it had never seemed to rain in
Macao. There the days had stretched forever, long and
golden, and the nights had fallen like black velvet.*

"Is everything—that is, will you be making any
answer, your lordship?"

Morland wadded up the note and shoved it deep
into the pocket of his dressing gown. "Message?" he
repeated absently.

"To the duke's letter."

"Message." A muscle flashed at Morland's jaw.
"Yes—I suppose I must." His eyes darkened and he
seemed to give himself a shake. "Ask the groom to wait,
if you will, Whitby."

It was a lovely room, Chessy thought blankly. Strange
that she'd never really noticed before.

Palest gray moiré silk wall coverings. A bed lush
with purple velvet hangings. Etchings of English men-
of-war in high seas. Bright, delicate watercolors of
English cantonments in foreign climes. Botanical
prints beneath gleaming wall sconces.

She felt a strange lump gather in her throat. Sniffing
defiantly, she scrubbed at her cheeks. She ran her
hands slowly over the cut velvet tester, the same shade
as the damask bedspread.

Just the color of your eyes, Tony had told her only an
hour before.

Chessy shivered and drew her arms across her chest.

What was happening to her? How had she managed
to lose years of discipline in the passage of a single
day?

Especially now, when her father's fate hung so pre-
cariously, dependent on her skill.

Quickly, before she could question the decision,
Chessy tugged on her black silk jacket and pants. Slippers in hand, she crept to the door and pushed it open.

The corridor was quiet. Far below she could hear
the tap of shoes along the marble entrance alcove.

Shaking her long hair back over her shoulders, she moved down the corridor. Only a few steps later, the creak of a door brought her up short.

"Oh, it that you, Miss Cameron?" Mrs. Harris's round face was full of kindly curiosity. "It's tired you must be, what with all the care you've been giving his lordship. I'll send up anything you'd care for—porridge? Scones? A boiled egg, perhaps? Now which one would you be preferring?"

How heavenly it all sounded. But there was no time, not for any of it.

"Maybe later, Mrs. Harris. I'm just on the point of—"

What? Of running away? Of leaving before the earl can find me?

Chessy frowned. "That is—I must go and refill my case." She gestured at the black leather bag beneath her arm. "Herbs, you understand. Needles of various sizes to sharpen and clean."

The plump, gray-haired housekeeper shuddered. "Needles, do you say? Lord bless me, what will they think of next! But I wouldn't want to be keeping you from your work, miss. Just you let me know when you're hungry. It's my baking day today, and down in the kitchen is where you'll find me."

With a final smile, she turned and padded off down the corridor.

Chessy's breath hissed free. After giving Mrs. Harris a few moments' head start, she headed for the rear stairs.

She was just rounding the first landing when a bright-cheeked housemaid in a white mobcap came toward her, humming quietly. When she saw Chessy, she dropped a quick curtsy.

"Are you—that is, would you be lost, miss? I'd be most gratified to show you the way, if so. Looking for the salon, was you? Or perhaps for Mr. Whitby?"

She waited expectantly.

Chessy bit down an oath and smiled back. "I was, er, needing some—some water. Yes, some boiled water."

What an execrable story! The woman would think her daft!

But the young maidservant only smiled and dropped another curtsy. "Then you're on the right path. Straight down these stairs and to the left is where you'll find the kitchens. But I'd be ever so happy to help you. Was it boiling water you was needing? For a bath, like? If so, I'll have the grooms fetch you up the copper tub and—"

"No!"

The maidservant frowned a little, confused by the desperation in Chessy's voice. "Then . . ."

Think, fool! Chessy pasted a bright smile on her lips. "No, not for a bath. It's for . . . for my medicine, you understand."

The young woman's eyes brightened. "Oh, yes. Of course, miss. I'll be happy to fetch it. We're all ever so thankful to you for saving the master's life. It's a wonderful man he is." She blushed suddenly. "Not in the way you're thinking, I'll wager. It's just—well, he was ever so good to my mum and brothers when they come down with the fever last winter. Let me off to visit them every day, he did. Even gave me food from Mrs. Harris's pantry to see them through." She smiled crookedly. "Would've died without him, I've not a shred of a doubt. And him with his own problems to worry about, what with his knee and all. And those two children to care for—"

Abruptly she recalled herself, blushing furiously. "Oh, but I do beg pardon, miss. Here I am letting my tongue run on wheels! I'm sure I never meant—" She gave a quick, nervous curtsy. "I'll have the water up in a trice, miss. No need to bother yourself about that."

Chessy gnawed on her lower lip as the slender figure disappeared down the stairs.

That meant the servants' staircase was out. Which left only the front entrance.

And it would have to be fast. She had only a few more minutes until the earl returned.

Chessy quickened her pace, suddenly terrified of seeing his face, with the telltale flicker in his eye or the hardening at his jaw that betrayed his regret or distaste for what had happened between them.

After all, she was no beauty. She had no illusions about that. Her shape was tolerable enough, she supposed, but she lacked any of the airs and graces that captivated men and made them take on a moonstruck expression.

No, what happened had been the result of Tony's illness, or because he felt some sense of obligation to her for her care. She would be a fool to believe anything else.

And Francesca Cameron was determined that she would not allow herself to become a fool over Tony Morland.

Not a *second* time.

Her hand trembled on the polished wood of the banister as she stared down at the alcove. A groom passed, and somewhere down the corridor she heard the low murmur of voices.

Time to go. She knew it was the only choice open to her, but her heart still resisted.

Go now.

Drawing a ragged breath, she crept down the thickly carpeted spiral staircase. The groom was gone, and no one was watching the broad oak doors. In a minute it would be done. She would be away. Free.

The murmuring down the corridor changed to low giggles. Frowning, Chessy turned, looking for a place to hide, but she was midstaircase, and her only choice was to go up or down.

At the top of the stairs she heard Whitby's voice.

That left only down.

Quickly she sped down the last few steps, only to run smack into a pair of stealthy figures sneaking past one of the marble columns at the entrance.

Chessy's mouth dropped open as the taller of the pair turned and brought his finger to his lips, signaling her to silence.

"But who—"

Swiftly, he caught her arm and tugged her back into

the shadows, just as Whitby passed from the landing
and descended the stairs.

The boy—for it was a boy, Chessy saw now—
clutched at her arm, signaling urgently for silence.
Chessy felt a moment's misgiving at being an accom-
plice in their stealth.

Then she shrugged the thought away. Since they
didn't look like robbers, what business was it of hers?

When Whitby finally disappeared, the boy gave an
audible sigh and patted his smaller companion's head.

A girl, Chessy saw. A girl with guinea-gold curls and
eyes the color of a summer sky.

Eyes the exact shade of *Tony's* eyes . . .

Chessy made her face grave. "Now then, what's all
this about? It wasn't nice, you know, hiding from
Whitby that way."

The boy gave a crooked little smile as he tucked his
ornamental tricorn under one arm. "No it wasn't, was
it? But it was necessary, you see. For he would just go
and tell our—er, the earl. And *he* would have our hides
if he knew we were here."

"The earl? But who—"

"Oh, never mind us. Please do go on about your
affairs. I rather think we'll be off now too." If the boy
saw anything odd in a woman creeping around inside
the earl's house, he was too well mannered to remark
upon it. "But may we help you find your way first? You
appeared lost a moment ago."

Chessy decided that the truth was the best policy.
"I've just been tending to—that is, to the earl. He has
been . . . unwell."

The boy stiffened. "Unwell? But I thought—"

"Don't worry. He will be quite himself very soon."

The little girl's lip trembled. "He's going to die, isn't
he? Just like *they* did!" Her shoulders slumped as she
clutched her rag doll.

Her brother gave her shoulders a squeeze. He
frowned up at Chessy. "Will he? Die, that is?"

Chessy felt a lump form in her throat. "Of course
not. Strong as an ox, the man is. He's—he's merely had
a bit of an accident and needs to rest. I imagine in half

an hour he'll be striding about, shouting for his breakfast and making life miserable for his underpaid and quite tireless staff." She shot the children a chiding look. "Unless, of course, one look at those Friday-faces of *yours* sends him into a decline."

The boy's face brightened. "I've got it! You're the one who saved his life, aren't you? Jem coachman told us all about you. I didn't really believe him, you know. Thought he was just trying to frighten us as punishment for our insisting on being conveyed to London." He gave a thoughtful look at Chessy's silk pants and tunic. "A healer, he said you were. I dare say that's why you're wearing those—" He recalled his manners, blushing furiously. "Excuse me. Where are my wits?" He tugged his dusty frock coat straight, smoothed his bottle-green waistcoat, and studied the girl beside him. "Take your thumb out of your mouth, Elspeth," he ordered gravely.

Then he turned to Chessy and offered his hand with great formality. "I am Jeremy Langford. This is my sister, Elspeth. We weren't supposed to come here, not to London. But our—that is—the earl was supposed to come back to Sevenoaks by the end of last week. And when he didn't, we began to worry that something was wrong again. So we decided to—"

At this point the small figure beside him, who had been hopping restlessly from one booted foot to the other, could hold back no longer. "Oh, cut line, Je'emy. Let *me* tell her! First we snuck out to the stables. Then we talked Jem coachman into bringing us here so we would see what was wrong." She stared up into Chessy's face, her eyes wide. "You're pretty," she said firmly. "I like you."

A moment later Chessy felt a chubby hand ease into hers.

The cornflower-blue eyes widened. "Are you going to marry our Tony? And be our new mama?"

Chessy went sheet-white. *Dear God, no wonder their eyes looked familiar! Both pairs clear and azure!*

Mama, the girl had said. *They must be his children! Why hadn't he told her?*

A chill rushed over her. She closed her eyes, unable to face the truth.

"Hush, Elspeth!" the boy said sharply. "Now you've upset her! Can't you keep a single solitary thought inside your head?"

"Can't. Don't want to neither!"

"Either," her brother said firmly. "And stop sucking your thumb like a child."

"I *am* a child!" The girl's lip began to quiver. "Are you? Going to marry our Tony?"

Impulsively Chessy reached out to pat her hand. "I—I'm afraid not, my dear. But I'm sure you'll find someone much nicer than I to become your mama. Your fa—your Tony must be very good at finding women, I think."

Her eyes clouded for a moment, and then she straightened. "Now, I'm afraid I really must be on my way."

"You've got to practice, don't you? Jem told me you were a great hand at all sorts of pecular things. Shadow boxing. Swordplay. Said you could cut off a man's ear at ten paces just by looking at him." Jeremy's eyes gleamed with awe. "He told us you saved the earl's life by using magic charms and special chants."

Chessy smiled bitterly. Heaven only knew what sort of rumors had been flying among the staff since she'd arrived! "There was nothing magical about it, I assure you. And as for cutting off men's ears at ten paces, let's just say that I sometimes *wish* I had that ability."

"By Jove, I'd just bet you could do it if you set your mind to it!"

Chessy found herself smiling at his unadulterated admiration. "Well, I'm afraid I really must be off. I've—I've more medicine to mix up, and—oh, just thousands of things to do," she added vaguely.

Disappointment darkened the boy's face. He gave her a sober smile.

Far too sober a smile for a boy so young, Chessy found herself thinking. And that thought made her wonder what sort of sorrows had made him grow up so soon.

At that moment a door opened down the hall. A hard voice echoed down the corridor.

A voice that made Chessy's stomach lurch painfully.

"Tell him to wait for a reply, Whitby. And—and bring it to me here. No matter when it comes."

So much for your twenty minutes, old girl, Chessy thought, clutching at the marble pillar for support. *It appears he's already forgotten all about you. Maybe he was glad to have a reason to forget you.*

She raised her chin proudly and blinked back the tears that stung the back of her eyes. "Forgive me, but I really must—"

The chubby fingers circling her hand only tightened. "But it's Mrs. Harris's cooking day," the girl named Elspeth said in a husky little voice. "She always makes blueberry scones and lemon tarts. They're our Tony's favorite. Mine too. Would you—would you like to come down and try some?"

Her eyes were huge, guileless.

And they pierced right through Chessy's soul.

Eyes of robin's-egg blue. Eyes of tropical seas.

Tony's eyes.

Oh, Tony, Tony, when did it happen? Why didn't you tell me?

Chessy summoned up a crooked smile. "I—I only wish I could, but I really haven't time."

The boy studied her thoughtfully. "The earl sounded fine to me, you know. His voice was as loud as ever. But—well, I'm afraid *you* don't look quite the thing, miss. Indeed I don't mean to be interfering, but—that is, you've gone quite pale."

Chessy closed her eyes for a moment. Sadness washed over her, and she tasted all the bitter textures of despair. Before, she hadn't known what she was missing or what it would be like to taste the rich, piercing sweetness of his love. But now—oh, now . . .

The next instant the boy caught her arm in a surprisingly firm grip. "That does it. You don't look like you should be going anywhere. You'd best come along with us. Mrs. Harris will know what to do. She'll brew you a nice cup of tea and seat you in her best chair before the fire. Then she'll shower you with talk of Yorkshire and all her nieces and nephews, and before you know it you'll be feeling right as rain. It always works for us. And it wouldn't do for *you* to go getting sick, would it? Then who would take care of—of the earl?"

His young face was set with determination. And at that moment his resemblance to Lord Morland was so sharp that it tore at Chessy's heart.

But she saw there would be no way of escaping him, not without creating the very sort of disturbance she was hoping to avoid.

She bit her lip, then sighed. "Very well, Sir Galahad. I suppose I do look fairly awful."

"Oh, no. I never meant—"

Chessy chuckled at his chivalry. "Of course you didn't. But lead on, brave knight. Something tells me there are dragons waiting to be bested. And that you will find the perfect way to do it."

The boy looked inordinately pleased by her comment. "Do you really think so? Oh, I say, that's the finest compliment I've ever had. I'm nine, by the way," he said importantly. "Elspeth is five."

The chubby thumb slid from the girl's mouth. "Five and *three-quarters*, I am."

"Five and three-quarters," the boy repeated with a long-suffering sigh. "You really must go down with us. I can't wait to hear the whole story. If even half of what Jem coachman told me is true, it will be splendid. But I don't believe—that is, I don't mean to be rude, but we haven't actually met."

Chessy smiled and extended her hand. "Miss Francesca Cameron. But you may call me Chessy."

Jeremy pressed her fingers warmly. "I'm ever so glad that he—that the earl had *you* to look after him, Miss Chessy. And to think that we were kicking up our heels at Sevenoaks, absolutely useless, while he was here, needing us."

The girl's thumb popped from her mouth for a second time. "Told you we should come! Knew it, didn't I just!"

The boy squeezed her shoulder. "And you were quite right this time, imp. Dam—er, deuced glad you convinced me." His face turned sober. "And of course we can't bother the earl now. We must leave him to rest." Jeremy's azure eyes narrowed. "You could do with a rest too. You look rather shot yourself." He blushed and coughed very consciously. "Not the thing to say, of course. Didn't mean to imply—that is, not that you are anything but, well, quite fine. A diamond of the first water, don't you know?"

Chessy had to smile at this extravagant praise. "Flummery, Master Jeremy?"

"Devil a bit!" His cheeks turned pinker.

At the same moment chubby fingers tugged at Chessy's silk jacket. "Can we go now? The kitchen is ever so nice when Mrs. Harris is cooking. She never uses titles or makes us sit like China dolls. And I'm verrrrry hungry." Elspeth's lip trembled. "Only she won't like it if we go down alone, since we're not supposed to be here, you know. So—so do you think you could come with us? To explain?"

Outgunned, outnumbered, and outflanked.

Chessy sighed. Well, what difference could a quarter-hour make now? Especially when the earl was sequestered in his study, awaiting important papers.

Jeremy, meanwhile, seized her other hand and tugged her toward the back stairs. "Indeed, Mrs. Harris does make lovely tarts! The Duchess of Cranford has offered Tony any amount of money to lure her away, but he won't even consider the idea. I even heard that Prinny himself made an offer—a thousand pounds, Jem told us it was. A veritable fortune, but still the earl wouldn't let her go."

Chessy had a sudden stricken realization. "He wouldn't?" she said faintly. "Not even to the Prince Regent?"

"Devil a bit," the boy said cheerfully. "And the best thing is, she always saves her very best for us. Even though she likes to complain about it."

At that second his stomach rumbled quite loudly.

He gave an embarrassed smile that made him look not a day over his nine years.

Chessy thought he looked quite charming at that second, and she had to resist an urge to ruffle his glossy hair. "Very well. Lead on, Sir Galahad."

Jeremy flashed her a smile. "Come along, Elspeth. Don't dawdle this time," Jeremy called over his shoulder as he moved toward the staircase leading down to the kitchens.

A moment later Chessy found herself propelled across the polished marble foyer, tightly in tow of a very serious nine-year-old boy on one hand and a sunny-faced nearly-six-year-old on the other.

And she found herself wondering what else could possibly go wrong this day.

28

"**D**amn. Damn and blast!"

Clad in a silken dressing gown of crimson and navy paisley, the Earl of Morland turned from the sunny rear window, a scowl upon his face.

It was worse than he'd thought. *Far worse.*

"When did this come?"

"Only a moment ago, your lordship."

Morland stared down at the bold scrawl darkening the heavy vellum sheet. The captive Triad had taken some sort of poison he'd had concealed in his jacket. It didn't look good, not at all. And he'd told them nothing.

"Is the fellow still below?"

Whitby nodded.

"Then hold him. I shall have to reply." Morland's fingers tightened on the sheet. "Though God knows what there is to say." He shook his head, wincing as pain shot through his still-bandaged arm.

Damn, when would he be free of this whole business? His thoughts kept turning to the room upstairs where Chessy waited, her hair a blue-black cascade upon his pillow.

Desire gripped him at the thought. His fingers twisted as heat shot through him.

He remembered how they had loved once and then again as dawn crept over London's heaving chimneys. And each time had been piercing, sweet in a way Morland had never thought to know.

Now all he wanted was to be back beside her, his fingers tangled deep in her hair, his body given over to the new universe he had just begun to discover in her arms.

But he could not.

Not with this bloody book in jeopardy and three years of foreign policy in danger of disarray.

His face hardened as he crumpled the vellum sheet to a tight ball. "I'll need coffee, Whitby. A great deal of it, I'm afraid. And clothes." He eyed the paper-strewn desk, with its secret drawer, realizing it might be hours until he was free again. There were codes to be completed, after all. And then there were informants to be contacted, even those in the most unlikely places.

His hands drove deep into his pockets as bitterness gripped him.

Why now? Why couldn't they leave him alone, now that the war was over?

But he knew the answer too well. The responsibility had been his, the plan of his own design. Honor bound him, and he could no more have turned from Wellington's request than he could have ceased breathing. Honor was the only thing that had kept him going for a long time now.

For ten years?

He muttered a low curse. "And Whitby?"

"Yes, your lordship?"

"Please, see to Miss Cameron. Food. Clothing. Whatever she requires. Let her know"—he raked a hand through his unruly bronze hair—"it may be rather a while."

"Of course, my lord."

"And after that send a note to Sevenoaks. I believe Jeremy's tutor has a brother just down from Oxford. Tell him I have need of him in London. On a project of some delicacy," Morland added. "And ask him to bring his basic readers and several simple novels."

"Very good, my lord."

When the steward closed the door softly behind him, the earl was still at the window, staring out at the neat row of rosebushes bordering the rear garden.

But the man framed by the window saw neither red petals nor green boughs.

All he saw was a woman's face, glorious in its honesty, haunting in its sadness.

And he realized that he could never let her go, that he wanted to spend the rest of his life fighting, arguing, trying to understand her split-second mood shifts and making her the happiest woman on earth.

And he'd damned well succeed!

But not until this bloody business with James Cameron and the book was over and done with.

"**A**nd then he said he'd flay us both if we even *thought* of doing anything like that ever again!"

Chessy sat back, laughing, as Jeremy Langford ended his story with an engaging grin. "And that we didn't, Miss Chessy. I can swear to you we didn't. Even though Miss Twitchett—she's our governess—makes us as cross as hornets with her carping all the time."

He looked down as Elspeth tugged at his sleeve. Her eyes were wide. "What does *flay* mean, Je'emy?"

Her brother shook his head. "Not now, Elspeth," he said importantly.

Chessy took pity on the girl. "It's something—not at all comfortable, my dear." She held out the plate with the last of Mrs. Harris's delectable lemon tarts. "Why don't you have the last one? I'm sure I couldn't eat another bite." She saw the girl frown as politeness warred with appetite. "It's quite all right, really. Just think how desolate Mrs. Harris will be if we don't finish them."

At that, Elspeth smiled and scooped up the last confection. Then she halted. "But—that is, p'raps you'd like to share it with me?" She gave Chessy a wide-eyed look.

Chessy patted her reed-slim stomach. "Oh, but I mustn't. One must guard one's figure, you know."

Intent at polishing off his fifth blueberry scone, Jeremy frowned. "Wouldn't think *you'd* need to worry about such things, miss. A real stunner, that's what you are." He coughed, and a faint flush stained his cheeks. "That is, but—ought I to have mentioned such a thing?"

Chessy smiled. "It's a delightful compliment." Her violet eyes twinkled. "The very nicest I've had in days, as a matter of fact."

The boy beamed, reassured. "It's no more than the truth. You needn't worry a whit about your figure. And I'll take great pleasure in thrashing anyone who suggests such a thing!" He looked quite belligerent for a moment, and Chessy hid a smile, finding a strange comfort in his protectiveness.

At that moment a door creaked open, and a barrage of orders issued from the floor above.

Instantly Chessy stiffened.

She stood up swiftly, trying for nonchalance. "It—it must be nearly time for Lord Morland's, er—medicine. I must go to him, see what he requires. You will excuse me, I hope."

Jeremy was on his feet instantly. "Certainly. Give him our regards, won't you? We don't mean to be any trouble. I'll even see to it that Elspeth doesn't plague him to take her to Astley's Amphitheatre this time."

Booted feet crossed the hall above.

Quickly Chessy made for the servants' staircase.

"Miss—Miss Francesca?"

Jeremy's voice, low and wistful, stopped her midstride. She turned at the door, her fingers upon the latch. "Yes?"

"He's—he's ever so lucky to have found you. He—he needs someone, you know. Ever since Salamanca, he's been different. Like he's—he's pushed things down and has to keep moving or they'll work their way free. Now he's always busy, always going somewhere, doing something. He used to laugh, oh, just at anything. He used to have time to take us fishing or go looking for kittens hidden in the stable. Not that we are complaining. He's been ever so good to us, considering . . ." The boy's eyes gleamed with sudden moisture. "But now—well, he needs something more. Or *someone*. Someone just like you. Elspeth and I discussed it, and we both think so."

As the flaxen-haired girl nodded her agreement, a lump formed in Chessy's throat. Her fingers tensed upon the door latch. "How—how very kind you are," she said softly.

And then she turned and fled into the darkness of the back stairs.

Something drew her back to his room one last time. She should have left immediately, of course. She should have slid out through the window or crept past the stillroom behind the kitchen.

Even marched right out through the front door.

But she didn't.

She *couldn't*. Not yet.

Instead, she slipped back to the place where she had learned the real meaning of loss and fear. Where she had found her first true taste of paradise. The place where she had discovered that dreams really could come true.

Just for a few moments, she wanted to feel him again. To smell the tang of his skin, fresh with lemon soap and leather. To slide her fingers across the crisp white sheets and remember how it had felt when he touched her.

When he had first taken her. In love.

Especially now, when Chessy knew it could never be that way again.

Just one last time, she promised herself. Just so that she could remember, when she was far away and the days were bleak and cold once more.

For he was too busy for her, pressed with more family and governmental duties than he could already manage. And he was a man of rank and importance—far too important to be saddled with an awkward little nobody like herself.

His dressing gown was tossed across his bed. Chessy picked it up carefully and ran her cheek across the smooth dark silk.

The fabric still held his scent—leather and tobacco and a faint tang of the lemon soap he favored.

A sharp, painful burning filled Chessy's throat.

But she knew she couldn't stay. There were too many years between them, too many differences of age and place and habit.

Most of all there was her father, still held captive by madmen.

No, Chessy had to go.

With trembling fingers she laid the dressing gown down and clutched her black bag to her chest.

Good-bye, my forever friend. I—I love you . . . and shall love you always.

Tears burned in Chessy's eyes as she turned. Outside the hall was quiet.

This time no servants were present to keep her from her course.

Ironic. Now she might almost have welcomed their intercession.

She turned at the threshold and took a last, clear look. Closing her eyes, she imprinted the scene on her memory.

The violet damask curtains, swaying slightly. The rich rustle of their stiff folds. The fresh scent of beeswax and lemon oil polish. Sunlight glinting off gilt frames and a silver candelabrum.

How much she wanted to stay. To pull him down against her onto those crisp white sheets.

To touch him. To feel his hands in turn. Touching her everywhere . . .

Biting back a sob, Chessy spun about and slipped down the corridor.

She was at the head of the stairs before she realized the hallway below was occupied.

Elspeth and Jeremy were standing stiffly to one side,

arguing with Whitby, who was pointing toward the far corridor. A moment later, Elspeth pushed past her brother and went running toward the earl's study.

Her pounding feet echoed down the hallway, somehow in tune with Chessy's racing heartbeat. By the time she reached the front alcove, Whitby had gone in pursuit of the children.

Chessy watched from behind a marble column as the study door was open. The earl emerged and was greeted with shouts of giddy laughter from the children.

His children.

Chessy's eyes filled with tears as she watched Tony clasp Elspeth and toss her up into the air, then turn and sweep an arm around Jeremy's shoulders.

Suddenly Chessy felt alone. Horribly alone.

Just the way she'd always felt, growing up on the outside of the close-knit British colonial community in Macao. Only then it hadn't hurt so much. But now, oh, now, the pain was blinding.

She watched the earl lift Elspeth up onto his broad shoulders. "What are *you* doing here, imp? And you, Jeremy?"

Elspeth laughed in delight, clutching at his hair. "More, Papa! Higher!"

"Now, now, Elspeth! How many times have I told you not to—"

Chessy shrank back deeper into the shadows.

Papa. The sound was a knife in her heart.

There was no possibility of a mistake, then.

His life. Her life. He had children, a family already. A thousand bonds and responsibilities that closed him off from her.

East and West, forever divided.

She had to go! Now, before she disgraced herself further.

She took one last look. Jeremy was hugging his father and talking excitedly. Elspeth was smiling down in triumph from atop the earl's broad shoulders.

A dust-stained and quite irritated servant stood grimly in the background.

A governess? And if so, what did it matter? It was not Chessy's place to fret if the woman's eyes were cold and her face was hard and unforgiving. So what that she was not at all the sort of person to be given the care of two such sensitive children.

No, not Chessy's business at all.

Brushing at her eyes, she slipped down the stairs to the massive oaken door, blinking when she stepped out into the blinding light of midday.

A hackney moved along at a trot. Two prim nannies marched past, their charges tightly in hand.

And then, through a blur of tears, Chessy made out Swithin's gaunt, beloved face.

"Chessy—what has that devil's son been doing to you? By heaven, I'll gullet the scoundrel with my own hands if—"

Chessy swayed and clutched the cold iron railing. *Scoundrel? If only it were so simple!* "It's—it's nothing, Swithin. Let's—please, let's just go home."

Home? That shabby little house on Dorrington Street?

She gave a ragged laugh.

Swithin took one look at her face, at her white, drawn cheeks and red-rimmed eyes. Muttering, he took her hand firmly. "Right then, miss. Home it is. Then to bed with you. Wouldn't wonder at it if you was coming down with something. Something mean and nasty."

Oh, yes, it was mean and nasty, all right.

Chessy scrubbed blindly at her eyes, then took the arm he offered. Together they walked slowly down the steps, not another word said between them.

They made a strange pair descending from that elegant house, the girl in black with a battered leather bag clutched to her chest and the grizzled old servant whose eyes were dark with anger and uncertainty.

But no one in the house at Number 12 Half Moon Street even noticed their departure.

As it happened, only one person noticed. And the pair of eyes that watched Francesca Cameron board a hired hackney were anything but kindly.

29

"**W**hat do you mean, our man just disappeared?"

The white-haired leader of the Triads sat in the shadows, incense curling in long plumes around him.

The man before him fell to his knees. "A thousand apologies, lord. One of the foreign devils followed him on the way back to the boat. They must have captured him."

The Triad leader steepled his fingers. "He is loyal?"

"Never, lord. He is brave. Nothing can make him talk."

The figure in the shadows laughed darkly. "All men talk, you fool. It is simply a matter of time. Now because of that son of a turtle we will have to change our plans. Ayeeah! I am indeed surrounded by worthless fools!" His eyes closed as he inhaled the fragrant incense for a moment. "But all is not lost. We will start with the woman. We know her weak point."

"The Englishman on Half Moon Street?"

The old man nodded. "Exactly. You will make an able Triad yet, Wu-fang. Now listen carefully. I have learned of a foreign devil who is much interested in

271

pillow books. He lives in secrecy and will be difficult to find, however."

"*I* can find him, lord."

The old Triad smiled at this bit of arrogance. "Can you? If so, then you will be well rewarded, since the man may be involved somehow already. Hire whatever help you require. The English foreign devils near the docks will do anything for a few pieces of gold. But first take care of the yellow-haired *yang-kuei*. And do not fail this time, as you did before. Pick your moment carefully, and make the poison strong. The Englishman must die, since he distracts the woman from finding the pillow book."

"I understand, lord."

"Be prepared to obey me perfectly. Otherwise, you and all your descendants will die a long, slow death."

As the incense curled up, the warrior sat forward and listened.

"What do you mean, the Cameron chit just vanished?"

Arrayed in a fuchsia silk peignoir that left very little of her voluptuous anatomy to the imagination, Lady Louisa Landringham jerked upright on her velvet settee.

Unguents and perfume vials struck the floor with a crack.

The man before her, dressed in the pale blue livery of a groom, shrugged nonchalantly, but his brow beaded up with sweat.

Louisa came slowly to her feet, her peignoir sliding apart to reveal ivory thighs and a thick tangle of hair nestled between.

The groom swallowed audibly. His eyes fell, riveted on the lushly curving breasts that thrust against the decolletage of the gossamer silk.

"You are . . ." His employer frowned slightly, moving closer. Her fingers slid along his satin-clad shoulders. "Wilson, isn't it?"

The servant could only nod, red-faced and stupefied.

Bloodred nails trailed across his neck and skimmed

his ear. "Wilson. Such a bold name." The crimson-tipped fingers fell, brushing along his breeches. "Such a hard name . . ."

"Begging your pardon, your ladyship, but you never said nothing about—"

Abruptly his face contorted. The clever fingers found the first button on his breeches and inched it free. "Ah, yes, Wilson. Now let me see if your name matches the rest of you."

Louisa Landringham's small pink tongue swept her lips, leaving them agleam with moisture. It was not Wilson she was thinking of, however, but a blond earl with eyes of mocking sapphire.

Another button slid free. "Of course, if you'd rather *not* be in my employ, I would not dream of holding you. If you have a more promising position in mind . . ."

The servant's voice caught in a raw gasp as his manhood slid free. He stared down in disbelief as the bloodred nails circled his aching flesh. "N—no, Lady Landringham. That is—" A shudder shook him as the skillful fingers curved, sending blood hammering to his groin. "Sweet Lord above, I didn't never—"

"That is good, Wilson, Very good." The half-clad woman smiled down at the rampant length of muscle quivering within her fingers.

So vulnerable. Just as Tony Morland would soon be. And then she would repay him for humiliating her. She had the perfect person to help her do it.

Her lips twisted. "And now you will listen, my dear Wilson. You will listen well." She began to talk as she stroked him, her words low and smooth as satin. She made them sound almost like love words, though the task they described was precisely the opposite of lover-like.

When she finished speaking, the servant was red-faced, gasping, incoherent with need.

"And now, Wilson, since you've been such a naughty boy, I'm afraid I really must punish you." Her eyes narrowed. "Something very hard, I think. Something that will make you hot. Something that will make you groan . . ."

She went slowly to her knees. Her eyes were dark, unreadable. She pushed the satin from her perfumed shoulders and raised her head.

Her ruby lips parted. "Come here, Wilson," she whispered.

The groom moved closer. Lady Landringham was still smiling when her lips circled him and the first raw groan was torn from his throat.

"**I** don't bloody believe it! How could she just vanish?"

Whitby tried not to quiver beneath his employer's fierce inquisition. He stared stiffly at a flowered motif on the silk-covered walls. "I was just striving to ascertain that for myself when your lordship rang."

Lord Morland strode across the hall to the front salon and stood staring down at the street, his face harsh. "Didn't anyone see her go?"

Whitby tugged nervously at his sober waistcoat. "She was last seen in the kitchen, I believe."

"In the kitchen? What in God's name was she doing in the *kitchen*?"

"She was, er—sampling Mrs. Harris's lemon tarts."

"Sampling lemon tarts? What sort of fool do you take me for, Whitby?"

The servant flushed. "None, of course. I did not mean to imply—"

Morland's hands tightened into fists. "Then give me the truth this time, and make it bloody quick, man!" He threw back the curtains and moved closer to the window. He found he had to put a hand to the sill for support.

Only by iron force of will did Whitby keep from going to his aid. He knew only too well how any attempt at assistance would be met. Which was exactly why he had been so thankful to Miss Cameron for stepping in when the earl had needed her. No one else could have kept him still while his wound healed. Certainly no one else could have saved him from that monstrous poison inflicted through the intruder's knife.

The servant frowned faintly. But where in the devil

had the girl disappeared to? And why? She was needed here, after all. Somehow in the course of a few short hours, it appeared that they had *all* come to rely on her calm good sense.

Perhaps the stony-faced earl most of all.

Whitby sighed as Morland began to pace the room furiously, one hand clenched about his throbbing forearm.

"Well, man?"

"His Grace, the young duke, said she just—vanished."

"Jeremy? Good God, never tell me *he* saw her?"

Whitby nodded morosely. "It was not long after the pair arrived, accompanied by a very flustered and nearly incomprehensible governess and two grooms. Miss Twitchett, I believe the woman's name was. I heard her say that she had never had the misfortune to be saddled with two more ungracious, unteachable, ani—er . . . charges. Well, *charges* was not quite the word she used." Whitby coughed. "My lord."

Morland's face took on a dark cast. "Oh, she called my wards *animals*, did she?"

Whitby nodded. "That was just after she pulled a mouse from her portmanteau, I believe."

Morland broke into a reluctant grin. "Did she just?" He rubbed his jaw. "Miss Twitchett? She's the Friday-faced creature with the shrill titter, isn't she?"

Whitby nodded at this damning description.

Morland raked a hand through his long bronze hair. "Don't know why in hell I ever engaged the bloody woman in the first place. A perfect bird-wit, and not a shred of patience about her. The woman has no business having anything to do with children."

"So you said at the time, I believe, my lord," Whitby said stiffly.

"Then why did I hire her?"

"I believe there was that business with breeding stock requiring your presence in York. And then there were the races at Newmarket, and—"

"Don't remind me, Whitby." Morland rubbed his jaw irritably. "Well, it's the very devil of a coil. Don't know what's to be done with the pair now." Morland's eyes began to gleam. "A mouse, did you say? I wish I might have seen that."

"And then there was the snake, your lordship."

"*Snake?*"

"Rather large and spotted, as I recall. The creature escaped from the governess's valise and went after the mouse. One of the under-housemaids fainted, and there was a great commotion in the foyer. The duchess was just on the point of leaving, you see, and—"

"The duchess? Of Cranford? *She* was there too?"

Whitby's lips began to twitch. "Indeed, your lordship. I believe—that is, it appeared that the duchess and the children had reached some sort of understanding. When Miss Twitchett reached out and seized young Jeremy by the ear, the duchess was overheard to say that she would expect the woman to release the boy on the instant. And then she could take herself off, for her services would no longer be required." The servant's face assumed an impassive mask. "Not that one likes to eavesdrop, of course."

"Of course not," Morland said dryly. "And where was Miss Cameron during this great melee?"

"Well, that's just it, your lordship. In all the botheration, she just—just—"

"Vanished?"

Whitby nodded his head gravely.

Tony's face took on a thoughtful look. "Did she? I wonder."

It was raining.

Chessy frowned, fingering the frayed muslin curtain. A moment later, she let it fall back across the window above the rain-soaked street.

Rain suited her mood exactly.

But she would not cry. She would not grieve in any way. Not even the note that had arrived while she was at Half Moon Street would make her cry.

Quickly Chessy turned, straightening her practice

tunic. She took a deep breath and focused low, struggling to push away bitter, clinging memories.

Once more her hands began to move, sliding forward like arching swallows. Her face was a study in composure as she found her pace, moving slowly and silently through the dim beam of light in the empty room.

Only her eyes betrayed her inner turmoil, tense and haunted.

The note had been short but very precise. Swithin had read it to her grimly. *Do not see the yellow-haired Englishman again. He is too curious about the pillow book already. And he distracts you, making you useless in your search. Heed this warning well. If you ignore it, he will die. Very slowly. Very painfully.*

And your father will follow.

Her cloth slipper hissed over the wooden floor, raising tiny specks of dust that danced in the sunlight. The air was still, rich with the scent of lemon oil.

That would be Mrs. Harris's handiwork, Chessy thought. And Lord Morland had turned down an offer from the Regent himself for the woman's services!

Her foot slipped. Her ankle twisted and struck the floor, raking up a long sliver.

She muttered an oath and reached down to tug the slipper free. But the wood clung to the black silk, like an obscure symbol that Chessy could not quite understand.

Angrily she plucked at it, frowning when it slid through her fingers. She tried again, harder this time.

With a sharp hiss the thin slipper tore in two.

It struck Chessy as funny somehow. Slim and immobile in the beam of light, she stood staring at the jagged edges of black silk. Laughter welled up in her throat.

Big silver tears followed, coursing wildly down her pale cheeks.

There in the dim light, in the room rich with the smell of lemon and freshly cut roses, she studied the ruined slipper. Her last one.

Yes, it was funny somehow. Horribly funny . . .

Her choked laughter echoed from the high attic walls, ragged as the edges of silk in her fingers. Then the sound changed, grew deep and raw.

By the time Chessy sank down to the polished floor, her silly slipper caught tight in her fingers, she was crying.

For her slipper, she told herself fiercely.

For her dreams.

For the father she could not find and the mother she had never had.

But as she clutched the frayed silk tight and felt it grow wet with her tears, she knew it was a lie.

30

Someone was banging on the door.

Chessy pulled the pillow from atop her head and squinted up into the darkness.

Was the ship under siege? Or had her father merely forgotten to toss anchor again, and let them drift off in the currents?

Chessy blinked and sat up in her bed. "All right! I'm coming—"

She rubbed her eyes and reached for the breeches that always hung over the bulkhead just beside her cot.

They were gone.

The banging grew louder. "Coming, Father!"

Was it Han Sung's pirates again, chasing them for treasure? Or was it that rogue privateer O'Neill, looking for booty?

Dizzily she came to her feet.

Again someone banged on her door.

"Miss Chessy? You awake yet?"

Chessy frowned. "Swithin?" She pushed from bed and tugged on the robe she found at the foot of her bed. And then she froze. Her face turned pale with remembrance.

279

Not Macao, but London.

And her father . . .

She ran to the door and pushed it open with trembling fingers. "What—what is it, Swithin? Have you heard anything—anything more about—?"

She couldn't finish the question.

Swithin shook his head. "Not from them as has your father, miss. Nor did I mean to wake you, neither, but—well, you see, I can't turn him away any longer."

"Him?" A strange humming invaded Chessy's blood.

"Lord Morland, miss. Been here already three times this morning, he has. Looking none too happy neither. Especially when I told him as how you wasn't receiving guests."

Chessy's mouth went flat and tense.

"You're not going to say nothing about what happened between you two while you was at Half Moon Street?"

She shook her head. "Don't—don't ask, Swithin. It's all done with anyway."

The bleakness in her tone made the old servant frown. His face turned grim. "It ain't right, miss. I said it before and I'll say it again. It ain't bloody *right*. You shouldn't otter be roamin' about the roofs o' London searching for that blasted book. Your father has friends, you know. Lay the matter before them and let 'em—"

Chessy sighed. Her fingers tightened on the belt of her robe. "Please, Swithin, don't let's argue. Not again. There's not one of them I could trust in such a delicate matter. And that leaves only me."

From far below she heard the drum of boots. A hard voice rang up the stairwell. "Tell her I won't go away until she comes out, Swithin!"

A shudder shook her. Dear God, when would it all be over?

"T-tell him I'm—I'm indisposed. I couldn't possibly see anyone today."

It went sorely against the grain for her to use such an excuse, but Chessy found she had no better one at hand.

He wouldn't dare crash into her bedroom, at least.

The harsh male voice boomed up once more. "And tell her if she doesn't come down in fifteen minutes, I'll come up there and *carry* her down!"

Swithin shook his head. "Had a fair idea how it was with him when he first arrived, miss. All bloodshot and disheveled he was, and it not a minute after daybreak." He stopped, waiting for Chessy to add some comment. When she did not, he shrugged. "Told him you was sick. Then I told him you plain wasn't wishful to see him. But the earl didn't seem of half a mind to believe any of it, miss. Not that I'm much surprised. I'm a man as has eyes in his head, fer all that."

Chessy glared at the banister as if it were the source of all her problems.

"He's been kicking up his heels in the drawing room for an hour now. It's his third visit of the day, and he's looking positively murderous. Maybe it would be better if you—"

Chessy's fists clenched and unclenched. Damn the man! Why, oh, why wouldn't he just let her alone!

Abruptly she thought of the gardenia he had kept in the buttonhole of his shirt. The tremor in his hands when he had stroked the hair from her cheek and then kissed her.

Softly.

Thoroughly.

Then hungrily, so hungrily that she . . .

"Oh, very well," she snapped. "I'll see the wretched man. I can see that's the only way I shall ever be rid of him!"

P recisely fifteen minutes later, Chessy swung open the door to the sunny salon.

Her sprigged muslin dress was creased and threadbare, the oldest of the gowns she had brought to London. Her slippers were very little better.

Some angry demon had made her choose the clothes so that her business might be done with that much quicker.

She knew she looked the veriest urchin. That her face was pale and her hair was riotous and her eyes were dark-rimmed.

But she raised her chin in an imperious slant and strode across the room proudly.

Morland stood before the window. He was paler than usual, and there were lines of strain about his eyes, but otherwise there was no sign of the recent wound he had endured. And for some reason the sight of his perfectly tied cravat, his immaculate damask waistcoat, only made Chessy angrier.

At her step, he turned.

The sun fell full upon his taut face. She saw a muscle flash at his jaw. He moved slightly, shifting his weight to favor his good leg.

At that moment Chessy had a good notion of exactly what an accomplished performer he was. She knew his knee must be paining him above a little, yet he refused to make any concession to that pain, nor to the newer wound at his arm.

But in spite of her knowledge of his pain, she could not allow her heart to soften.

"My lord." Her voice was stiff. "You are recovered, I see. My congratulations."

Morland's sapphire eyes blazed down into her face. "With your help I am. I have come to give you my thanks."

"There is no need, I assure you." Chessy turned away to arrange an errant bloom in a crystal vase, thankful to escape his keen gaze.

So it was that she did not notice the hunger that swept the earl's face, the bleakness that darkened his eyes as she turned away from him.

"Your admirers are persistent, I see." He stared sourly at the fresh clusters of roses that filled the corner table. "My compliments."

When Chessy did not turn back, his face hardened. "I wonder how they would feel if they knew you had spent a day and two nights in my company. My reputation for conquest is vast, you know. And since we both know the reality of all that transpired last night . . ."

Chessy's fingers tightened on the stem of a vibrant yellow rose. "So?"

"So, my dear, you have been compromised. Thoroughly. Without hope of redemption. The only question now is what we are to do about it."

"Do?" Chessy gave the rose a tug. "Why, nothing, I imagine." She was pleased with the chill of her voice.

Morland's eyes glittered as he smoothed his gloves between his fingers. "Nothing?" He gave a harsh laugh. "How long do you think matters will stay hidden?"

"Long enough. I shall be leaving London very soon, you see. Therefore I pray you will not concern yourself with my trivial affairs." She turned slowly, her face pale but composed. "And now, if you are quite finished—"

"Finished? No, by God, I'm not finished!" Morland strode across the room and jerked her into his arms. His burning eyes raked her face. "You can't get out of this scrape as easily as those others, Cricket. You were seen—*we* were seen. Not only at my house but at the duchess's conservatory, it seems." He caught back a curse and fought for some semblance of control. "And so you would do me a very great honor if you would consent"—his jaw hardened—"to become my wife."

A vein was beating at his forehead, just below the dark gold comma of his hair.

Numb, immobile, Chessy found herself studying that quicksilver flash of motion. He was very handsome, she thought in a detached sort of way. His brow was high, but not too high. And his eyes were so startlingly blue . . .

"Wife?" Her voice rose, dim and very faint in her own ears. "I—I believe not."

The vein at his forehead seemed to pound faster. "You little fool! They'll slash you to ribbons! They thrive on gossip such as this! They'll leave you in pieces before they've even had their breakfast chocolate! By midday, the scandal will be all through the *ton*."

Chessy made a low sound of protest.

Morland's fingers tightened. "Marry me, Chessy."
He felt heat flare where her breasts brushed his chest.
"Marry me, damn it! Now! Today!"

Chessy's face was unreadable. "Just like that? A
bloodless, formal contract? We repeat some words, and
then you go your way and I go mine?"

Morland's lips tensed. "If it is your wish, I shall not
impede you."

Chessy felt a painful lump block her throat. "You to
spend your nights with your Germaine, and I to conduct my own liaisons, just as long as it is all most
discreet?"

"I don't propose to deny you what I would enjoy
myself, if that's what you mean."

Chessy paled. "I see." Her hopes fled. How could she
have thought . . .

"Well, you can take yourself and your pompous
proposal and just—just take a leap into the Thames!"

Morland's fingers bit into her shoulders. "You have
no choice, Chessy. Not this time. This is one scrape I
can't get you out of. It's beyond wishing or changing
this time, for we were seen. And—the Duke of Wellington was across the street when you left on Swithin's
arm. He saw quite enough to guess what had happened."

Chessy tensed in his arms. A shudder went through
her. "No—he couldn't have!"

"I'm afraid he did. And unfortunately the old martinet's eyes are sharp as an eagle's. He has already been
around to see me. Raked me over the coals most roy-
ally, I can tell you. And as if that weren't enough, the
duchess came to put in a word or two. Damned crusty
she was too."

Chessy swayed at this new onslaught. How had it all
changed—gone so wrong? Was he now to be dragged
down, forced into some bloodless contract for the sake
of propriety?

"It's not fair!" she said tightly.

"Life is often unfair, Chessy. I would have thought
you knew that by now," he added harshly.

Chessy stiffened. Who was *he* to be lecturing her? "I

don't care. And I won't do it, do you hear? I won't marry you!"

"It's *your* reputation that will be in shreds, my girl. Mine is too tattered to suffer any further damage. But you are the one who'll be mocked, shunned, gossiped about."

A chill slid over her. So it was to be just as before. Once again the sneering faces. The cold, cruel taunts.

She raised her chin defiantly, shrugging off his hands and glaring up at him. "I shan't be in London long enough to care, I assure you."

Morland's eyes hardened. Damn! Why was none of this going as he'd planned? How could she have lost all her feeling for him? At the very least she ought to have acknowledged the gravity of their situation and shown some hint of appreciation for his offer.

But there she stood, pale as glass, her eyes glittering and distant. And she was wearing that damned awful dress that should have made her look ridiculous.

Instead, it only made her look utterly vulnerable, intensely fragile.

And blinding beautiful—to *him*, at least.

Somehow Tony thought it would always be so with her.

"And that is your final answer?"

Chessy looked up then, catching the full azure fire of his gaze. The force of it made her breath catch. "I—I am sorry to decline your offer," she said stiffly. "But I haven't the slightest shred of interest in what the gossips of the *ton* have to say about me."

Morland moved then, with speed and utter fury. He pulled her against his chest, his jaw clenched with anger. "But *I* care. I won't have your name dragged through the mud, Chessy. And I won't have mine dragged down with it. This time there's not only you to consider, but the duchess. She is in a way of being a sponsor to you, after presenting you at her ball. Haven't you any concern for *her*? The scandal would be devastating to her."

Chessy shivered. She hadn't realized.

Her eyes closed for a second. When they opened,

they were dark with regret. "Of course I care. But she'll weather the storm. She told me once that the *ton* lives in dread of her setdowns. Just—just tell her to disown me. Tell them I was a sneaking little adventuress who thought to use her to gain entrance to Society." She gave a bitter little laugh. "They'll believe it soon enough. People like nothing more than to believe the worst about each other."

Morland cursed fluently. "There are others to consider. Elspeth and Jeremy, for a start. They're bound to hear the gossip."

Chessy paled. She remembered Jeremy's all-too-sober face and worshipping eyes. Dear God, she did not want to cause them any further pain. Something told her they had known too much already.

"And what if you're carrying my child?" His voice was dark, harsh.

Chessy swayed in his arms.

"You didn't think of that, did you? By God, you don't think of anything but yourself!"

She could only stare, white-faced.

A child? A child with his sapphire eyes? With bronze hair that curled in rich, unruly tendrils just as his did?

She bit back a sob, shoving against his fingers. "No—it can't—"

Morland's jaw settled to a hard line. "I won't have a child of mine cast adrift upon the world, Chessy. I saw enough of that in Portugal. Believe me, I saw things that would—" He bit back his words and stiffened. "My child—*our* child—will have roots, security, and all the love that I can give. And he'll have a mother and a father who live together under one roof, by God!"

Chessy could only blink at the suppressed fury in his voice. Dear God, what if it were true? What if . . .

White-faced, she wrenched at his grip and managed to break free. Unconsciously, her hands fell, splayed over her stomach. No, it was impossible! Surely such a thing could not happen after only one night!

Morland gave a bitter laugh. "Don't count on it," he said flatly, reading her thoughts all too well. "More cunning minds than yours have been disappointed in such hopes. All it takes is once, Chessy. And I hope I needn't remind you that I gave you myself and my seed far more than once last night. And you took me, held me, everything that I had to give. Sweet Lord, time and again."

Chessy closed her eyes, helpless in a flood of bitter-sweet memories. Adrift in the recall of his hands upon her. The sound of her own voice, ragged and breathless in passion.

His words were torment, hammering through her head.

Gave you myself and my seed.

She clenched her slender hands, fighting the sweet heat of the memories.

Time and again. Deep. So damned deep.

But he deserved much more than a bloodless con-tract. And *she* would never settle for anything less than love in marriage. Her father had tried that, and what had he to show for it but a lifetime of sorrow?

No, she must not even consider it.

Somehow Chessy managed to raise her chin. Her face was tense, as brittle as purest porcelain bisque. "Then all the blame must fall to me. And the responsi-bility as well. That is the usual way of society, is it not? The woman is to bear the blame in such matters."

"It's not *my* way, damn it!"

She shivered, wondering how many other conversa-tions such as this he had had.

With the mother of those two charming and utterly defenseless children, perhaps?

"Listen to me, Chessy—"

But she didn't listen. She moved to the bellpull and tugged sharply. A suspiciously short time later, Swithin poked his head through the door.

"Yes, miss?"

"Lord Morland is just leaving." Her eyes were cold and clear as amethyst shards.

Morland went utterly still. "Don't do this, Chessy."

"See him out, if you please, Swithin."

"You make a grave mistake." Morland stood rigid.

The sun glittered off his hair, wreathing it in golden light.

It was a strange color, Chessy thought dimly. It reminded her of finest Chinese imperial satin. She stared at him, memorizing the flare of his eyes, the glint of his hair.

The hard set of his angular jaw.

Memories.

They would be all she had left.

Unless he was right . . .

Without a word Morland jerked on his kid gloves, then turned and reached to the chipped side table behind him.

Abruptly he thrust a bunch of flowers into Chessy's nerveless fingers.

"For you. With my compliments. In my—absorption—I forgot them. Enjoy them well. If you persist in this madness, you will have no place left to wear them, for no one will ever receive you. Even the duchess will be helpless to assist you."

Chessy did not move when the door slammed shut behind him. Only long seconds later did she slowly raise the flowers to her face, letting their petals soothe the hot tears that gleamed there.

Gardenias. Rich and soft and beautiful. They must have cost him a fortune.

The fool. The wretched, bloody fool . . .

Once again he had shattered her defenses.

Once again he had broken her heart into jagged little pieces.

Blindly Chessy hugged the soft, fragrant buds. Tears glittered on her cheeks as she raised her head and stared out at the weathered fence and the untidy back garden, seeing none of it.

All she heard was the sound of Morland's boots ringing through the front hall and the crash of the door as it slammed shut behind him.

All she saw were the harsh lines of his face as he took his farewell.

I gave you myself and my seed.

Her fingers tightened on the creamy petals. *All it takes is once.*

And Chessy found herself praying that it would be exactly so.

31

The door knocker began to pound barely five minutes after Morland's angry departure.

One look at Swithin's face told Chessy that the situation had only grown worse. "It's the Duchess of Cranford this time. She's sent a groom to say she has to see you."

Chessy caught a ragged breath. "I—I can't, Swithin."

"Don't look like the man'll be leaving fast neither."

At that moment the knocker began to bang anew. Muttering angrily, Swithin turned and stamped out into the hall. "If it's the earl again, I'll be standing aside, miss. Not so young as I used ter be, you know. And the fellow's liable to plant me a facer if . . ."

His voice trailed off as he trudged down the stairs.

Chessy waited, frozen. Morland's exquisite gardenias were clutched in her fingers. Swithin opened the door.

A male voice rose, clipped and imperious. "I would be pleased if Miss Cameron could find the time to receive me. It is a matter of some importance."

Chessy frowned. Abruptly she saw the face that went with that voice.

Surely not the Duke of Wellington? Not here?

Swiftly she straightened her dress and smoothed down her hair. But why—

Then her cheeks flushed with color as she recalled Lord Morland's warnings. Sweet heaven, the duke had seen—he knew all!

She barely had time to turn when she heard Swithin approaching. She couldn't possibly turn the duke away. It would be beyond anything rude.

She gave Swithin a tense nod, then moved into the salon and took a seat by the window.

The duke was forthright and decisive, in this as in all he did. He studied her face for a moment, then came directly to the point.

"He has come to you?"

Chessy did not pretend to misunderstand. "He has."

"And you turned him down?"

"I did."

"Heavens, but you are a very determined sort of female, Miss Cameron. Just yesterday I was saying to Mrs. Arbuthnot—but that's neither here nor there. You make a great mistake to refuse his offer, my dear. The two of you will deal well together, I am convinced of it. And frankly—under the circumstances—" He gave a little cough. "Well, I cannot see that you have very much choice."

Chessy's fingers settled tensely upon her lap. "I am afraid that there you are wrong, Your Grace. Quite wrong. I shall be gone very soon. And there are reasons—things that prevent me—"

He snorted. "All very good talk, but it won't do, you know. I saw you. My groom saw you. That means at least a dozen other people also saw you descending from Lord Morland's at a markedly indelicate hour of the morning. It just isn't done, you know! The word will be all over London by noon."

Chessy's face paled as the duke began to pace the sunlit room. "Don't know what's come over that damn fool Morland. Ever since the siege of Ciudad Rodrigo—

well, he's been simmering on the edge of an explosion. The best soldier I ever had, but always headstrong. And now *this*!"

"It was not *his* fault, I assure you."

"Humphh. The man's a bully and a cad."

"Not at all. He was—very nice."

"*Nice?* He is thoughtless and brash, entirely encroaching—"

Chessy's eyes took on a strange glitter. "On the contrary. His manners to me were and always have been nothing less than impeccable."

Wellington turned his head to conceal the tiny smile playing about his lips. "In that case I fail to see the problem, Miss Cameron. Marry the man! Marry him and make him happy! Then I may finally get some work out of him."

Chessy's hands twisted in desperation. "I—I cannot."

The duke's eyes narrowed. "Ah. Has it something to do with that bloody book, perhaps? I told him the infernal thing would be more trouble than it was worth."

Chessy stiffened. "Book?" she repeated softly.

"I suppose I might as well tell you, since you are familiar with the ways of the East. You see, Morland has promised to find a book as a gift for the Chinese emperor. A very special book." He coughed gruffly. "Some sort of—erotic manual."

Chessy clutched at the wooden arm of the chair. "*The Yellow Emperor's Guide to Secret Arts?*"

"That's the one. You've seen it?" Wellington's dark brow rose in surprise.

Chessy gave a mirthless laugh. "So I have. But not recently. And as it happens I'm looking for the same book. My father has been kidnapped, and it is the price of his ransom, you see."

As she spoke, her mind spun in tight little circles. *Tony knew about the book but he had not told her. Had he had plans of his own for the priceless object? Had he even planned to use her to find the book for him?*

Surely not!

But the suspicion, once risen, was not easy to escape.

Wellington's dark brows flew together. "James Cameron is being held captive? Dear Lord, when did this come about?"

Taking a deep breath, Chessy told him the whole story. Her voice was low and clear and steady. Only her white, locked fingers betrayed her inner turmoil.

When she had finished, Wellington gave a low curse. "Damn, but this does complicate matters. Won't do to have your father die for this infernal book Morland's hell-bent on finding. But it's the devil of a coil, Miss Cameron. I won't deny you that."

He turned abruptly. His startling blue eyes scoured her face. "You will not have him? Not under *any* circumstances?"

Chessy shook her head.

"What if your father's business could be swiftly resolved? Would that change your answer?"

Chessy waved her hands restlessly. "I cannot say—that is, it is impossible to hope—"

"You let me worry about the hoping part, my dear." The Duke of Wellington shot her a last, assessing look, then turned and strode to the door in that abrupt way of his. At the threshold he paused. "I bid you good day, Miss Cameron. I shall send you an answer soon. And until then"—he frowned, and the hardness of his face was more pronounced then ever—"do not leave your house unescorted. Not even for a moment. Not under *any* circumstances, do you hear me?"

"I—of course." Chessy decided not to enlighten the duke about her own singular skills of protection. It was her father's safety that she worried about, not her own. "I will do as you ask."

As long as it suits my plans, she amended silently.

"Very well. My compliments to you then."

He strode from the room, a warrior engaged on a new campaign. Chessy wondered what complex strategies he was calculating in that quite fertile brain of his.

Despite his every resolve, Morland did not go to his

study upon his return. Nor did he seek out Whitby and leave orders for a dozen pressing matters that he ought to have attended to.

Instead he climbed slowly up the broad winding staircase until he came to his bedroom.

At the open door he stopped.

For a long time he simply stood staring at the crisp white pillow. His hands tensed as he thought of blue-black hair scattered over white linen.

His arm was throbbing, but he paid no attention. His pain was of a different sort now.

He thought about all the times he had dreamed of Chessy right there in his bed. He thought of all the dark, bitter nights he'd told himself to give up, that such a thing could never be.

His hands clenched.

He tried not to think of other things then, other dreams he'd somehow held at bay for year after year. Dreams of a house filled with laughter, bright with flowers, and the sound of children's flying feet.

And he realized that Chessy had been in every one of those forbidden dreams, smiling, angry, adoring.

The mother of his children.

His nails dug into the wooden doorframe. God, it was too sweet to think of. She would never stay. And yet—was it right to think of trying to make her, if her heart was pulled to different climes?

He ran a hand through his bronze hair.

He wondered, then, if it had perhaps been in his mind all along to compromise her. To make it impossible for her to leave. He drew a long, unsteady breath, remembering that there might even now be a child, conceived in their night's recklessness.

And he wanted that. Dear God, how *much* he wanted that. A child with Chessy's violet eyes, with the delectable, unpredictable dimple nestled in the curve of her left cheek.

He cursed. No good letting one's mind charge on. All the wishing in the world would not make dreams like that one come true.

He heard a low cough behind him. "Yes, Whitby?"

"I beg your pardon, my lord, but"—the butler frowned—"there is a *person* below. A most singular person. He professes to have private business with you." The servant gave a sniff, as if to give his opinion of such pretensions.

"Person? What sort of person?"

"A young person—very young. And such clothing!" Whitby gave a delicate shudder. "All of the most disreputable sort. He darted in through the back entrance when Mrs. Harris was occupied and had the brass to demand to be taken up to see you."

Morland's eyes narrowed. "An urchin, is he? With a scar over his left eyebrow."

"Well, as it happens, yes. But—"

"Don't dawdle man, go show him in!" Morland turned and strode toward the stairway. "I'll see him in my study."

Shaking his head morosely, Whitby made his way to the servants' staircase, grumbling about the incomprehensible follies of the Quality with every reluctant step.

32

The boy was filthy. He was also sublimely unconscious of how out of place he was in the earl's exquisite study.

"So, guv. I come to report, like yer tol' me."

Morland motioned him to a chair, after a dubious look at the boy's battered hat and soot-stained trousers. "Would you care for something to eat? To drink?"

The boy shook his head. "Naw. Had my ration o' grog for the day already. And I reckon I'll be concluding my business, then shoving off." He waited, his young eyes very sharp on Morland's face.

"You'll be wanting your money first, I take it?"

"Bob is bob, guv." The boy's jaunty smile revealed a row of gleaming white teeth.

Without warning Morland tossed a small bag through the air. The boy caught it without so much as a blink.

"You have your talents, young man, I'll say that for you. And now for your part of the bargain?"

The boy peered into the cloth bag, made a rapid assessment of its golden contents, then stowed the hoard of coins deep in the pocket of his trousers.

"I like doing business wiff ye, guv. Knows just as

how to treat a business partner. Aye, naught but pounding dealing with ye." He brushed a black strand from his eyebrow and turned to Morland, his eyes glittering. "It were just like ye said, guv. There was three of them, dressed peculiar-like. Came up from the docks, though they made a great business of trying to hide it. Not that they could hide nothing from Barnaby Brown, mind ye. They was watching the lady's house. Took turns of it, one of them going back to the docks every six hours. To report, I reckon."

Morland's face grew grim. "Did you find the place they came from?"

The boy's eyes gleamed. "Didn't I just! Funny sort of ship and a bloody queer crew, I can tell ye. Didn't manage to get on board myself, o' course, since ye was wishful to keep everything all secret-like. Here—I brung ye a map I drawed o' the place. I watched it careful for near on two days. No one else came on or off neither. Just the men who come to report. Deuced queer, if ye ask me."

"You don't know how queer," Morland said softly. "What about the girl?"

"All right and tight, she is. Me and my boys is keeping our eyes on the place, just like ye said. That niffy-naffy servant of hers is a game one though. Twice he nearly caught me sniffing round the mews before I piked off. Only other one—excepting yerself—who went in was that soldier nob. The Duke of Wellyton." The boy's eyes widened with fervent admiration. "Coo, but he's a proper dasher, ain't he?"

Morland hid a smile. "So I am told." He studied the eager figure before him. "You've done well, Barnaby. I trust you have a safe place to stow that gold."

The boy smiled. "Don't I just! And ye remember me iffen ye need any other work done. Secret-like, ye know. Allers find me up Cheapside way. They knows how ter fetch me there."

Morland look as if he meant to say something more but sat back instead. "I shall keep that in mind. Until then you have my thanks. I am certain that I needn't remind you that none of this business is to become public knowledge."

"I should think bleeding not! A deal's a bleeding deal, guv!" The boy gave Morland an affronted look. "Damned if I go back on *my* word."

"I beg your pardon. It was foolish of me to suggest such a thing," Morland said affably.

The boy studied him for a moment, then broke into a sudden smile. "Don't reckon ye're much foolish, guv. Not a bit of it."

A crisp tap came at the study door. A moment later, Whitby's stiff features appeared. "I beg your pardon, my lord, but another missive has arrived." He shot a disapproving look at the sooty urchin lounging easily in a now-smudged wing chair. "Shall I show the, er— young man out?"

"The runner is from Whitehall?"

Whitby nodded.

"Very well. Tell him I shan't be above a moment. And—tell the children I'll be down directly, if you please."

With stiff reluctance, Whitby turned to convey his messages.

Morland's companion nodded appreciatively. "Busy place ye run here, guv. Reckon ye got affairs o' yer own to tend. So I'll just be pushing off. But first, I reckon I should be tellin' ye. Those queer sorts wasn't the only ones watchin' the house. There was another cove wiff the same idea. English-like, not foreign. Right clever bloke he was too. Thought ye'd want ter know, guv."

Abruptly Morland pushed to his feet. In one swift move he tossed another full bag of coins to the urchin, who caught it with a yelp of triumph. "No need for that, guv. Paid up all right and tight, we are!"

"But our business is not quite finished, Barnaby. I have a message for you. One that must not be committed to paper. Can you remember it? And harder still, can you *forget* it—absolutely and utterly—as soon as it is delivered? It is to that, er—flash cove you mentioned. The Duke of, ah, Wellyton."

The urchin broke into a jaunty smile that lit the

dirty curves of his face. "Can't I just! For a bag of shiners like that, I reckon I cud forget my own name! So speak on, guv. I'm all bleedin' ears! Coo, wait'l me blokes hear I was in the way of speaking wiff the Great Man himself!"

Chessy was just on the point of setting out for the Duchess of Cranford's, as summoned, when Swithin knocked at her door.

"Someone askin' fer you, miss. Out in the alley, he is. Young lad with dark sort of hair. Says as how he was sorry fer bothering you, but he had to see you before he went off."

Chessy placed her chipped silver brush back on her dresser. Her eyes met Swithin's in the mirror. "Before he went off?"

The servant shrugged. "Said he couldn't stomach things no more at Half Moon Street and was setting off for a life of adventure on the high road. But before he left, he was wishful to have a word with yourself."

Chessy frowned. "Was he a slender boy? With thick dark hair? About nine years old?"

Swithin scratched his chin. "Close enough, I reckon. But who—"

Jeremy. But what could have driven him to such a desperate and irrevocable course?

Chessy was already on her way to the stairs. "Never mind, Swithin. I'll talk to him myself."

The carriage stood in the narrow mews.

Chessy looked about for the boy Swithin had described but saw no one. Then she noticed that the carriage door was slightly ajar.

"Jeremy?" She pushed open the door and stared inside.

A shadowed figure was huddled against the far wall, swathed in something that looked like a cloak. No doubt to hide his face when he crept from his father's house, Chessy thought.

But it was the tricorn hat that made her breath catch.

"Jeremy! What are you doing here? You can't really mean to run away."

The figure only flinched and pulled his arms closer across his chest. The tricorn hat tilted lower over his face.

Chessy frowned, unable to see him clearly. "You can tell me, you know. I only mean to help you."

"*He* won't miss me," came a low, muffled voice.

Chessy thought he might have been crying. She climbed inside, searching for the words to begin. She could not possibly let the boy flee, of course. "Could you—would you like to tell me what happened?"

The draped figure in the shadows shook his head vehemently.

"Very well, but—"

Outside, the door clicked shut. Chessy turned in time to see a figure move away from the curtained window. Up front, the driver gave a shout and whipped up the team.

A moment later the carriage lurched into motion. And the door, when Chessy jerked at the latch, was locked tight.

33

Instinct slammed her into action.

She fell back against the wall and forced her body to relax, while she calculated the point of highest risk for her opponent. He was small, so it would be best to be low. At his knees, perhaps.

For by now she was certain he was *not* Jeremy, nor anyone who wished her well.

Most likely it was one of the same men who were holding her father. And now her only escape was the far door. She prayed it was not locked from the outside.

Chessy's fingers tensed. Outside, the team was gathering speed. It would have to be soon.

She eased closer to the huddled figure. She made her voice no more than irritated, the chiding tone one used to a child.

"What have you done, you silly boy? Running off will help nothing. Certainly not with me. I can hardly join you in your adventures." With every word she inched closer to the door. Only a little more, and she would be within reach. . . .

She glared at the cloaked figure. "Stop the carriage this instant! If you set me down now, I shan't tell Lord

301

Morland about this mad thing you've done. But soon I
shall have no choice. And then I cannot—"

She was still talking when she pushed to her feet
and slammed her shoulder against the door.

The whole frame shook beneath the force of the
impact. The glass pane rattled; the door latch rocked
up and down.

But the door did not open.

Wildly Chessy grabbed for the latch. At the same
moment the dark cloak was flung back to reveal bent
knees and dark boots. Polished boots of fine leather.
They slammed to the floor while a tall body emerged
from beneath a voluminous caped riding coat.

The tricorn fell to the floor.

"You!"

Azure eyes faced her in raw challenge. "Let go of
that latch, Chessy."

For answer, she shoved harder, wrenching the door
until it creaked in protest.

The team was at the gallop now, and the cobblestones rang out with the thunder of the wheels.

"Damn it, do you wish to be killed? Let go, I say!"

Hard hands bit into her shoulders and wrenched
her backward, but Chessy was too experienced at de-
fense to be taken easily. She drove her slippered foot
against his ankle and knifed down, struggling to release
the latch.

Morland growled a curse, his face going pale.

Chessy forced away a stab of remorse, tearing wildly
at the door latch.

Outside, the narrow streets flashed past in a blur.

And then the metal gave way beneath her fingers.
The next second, the door lurched open. Chessy caught
at the rim of the door as she sailed out of the carriage,
her feet jolting against the raised steps.

"As heaven is my witness—" Hard hands clenched
on her waist, trying to tug her back inside, but she
kicked wildly, clinging with raw desperation to the
opened door.

"Stop, Chessy!"

She barely heard. Her whole attention was on fighting free of the fingers trying to haul her back inside.

The carriage hit a bump and cast Chessy up into the air. Her fingers screamed with pain as she fought to hold on.

A wild cry broke out from the driver. "Carriage coming, m'lord!"

Only then did Chessy see the mail coach rocking madly as it careened toward them. Now only a narrow intersection separated them, barely large enough for the two vehicles to inch past without impact.

Chessy's face bled white. A scream clung in her throat as the huge coach churned up dust, racing ever closer.

"Chessy! Hold still, damn it!"

And then Tony was clinging to the door with her, his hands rough as they slid over her waist. The next minute, she was jerked from her precarious hold on the shaking door. The air whined past and dust burned into her face. Noise . . . fear . . . burning like acid in her throat.

With a brutal jolt she hit the floor. Strong arms jerked her back just as the door crashed wide open against the side of the carriage.

A moment later, the mail coach smoked past, sparks flying as the wheels cracked together.

Chessy went sheet-white as she saw the horrified passengers staring across at her, mere inches away.

And then the carriage thundered past. Only rows of neat houses and passersby filled the open door.

"Dear God . . ." A shudder ripped through her as she realized how close she'd come to being smashed against the passing coach.

Her eyes closed.

What a horrible way to die.

Her breath was ragged, her body like ice, when Tony twisted and caught her beneath him on the carriage floor.

"Are you mad?" he asked. "You might have been killed!"

She couldn't find an answer. His face blurred before

her until all she saw was the hard glitter of his eyes, the angry set to his jaw.

His hands dug into her shoulders. She felt him tense against her.

And then light and sound were blocked out as his lips met hers, angry and punishing.

"Bloody little fool," he growled. "Do you know just how close you came to dying out there?"

The words were hurled against her face, her cheeks, her eyes. "I could almost hear your screams as you fell beneath the wheels."

Chessy tried to fight the desperate urgency in his voice, the driving power of his hands, his lips. But the knowledge of his caring hit her like flame, left her week-kneed and hungry.

Driven by a desperation of her own.

"I didn't think—didn't realize—"

And then somehow her own hands were driving, urgent upon his shoulders. Tremors ran through her as she felt the heat of him, the angry need of him.

"When are you going to realize that you're not alone, that you don't have to fight every battle by yourself?"

The words were a dark, hot flow against her eyelids. She shivered as he moved down her face, and ran his tongue along the edge of her lips.

"Oh, God, don't. No more."

But he didn't seem to hear. His thighs were against hers, hard and taut as he buried his fingers in her tumbled hair. "What a fool I am. Do you see even now how I cannot fight my need for you? But what if I had lost you? What if we had lost *us*? And all for what? For a few angry scraps of pride and stubborn independence?"

He molded her lips beneath his. His voice caught in a groan.

"Marry me, Chessy. Bear my children. Let me make you blindly, savagely happy." The words poured over her, smooth and dark as the amethyst quilt upon his big bed.

"I swear I'll make you happy. You'll not regret a single second."

Blinding sweetness. Dark yearning. And worse of all, a yielding. It began vast and deep inside her and stretched away forever.

But Chessy knew she could not yield. Not when so much hung on her staying strong and stubborn and clever. Not when the Triads would kill him if she stayed. Maybe someday . . .

She closed her mind to the sweet seduction of hope, knowing it would only weaken her further.

"S-stop. I—I cannot—"

He pulled back. His eyes were hard with need and bitterness. "Damn it, Chessy, when are you going to start trusting me? And start trusting yourself?"

Her protests choked at her lips. Trust herself? What gave him the arrogance to think that—

In a blaze of awareness, she realized he was right. It was herself she did not trust. For the need in her was as fierce as in him, and she knew that once freed, she would never be able to tame it again. After only one night together he had torn her to pieces, knocked down all the defenses she had been ten years in the building.

Honesty warred with self-preservation—and lost. No, she could never trust him since she could not trust *herself* when he was nearby.

"I—I don't want to talk about it." She jerked blindly at his fingers, trying to push away from him.

But the floor was narrow, and her wrenching only served to drive her thighs against his. Her foot slammed against his knee.

His face went rigid. She felt him shudder.

"I'm—oh, Tony, I'm so sorry."

He pulled away from her, his eyes harsh. "There is no need to apologize, I assure you. If I am flawed, it is my fault, not yours."

His face was set in hard lines. He pushed away and sat back slowly against the far wall.

As if he needed to put the greatest possible distance between them.

Chessy felt cold, very cold. Her hand rose. "Tony, I didn't mean—"

But the distance was written on his face. He turned away. "Of course you did not. My deficiencies are hardly your concern. We need not speak of it again."

White-faced, Chessy watched a vast gulf stretch between them, saw him shut himself away behind that exquisite, polished exterior that blinded the rest of the world to his unhappiness.

But it did not blind her. For she knew those walls too well to mistake them in another.

Morland turned from the window then. His fingers were hard upon the small sill. "I shall ask you one last time, Miss Cameron. Will you do me the very great honor of becoming my wife?"

Chessy's eyes were huge pools of violet. She fought for courage. "I—I shall not."

Morland's fingers tightened on the curtain, shredding the light muslin. "I see. You make yourself eminently clear." And with that he turned away, stony-faced.

Tears burned Chessy's eyes. She found the flat decision in his voice unbearable. Surely *now* he would let her go . . .

Slowly she began to inch along the seat toward the carriage door.

Morland turned. A gun glinted in his fingers, chill in the light that slid through the shredded curtain. "I advise you not to, my dear. I shall shoot, I warn you. Better a shattered arm than for you to lie trampled on the highway. No matter what lies between us."

Chessy stared at the gleaming metal.

"Now get some sleep. We have some hours before daybreak."

Icy with fury and disdain, Chessy pulled her cloak around her. Sleep was the farthest thing from her mind.

And in spite of Tony's rigid silence, she knew that it was the same for him.

But Chessy did sleep. Somewhere near dawn, a jolt of

the carriage woke her. Her eyes flashed open, and she sat rigid, her heart hammering in the chill gray light.

She shivered as a gust of air swirled about her. Something rough brushed her cheek.

His cloak. She felt the stiffness of the collar. He must have tucked it around her in the night.

She smelled the faint scent of leather and citrus. The sweetness of brandy.

The scent made her body tighten.

No sound came from the far side of the carriage. The tall, dark figure sat with his tricorn slanted over his face, his long legs outstretched.

Chessy inched closer to the door. The Triad warning rang oddly through her mind.

Now. Get it done before he wakes.

She wrenched open the door and jumped.

34

The door crashed open. Dust and twigs slashed at Chessy's face. And then she felt the iron grip at her waist.

She cried out as she was wrenched savagely back inside and the door slammed shut behind her.

"I thought I made my wishes clear, hellion! No more acrobatics!"

"Let me g-go! My father—"

"Your father does not require your help. You are only complicating matters."

Chessy stared at Morland's lean, hard features, barely visible in the half-light. If only she could believe him! "What do you mean?" Her tone was accusing. "What have you found out?"

"Have you so little trust?"

"Tell me!"

"I have told you enough, woman! And you're to stay out of it. It's too bloody dangerous. You will just have to trust me in this."

"Trust *you*? After you kidnap me like the lowest London cutthroat?" She gave a bitter laugh. "I think not."

"You have no choice in the matter, Chessy. Now sit back and enjoy our ride. We should be nearing our destination very soon."

"Beast! Where are you taking me? I warn you, as soon as you put me down, I'll make a scene. I'll tell everyone what you've done! I'll make you rue the day you—"

From outside came the creaking of carriage wheels and the neigh of a team. The driver leaned down to shout into the window. "White Hart Inn, m'lord."

Chessy's glared at her impassive companion. "No, I don't trust you. and I'll never trust you again!"

Morland's face was unreadable. "A pity. For that is going to make our descent rather messy, I'm afraid." He moved closer. "And you are going into that inn with me, Chessy, my love. Willingly or unwillingly."

Without warning he hauled her against his chest. His mouth came down upon hers, open and hot. He tongued her lips apart in a long, slow slide and eased into the honeyed recess beyond.

Chessy shivered. And the next moment, to her infinite fury, she found herself touching and tasting back. His tongue. His lips.

"Ah, God, Cricket—" His hand went rigid on her back. With his other he spanned the aching peak of her breast.

She barely heard her own whimper of protest. Of desire.

"How do you do this to me, temptress? Make me forget everything and everyone while you're in my arms."

He moved again. Suddenly cloth gave way and flesh met taut flesh.

"T-Tony . . ." She was on fire. His fingers were hard, demanding. And somehow they were not hard enough. They made her want more.

"Chessy." Her name rolled dark and fierce from his throat.

Her hands slid to his neck. Shivering, she arched back in his arms, opening herself like a perfect white flower to the blinding force of his pleasure.

With a groan he buried his fingers in her hair and brought his head down.

His lips circled the rim of the pouting, crimson nipple. They nipped and tugged with tormenting skill. Chessy twisted her head and cried out in pleasure. And then—teeth. Hot, moist breath. The velvet slide of his restless, hungry tongue.

Until she felt fire uncoil through every inch of her body.

"You see—" His voice was ragged. "By God, even now you blind me, enslave me." He took the whole velvet curve of her, crimson peak and dusky nimbus. He smoothed her in heat and then left her gasping as he arched her even farther in his arms, skin to straining skin. His lips closed around her, suckling her fiercely.

"Give me more, Chessy. Give me the sound of your passion. Give me your sweet, ragged whimpers."

Dear God, she was close to yielding, to giving him all he asked. His hands slid deeper into her hair, cupping her head with fierce protectiveness.

With infinite need.

While his mouth drove her straight to paradise.

A dark paradise, rich with sound and a thousand lush textures. Hard lips. The jut of his chin. The hot slide of his fingers.

"Marry me, Chessy." His voice came raw and hoarse. "Now. Today."

Chessy stiffened. Dazed by desire, she could only stare at him.

"Yes. Just say yes."

"N-no."

"Damn it, don't be a fool!"

Reason and reality returned in a slow, chill flood. So this was his game. She caught back a sob. "I cannot marry you. I *will* not!"

With a little moan, she tore away—but not quite soon enough.

His eyes burning, he caught her up and slung her over his shoulder. With his boot he kicked open the coach door and descended the stairs that the groom had hastily let down.

Chessy began to twist and scream, her feet beating at thin air.

She pounded at his back.

Still his pace did not slow.

Wildly, she fought, her legs hammering as she struggled to break his grip on her straining bottom.

Morland tipped his tricorn hat at two wide-mouthed hostlers, who stared in amazement as he and his sputtering captive moved past.

"I'll murder you, Tony Morland! I'll stake you out and—"

"Promises, promises, my darling! And if you keep lurching about like that, you'll show even more of your shapely ankles to those hostlers than you already have."

Chessy bit back an oath, trying to tug her skirts back down on her legs.

The earl chuckled and winked at a staring groom. "Too much to drink, you know. The wench has never had a head for wine. But she will insist on drinking, no matter the aftereffects. And it makes her so very amorous that somehow I never can find the heart to deny her."

"I'll slit your throat!" Chessy hissed, as the groom gave her a speculative leer. "Oh, just you wait, you—you beast!"

She twisted and called out to a stunned lady in somber black kerseymere. "Help me! He's not my husband!"

Morland gave the matron a shrug. "Of course I'm not. The baggage is already married. Unfortunately, her husband, though rich, is advanced in age and not quite what she expected. Physically, you understand. So she comes to me to supply the things he cannot give her. Ah, but what is a gentleman to do when beseeched by such a baggage? Especially such a comely one?"

The matron sniffed and turned away, scandalized.

"Murder will be too good for you!" Chessy rasped. "It will be slow torture. I'll find a knife. No, I'll use my largest needle. Oh, I'll make you sorry for this, Tony Morland. Just see if I d-don't!"

Chessy was still sputtering when the earl carried her inside the elegant hostelry and hammered up the stairs to the private suite of rooms he had engaged on the second floor.

And there he threw her down onto a vast four-poster bed and kicked the door shut behind him.

He shrugged off his elegant jacket of chocolate brown velvet. His hands went to his cravat.

"What—what are you doing!"

"I am removing my cravat. And after that I'll remove my shirt, and my—"

"You wouldn't dare! I saved your life!"

"And I am going to save yours, Chessy. By marrying you. I have a cleric downstairs and a special license in my pocket. And you, my sweet, are not going to leave this room—this *bed*—until you consent to become my wife."

Chessy's face set in a mutinous frown. "I *won't*."

"Very well." The cravat came free and went flying. His hands fell to his breeches.

"I'll scream."

"Oh, yes. With passion."

"I'll kick! I'll—I'll bite you!"

"So you will." His eyes went smoky blue. "When I bury myself inside you. When I drive deep and take you with me to stunning pleasure. Just think about it, Chessy. About how good it will feel."

Mesmerized, she stared at his long fingers, his lean, powerful thighs.

And found herself unable to think of anything else.

But her face was hard with determination. "I—I can't. Don't ask it of me. You don't understand."

Morland's fingers stilled. "Why? You're not married already."

"No, of course not. But—"

"Then nothing else matters," he said harshly.

"You're wrong. You don't know—"

"Know what? What can be important enough to drive us apart?"

Chessy's face drained of its color.

"Well?"

She swallowed. Her fingers dug restless patterns in the feather quilt.

"Answer me, Chessy."

At that moment boots echoed along the corridor. The next moment, a tap came at the door. "Beg pardon, your lordship, but the cleric is growing restless. He wonders—that is, will you be wishing for the ceremony to begin soon?"

Morland smothered a curse and strode to the door. "Soon enough! Tell him that the, er—*bride* is at her toilette. She will not be much longer, however. Meanwhile, give him some of that claret you keep hidden in your cellar. The good bottles, this time. And don't water it. That should put the fellow in a better frame of mind."

Morland did not wait to hear the landlord's answer. Slamming the door, he resumed his argument with Chessy. "Now, stubborn one, tell me—"

The order died in his throat.

When he turned around the room was empty.

35

"**D**amn and blast!"

Had he been less irritable, Morland would have seen
the irony in *him*, rake confirmed, trying to force a
woman he had ruined into the protection of marriage.

But at that moment his leg was throbbing and his
shoulder was on fire, and he was furious at the way the
whole situation had backfired. Worse yet had been the
tormenting carriage ride with the occasional brush of
her hands, the soft slide of her thighs and hips.

All of which had evoked haunting memories of her
passion, so honest, when he had loved her through the
long night.

And he would have that passion again, Morland
swore. But only when she was his *wife*.

He gave the room a swift glance, then ran for the
window. Slamming up the pane, he bent out and surveyed the rooftops.

His face paled.

She was climbing along the gable above his head,
her skirts swept up in one hand. He started to cry out,
then bit back the words, afraid in her distraction she
might slip.

Smothering a curse, he wrenched off his boots and socks, then lunged over the sill after her.

His eyes narrowed against the gleaming sunlight. He saw her edging along the intersection of two deeply slanting roofs. Even then, burning with fear and fury, Morland marveled at her exquisite grace and sureness of step. He would have to be fast and silent.

He studied the adjoining roofs, looking for a rear approach that would hide him.

And then he froze.

On the roof beyond her, black against the setting sun, he saw a figure hiding behind a chimney.

He plunged forward in the same second that he shouted a warning: "Down, Chessy! Now!"

She swung her head, then jerked sharply, struggling to regain her balance. Only then did she look up and see the man crouched on the roof.

Golden sunlight flashed upon the barrel of a gun.

Morland lunged forward, his bare feet shredded by the sharp tiles. His eyes narrowed against the sun as he saw the gun rise and then slowly level.

Sweet God, there was no time.

He bent down and clawed a heavy tile free.

With a prayer on his lips he hurled it toward the figure beside the chimney.

A shot rang out, harsh against the *whoosh* of the soaring tile.

And then a shout of pain. The desperate scramble of arms and feet. But the fellow had not fallen. Somehow he had managed to push back to his feet and now was advancing on Chessy.

And this time, his pistol lost, he was holding a knife.

Morland scrambled along the crest of the adjoining roof, oblivious to the blood on his feet. With a shout of rage, he reached the crest, then plunged down.

But even as he watched, the man's foot struck an uneven tile. For a moment he went rigid, then began to claw at the air.

His struggle came too late, however. His body twisted and he lost his footing. The next second he went hurtling down over the edge of the roof and out of sight.

There were angry shouts from the inn's yard, and
then the wild neighing of horses. A woman screamed.

Morland heard none of it. All his attention was on
the slender figure at the crest of the roof, her hands
locked, her body rigid.

Her black hair whipped out around her as she stood
trembling, frozen with fear, unable to move.

"It's all right, my beauty. Just wait for me."

She turned wild eyes upon him. "T-Tony, help me.
I—I—can't"

"Hush, love. I'm almost there. Just a few more
steps."

He could see her face now. It was sheet-white
against the wild amethyst of her eyes. Morland realized
she was in shock.

"Oh, God, he tried to—he almost—" She swayed.
Almost against her will, her eyes slanted down in the
direction where the body had fallen.

"Don't look down, Chessy. Look at me," Morland
commanded. "Think about us. Think about—"

At that moment a loud shout burst from the stable
yard. "Go fetch the magistrate! And then that church-
fellow. This poor beggar's dead!"

Chessy shuddered. Her knees seemed to sway, then
lose their strength.

The next moment, she went plunging over the roof.

"Chessy!"

Without thought or the slightest hesitation Morland
threw himself down after her.

She was going to die. That was the only thought
shrieking through Chessy's mind as she smashed along
the jagged tiles, her skirts shredding farther with every
jolt.

Dear God, in a few seconds I am going to die.

But she didn't want to die. She wasn't nearly ready
to die.

The sky tilted, spinning around her in a blur of
turquoise. Wind whipped at her hair, lashing it across
her eyes as she careened wildly down the sloping roof.

"No!" She drove her fingers into the tiles, sobbing as they ripped free again and again.

And then, dimly, she heard the crashing from the opposite roof. Her eyes widened as she saw a tall shape hurtling down toward her.

"Tony!"

They had mere seconds of impact, his hard thighs rammed into hers, driving her sideways. His feet slammed hard against the lower corner of the roof. "Hold on!" he shouted.

Blindly Chessy twisted to her stomach. Her fingers found the lip of the gutter and clung tight.

And then her feet skittered free. She dangled over the stable yard.

She sobbed as she heard the crack of tiles upon the earth and Morland's raw curse.

A moment later, she heard the dull *thwack* of a large body striking the ground.

She twisted, straining to look down, but all she could see was black hair tossed about her eyes.

"Tony! Dear God, please, no!"

Tears burned her eyes, and her fingers screamed in pain where the metal rim of the gutter bit deep.

But no answering call came from beneath her.

Suddenly her will began to waver. The pain was too fierce, the effort too great now that he was—

A sob broke from her throat. How ironic that with all her skill and training it should end like this.

Two fingers tore free, and then her right hand. She cried out as her whole body pitched wildly, jerking from side to side.

And then she heard a low groan, followed by the scrape of stone on stone.

"Ch-Chessy?" Another groan, then a low curse. "Sweet Lord—hold on, my love."

"Tony?" She blinked as tears flooded her eyes, her cheeks.

"Here, Cricket. Hold on—just a little longer."

Her hand was white, fast growing numb. She caught back a sob as one more finger wrenched free. "I—I can't!"

"A second or two, my heart. And then—"

She heard the scrape of fabric and the creaking of wood.

"Done! Let go, Chessy."

Another finger ripped free. Chessy sobbed as pain cracked through her wrist and forearm. She had only a few more seconds until she fell. "Now? Tony, I can't see—"

"Do it now, my love. Trust me. Just—ahhhh—trust me."

Black hair covered her eyes, whipped up by the wind racing over the roof. She felt the metal gutter shudder and heave beneath her gripping fingers.

Trust me.

Her heart lurched. There was nothing but emptiness and death beneath her kicking feet.

Just trust me. . . .

With a wild cry she let go of the shaking gutter and dropped into space.

She heard Morland shout. The next second, her feet struck the ground with a bone-jarring crack. Pain exploded through her from rib to toe.

And then the ground began to move, tilting crazily before pooling into a soft heap.

Blinking, she looked around her. She caught back a watery sob. "A quilt?"

"It was the best I could do on short notice." His hard hands were around her; his fingers gripped her shoulders. "You fool, you little fool. I'm tempted to turn you over my knee and flay your sweet hide! To burn your bottom until you promise me you'll never do anything so hen-witted again."

Crying, hiccuping, Chessy closed her eyes and burrowed into that warmth. "He—he tried to k-kill me. He h-had a pistol. I couldn't—"

The fingers tightened. "Hush, Cricket. It's over now. Just rest."

Dimly Chessy felt a shudder rush through his chest and then the hot slide of tears upon her neck.

His tears.

She clung to him, afraid to let go, afraid that she'd

find that this was just another dream and any second she would be ripped away from him.

"I—I killed him. He is over there right now, isn't he? His—his body."

"He killed himself, Chessy. Don't talk rubbish."

"But—"

"No buts. And no more talk. I'm taking you inside. I'll tend to the body later."

She closed her eyes as she felt herself lifted up, crushed against his taut frame.

Tight as they were, she could not mistake the momentary tremor that shook him, the tensing of his thigh.

"Tony—you're hurt. Put me down! I can walk—"

"When pigs can fly!" he muttered grimly, stalking toward the inn's rear entrance, where a score of wide-eyed servants were thronged, whispering and pointing.

"Out of the way," he growled. Instantly the milling humanity parted like the biblical Red Sea, and Morland stalked up the White Hart's rickety rear steps.

Chessy felt him flinch and twisted her head downward.

"Your feet! Oh, Tony, you've—"

He swung her close and cut her off with a kiss, raw and hard and infinitely fierce.

Around them the onlookers giggled, then began to laugh.

A moment later, a ragged chorus of cheers broke forth.

Chessy barely heard, her world limited to the hard, hungry slide of Tony's mouth against hers.

Light flared behind her locked eyelids. The breath was jerked from her lungs. Heat, oh such heat . . .

Maybe you did die, little fool. Because this certainly feels like heaven.

A moment later, Morland pulled away. Chessy's cheeks flushed crimson beneath the unveiled sexual need that blazed in his eyes.

"East of forever, Cricket. And don't ever forget it. Because I'm never going to let you go again."

She heard shouts of encouragement, then wild clapping.

"Now, will you marry me, woman? Or am I going to have to save you from death yet another time?"

Her breath caught before the force of his unrelenting gaze. She wanted to yield. Oh, heaven, how she wanted to. If it weren't for the Triad threat. If it weren't for her father . . .

"I—I—"

"Done. As good as a yes!" Morland slanted a look at the surrounding crowd. "You heard it, didn't you? A yes—clear as sunlight on an August day."

Several women laughed. A brawny workman shouted a very lusty suggestion of how the earl might persuade her.

Smiling darkly, Morland stared down at Chessy. "Oh, I mean to. Just as soon as I can fetch her upstairs to bed." His fingers cupped her fiercely, protectively while his eyes made a host of hungry, erotic promises. Meanwhile there was no mistaking his savage need, the hot rise of his manhood against her hip.

Chessy licked lips that had gone suddenly dry. Her heart began to thump in a crazy, erratic staccato.

For she knew the same need now.

She shivered as the flame in his eyes blazed higher. She should have known she could never hide anything from this man.

But she had to try. "You don't—we c-can't—"

He wasn't fooled for a second by her sputtering denials.

"I do and we can. Oh yes, Cricket, we most certainly can." Without looking away, he raised his voice in command to the crowd. "Now will somebody go and fetch that bloody cleric before I have to chase the woman over another roof?"

36

This time when Morland put her down, Chessy found herself on a settee in the sitting room on the second floor. Not, as he had threatened, in the adjoining bedroom.

"Don't want to shock the cleric, do we?" Morland said gruffly as he bent to examine her ankle.

Chessy winced as he ran his fingers over the bone.

Only then did she look down and see that her whole foot was blue-black and swollen. Morland muttered something beneath his breath and yanked at the bell-pull.

Seconds later, the landlord appeared, all smiles. Chessy realized he must have been waiting at the upper landing. By the cheerfulness of his manner, she decided that all the furor had not cost him any business.

Quite the contrary, she suspected.

"What is your wish, my lord? Claret? A fine pair of hens my Elsie has been all day in the roasting? Or perhaps a pigeon pie?"

Morland cut into this happy recitation. "Clean gauze and a basin of water will do for now. But the cleric—is he still below?"

"Enjoying his second bottle of claret, my lord."

"Very good. See that his glass is kept refilled."

As soon as the landlord left, Morland came back to the settee where Chessy was lying. "Is it damnably painful?"

Chessy managed an unconcerned smile. "Oh, just a twinge or two. I'll be fine. But what about you? Your feet are—"

"My feet can wait. But I'm sorely tempted to blister your backside, hellion. What possessed you to bolt that way?" His eyes blazed down at her as he lifted her shredded skirts and gently slid his hands along her leg.

Chessy swallowed at that masterful sweep of callused skin. "I—I had to go."

"I can see I'm going to have to keep a close eye on you. Now hold still while I remove these ruined stockings. Then I'm going to wash your face and brush that wild hair. And then, my dear sweet idiot, I'm going to carry you downstairs and hold you in my arms while that overpaid cleric, who is by now almost certainly three sails to the wind, pronounces us man and wife in the eyes of man and God. And then, my sweet—then I am going to carry you up here to bed and—"

A pounding came at the door. "The cleric is ready, my lord. He requests that the bride hasten. He has other parishes to visit and another marriage to perform this day."

Morland muttered beneath his breath. "Ten minutes, landlord. And tell him he will be amply repaid."

Heavy footsteps echoed back down the stairs.

Morland's eyes darkened as he raised Chessy's skirt higher, following the soft curve of her calf.

"N-no, Tony. You—you mustn't—"

But with every inch he left her more breathless, more confused, until she couldn't seem to frame a complete sentence.

And the libertine knew it full well.

Smiling darkly, he ran his fingers along one lace-trimmed garter. Slowly he slid his finger beneath the edge.

"Tony—don't—I can't think when—"

"I'm delighted to hear it." His hand slid deeper.

"No, stop! You don't understand. It's not that I don't want—that you aren't—"

His fingers splayed, cupping the hot, sleek skin beneath her knitted stockings.

Chessy caught a ragged breath, determined to finish, to explain all the reasons why she couldn't marry him. But she did not want to hurt him. "That is—well, attractive. I don't deny that sometimes I find you—that you can be extremely—"

His thumbs edged out, leaving trails of fire along her naked flesh.

Upward, ever upward.

Chessy tried to repress a shiver—and failed. "Just like, well, *now*. I have to admit that your touch does not leave me—ah, unaffected."

"Indeed?" Morland's voice was as rough and rich as damask. "And what about this?"

His thumbs eased higher.

Chessy squeezed her eyes shut as pleasure burst hot and ripe as sun-warmed honey all through her body. "P-pleasant enough, I suppose. But there are so many things that separate us—and there is also my father to think of." *And the Triads.*

"I am attending to your father's situation. Trust me, Cricket. I should have some information for you very soon, in fact."

"Truly, Tony?"

"Surely you don't think I would lie about such a thing."

"No. No, I suppose not." She sighed. "It's just the uncertainty. The not knowing."

Morland bent closer. Chessy closed her eyes, feeling the warm sweep of his breath against her neck. But she was in control, she told herself. She was explaining to him at last. After this everything would be safe and settled and sane again.

His thumbs grazed the junction of her thighs.

Her eyes flew open. Control fled out the window. "W-what are you—" Her breath caught as his rough fingers played through her tangled black curls. "*D-doing?*" she finished in a croak.

"Just a little experiment, my sweet. But don't let me stop you. Pray continue with your explanation. I am finding it utterly, er, fascinating. . . ."

Chessy's heart was beating double-time and her blood seemed to have been invaded by a sky full of chain lightning. But she caught her breath and forced herself to continue. She *had* to convince him, after all.

"It's just that we—that you and I are so—"

Dense curls parted to reveal sleek, heated skin. "Yes? What is that we are, my sweet?"

"D-different." Chessy's voice was a squeak. "From two different worlds."

"We seem close enough now, my love."

Chessy caught back a moan as he inched deeper and found her love-slick secret. "But that's because—it doesn't mean—"

"What? What doesn't it mean?"

"Oh, anything permanent. Anything real and t-true. It's just—oh, stop. Tony. *Please.*"

"Not until you tell me what it does mean, my heart. Now, while I touch you." His voice had a rough edge that spoke of his own growing need. "While I watch you shiver."

Chessy trembled at the need in his voice, matched by the velvet tug of his searching fingers.

"It's like being hungry or th-thirsty too long. You envision it, dream about it. And then suddenly you can't stop thinking about it."

"Are you, Chessy? Hungry for me?" He was sheathed in her sweetness now, moving slow and potent inside her.

She wanted to deny it, but she couldn't. How could she, when all she could think of was the fire he was stirring to life inside her?

"Tell me."

Her body arched beneath him. "Y-yes, oh, God, yes."

He touched her with his lips then, drinking in the pulse that throbbed at her neck. "And now I'll tell you *why* you are, little fool. Because you love me. Though not nearly as much as I love you."

"No!" She tried to pull free, fighting waves of pleasure. Everything was going wrong, her explanations twisting back against her. "You don't understand."

"Then why do you shiver when I do this? Why does your breath catch when I touch you *here*?"

And she did shiver; her breath most certainly did catch when he coaxed a deeper entrance.

"God, you're beautiful. And I'll never, never let you go." He growled the words against her neck, her ear, her closed eyelids.

Chessy tried to swim up from the dark, rich abyss of pleasure where she'd fallen. "You m-must! I've brought you danger enough. One day you'll wake up and you'll be sorry you ever met me. And then you'll start hating me, hating *us*."

Tears pressed at her eyes. "I—I don't think I could bear that, Tony. So please, just l-let me go. Now, before you—before we—"

The hard fingers froze, sheathed deep inside her.

Hating her? What was the absurd creature talking about? Who had left her so scarred, so unsure of her own powers?

Morland's face turned grim. At least now he had a clear enemy to fight. Now he knew just *why* she had been fighting him at every turn. Not because of her father, but because of her own lack of confidence.

And he knew exactly what to do to prove how wrong she was.

But at that very moment of revelation, a pounding came at the door.

"I know you're in there, you young scoundrel, so open up! I'll have no more of your rakehell antics, I warn you!"

Morland blinked. It could not be. It was utterly *impossible*!

The doorframe shook. A hard object cracked against the knob. "Open up, I say! Otherwise I'll have the landlord up to force the door down. Do you hear me, Tony Morland?"

Chessy's face went sheet-white. "Oh, no—it isn't—"

Morland planted a hard kiss against her cheek. "We aren't finished, hellion. Not *nearly* finished, I warn you." His eyes blazed. He watched her face while he eased from her sweet, sheathing softness. "Beautiful," he whispered.

A muscle flashed at his jaw as he pushed to his feet. "I'll murder her. I'll absolutely murder her."

"No, Tony. It's my fault. Let me g-go!"

"Never!" Quickly he tugged her stockings up, then smoothed her skirts, trying to restore her to some semblance of respectability.

He had not yet finished when the door shook, then exploded open with a crash.

The Duchess of Cranford stood on the threshold, cane in hand, a liveried groom standing impassively beside her.

"Just as I thought. Whitby told me what you were up to and I had the carriage followed. Release the gel this instant, you cad! Have you no shred, no ounce of decency left?" She stared down at Morland's hand, which was still curved over Chessy's ankle. "Let the gel go, I say. She's been through enough!"

Chessy bit her lip, feeling as if she'd been plunged into a nightmare. "Oh, no, please—it's not his fault. He was only trying to—"

"I know perfectly well what the rogue was trying to do, my dear. And believe me, I mean to see that he doesn't get away with it. Not while you are under *my* protection." The duchess glared at Morland. "Release her."

Morland's body went rigid with anger. "You presume too much."

The duchess's eyes flashed. "On the contrary, jack-anapes. It is you who—"

"Stop!" Chessy pushed to her feet, wincing as her weight fell onto her throbbing ankle. "Oh, please, I cannot bear to see you fighting this way."

She swayed, her face very pale. "Not over me," she whispered.

Morland's face set in hard lines as he pulled her into

his arms. "See what you've done. She shouldn't even be up, not with that ankle as it is. It's bloody well probably broken." He glared at the duchess. "Are you satisfied now?"

The old woman's hands clenched and unclenched upon her silver-handled cane. "Oh, Chessy—what have I done?"

Chessy tried vainly to scrub the silver tears from her cheeks. "You did nothing, Your Grace. It was I—it was all my fault that—"

Morland's hands tensed on her waist. "Hush, Cricket." He turned and glowered at the duchess. "I give you notice, Your Grace. There is a bleary-eyed cleric downstairs who is waiting to hear our vows. In ten minutes this woman will be my wife, and not anything or anyone is going to stop that ceremony from taking place."

The old woman seemed to shudder. Then her shoulders rose, decisive as ever. "Over my dead body, Tony Morland. She deserves more than a makeshift ceremony in a hole-in-the-wall hostelry in the middle of nowhere."

Behind her came an angry protest. "The White Hart? A hole the wall? I must object—"

The duchess cut off the landlord with a sharp shake of her cane. "The gel deserves a lavish wedding at St. James's, with all her friends and family about her. She should be dressed in white satin and carrying lots of fresh gardenias." Her gnarled fingers shook. "Not like this, you fool. Why, she's wearing shredded stockings and a dusty gown that looks like—" She snorted, unable to find words harsh enough.

"That looks like she had fallen from the roof?" Morland's voice was low and hoarse. "I am desolate to tell you that that is precisely what she *has* done. After nearly dying at the hand of an assassin. But I aim to see that she never faces such danger again. And I shall start by making the hellion my wife!"

The duchess's face took on an arrested look. "Assassin? But how—why—"

"I shall explain it all later after I've looked at the

body and spoken with the magistrate. Right now, I have a wedding to attend." His face went very hard. "Do you mean to stand at our side and give us your blessing? If not, then I warn you that you will not be welcome, neither here nor at Sevenoaks."

Chessy tried to pull away from him. "No, please. Stop! No more fighting—"

"I'll have your answer now, Your Grace."

The duchess's shoulders suddenly went slack, leaving her looking old and very frail. "I—I never knew. And that body out in the stable yard?"

Morland scowled when he felt Chessy stiffen in his arms. "Let us just say that the villain won't be bothering Miss Cameron. Not ever again."

The duchess seemed to shiver. Without a word the groom reached out to steady her.

But she raised her chin and pushed his hand away. "I—I am afraid I have been a great fool. But I only meant to help, you see. And I was so afraid that—"

Tony stared at her, his face stony. "Will you or won't you?"

The duchess rose to her full five feet of fragile, imperious womanhood. "Of course I shall! What do you take me for, a fool?"

Morland's tense grip on Chessy's waist loosened slightly. His eyes took on a dark gleam.

The polished cane shook at him. "Don't say it, you rascal. Don't even *think* it!"

"I wouldn't dream of it," the earl said smoothly. "And now, if you don't mind, I suggest we go. That cleric won't wait forever."

The duchess frowned, for the first time taking note of the earl's bare and very bloodstained feet. "But— good God, boy, what have you been doing—crawling about over broken glass? Just what has been going on here?"

Chessy stared up at Tony. Her eyes were very bright, and her face was swept with color. At that moment her husband-to-be looked down at her, and his face took on an infinite softness. "You wouldn't believe it if I told you. What do you think, my heart?"

Chessy couldn't speak, robbed of breath by the dark tenderness that swept his face. "I suspect not. I don't even believe it, and I was there." She bit her lip. "Are you sure, Tony? Truly sure? There must be so many others who would suit you better. And I know nothing about sewing or sketching or presiding over a dinner table."

"I would have it no other way, absurd creature."

"But—the Triads. They've threatened to kill you if I see you again!"

Tony's eyes darkened as another piece of the puzzle slid into place "Did they now? Well, you can forget about the Triads. They'll soon be where they can't harm anyone. So now all you need to think about is getting married, my love. After that we'll spend our time digging up Roman ruins and tramping across the Pennines. We'll hike Hadrian's Wall and sail the Aegean in summer. What need have I of a woman who sews or sketches or presides over a dinner table, when I have you—you, who preside over my heart?"

Chessy bit back a watery laugh. "You are mad. You could have so very much better than I. But if you are certain, truly certain, then truly I would like it very much if you—if we—"

She flushed a glorious crimson, unable to finish.

Her face burrowed into the crook of his arm.

"No stopping now, my beauty. Say the words." Morland's voice lowered to a dark plea. "Please, Chessy. Tell me. Just once."

She raised beautiful, tear-streaked cheeks and swallowed. Her chin rose with determination. "I would be most honored to become your wife, my l-lord. Though why you should want to—"

Morland groaned and cut off her arguments with a kiss upon lips that trembled, then opened sleekly to him.

His hand rose to cradle her neck, curtained in a mass of blue-black curls. "Why? It's very simple, you know. I love you, Cricket. I suppose I always have. Ever since I first saw you, ever since you swam naked in the tropical sea beneath a moon just made to drive lovers crazy."

A loud snort came from the doorway. "Well, are you going to get married or did I come all this way for nothing?" The duchess's voice was suspiciously throaty. She made a furtive swipe at her cheek with a white handkerchief that appeared from the groom beside her as if by magic.

Morland looked up and gave her a brilliant smile. "The same question I've been asking for an hour now. Shall you precede us?"

But before they could turn, the landlord came puffing up the stairs. His hands twisted in his apron as he shook his head apologetically. "Couldn't keep him, your lordship. Dashed if I didn't try. And now if three bottles of my best claret aren't wasted too!"

"What are you saying, man? Speak up."

"The cleric. Said I was to thank you for the claret, but he couldn't wait all day for you two to be making up your minds. That's what I've been trying to tell you—he left fifteen minutes ago."

37

"**D**amn and blast!"

"I couldn't have put it better myself," the Duchess of Cranford snapped. Abruptly she rounded on the apologetic publican. "Which way did he go?"

"Took the stage to Chelmsford. Your Grace," he added deferentially.

'You have the special license with you, Tony?"

Morland nodded grimly.

"In that case, I have a better suggestion to make. An old friend of mine holds the living in Ipswich. He is a gentleman of great warmth, although he is not much in the world. You would like him, Miss Cameron. It would be a pleasure to summon him to Sevenoaks. . . ." She let the suggestion trail away, while she watched Morland's face for signs of displeasure.

The earl looked down at his bride-to-be. "Well? Is she right? Ought I to let you be married in white satin and pearls, with embroidered slippers on your feet instead of torn stockings?"

"If you would not dislike it too much . . ."

Smiling, Morland looked up at the duchess. "Send your message then, Your Grace. But it must be soon."

"Ah, the rare impatience of youth," the white-haired woman said, turning to whisper a word to her groom, who instantly set off down the stairs. "And now, I wonder if I might find a seat in this ramshackle place. I have been traveling since daybreak, and I am ever so—"

She was cut off by the hammer of feet. A moment later, a small figure with guinea-gold braids burst through the doorway.

"We waited to fifteen minutes past the hour, just as you asked, Your Grace. Are you ready to—" Cornflower-blue eyes turned upon Chessy and the earl. "Oh! There you are. Hullo! Je'emy said that you were—"

Her brother came to stand beside her. "Not now, Elspeth."

"But you did! You said that the two of them were—"

"*Not now.*"

Chessy stiffened as the children studied her curiously.

"Why is our Tony carrying you that way?"

She felt a sharp pain strike her chest. "Because— that is—" How was she to break the news to these, his children?

"Because, my nosy little miss, Miss Cameron has hurt her ankle escaping from a very bad man, and she cannot walk on it. Luckily, she has *me* to carry her around."

Elspeth's brow furrowed with concentration. "Everywhere? Oh, surely not to—"

Her brother dug his elbow into her side. "Cut line, Elspeth."

"But—"

"Let Uncle Tony alone, imp. We've plagued him enough in the last two days."

Chessy's heart did a queer little dance in her chest. She blinked, unable to believe what she had just heard. "*Uncle?*"

Tony watched a wave of crimson inch across her cheeks. "Yes, uncle." His sapphire eyes narrowed. "As in brother's children. But—no, don't tell me you thought—" His fingers tensed at her waist. "Unforgivably foolish, my dear. And inexcusable of you to have carried the secret rather than task me with it outright."

Chessy gave him a rather unsteady smile. "You're quite right, of course. I know that now."

"But Uncle Tony, what did you do to your feet?" Jeremy's voice grew rather shrill. "You—you're bleeding!"

Morland sighed. It was obvious that he was not going to be given any time alone with his bride-to-be. Nor was he going to be allowed to have his ceremony this day. So he supposed he would have to content himself with holding her beside him on that rather lamentable excuse for a settee.

"It is rather a long story, Jeremy."

The children darted to the settee and squirmed down side by side. Elbows to knees, they stared up at him, a vision of eagerness. "Oh, we have plenty of time, don't we, Your Grace?"

Morland eyed the spindly side chair sourly, then moved to a rather faded but quite generous wing chair. Still holding Chessy against him, he slid down into the seat.

"Really, Tony," the duchess chided.

"You've denied me my wedding," he said darkly. "But you're not going to deny me this."

Chessy began to squirm, uncomfortable in the scrutiny of three sets of interested eyes.

"Sit still," Morland said darkly.

Chessy's breath caught as she felt the telltale hardness at her hip. Her eyes flashed to the earl's face.

"Exactly."

Another flood of crimson washed over her cheeks.

Morland's eyes turned smoky, promising her that he meant to do something about that need as soon as possible. But not, it appeared, as soon as he would like.

"Tell us, Uncle Tony. Tell us what happened!"

"Very well, you pair of intractable, incorrigible, encroaching—"

"What's *in-incorrigible* mean?" Elspeth demanded.

"Brats," her brother translated, with a rueful smile.

"I am *not*! I always curtsy to my elders. And Mrs. Harris says—"

Morland sighed and shook his head. Chessy began to laugh softly. Even the duchess developed a rather marked gleam in her eyes.

The children were still arguing fifteen minutes later when the landlord came up to serve them tea and his wife's very best walnut cakes, fresh from the oven.

On the tray were the inn's finest silver and a bottle of the cellar's best brandy.

The White Hart's owner might be living in a backwater, but the man knew momentous events when he saw them.

"**D**id not!"

"Did too!"

"Did *not*!"

"Did—"

"*Enough!*"

Instantly two pairs of azure eyes, so like Tony's own, slanted up, contrite. Tea over, walnut cakes consumed down to the last crumb, the children had also digested a rather toned-down version of Chessy's near-escape.

Soon after that they had begun to argue over whose idea it had been to approach the Duchess of Cranford when their uncle had so precipitously disappeared. But the duchess had already had suspicions of her own.

"Since you have now assured yourself that I and Miss Cameron are safe, I believe you should find your governess and—"

"You mean Miss Twitchett?"

"That's right, Miss Twitchett. She will see to it that—"

"Oh, her. *She's* gone," Elspeth said blithely. "The duchess let her go."

"Lord, I forgot about that." Morland looked at the imperious old woman, his eyes promising vengeance. "In that case, perhaps *she* would like to take you downstairs and see to it that your faces are washed, your hair is combed, and those vastly grubby fingers are cleaned before we leave here."

The duchess sniffed and came to her feet. "Come along, children. I have my companion with me, and I daresay we can find something to occupy you in this quaint place."

"I have it!" Elspeth seized her hand companionably. "The landlord told us there was frogs in the pond."

"Were," the old woman corrected absently.

"Were? Did you see them too? Oh, capital! Jeremy promised he'd fetch one for me. Maybe he would trap one for you too. But perhaps you'd like to do that yourself."

The duchess shot Morland an entreating look, but the earl shook his head, smiling hugely. "You got yourself into this, Your Grace. And I'm going to leave you to get yourself out of it again, just as cleverly. Companion or not."

Her chin rose. "Come, children. It is perfectly clear that we are not wanted here."

"If you don't mind, Your Grace, could you make mine a big one, please? Big and brown. Without tooooo many of those horrid warts . . ."

The duchess gave a delicate shiver as Elspeth pulled her happily from the room.

Silence reigned in their wake.

Chessy bit at her lip, trying to suppress a giggle. "You shouldn't have done that, Tony. Perhaps I ought to go after them and—"

"You'll do nothing of the kind, hellion. You heard her say that she has her companion along to help her. So it's right here that you'll stay—meek and submissive for once—while I wrap that ankle." He glanced down at his own feet and torn breeches and gave a sour look. "Thank heaven none of my acquaintances are likely to see me here. Otherwise, I don't think I should ever live this day down."

"I wish they *could* see you. For you were wonderful there on the roof, absolutely *heroic*." Her eyes gleamed, as she repeated their old vow softly. " 'My forever friend. My heart and my bravest warrior, against all foes.' Oh, Tony, you saved my life. I froze up there, utterly froze. That's *never* happened to me before."

Suddenly all the grisly events of the day came back to haunt her. "And he would have—he meant to—" She shuddered.

"Hush. It's all over. You were in shock. But you're safe now."

"How can I ever repay you?"

Morland's eyes darkened. "Oh, I fancy I shall be able to think of a thing or two. And for a start—"

Once more the landlord's bulky frame could be heard pounding up the stairs.

Morland raised his eyes skyward. "Are we *never* to be left in peace?"

A moment later a nervous tap came at the door.

"Enter," Morland said darkly.

The publican's face was sweat-speckled and red with exertion. "Begging pardon, your lordship, but there's a man below as is wishful of speaking with your lordship. Well, *wishful* ain't perhaps the right word, but—"

"Send him away," came the ruthless reply.

"But—that is, he's not likely to—"

"Unless"—Morland's face brightened—"can it be our errant cleric?"

"No, but—"

"Then off with the fellow! And off with *you* too. Right now!"

The sweating landlord shook his head, then left the room, muttering all the while.

"Interfering lot, these Essex types. I knew there was a reason I never stopped here on the way to Sevenoaks. I must remember to avoid the place in future. Now, where were we?"

"*We* were busy being inexcusably rude and unforgivably ruthless."

"Nonsense, my dear. A little rudeness is expected of the nobility. Had I shown the man any courtesy, he would have collapsed from the sheer shock of it."

Chessy struggled to pull from his lap. "You are

without a doubt the most conceited, the most discourteous—"

Morland pulled her back against him and planted a decisive kiss on her neck.

"—the most arrogant—"

His next sally was an assault against her earlobe.

"—the m-most, the very most—oh, Tony!"

He teased her sensitive skin with tongue and teeth, making her breath came low and ragged. "Wretched man! How do you always succeed in making me feel this way?"

"What way?" came the midnight question, murmured against hungry, flushed skin.

"So—so breathless. So . . . reckless."

Morland gave a low laugh. "It's very simple, my love. I'm just making you feel the same way I do. Fair is fair, after all. Even Confucius said something to the effect that—"

But he got no further. The next moment, the door crashed open to reveal a tall man in a battered felt hat and a voluminous, dust-stained greatcoat. Rage was written in every rigid line of his body.

"Let her go."

Morland blinked but did not move.

"Now, you fool!"

Chessy felt Morland's body stiffen. "I don't believe I care for your tone, fellow. Nor for your form of address." His voice was soft, deceptively calm.

But any of his friends could have said how dangerous it was. "And I very much suggest that you go back out the way you came in. Otherwise . . ." He let the word linger, soft and threatening.

"Otherwise *what?* I don't give a damn for what you think of me or my tone. Stand away from her, you bastard!"

Morland's eyes narrowed. Certain oaths could not be ignored.

Slowly he slid Chessy from his lap onto the wide arm of the chair. "Indeed. Perhaps you would care to—discuss . . . this outside. Man to man."

"Happily."

Chessy gripped Morland's shoulder. "Don't, Tony. You mustn't—" She looked across the room. What was it about the man that caught at her? "Who—who are you?"

A low, almost hoarse laugh.

Tony pushed to his feet. "Forget it, Chessy. Don't concern yourself. The stable yard will do well enough for our brief business. I doubt that the fellow fights as well as he hurls insults."

"Well enough to toss the likes of you."

Morland's hands curled to fists. "Lead on then."

Chessy caught at his hand. "No—I forbid it! Your feet are still raw, and your arm is bleeding. This is madness!"

"Five minutes will be enough to dispose of this arrogant fellow." Morland said harshly.

"But your—" Chessy hesitated, uncertain about whether to mention his weak knee.

He turned, his face suddenly expressionless. He was waiting, she knew, to hear what she would say next.

Chessy went totally still, feeling a chill go down her spine. She realized that she was perched on the edge of a perilous abyss.

What she said next would be terribly important. One mistake, one slip, and she would lose him.

"—your shoulder," she finished breathlessly. "It is only beginning to heal, after all. And considering that I invested a great deal of effort in seeing that you did not die, I take your cavalier attitude as a personal insult."

She saw the earl relax fractionally. "My shoulder will be no obstacle, I assure you."

"Oh, you are impossible! Totally arrogant, completely foolish. In short, exactly what I would expect in a male."

Morland's bronze brow rose. "Hardly surprising," he said dryly. "I *am* male, after all."

"Well, you needn't act like it all the time! Nor go about blustering like—like—"

"Like an ill-tempered water buffalo?" the man in the doorway suggested. "Or a sulky schoolboy?"

Chessy stiffened. There it was again, something

about the voice, with its faint edge of bitter humor. "What is it to you?"

Morland saw her frown, saw the sudden stiffening of her shoulders. "I am forced to second her question. What business is it of yours?"

"What business? Everything, I should think." The tall man tugged at his dusty greatcoat and flung it from his shoulders. "Because, you damned importunate rake, *I* am her *father!*"

38

As he spoke, the traveler tugged off his battered hat, revealing a quantity of shaggy silver and black hair. He crossed his arms before his chest, glaring at Morland. "And *you* were to take care of her. To protect her from harm. Bah! Instead you've been seducing her! Taking ruthless advantage of her vulnerability."

But he was interrupted in his diatribe. "*Father? Is it really you?*" With a wild cry Chessy wobbled to her feet, wincing when she let go of the armchair.

"Chessy, don't!" Morland reached out for her.

But it was too late. She swayed, then began to slip sideways.

Morland caught her just before she struck the arm of the chair. Holding her tightly, he glared at a now-stupefied James Cameron. "Haven't you anything better to do than destroy your daughter's life, Cameron? Don't you have some dirt to paw at in the name of scientific advancement? Some pompous merchant to fawn over in a bid for financing some new and incredible venture? Sweet God, man, can't you see she's in pain?"

The older man's wild eyebrows knitted in a frown.

340

"Chessy, my girl—" He looked at Morland. "Exactly what's been going on here?"

"It's about time you took some interest in your daughter's welfare! Fine sort of father you are, traipsing off and leaving her to manage everything, then expecting her to rescue you from your own folly when—"

"Enough, man! I'm just itching to put a bullet through someone right now, and it might as well be you."

"Just try it!"

"Fine! The stable yard, it is. After you."

Chessy wavered between tears of joy and irritation. "Stop it, you two! You're—you're worse than those two children!"

"What two children?" her father demanded. "Don't tell me the bounder is trying to foist his byblows off on you. Exactly what I'd expect of such a scoundrel! By heaven, Tony, I'll teach you to—"

He pulled out a pistol and leveled it at Morland's chest. "Put her down and step aside, rogue. Then prepare to meet your Maker."

"Father, don't!"

"Now, you cur!"

Morland set Chessy down in a nearby side chair and crossed his arms over his chest. "Go ahead and shoot."

"No!" Chessy managed to wobble toward her father, tears gleaming on her cheeks. "Stop this idiocy!" Wildly she reached out and seized his free arm.

Cameron blinked and then looked down. He seemed to shudder when he saw the tears glinting on her face. "Chessy, girl," he said softly, raggedly. "What have I done? You—you love him?"

"Vastly. Deliriously."

The next second, Cameron thrust his pistol into his pocket and caught her up in a fierce embrace. "I didn't know. I thought he was forcing you to—"

"Of course you didn't know. But you're really all right? They didn't hurt you?"

"Not a scrape," Cameron lied smoothly.

"But how did you manage to escape? It *was* the Triads, wasn't it?"

"Later," he said gruffly. "I'm far more interested in what has been happening to you."

"It's rather—" She shot a look at the grim-faced earl. "Well, it's rather a long story. And I think you both could do with some tea before we embark on it."

At that moment scuffling came from the hallway. Two small figures poked their heads through the doorway.

"Oh, look, Je'emy. She's kissing *him* now. I thought you said—"

"Hush, Elspeth."

"Won't! You said she was going to marry our uncle Tony!"

"Uncle Tony?" James Cameron echoed in surprise. "Marry my Chessy?" He looked across at the earl. Suddenly his craggy features creased in a smile. "Well, why didn't you just say so, blackguard? All this time I've been thinking you had something a great deal more irregular in mind!"

"Because you didn't give us time to say anything," Chessy said, with a watery chuckle.

"Jumped the gun, did I?" He gave Chessy a rueful smile.

"You always do," his daughter said softly. Lovingly.

"Ah, girl, you know me too well." He studied the earl, who was still standing rigid across the room. "Well, don't hang back there! Come here, my boy. Come here and shake my bloody hand! Not that I deserve it, fool that I've been. But you've known me long enough to know I've a temper second to none." He looked down at the two wide-eyed figures in the doorway. "Your niece and nephew, are they?"

"My wards. They are my brother's children," Morland said, unbending slightly.

"Look like a smart enough pair. Ever seen an old English coin, young fellow? A gold *solidus* of Magnus Maximus, the great usurper who wrested England from Rome's control and then attacked the heart of the empire itself. Pure gold they are and very beautiful, with winged Victory blazing in the background. And what about you, young miss? Ever pulled a flint arrowhead from the dirt, dropped straight from the hand of a hunter ten thousand years dead?"

"*Nooooooo*," the children whispered as one, totally mesmerized.

"Indeed? Then tell your uncle he's been seriously neglecting your education."

The two were just working up their courage to set upon this vastly curious man with the wild silver-black hair when the duchess appeared. "So there you two are! What have you done with the frog I captured for you, Elspeth?"

"You?" Morland couldn't hold back a startled laugh. "A frog. Not one with lots of those ugly brown warts, I hope?"

"Just so. But what business it is of *yours*, I'm sure I couldn't say!" the duchess said crisply.

Chessy's father nodded appreciatively. "That's telling him."

"And who, may I ask, are *you*?"

"James Edward Harris Cameron." He swept his battered hat low. "At your service."

The duchess went very still. "Cameron? You mean—" She looked at Chessy for confirmation.

"My father. He managed to escape. Heaven knows how he found us here."

"When I couldn't find you at Dorrington Street, Chessy, I went to see Tony. That man Whitby told me how to find you here."

"I'm beginning to wish he hadn't," Morland muttered. And then his eyes began to gleam. "You truly are unharmed? Did you get a look at any of them?"

"Not now, my boy. Not now." Chessy's father frowned. "I'll tell you all about it later. Chessy needs to rest now."

"That's the first *sensible* thing you've said."

"Will you two *please* stop fighting?" Chessy swayed, and Elspeth ran to her side and caught her arm. Chessy clasped the girl close and glared at Morland and her father. "When are you going to start acting your age?"

"Never, I should hope," her father muttered.

"That's the truth of it," Morland growled. "And you

never *have*. All your life you've run from responsibility, leaving everything up to Chessy." Morland glared at Cameron. "But I mean to see that all change. I'm going to make her safe from you and your—"

Chessy sighed. As the two continued to argue, she turned and looked down at a wide-eyed Elspeth. She shrugged. "Men!"

After a moment Elspeth tossed her shoulders in a perfect imitation, then sighed grandly. "Men!"

Chessy stood at the window, watching a village boy herd his woolly charges through a lane gaudy with bluebells. She smiled, feeling a warmth and sense of belonging that she had never experienced before.

So this was the England she had heard others talk about with such nostalgia and joy. Seeing it now, all green hills and luminous mist, Chessy could understand their pain at being so far away from its beauty.

Across the room her father rambled on, describing a particularly perilous adventure in the wilds of Baluchistan, where warring nomads had nearly beheaded him. Before him the children sat wide-eyed, mute with awe.

Slender fingers patted her shoulder. "Thinking of Macao, my dear?"

Chessy looked up, smiling to see the duchess. She pointed toward the window. "I'm thinking of this, actually. It's all so . . . beautiful."

"You're not homesick, I hope?"

Chessy shook her head. "And I feel almost ungrateful for that. After all, I barely know anything about England, and yet . . ." She shook her head. "Somehow I feel entirely at home here."

"Perhaps that sense of comfort has something to do with Tony Morland."

Chessy's smile widened. "I expect it does." For a moment a shadow crossed her face. "If only . . ."

"If only what, my dear girl?"

Chessy tugged at the lace trim on her bodice.

"Go on. You can tell me."

"It's just that—that I know he's giving up so much. There must be other women much more the thing for him. And I can bring him neither wealth nor title."

"Nonsense." The duchess squeezed her shoulder. "Have you ever stopped to think that you might be bringing him *other* things . . . things like light and laughter and a sense of belonging that he has never known before? For you do all that, Francesca Cameron. I have seen the change in him in the last week. It is all because of you, my dear girl."

Chessy covered the duchess's papery fingers with her own, feeling a lump grow in her throat. "Oh, thank you. You've all been so k-kind to me."

The duchess sniffed suddenly. "Nonsense. It's you who—" As footsteps sounded behind them, she cleared her throat and stepped back from Chessy.

"Spinning new schemes, I see." The earl looked from one female face to the other. "Allies against me already?"

"And a good thing too," the duchess said crisply. "You need taking in hand, my boy. From all I can see, Miss Cameron is precisely the one to do it. I've just been telling her about all your bad habits."

Tony gave a tragic sigh. "And here I'd been hoping to pass myself off as a gentleman of some credit."

The duchess snorted. "Vain hope, if you ask me!"

They argued, all six of them, loud and long and cheerfully. The sunny afternoon passed slow and unnoticed and dusk settled gracefully over the lush Essex countryside.

Lambs trotted home, bells clanging, through the narrow hedgerows where avocets and skylarks trilled. The air hung golden, wreathed in a fine shimmering mist that clung to the green hills and interlinking silver waterways.

And somehow Chessy felt more at home in that simple little inn than she had ever felt in all her life.

After a noisy and very informal dinner, it was decided that they should pass the night at the White Hart.

The landlord was more than amenable, and Chessy saw that her father was relieved not to have to take to the road again so soon.

Several times Chessy tried to detach him from the group, hoping for a chance to hear the story of his escape, but each time he was pulled back into another story by the wide-eyed children who found in him everything of adventure and courage.

As the sky darkened to purple, Lord Morland went off to make arrangements for the children. To Chessy's delight, they were to have a room that opened onto hers on one side and the duchess's on the other. Morland had argued for the smaller room for himself, but since the bed was clearly at least a foot shorter than he was, he was overruled.

"And now off to bed, you two! We'll make an early start tomorrow, so we can reach Sevenoaks in time for luncheon."

"Oh, not yet! Just one more story! *Please*, Uncle Tony?"

Their guardian appeared unmoved by their cajolery. "Now, you two! Unless you dare to face the legendary monster of the fens."

Elspeth giggled wildly. Jeremy looked torn between excitement and acute embarrassment.

"So, you are bold, are you?" The next moment, he charged toward the children and caught each securely under an arm, then hauled them laughing and protesting toward the door in what was obviously an old and hallowed bedtime ritual.

At the threshold he turned. "Say good night, monsters."

The children gave their adieus, screeching as Tony tickled them unmercifully.

Soon after, Chessy and the duchess made their way off to bed. Only James Cameron stayed behind, nursing a very fine bottle of Madeira that the landlord had fetched from the cellar.

But the more he drank, the more worried he became.

Chessy was just drifting into a restless sleep when she heard a soft tap at her door. She sat up, her heart pounding as memories of her rooftop escape flashed before her eyes.

Silence. Then once again the hesitant tapping.

This time Chessy realized the sound came from the inner door that opened to the children's room.

"M-miss Chessy?"

A gust of wind flung itself at the old building, making the eaves creak and the glass panes rattle.

A moment later, the door burst open. Elspeth stood like a phantom in the doorway, her face as pale as her voluminous white nightgown. A frayed and well-worn doll was clutched tightly beneath her arm. "M-miss? Are you—that is, did you hear that noise?"

"The wind? Very nasty, wasn't it? But totally harmless, I assure you."

"Do you mind—the w-wind, I mean? When it groans and growls like that?"

Chessy's heart twisted when she saw that Elspeth was trembling violently. "What is it, little love?" She pulled back the covers and went to kneel beside the girl, smoothing down her glossy gold braids.

The shivering continued. "I thought that—if you didn't like the wind as much as I didn't, then"—she swallowed as another great gust roared overhead—"then I wouldn't mind if you wanted to come and share my bed."

Chessy caught her in a quick, fierce hug, then came swiftly to her feet. "What a lovely idea. Shall I just go and fetch my pillow?"

Elspeth nodded. As Chessy turned, the girl caught her hand and trotted along with her, unwilling to leave her side for even a moment.

Together they fetched the pillow, then walked into the next room, where Chessy slid in beside the pale little girl.

Jeremy was fast asleep on the far side of the room, oblivious to both the wind and a branch that was scraping against the window.

"W-would you like to read a story? The candle is on the dresser."

Chessy's breath wedged in her throat. Once again the old pain ran through her, along with the familiar cutting sense of shame.

"I—I think not, my dear. We don't want to wake Jeremy, after all. Perhaps I could tell you a story instead. If I am very quiet."

"Oh, yes, please. In the morning Je'emy will be ever so angry that he slept right through it."

"Very well. Snuggle close now."

Warm fingers caught Chessy's hand. "I'm ready, miss."

"Well then, let's see. Once upon a time—"

"Long, long ago," Elspeth filled in knowledgeably.

"Not fair! Have you heard this story before, imp?"

Elspeth gave a giggle. "Oh, miss, you're teasing me. Do go on."

"Hmmm, now where was I? Oh, yes, long, long ago, in a splendid land far across the seven seas there was a country where mince tarts and walnut cakes grew like apples on a tree."

"Mmmmmm. Sounds . . . ever so nice . . ." Elspeth yawned.

"Oh, yes, it was a very special place. A place north of night and west of morning."

Chessy's voice softened as she heard Elspeth's breath slow into the rhythms of sleep.

"And in that land south of the sun, north of the night, there was a very clever little girl. A girl brave and fair. A girl named Elspeth. . . ."

Chessy smiled, feeling the little fingers relax on her hand. Very carefully, she eased from the bed and then bent low to tuck the coverlet around the now soundly sleeping child.

"Sleep well, little one," she whispered. "I only wish I could do the same."

"You should have stayed, Lizzie." The duchess gave

her white hair a final tug and set the silver-handled brush on the chipped dressing table.

Her companion did not answer, seeming intent on brushing a bit of dust from a pair of the duchess's fine kidskin slippers.

The duchess frowned. "You can't go on hiding forever, you know. What's done is done, my dear. Someday you're going to have to face that fact. And I have a feeling that that sometime is now."

Small and slender, the dark-haired woman sighed. She rolled the shoes in paper and then arranged them neatly in the top of a packed portmanteau. "I—I could not. I tried to, but—oh, it's impossible!" She turned then, and the duchess saw that her fine-boned face was streaked with tears.

"Oh, Lizzie, no tears! Come here!" She held out her hands, and her companion came to sit beside her as sobs shook her.

"You're so good to me, Amelia. Too good, I'm sure. After all that's happened."

"Nonsense. I'm simply a selfish old woman who follows her own wishes entirely. For I've discovered I have the very best companion in all the world." She reached out and raised the woman's chin. "But you can't go on hiding behind me forever. Nor can you go on with this charade of being a companion. It doesn't suit you, I've always told you that. And especially now."

The woman named Elizabeth blinked back tears. Her eyes were red-rimmed in the lamplight.

And they were also a remarkable shade of amethyst.

"When are you going to tell her?" the duchess demanded sternly.

"Tell her? I *can't*. How could I possibly face her after—oh, it's all such a muddle! She would hate me so."

"You can and you must. The gel has a right to know, after all."

The dark-haired woman sniffed and accepted the lace-trimmed handkerchief the duchess offered. "Tell her what? It was all so long ago. I was certain I was over it, that things were best left as they were. And now, to go opening everything up again, to relive all that pain—" She caught back a sob. "I—I don't think I can bear it."

"If *you* don't tell her, then I shall."

"No! Please—"

"She's got to know, Elizabeth. I should have put my foot down long ago, but I'd heard such stories about the man, such tales of his wild behavior. But now— well, he's not the bandit I pictured him to be. Not at all."

"Bandit? Oh, never. James was *never* that." A soft, dreamy smile came over the companion's face. "He was a good man. Stubborn and eccentric, yes, but a *good* man."

The duchess muttered an oath. "That does it! You've got to tell them. *Both* of them. Cameron is entitled to know. And Chessy—well, it's time Chessy found out that she has a mother!"

39

The woman went sheet-white. "T-tell her? That I'm her mother?"

"Of course."

"Just like that? 'Hullo, my dear. Sorry I was gone, but now I'm back, and everything will be just splendid again.' Oh, Amelia—I can't!"

The Duchess of Cranford gave a snort. "Lizzie Granville, where's your spunk? It got you through in the old days, before you came to me, and bad days they were. And you had to know that a time would come when this would happen."

The woman with the amethyst eyes—eyes so like Chessy's—gave a sigh. "I suppose I did. But not now—not yet—" She turned to the duchess then. "And she's so beautiful, Amelia. So brave. She's—oh, everything I'm *not*. I couldn't even manage to weather the storm of my father's disapproval."

"There were reasons, as I recall. Your mother was desperately ill, and your father was unwilling to provide her the care she needed. Not that I was surprised. "Old Granville was a hard-hearted bounder if ever I saw one," she said darkly.

351

Elizabeth Granville stood up and began to pace the room, the lace handkerchief clutched in her fingers. "But Francesca—even if I did tell her, how would it change things? I have no place in her world. Nor in *his*."

"You still care for him, don't you?"

The dark-haired woman went very still. "Care?"

"Don't mince words with me, woman. Answer the question!"

"I—well, yes." It was a mere whisper. "In a purely platonic sort of way, of course. It would be nice if we could be friends again."

The duchess gave a snort that showed her opinion of this idea. "Very well, I'll give you until tomorrow night. Then I shall tell him, will you, nil you. Do you understand me?"

Her companion had barely heard. She was staring out at the lush Essex countryside, where a full moon rode cloud-waves of flashing silver in the wake of the stormy wind.

"He was always handsome—he is still so, don't you think? And did you see how wonderful he was with the children? He must have been a splendid father to—to our child." Lizzie's fingers tensed on the white muslin curtains. "Francesca—dear little Francesca, with her sweet laugh and her chubby cheeks. And that unpredictable little dimple . . . How much I've missed. Things that can never be recovered. Oh, Amelia what a fool I've been—"

The next moment, her head sank down against the glass pane, and she began to cry, in fierce, muffled sobs.

Neither woman noticed that the door, rickety at best, had blown open in the wind and now stood slightly ajar.

Outside in the corridor the Earl of Morland eased back against the wall.

It was impossible.

It was incredible. And yet . . . he had heard the

words with his own ears, heard the duchess's threat and her companion's answers.

Elizabeth Granville. James Cameron's wife.

Chessy Cameron's *mother*.

And what in heaven's name was he to do about this discovery he'd made? The duchess was right, Chessy was entitled to know. But how could he lay the whole business before her without hurting her more?

No, best to follow the duchess's advice and see what happened on the morrow. Then perhaps, if the woman still resisted—

A noise behind Morland brought him around fast, his hand curled to a fist. He had a vision of black-masked Triads and hard-faced ruffians intent on seizing Chessy.

But it was only a man. A tall man with wild graying hair and a gaunt face. A face that was just now white and pasty, as if he'd seen a ghost.

Which in a way, James Cameron had.

It was the ghost of his own past he'd seen, the ghost of the woman he had always loved, and the mother of his child.

"She—she's alive! By God, after all these years." He stared at Morland, a dazed look in his eyes. "You—you heard, didn't you?"

Morland nodded.

"Elizabeth—Lizzie—" His fingers swept before his eyes, and his shoulders seemed to pitch. "How could she have done this to me? To *us*?" He was white, shaken. "I thought she had died. By God, I ought to march right in there and—"

"Come along, man. You're shaking like a leaf. You're in no condition to confront *anyone* right now. I'm not sure that even *I* am. I've some tolerable Madeira in my room, and I think now is a perfect time to broach it." Carefully, Tony pulled the duchess's door closed, then took Cameron's arm and steered him down the opposite corridor.

"And while we're there, you may as well tell me everything—including the things that you didn't want to tell Chessy about the Triads."

"It came out of the blue. Neither of us expected it. I suppose it happens that way sometimes."

They sat, legs outstretched, before the fire that the landlord had kindled earlier in the earl's private room. The Madeira was already half gone.

Cameron's voice fell into a low, reflective cadence. "We married with her grandmother's help. Elizabeth was of age, after all, and it was only her father's intransigence that had kept us apart. I think he was loath to part with a daughter who happened to be such a good servant. For he worked her like a servant, you know. And without her, who knew how long her mother could have lasted?" He sighed, studying the fine Madeira. "It was a damnable mess, from beginning to end. And in spite of that, there was time for us to snatch some trace of happiness, even if just for a little while."

Suddenly Morland frowned. He heard a sound—was it the faint creak of a floorboard out in the hall? Raising a finger to his lips, he crept silently to the door and eased it open.

The corridor was empty. Two candles cast dancing shadows from sconces on the wall.

Grim-faced, Morland moved down the hall and tried the door to Chessy's room.

Locked, just as he'd ordered. And the children's room was just the same.

Only at the duchess's door did he pause and frown. He tapped softly. "Your Grace?"

The duchess appeared, her face anxious. "Is everything—is Chessy—"

"I mean to check. If you don't mind?" At the duchess's nod, he made his way to the adjoining room. Elspeth and Jeremy were sound asleep, covers bunched to their chins. Softly Morland eased open the door to Chessy's room.

She lay with her cheek to the fine linen, her hair haloed around her in a dark cloud. Her fingers were curled just beneath her chin. She looked lovely, fragile, and very beautiful.

Morland smoothed a dark strand from her cheek

and feathered a kiss across her brow. She stirred softly, then sighed.

But when he returned to the duchess's room, Morland's face was hard. "Keep the latch closed and throw the bolt after me. After what happened this afternoon, I mean to take no more chances."

The duchess nodded grimly.

Morland waited to hear the bolt driven home before he turned and strode back to his own room. His eyes were hard as he refilled his glass.

"Was anyone there?"

Morland shrugged. "No one I could see. Probably just the wind. These old inns have a thousand creaking corners." Drink in hand, he returned to his seat before the fire. "Where were we? Ah, yes, you were describing your impetuous marriage. What happened then? What separated the two of you?"

"Everything—nothing. Life." Cameron frowned. "It began over the child. I had brought Lizzie out to Macao to start a new life. By then, we had Chessy, as fine and healthy as ever a child could be. Lizzie had had a hard time, so I engaged a Chinese amah. But she wanted no part of the amah and just flew into a rage. Then we had a message that her mother had taken a turn for the worse back here in England."

He sighed, staring at his drink. "It came at a very bad time for us. One thing seemed to lead to another, one fight running into the next. I see now that it was partly my fault. Everything was so difficult for her over there. I didn't understand *how* difficult until—" He swirled his glass glumly. "We had a letter from her father, warning Lizzie that her mother was on her deathbed. I never knew until later that he had enclosed money for her passage back to England."

Cameron's fingers whitened on the crystal decanter. He looked very old at that moment, his big frame shrunken. "I—I can't remember all I said, but I remember telling her that if she left me then, I wouldn't have her back. And that Chessy would stay with me, since I couldn't be sure of how her father would treat the child. He'd sworn she was a bastard, you see, sworn that our marriage wasn't legal, though of course it was." He cursed softly. "We had a terrible row. Both of us said things we shouldn't have—things I'm sure we never meant. But by then, it was done and—and she was gone." His eyes glistened as he stared into the fire. "I never saw her again, you know. Not once until today, when she stood behind the duchess dressed in a black veil so thick I couldn't even recognize her. Over twenty years gone . . ."

"You had no idea she was here, living with the duchess?"

"None whatsoever. I made inquiries in Macao and Calcutta, but she had booked passage under a different name. After her return to England she must have lived very quietly, almost as a recluse, with the duchess. I—I searched but could find no trace of her anywhere. Needless to say, her father was no help, and by then her mother had died."

Morland shook his head. "I knew nothing about the woman, and I was a great deal closer at hand than you. Lord, I've known the duchess since I was in swaddling, and I don't think I saw this companion of hers more than half a dozen times. Amelia certainly never breathed a word of the story."

Cameron swirled his drink. "Well, there you have it. The whole silly, damnable tale. I—I tried to rear Chessy well, the way Lizzy would have wanted. Oh, of course we traveled about a great deal, and she didn't have the fripperies that most young women enjoy, but . . ."

He stared at Morland, a look of shaken entreaty on his face. "I didn't fail her, did I? Chessy truly is happy— was happy—with the life we led?"

Morland studied the fire, his expression unreadable. "I'm afraid you'll have to ask her that question, James. But one thing is certain: She *will* have to know about her mother. I quite agree with the duchess about that."

"Of course. I shall speak to Lizzie tomorrow. And then we must break the news to Chessy. Together, I think."

The two men sat in the firelight, their faces cast in bronze and shadow from the dancing flames, each considering the strange workings of fate and the turmoil that faced them on the morrow.

"And you still haven't explained the rest of this mess. About this escape from your captors. They *were* Triads, I take it? Just as Chessy suspected?"

Cameron nodded. "Not that I knew it at first. It was a damnable crossing, I assure you. I was trussed like a confounded chicken and tossed in a stinking hold with a hundred other poor beggars. It seemed an age before we docked, and then another age before I realized we were in England, riding at anchor out in the middle of Mother Thames."

"I'm sorry I couldn't have come myself to help rescue you, but Chessy needed to be kept safe. Wellington's men found you very fast, I believe."

Cameron smiled. "And damned glad I was to see them. The Great Man is every bit as arrogant as ever. But how did they know where I was being held? There must be hundreds of ships anchored in the Thames."

"We captured one of the Triads." Morland's voice hardened. "He—talked."

"Well I can only thank heaven for it. I heard bits and pieces down in the hold. It seems the Triads were planning to use the book for the same purpose you were. They hoped that the emperor would cease his harassment of their secret activities if they presented him with such a treasure. But three months ago the book disappeared." Cameron studied Tony. "Your doing?"

"I still have a few tricks left, James."

"Damned clever of you. Unfortunately, the Triads have no liking for me. When their precious book disappeared, they decided to use Chessy to track it down. They knew of her training and decided she would be the perfect one—especially when they learned that the book had been taken here to London, where they could hardly operate unnoticed." Cameron rubbed his neck gingerly. "But until I find that book, Chessy's life is still in danger."

"What can they do? We're in England, man, not the middle of Asia!"

"You don't understand them, Tony. They are fiercely loyal and superbly trained. Believe me, they won't give up until they find that book—or die in the process."

Morland swore softly. "Did you hear them discuss who had the wretched thing?"

"An Englishman. That's all they knew."

Morland smothered a curse. "Which leaves us no better off than before."

"Not quite. I had someone keeping an eye on Chessy, someone I trusted completely. He sailed with her when she came to London with Swithin. Not that she knew it, of course."

Morland sat forward abruptly. "He?"

"A fellow student of hers at Shao-lin. A warrior with skills even beyond her own. Part French, part Scot, and part pure Manchu prince. His name is Mackinnon, but we always called him Kahn, in jest."

Morland stared down at his sleeve and picked at a minute speck of lint. "Did she—" He cleared his throat. "Were they—"

"Fool." Cameron's eyes were chiding. "Chessy has had eyes for only *one* man ever since she was fifteen. A reckless, half-tamed Englishman with more nerve than sense." He stared at Morland, his face challenging. "No, of course, they weren't lovers. As far as I know, she thought of him only as a sort of elder brother. Though for *his* part, sometimes I think—"

"Never mind," Morland said with sudden violence. "*His* wishes do not interest me in the least. She's mine now, do you hear? And I'll not give her up—not for anyone or anything!"

Cameron's lips twitched into a ghost of a smile. One wild white eyebrow arched to a point. "Very interesting."

"Go ahead and gloat, you bounder. But you'll have to murder me to stop me from marrying her now."

Suddenly Cameron put down his glass and broke into harsh coughing.

"Good God, man, are you sick?"

The older man shrugged. "Let's just say that there are good days and bad days. Nothing particular, you understand. But with all those years in the East, with the tropical fever—and my heart has never been—" He gave Tony a sidelong look. "Never mind that."

Morland raked his fingers through his hair. "Damn it, Jamie, why didn't you tell me?"

"I won't speak of it again, Tony, and I'll expect the same of you. Chessy knows nothing about this, and I mean to see it stays that way. All I meant—all I *want* is for her to be happy, to find the home she never had, the security I never could give her." He looked up at Tony then, his eyes hard and very determined. "Do you mean to give her those things?"

Morland frowned. "You know I do!"

"Excellent. By the way, I'm sorry about the way things turned out between us. It hurt me a great deal to make you leave Macao."

"If so, you had a damned peculiar way of showing it! You nearly bit my head off after finding us on deck that night in a markedly disheveled state."

Cameron's fingers clenched. "I was hard pressed not to shoot you then and there, my boy, and I don't mind admitting it. She was still a child, and you were a man with a great deal of experience. You took advantage of her innocence, advantage of the intimacy of our ship—"

Morland stiffened. "I never touched her! Good God, you can't really believe that I would—"

"Oh, not after I'd thought about it." Cameron crossed his arms over his chest and stared into the fire. "I realized that you'd stopped before things went too far. But damn it, they would have gone too far again, sooner or later, had you stayed. For even I could see that she was head over heels in love with you, as you were with her. If I hadn't sent you packing when I did, you would have *had* to marry her." He studied Morland intently. "You'd been through the disaster of Corunna, but I'd a feeling you weren't quite ready to settle down yet, not while Napoleon was still storming about the Continent."

Morland shrugged. "I only know that you kicked the rug out from under me that night—and in the process you destroyed the first happiness I had known in a very long time."

Cameron reached over and gave Morland's shoulder a swift, fierce squeeze. "Devilish sorry about that. I thought—I hoped—you'd come back, at least when the war ended. I had my ways of keeping tabs on you. I knew about Salamanca—about your knee—"

Morland's face went cold and shuttered.

"Don't give me that look. You were a long time recovering—yes, I know about *that* too. And about that devilish business with that bounder of a brother and his flighty wife. I *had* to know. Because of Chessy, don't you see?"

They sat that way for a long time, neither speaking. Cameron stared into the crackling fire, while Tony gazed out the window past the shabby, drifting curtains.

Finally Morland put down his glass. "I believe that leaves us nothing more to argue about, except how we're going to find that book and get rid of those rascally Triads."

The two men's eyes met.

"Are you thinking—"

"—what I'm thinking?"

Cameron smiled coldly. "The other man? The Englishman?"

Morland nodded. "He's our only clue."

"I'll see if I can track him down. Maybe he can tell us something about this book."

"Not by yourself, you won't! And I'm not moving a foot away from Chessy—not while she's still in danger."

"I can manage perfectly without you, my boy. Been in worse scrapes than this by far, I have." Cameron frowned. "But not while Chessy was involved."

"I'll see to it that Wellington is informed and that all the men you need are put at your disposal."

"Thank you, my boy. And never fear. Somehow I *will* find our mystery man and that pillow book."

40

The voice was hushed, sultry, dark as the night. "You came."

"Of course, my dear. Did you expect me to stay away?"

Louisa Landringham smoothed her perfectly arranged silk peignoir and wet her crimson lips carefully. "I wasn't certain." She sounded petulant.

The man before her smiled. "And it goaded you, didn't it? Not to know." He crossed his arms before his chest and studied her, cool and mocking.

"Perhaps. Perhaps not. What are you looking at?"

He kicked the door shut behind him. "You. For you are lovely, my dear Louisa. Which I think you know full well."

He sauntered across the room. His body cast a black bar of shadow across the bed where she lay, silk skirts arrayed in a careful froth that displayed her body to perfection.

His eyes darkened. "*Very* lovely." Without a word his went to his neckcloth.

"No!" Louisa forced her voice to calmness. "That

is—let me, won't you?" In a sinuous slide of lace and satin, she came to her feet.

His eyes narrowed slightly. "If you choose."

Her eyelids fell, covering the sudden glitter in her eyes. "Oh, I do." With expert fingers she eased the white linen free, and then the perfectly cut black waistcoat. Her lips curved as she freed the buttons of his shirt and felt the sudden race of his heart.

Slowly she slid her fingers beneath the shirt, slanting him a sultry look.

Instantly she was rewarded with a curse and the hard thrust of angry muscle against her hips. She wet her lips again.

Slowly. Carefully.

That did the trick. It always did.

The next second, she was flat against the wall, her peignoir torn clean through as he bared her luscious body to his blazing gaze.

Her carefully rouged nipples gleamed bloodred in the firelight. It was a trick she had learned several years before in France, where it had had a most pronounced effect on her admirers.

And tonight just as on those other nights, it had the same effect.

"God, you really are a little whore at heart, aren't you?"

The woman in the ripped peignoir merely smiled, her eyes heavy-lidded as she reached low, searching for the warm thrust of his manhood. Oh, she would make him pay for that comment, but not quite yet. Not until she had him at his most vulnerable . . .

She found him. Her nails curved, gently scoring the heated, pulsing inches.

"I wonder what it would take to surprise you," he said.

"Beyond anything *you* could offer, I think."

"Do you really?" His eyes glinted, hard and chill as ice. He caught up his neckcloth from the bed and circled her wrist before she knew it. She hissed and kicked and tried to bite him, but he merely laughed and lapped the white linen around the bedpost.

"No! Damn it, you'll be sorry—"

But her eyes were glinting strangely. A wild crimson flush covered her perfect, perfumed skin.

"No?" he repeated mockingly. Slowly he bent and flicked the hard, thrusting point of one breast.

Louisa's breath caught. She closed her eyes as he tugged off the shredded remains of her expensive French peignoir and then used it to secure her other wrist. "No—"

He smiled, enjoying the sight of her white limbs spread to him. "Still no?"

"No, damn you!" But she arched as she spoke, and her eyes were full of fire.

"How amusing it will be to discover all your little games, Louisa. But first, I really think you'd better tell me what that groom of yours was doing up at the White Hart."

She stiffened and began to frame a protest, but by then his fingers were upon her, moving hard and expertly.

"I warned you that you were not to interfere, didn't I?"

Louisa arched her back and moaned.

"More? Then tell me what you've been up to, my dear. And this time I think you'd better make it the truth."

She was panting by the time he'd finished. She was twisting. Begging. She'd given him every detail . . .

And she didn't even care.

PART
THREE

South
of the Sun

41

Chessy awoke to the sound of Elspeth's slightly off-key singing. The girl was sitting, fully dressed, having a tea party with her dolly.

Beside them, in a little wicker basket, a fat brown frog croaked throatily.

"Hush, Napoleon. We don't want to wake Miss Chessy."

"Miss Chessy is already awake."

Elspeth whirled about, her face wreathed in smiles. "Oh, capital! Would you care for some tea?" She held out a tiny porcelain cup with a cracked handle, which Chessy accepted gravely.

She made a great business of sipping the imaginary brew, then pursing her lips. "I always take my tea with three spoonfuls of sugar, if you please."

Elspeth giggled. "Of course—so stupid of me," she said grandly, spooning in a quantity of imaginary sugar. "How's that?"

"Much better," Chessy studied the girl's happy face. "Did you sleep well?"

"Oh, ever so well, thank you. And I told Je'emy 'bout the lovely story he missed. All about dragons and warriors and a beastly old king who wanted to—" She stopped, frowning. "What *did* he want to do, Miss Chessy?"

"Oh, all sorts of nasty things. He wanted to cut down all the mince tart trees and plant spinach instead. Just think of that."

As Elspeth giggled the duchess came in. "Well, I see that you two are going on famously. But I am famished. Anyone for breakfast?"

"Dolly is quite hungry, aren't you, Dolly?"

"In that case we'd better let Dolly go first, shouldn't we?" The duchess turned to her veiled companion. "Give me your hand on the stairs, won't you, Elizabeth?"

As she followed a happily chattering Elspeth from the room, Chessy barely noticed the slender figure draped in a black veil who stepped forward and assisted the duchess downstairs.

They assembled as the sun rose over green plains crisscrossed by silver canals. Sea birds were everywhere, noisy and vigilant.

Morland motioned the duchess aside while Chessy was engaged in admiring Elspeth's new frog.

"Remarkable," the duchess said, shaking her head. "They make me feel a thousand years old."

"Nonsense." Morland patted her thin hand. "You put us all to shame."

The duchess sniffed. "You've too much charm, Tony. I've warned you about that before. It will get you into a great deal of trouble one day—if it hasn't already. Now what is it you want? Not the simple pleasure of an old lady's company, I'm convinced."

Morland put a hand across his chest. "Madame, you wound me."

"Humph. Too much charm, just as I said." And then, as Morland's smile began to fade away to grimness, "What is it?"

The earl's eyes moved to Chessy, who was stroking Elspeth's newest pet.

"Is there something wrong between you and Chessy?" she asked." If you have any sense at all, you'll not let her get away, my boy!"

"I have no intention of letting her escape," Morland said gravely. "And nothing is wrong—not in that way, at least." His jaw hardened. "But she is in danger."

"The man on the rooftop yesterday?"

Morland nodded. "Yes, he was after Chessy. And I am very much afraid that there will be others."

The duchess frowned. "But this is dreadful! What are you going to do?"

"Do? I'm going to get her to Sevenoaks as fast as possible and then keep her there—forcibly, if necessary—until I am sure that she is finally safe."

"But will she be safe even at Sevenoaks? It is a vast place, after all."

A muscle flashed at Morland's jaw. "She'll be safe. I'll see to that." His face was very hard as he handed the duchess up into her carriage, where she was to ride with the children. Chessy and her father were to follow in the earl's carriage, while he ranged ahead on horseback.

"I don't expect any trouble en route," he said softly, "but after yesterday, I prefer not to take chances. I'll keep an eye out for anything odd. Meanwhile, Cameron is armed. She will be safe with him." He swung the carriage door shut. "By the way, Your Grace, I checked on your door last night. I overheard."

The duchess went very still. "You—you heard? About Chessy and—and—"

"Her mother. Yes, I heard all of it. It will be a shock, a terrible shock."

The duchess sighed. "The gel has a right to know. And it must be done, the sooner the better."

Morland frowned. "I agree entirely. But there will be time enough after we reach Sevenoaks. I want her first memories there to be happy ones, unclouded by doubt."

"Very well. Elizabeth will have to tell Chessy soon after."

"Tell me what?"

For a split-second the two froze, hearing that voice just behind them. Chessy was standing at the bottom of the carriage steps with Elspeth and Jeremy on each side of her.

"T-tell you?" the duchess repeated faintly.

Chessy looked from the duchess to the earl. "I beg your pardon," she said slowly. "I—we didn't mean to eavesdrop."

"Er, it was nothing. The duchess wanted to describe Sevenoaks, my estate, to you, but I told her I wanted it to be a surprise." Morland summoned up all his considerable charm. "You don't mind, do you, my dear?"

"Of course not. I've always loved surprises." But Chessy had not missed the moment of uneasiness between the duchess and Tony. She could only wonder at what it meant.

"You are well? Quite well?" Chessy settled back against the seat and studied her father as the carriage lurched out of the White Hart's yard.

James Cameron patted her hand. "Perfectly."

"Don't lie to *me*, James Cameron! You look thin and drawn. And you've been coughing far too much. It cannot have been pleasant."

Her father sighed. "Too keen-eyed by half, my girl. Very well, it was not at all pleasant. I was gagged and hauled into the hold like a squirming pig bound for the pot. And the cold." He scowled. "I don't think I'll ever get used to this wretched English weather again."

"I'm so glad you're s-safe," Chessy whispered, a catch in her voice. "You might have—they could have—"

"Now, now, girl, don't go mourning for me. I'm a long way from being dead yet, I warn you!"

Chessy brushed furtively at a tear. "You *do* seem well enough. Except for the coughing . . ."

"And so I am. Actually, I don't think I've laughed so much in years. Those two children are really quite remarkable. A pity about their parents. But they seem to get on well with the earl." His keen eyes narrowed. "You don't mind?"

Chessy felt her cheeks flame red. "M-mind?"

"They must come to you after you are married, you know, since Morland is their guardian."

Chessy made a great business of straightening her skirts. "Of course—that is, it has not been entirely settled that—when—if—" She bit her lip. Her flush grew more pronounced.

"Well, if the man hasn't said it, he's been *thinking* it clearly enough," her father said dryly. "But there, I won't task you with things you obviously don't wish to tell me."

Chessy sighed, uncertain why she wished to avoid this particular subject for a while longer. Perhaps it was because so much had happened in the last days— the attack on Morland, his scheme to abduct her, and then the attack at the inn. Only this morning, she had awakened dazed, half expecting to find herself back in her sunny room overlooking the Macao harbor, with the week's events reduced to nothing but a very disturbing dream.

But it was no dream. And Chessy found herself struggling to make sense of her chaotic emotions and the adjustment to a new country. Added to that was her concern about her father's situation. Until she satisfied herself that he was truly safe, she did not feel free to face her own future or consider the prospect of happiness with the man she loved.

For there was no doubt that she did love Anthony Morland.

"Oh, Father, I'm sorry," she said impulsively. "It's just—well, there's been so much, so quickly. Sometimes I feel I must be the happiest woman in the world. And then, other times . . ." Her eyes took on a liquid sheen. "Oh, it's utterly silly, I know, but somehow I'm just not ready for . . ." She sighed. "I suppose it's times like this that I wish I had a mother. Not that *you* haven't been wonderful," she added quickly.

Her father frowned, looking as if he meant to speak, but he contented himself with patting Chessy's hands, which were clenched tightly at her waist.

And then, while the lush Essex countryside sped

past in a blur of green and gold and muted silver, he
began to talk of safer things, beginning with the latest
gossip of Macao and ending with the status of another
old Chinese junk with which he hoped to explore an
offshore reef.

Chessy listened dutifully, her face intent. Oh yes,
she listened almost fiercely.

But her thoughts kept drifting to the man riding
ahead of their carriage and the secret he and the duchess had been trying to conceal from her.

By midmorning, the air was fresh and sharp with the
tang of salt. Off in the distance the dark lines of the
forest gave way to softly rolling hills and then to an
endless sweep of green reeds. Beyond that glinted the
silver curve of the sea. The carriage rumbled past, men
with dark, weathered faces, who were cutting reeds and
stacking them to dry for use in next year's thatch, while
sturdy-looking children gathered cockles beside the
silver canals that seemed to meander everywhere
through the lowlands.

They were traveling northeast now, Chessy realized.
She had seen the earl only briefly, when he reined in
his massive bay to speak a word or two with the coachman.

James was resting, and after a while Chessy drifted
to sleep, too, lulled by the rhythms of Morland's well-
sprung carriage. She did not know how long she slept
before she lurched awake at the scream of the brake
being thrown.

Morland's face appeared, framed in the carriage
window. Chessy's first thought was awe at how well he
sat his horse, almost as if man and beast were one. And
then she remembered that he must often have been on
horseback in Portugal and Spain. She felt a sharp stab
of curiosity about those weeks and months, about all
the dangers he had faced since they had parted.

But then he was smiling down at her, and in the
heat of his gaze she forgot everything—curiosity, doubt,
and regret.

All she thought of was how blue and clear his eyes were, and how filled with happiness they were now.

"May I steal her away for a while, Jamie?" Morland's eyes were on Chessy, though he spoke to her father. "I know you've a great deal of catching up to do, but there's something I want to show her."

"By all means. She's not been hearing anything I've said for ages now."

"That's not true! I have—" Chessy smiled ruefully. "Well perhaps not *everything*."

"Off with you!" her father said gruffly. "There's no need to apologize for being bored in an old man's company."

Chessy started to protest, but he cut her off. "Go on now. Perhaps I'll ask those children to share the coach. At least my stories will be new to them." His smile took the sting from his reproach.

The sky was vast and cloudless overhead as Chessy emerged from the carriage. She frowned. "But how—"

"Like this." The earl reached down and scooped her up before him.

"But I can't—that is, I don't ride!" she said breathlessly.

"You do now, my heart. And don't worry about falling, because I never mean to let go of you again." His voice was low and dark, meant only for her ears.

And the vow was very clear.

Chessy flushed, wriggling before him, trying to slide her skirts down across her exposed ankles.

Morland merely laughed at her efforts, then eased her closer until her hip was wedged against his hard thigh. "Hold on, beauty. Hold on as tight as I mean to hold on to you."

And then they were off.

B ehind them, the duchess's carriage had drawn up beside the earl's and the steps were being let down.

"Do you mind?" the duchess asked James Cameron, peering inside. "Elizabeth is feeling unwell and would do better to lie down." She had her arm around her black-veiled companion.

"Oh, no, I couldn't—I wouldn't dream of—" Elizabeth protested.

But the duchess thrust her forward toward James.

For a moment the white-haired man did not move. And then he nodded. "Of course she may join me. Unless you would prefer to have the whole carriage—"

But the duchess cut off this suggestion decisively. "No need to disarrange yourself. She will do nicely in there. I will keep an eye on the children."

In spite of her protests the duchess's companion was handed up the steps, thrust inside the carriage, and the team set back into motion.

Elizabeth slid back against the far wall, her eyes— what could be seen of them—fixed on Cameron's face.

He stared back just as fixedly.

He heard her take a little ragged breath, saw her shoulders stiffen.

"Surely in here, the veil may be dispensed with," he said softly.

"Oh, no. That is, it wouldn't feel right."

"But whom have you lost?" Cameron's tone was gentle but inexorable. "Father? Husband? Or perhaps a child."

A shudder seemed to go through her.

And James Cameron found that he couldn't bear the sight of her pain any longer, though heaven knew he had every reason to be angry after all the years of pain she had inflicted upon him by her flight. "Don't cry."

Her fingers twisted against her black dress, as restless and pale as moth wings against the cold night.

When the low, choked sounds continued, Cameron bent closer still, his face gaunt and lined with a pain of its own. "*Don't.* I can't—bear it. Don't . . . Lizzie."

At that last word, the woman before him froze. And then she seemed to crumple, while choked little sounds spilled from her throat.

Cameron ignored her shivering, ignored her stiff fingers and her incoherent protests. He pulled her into the seat beside him, then very gently slid the black veil from her face.

"Lizzie." His own voice shook and his hands were no longer quite so steady. "My dearest love."

"Oh, J-James. I've been such a f-fool. You must hate me. And yet I thought it was all for the best. I knew you would be a s-splendid father to our little girl. She *is* a delight, isn't she? So calm and strong. So *sure*. Oh—all the things I am not, nor ever will be!"

"Hush." He ran his finger gently over her tear-streaked cheek. "You are just as strong in your own way. Remember how you berated that vegetable seller in Macao for trying to cheat me?"

His wife gave a hiccoughing laugh.

"And Chessy will soon love you just as much as I do."

"Oh, can you, James? After—all the years? After what I've done?"

"Hush, Lizzie, and I'll show you how much I can."

And then somehow she was in his arms, and he was kissing the tears from her white cheeks, murmuring incoherent phrases of his own.

Though they meant nothing at all, they seemed to give the woman in his arms an infinite amount of pleasure.

"*Tighter?* You wretch! Any tighter, and my dress will rise to an entirely indecent level.

Morland's eyes glittered. "It sounds promising."

"Not here, Tony! Someone will see!"

But he only spurred the great bay to a gallop, so that Chessy had perforce to grip tight or fall.

Self-preservation won the day. She clutched at Morland's back. "Wretched man! Someday I'll—"

But he cut her off with a kiss and threw his arm tightly around her waist as they set off through a green tunnel of beech trees lining the road.

"Where are you taking me?"

He only laughed and caught her close, until their

heat merged and their bodies lay snug and hungry against each other.

Chessy sighed and settled back against him, her side to his chest.

"That's better, termagant. I believe I have some hope of making you into a biddable wife yet."

For answer, she curved her fingers, lightly scoring his back.

He muttered an oath. His hand tightened, stretched flat across her belly. And then it slid lower, into the hollow where he found her heat.

"*Tony!*"

With a hoarse laugh he released her. "In this case you're right, my love. Any more of that, and we'll *never* get to Sevenoaks."

"Are we close?"

He chuckled and loosed his hand to point out over the wooded slope that ran down to patchwork fields dotted with grazing sheep. "As a matter of fact we have been on Sevenoaks land for the last hour." He reined the horse to a walk, moving down a narrow path nearly smothered by overhanging linden and willow trees. "And there is something I particularly wanted you to see."

He stooped and urged her down as a low-lying bough barely skimmed over their heads.

A moment later, Morland nudged the horse up the hill and off the path, past a loose clump of crimson rhododendron, and out onto the rim of the hill.

Chessy's breath caught.

They were overlooking the whole valley, all clinging mist and soft, diffuse sunlight as in a Constable painting. Here and there were scattered cottages of local flint, while sheep grazed everywhere, right up to the front doors. But most impressive of all was the sky, luminous and infinite, stretching away forever until it merged with the faint shimmer of water on the horizon.

And then Chessy saw the glint of sunshine on mullioned windows, saw the warm yellow stone that glowed just across the vale.

Morland looked rueful and charmingly uncertain.

"Sevenoaks. I wanted you to see it first from here. It's most beautiful seen across the valley like this, I think. And I—I wanted you to like it."

"Oh, Tony, it's—it's lovely."

"Do you think so? I hoped that you would." His brow furrowed. "I know it will be utterly different from Macao, and that there will be many adjustments for you to make, but—"

Chessy hushed him by instinct, lifting herself against him and covering his lips with hers.

Instantly his hands tightened. His mouth opened, warm and hungry and searching. In the space of a heartbeat horse, house, and rolling landscape were forgotten as their tongues met.

Desire flamed between them, lush and sultry.

Finally, with a low oath, Morland pulled himself away. "Sweet Lord, Miss Cameron, but you *do* pick your moments."

Her only answer was a soft moan as she eased closer and nibbled delicately at his lower lip.

He groaned. His hand slid into her dark curls. He slanted back, drawing her down against him until their bodies were aflame, everything forgotten but the heat of their desire.

It was the restless sidestepping of the horse that dragged them back to sanity. The bay neighed, jerking softly at the reins, ears high and alert.

Morland muttered harshly and slid Chessy back to a more secure position before him, then bent down to stroke the horse's neck. "What is it, girl? Is there something—"

He never had a chance to finish. The next second, a rifle cracked from the underbrush and a bullet whined past his face.

42

The big bay reared wildly, pawing at the air and nearly hurling Chessy to the ground. Morland gripped the horse, fighting to hold him.

Damn it, which of the servants would be fool enough to shoot blind into the underbrush?

But with the next instant he knew the answer. Not one of his servants at all. The shot had been no accident.

The horse danced in tight, restless circles under Morland's rein, and another shot blasted from the forest to their left.

Cursing, Morland spurred the mare forward, channeling the animal's fear into action before it could rear again.

Over the green woodland they crashed, with boughs and twigs slapping their faces as Tony raced the horse at a gallop just short of foolhardy. Chessy's face was pale, but she made no sound as she clung to his waist.

For by now, the realization had hit her too.

Behind them came the sharp snap of small branches and the drum of hooves, but Morland knew every inch of this land and had a thousand places to hide.

Abruptly he cut down a narrow shepherd's path, then reined in sharply, sheltered behind a granite outcropping overhung with densely clustered azaleas.

And there they waited, breath drawn, while a faint cloud of steam rose from the flanks of the great bay. Petals of white and crimson rained over them, carried on the wind from the bushes overhead, but that was the only movement in their green bower.

Behind them all sound ceased. Now there was no sign of their pursuers.

The silence stretched out, broken only by the low rush of the wind through the giant oaks and the bay's steady breathing.

And then some instinct made Morland pull back farther beneath the rocky overhang. The same instinct that had saved his life at Badajoz and Salamanca made him reach down and stroke the horse's neck, whispering soft words to soothe the restless mount.

A moment later, just beyond the granite cliff face, just beyond a shimmering green bank of willow fronds, a rider slid into the sunlight, rifle leveled before him.

The sight, coming amid the silence and the softly falling rain of azalea petals had all the raw impact of a nightmare.

Morland tensed, but his fingers never ceased their slow stroking of the mare's neck. Somehow they quieted the great horse when it seemed just on the verge of launching into a nervous dance.

A dance that would have given Chessy and Morland's hiding place away instantly and spelled their death.

For now a second rider appeared, coldly professional in his dispassionate survey of the surrounding forest. They were at point-blank range now, and if the riders had spotted them, Tony would have had no chance to tug his own rifle from its pouch at his saddle.

Certainly not with odds like this.

So they waited, scarcely daring to breathe. Only yards away, the riders slid through the slanting light of the great forest, silent and lethal amid the cheerful clamor of bird cry and rustling leaves.

Chessy watched in numb horror, her breath locked deep in her throat.

So close. Once again, so close to dying . . .

After what seemed an eternity of waiting the men disappeared back into the foliage. For long moments neither Chessy nor Morland spoke; his fingers simply continued their smooth, rhythmic movements against the bay's neck.

And then he looked down at Chessy. Her eyes were huge and bewildered.

"Steady, love," he whispered. "It's not far now."

Even through her haze of shock and fear, Chessy noticed that he continued to whisper.

So they were still in danger. And this was no random attack of poachers, not disgruntled peasantry nor reckless highwaymen abroad by day.

"Ready?"

Chessy nodded, swallowing her fear and the thousand questions that were choking her.

Morland's eyes seemed to flare with fury as he saw how much the motion cost her. "Good girl," he whispered, his hand pressed to the curve of her cheek. And then his arm fell, catching her waist tightly as he nudged the bay around, back in the direction from which they had come.

Chessy did not ask why or where but only pressed close to Morland's chest, sick with shame for having brought such danger down upon him.

For it was obvious that the riders were pursuing *her*, not him. Equally obvious was that they were commanded by the same people who had sent her attacker on the rooftop.

Tears burned at her throat, and she bit them back in taut silence.

Dear God, what was she to do now?

They backtracked and zigzagged for what seemed like hours, keeping to shepherd's paths and the deepest part of the forest, following tracks that Morland had known since he was a boy. Once they heard the crack of a gun several hundred yards away, and Morland eased the bay into the shadows behind a huge, twisting yew tree.

The grass hissed with the low malignance of death. Again a rider appeared, moving quietly through the slanting sunlight.

Morland's hand tightened on Chessy's waist. She felt the full heat of his impotent rage slam through him.

But he did not move, and soon the rider melted back into the cheerful green forest.

By then, Morland's face was very harsh. For Tony had seen what Chessy could not have: These men knew the hills and streams of Sevenoaks nearly as well as *he* did.

The sun was past midheaven when they finally broke from the forest and cantered up the gravel avenue leading to the Jacobean house at the head of the valley.

Chessy was pale and tired, too tired to find warmth in the lovely walls of native stone and the banks of mullioned windows that crowned the south front overlooking the valley.

"Home." Morland's voice was soft in her ear. He let the horse go and thundered up the last yards to the house.

Gravel flew up as the great oaken door opened, and Elspeth and Jeremy flew out, with the duchess and James Cameron close in their train.

"There you are, Uncle Tony!" Elspeth's face was intent. "We beat you home by ages!" And then her cornflower-blue eyes widened. "What—what's wrong with Miss Chessy? Why is she . . . bleeding?"

Only then did Chessy realize her ankle was slick and cold. Blinking, she stared down at the dark red stain at her hem. She hadn't felt the bullet graze her, hadn't even realized she'd been hit until now.

Her pulse was a ragged drumbeat in her ears but she managed a reassuring smile for the worried child. "It's just a scrape from a branch, Elspeth. I'm afraid I urged your uncle to take the last hill recklessly fast."

His eyes dark, Chessy's father moved to the dancing horse and lifted her down. Chessy shivered and accepted his arm as she moved up the drive to the house.

Morland slid from the great bay and tossed the reins to Jeremy, who was staring at the blood on Chessy's gown. "It's nothing," he said softly. "But the horse is winded. Will you see that he's brushed and bedded down?"

Jeremy swallowed and seemed to rouse himself from some sort of dark reverie. "Of course." He turned to his white-faced sister. "Come along to the stables with me, Elspeth. We'll find some sugar for Jupiter."

But as her brother moved off, Elspeth stood white-faced, overlooked by the sober adults moving off toward the house.

"She's going to die, isn't she?" Elspeth asked softly, of no one in particular. And no one seemed to hear her when she clutched her doll to her chest and whispered, "They all die."

"**W**here did it happen?"

James Cameron watched grimly as Morland ran a pad of white gauze over Chessy's ankle.

The bullet had left a jagged red path four inches long, but thankfully it had not pierced deeply or the bone would have been shattered.

"Just at the ridge where we left you. There were two of them, both armed. And they were waiting for us."

Cameron muttered a graphic curse. "Did you recognize them? Were they local poachers?"

Morland gave him a swift, warning look.

Chessy saw that look and knew that he did not want the subject broached in front of her.

More secrets. More deceptions.

She closed her eyes as the pain bit deep. She had hoped it was over, that the future could finally begin for the two of them.

But now she knew it was not to be, not with the Triads still involved. Not until she found the wretched book that would set them all free.

"There, that looks clean enough." Morland gave the wound a final critical look, then lapped several lengths of gauze around it. "I'm afraid you're not going to be able to dangle from any roofs for several days, my dear."

But the awkward joke, kindly meant, only made Chessy shiver.

For she had discovered what it meant to be afraid, there in the quiet wood as she had ridden pressed to Morland's chest. Not afraid for herself, but for Tony and the two children, who came into grave danger simply by their association with her.

And Chessy had never before known the full, blinding sense of fear, not since she had taken up the disciplines of Shao-lin.

But for Morland and her father's sake, she tried to hide the blankness in her eyes, the quiver that shook her fingers. "You're probably right. I suppose that means no acrobatics either?"

Morland studied her face, undeceived by her forced effort at humor. "Only one sort of acrobatics," he said softly, too softly for her father to hear. "And that will be with me, Cricket. In my bed. With my arms secure around you."

Her lips trembled at the harsh need she read in his eyes.

Then her father coughed. "Let her sleep, Morland. That's what she needs now. And in the meantime I'd like a word with you. Outside, in the corridor." It was a command, hard and clear.

Tony sighed. He tucked a quilt around Chessy and settled her leg at a more comfortable angle. "Better?"

She nodded, not trusting herself to speak.

"Go to sleep. I'll be back in a few minutes. And then I'll stay here with you, so you needn't worry."

She swallowed audibly and managed a smile. "I won't."

But it was a lie.

Outside, in the hall, Morland's reassurance swiftly gave way to raw fury.

He paced angrily, his fists clenched at his sides. "Damn it, Jamie, I don't want to alarm her any more than she already is. She's no fool—she realized almost as quickly as I did that those two were no idle poachers."

"And we can assume they were after Chessy and not you?"

Morland did not immediately answer, and his silence spoke volumes.

"Well?"

The earl raked his hand through his long bronze hair. "Yes—no—I don't know. But there was something that made me think . . ."

"Out with it then."

Morland frowned at the door to Chessy's room. "They seemed to know the terrain—every bloody inch of it."

Cameron gave a silent whistle. "Which means that they might have been after *you*, since they'd taken the trouble to learn the layout of Sevenoaks. Is that it?"

At Morland's tense nod, he pounded his fist against his palm. "But how can we make any plans if we don't know *whom* they're after?"

"Exactly what I've been asking myself, Jamie." Morland's eyes narrowed. "And that is why you're going to stay here and keep watch on Chessy while I ride back out and see if I can't find the answer to that question."

"What if she wakes? She'll be angry as blazes if she finds you went back there alone."

"She won't wake," the earl said grimly. "I took the liberty of adding some laudanum to the hot chocolate I gave her."

"Did you now? She'll be mad as a hornet at that bit of high-handedness, and no mistake."

Morland shrugged. "Have you any better ideas?"

"I suppose not. At least take someone with you. Haven't you a brawny bailiff or a gamekeeper of some sort?"

"The bailiff is seventy-six years old and has rheumatism. The estate gamekeeper died at Vimiero," Morland went on grimly. "Along with his three brothers. No, I'm afraid it will have to be just me."

"Well, I don't like it, not a whit. Be careful out there, do you hear me?"

Morland's jaw locked in a hard line. "Don't worry, old friend. I bloody well intend to."

It was the slow, sliding shadow that woke her. Silent and careful, he moved just at the edge of her vision, as if fearful of waking her.

Chessy's heart lurched, then twisted into a knot of fear.

The next instant, she saw the thick bronze hair, the keen sapphire eyes. "Tony!" She sat up sleepily and rubbed her eyes. "I—I thought you'd gone out to speak with Father."

He turned slowly. His face warmed in a small smile. "I meant to, but . . . I discovered I'd dropped something—my gloves, actually. Do you mind?"

"That you awoke me? No, of course not. But I did wonder why you were creeping about like that." She stifled a yawn: "Heavens, I feel like I've slept the very sleep of the dead." Abruptly her violet eyes widened. "You put something in my drink, didn't you?"

He did not move. "I?"

"You did! Admit it!"

The handsome features relaxed slightly. "Well, perhaps just a hint of laudanum."

Chessy glared. "I don't care for it, I warn you. Next time, tell me before you do such a thing." Then, as she stifled another yawn: "But I suppose it's only fair to admit it. I haven't slept so well in years."

She settled back against the pillows and patted the bed at her side.

He still did not move.

"Is something wrong? It's not the children, is it?"

As her voice rose in fear, he seemed to shake free of his trance. He strode toward the bed. "No, the children are fine. Just—hush."

"Oh. I thought—"

He came down slowly beside her. His face was turned away, in profile. "They're fine, really. Everything is fine. Now why don't you go back to sleep?"

She smoothed her slender fingers over the soft coverlet. "I . . . I don't have to, you know. Sleep, that is." She swallowed. "I feel fine. Just a twinge or two." Her eyes were full and very uncertain, but brave as well. "We could . . ." She swallowed again and touched the soft linen at his sleeve. And then, her voice low and tremulous: "I—I love you, Anthony Morland. Do you know how very much?"

He might have stiffened, although it was hard to be sure, with his face turned at an angle. His eyes seemed to fill with shadows.

And then he laughed, low and bitter. "Let me get this straight, Miss Cameron. Are you inviting me to share your bed?"

Chessy could only stare at him.

Her look of bewilderment and pain was answer enough.

He smothered a curse and rose abruptly. "Forgive me, my dear. It's just that—I must not stay. The grounds must be searched." His eyes darkened as he stared down at her. "Believe me, nothing else would keep me from you right now." He turned and moved to the door.

"You'll check on the children, won't you? Elspeth has been having nightmares, I gather."

"Of course."

"And you'll return? You'll . . . be close by?"

He stared at her from the doorway, his face unreadable in the shadowed interior where the sunlight never reached. "Every minute, my dear. Every single minute."

It was only later—and far too late—that Chessy realized he'd gone off without the gloves he said he'd come looking for.

43

He crisscrossed the valley for two hours, but he found no trace of the riders. Deep down, Morland realized he hadn't really expected to find anything.

Oh, yes, they were good, these men. Already some instinct warned Morland that they were even better than he feared.

When he cantered back up the gravel drive two hours later, his face was very grim, for he was forced to wonder if he could keep Chessy safe, even here at Sevenoaks.

Elspeth was waiting for him outside the stables.

Sliding from Jupiter, he tossed the reins to a waiting groom and then scooped Elspeth up into his arms.

The child's face was very white. This time she did not smile. "She's—she's going to die, isn't she? The way they always do."

"Die? Of course not. Who has been talking such nonsense to you?"

"I saw the blood. And then they c-closed the door and wouldn't let me in. You don't have to lie, Uncle Tony."

"I am *not* lying. Miss Cameron is *not* going to die,

Elspeth! She simply hurt her ankle and needs to rest for a few days."

The cornflower-blue eyes studied him, unconvinced.

He made his decision then. He had meant to wait, but perhaps this way was best after all. Carefully he slid back onto a low brick wall outside the stable and settled Elspeth in his lap. "Can I trust you with a secret, imp?"

The blue eyes widened.

"We'd meant to tell you later, but—well, you see, Miss Cameron and I are to be married. Very soon, in fact, and right here at Sevenoaks. Now you'll have to believe me when I tell you that she is simply resting and not sick at all. You want her to look her best for the wedding, don't you?"

Elspeth's lip trembled. "Oh," she said raggedly. "How—how nice. Can Je'emy and I come to visit?" she asked wistfully. "Just sometimes? If you wouldn't m-mind awfully?"

"Visit?" Morland caught her cheeks in his hands. He fought to keep his voice steady as rage filled him, rage for the twisted, irresponsible parents who had left this child so uncertain of her future. "Dearest, silly child, you're going to do far more than *visit*. You're going to live with us, of course, right here at Sevenoaks. And sometimes in London." He frowned. "Unless you don't wish to."

"Not live with you?" Elspeth threw her arms around him and clutched him with all the strength of her five years. "Oh, Uncle Tony, do you mean it? *Truly?*"

"Of course I mean it, imp."

"We'll be good, *very* good. I won't torment Cook, and I'll wash behind my ears. And I'll say my prayers every night. Even Dolly will be good! We won't be incorrgi— incorrsible, not ever again, even if you bring back that horrid Miss Twitchett. I—I promise!"

Tony smiled. "No more Miss Twitchett. We'll find someone much better, I promise you."

Abruptly Elspeth frowned. "But—would you possibly have room for one more, Uncle Tony?"

The Earl of Morland, hero of Badajoz and Salamanca, swallowed, wondering what bombshell was to be loosed upon him next. "One more? And who might that be?"

"Well, might Napoleon come too? He won't eat much, honestly he won't. And he's ever so clean. For a frog, that is."

Morland hid a smile. "I suppose we might find a spot for one more," he said softly. "As long as he's *very* clean."

"Oh, Uncle Tony! Thank you, thank you, thank you!"

Suddenly the hardened soldier of the Peninsular campaigns found himself blinking back tears as he was wrapped once more in a fierce, childish embrace.

Chessy slept on through the afternoon, much to Tony's relief. After his return, he went several times to check on her, and each time he found her sleeping soundly. He had felt a twinge of guilt at slipping the laudanum into her chocolate, but he knew her well enough to realize that she would have refused to rest otherwise.

And Tony wanted her safe inside where he and Jamie could keep a careful eye on her.

He had allowed Elspeth into the room once to reassure her that Miss Chessy was simply sleeping. The little girl had studied Chessy for long moments, then looked up at Tony. "I believe you now," she said gravely. "She's—she's beautiful, isn't she? Even while she's sleeping."

"So she is, imp. And so are you."

Elspeth had flushed with pleasure, then skipped outside, giggling and eager to pass this amazing bit of information on to her toplofty brother.

As Morland followed her from the room, he heard the drum of horses along the drive.

"Who can that be?" he muttered, closing the door to Chessy's room and nodding to Cameron, who sat guard in a chair outside, perusing the latest publication of the Royal Geologic Society.

Morland found, several minutes later, that it was

Viscount Ravenhurst and his vibrant wife, come to felicitate him on his impending nuptials.

Morland was thunderstruck. "But how did you—"

A grimy face appeared in the carriage window. "Hullo, guv! Hope yer don't mind, but this here nob was pokin' about, askin' where yer and the young miss piked off to. Seein' he said he was yer friend and all, I decided to tell him."

"You! And how did *you* know my plans, urchin?"

"Coo! No problem wiff that! All I did was to listen out at the stables while yer gave yer orders to the coachman. Yer really oughter be more mindful where yer do yer talking, guv." He stared up at the great house, wide-eyed. "Gor blimey! So this is Sevenoaks. No wonder yer was wishful to get back."

Morland studied the boy thoughtfully. Perhaps this new development was no bad idea. He'd been worried about his lack of manpower and had sent into the village for several reliable men, but he didn't know how long that would take. Now at least he would have his old friend Ravenhurst to keep watch on Chessy. And the grimy, resourceful Barnaby would be perfect to keep an eye on the children.

"Well, you've done me a good turn, young fellow. At least I think you have. Why don't you go on inside, and I'll have Cook see to your luncheon. I don't suppose you've eaten, have you?"

The boy shook his head. "Precious little. I cud eat a horse right now, and no mistake!"

"I doubt that Mrs. Sibley has horsemeat on the menu, but I'm certain she'll come up with an adequate alternative."

Morland directed the boy off to the waiting housekeeper, who eyed his grimy face with misgiving and led him off downstairs.

The viscount studied Tony thoughtfully. "I can't say that you look delighted to see us, Morland. Have we come at an inopportune time? When the boy told us of your plans, Tess—that is, we—"

His auburn-haired wife emerged from the carriage at that moment and cut him off. "No, lay the blame where it's due, my love. It was all my fault. I couldn't sleep a wink until I knew whether the jaded earl had finally succumbed to parson's mousetrap."

"By that bit of cant, you mean am I married?"

"Of course." The viscountess gave him a questioning look. "Well, are you?"

Morland sighed. "Not quite. In spite of all my best efforts, I might add." He ran his hand through his hair. "It's a damnable mess too. Actually, I'm glad you've come. But let's go inside before we discuss it, shall we? It's . . . rather complicated."

"**Y**ou have no doubt that they weren't poachers?" The viscount's face was grave as he accepted a glass of burgundy from Morland several minutes later.

The sun spilled through floor-to-ceiling windows overlooking rolling green lawns. Off in the distance the silver curve of the sea shimmered faintly. It was a scene of infinite peace and unmatched beauty.

And it was horribly at odds with the chilling incident of danger that Morland had just described.

"No doubt whatsoever. We haven't had poachers at Sevenoaks for ages, not since my father began dispensing game according to a formal arrangement by household. No, those two were no poachers."

"It appears to be a good thing that we came," Ravenhurst said grimly. "What do you want us to do?"

"For now, nothing. Just keep your eyes open, if you would. And I don't wish for Chessy to know any more than she already does. It would only upset her."

The viscountess started to say something, but her husband silenced her with a telling look. As she saw that the earl was longing to have a private conversation with her husband, Tess came gracefully to her feet. "No doubt you're wishing me at Jericho, and I don't blame you. I must look frightful after that journey."

Morland took her hand, raising it for a kiss. "You look, Tess, just as you always do. Perfectly lovely."

Behind them the viscount cleared his throat dryly.

"So sorry to disturb your dalliance, old man, but I really do wish you'd stop pawing my wife."

Tess laughed. "Oh, don't mind him, Tony. He's been too bored for words since we set foot in London. This outing is precisely what he needs. But when do I get to meet her? Chessy, that is."

"She's resting now. The bullet ran shallow, thank goodness, but she needs to keep off that leg for a day or two. I promise I'll take you to her first thing."

"I'll hold you to that, my lord. And now, since you two are obviously wishing for a private coze, I'll be off." She gave a mischievous smile. "I think I'll find that young lad and see what trouble we can stir up."

After she left, Ravenhurst sat back and steepled his fingers. "Now I believe you had better tell me the story again, my dear fellow. And this time don't leave out the worst of it."

The valley was blue with dusk when Chessy began to toss in the grip of laudanum dreams. She moved restlessly, caught in visions of glittering *ton* balls that dissolved into screams as men on horseback plunged onto the dance floor, rifles leveled.

The room was deeply shadowed. A single candle burned on the gilt table beside her bed.

Playing through an open window, the wind set the damask curtains to a slow flutter.

And then a low click. The faint hiss of wood upon stone.

Beside the fireplace a narrow panel opened, and a shadowed figure stepped into the half-light. For a second candlelight gleamed off hair of lustrous bronze.

But Chessy did not see, caught in a place of dreams. Not even when he came toward the bed did she rouse.

"Lovely," he said. "And more of a temptation than I imagined."

His hands fell, gently playing over the creamy skin above the lace of her peignoir. "Yes, *very* lovely. Louisa will be devilishly jealous."

At his light touch, Chessy's lips moved and she tossed restlessly.

For long moments he simply watched her, his eyes darkened to cold and soulless slits. And then he touched her again. This time he found the taut crimson crests beneath the filmy lace.

He circled them slowly, flicking them with cool enjoyment.

He felt the first flush of lust, and that, too, amused him.

"Intriguing." Andrew Langford, the very much *alive* Duke of Morwood, felt his mouth curve up in a thin smile. "And this time, my dear brother, I have every intention of finishing what I start."

44

The message came shortly after daybreak.

Morland was just falling asleep after taking his turn at watch outside Chessy's room when James Cameron tapped at his door.

The older man's face was grave when he entered. "One of the grooms has just ridden in from Dedham. They've found two men that answer your description. The magistrate, Mr. Buxted, is holding them until you can get there. But he has sent word that he won't be able to hold them very long."

Morland threw back the covers and began tossing on his clothes. "Two, did you say? Have they given any information?"

"The usual evasions, according to the groom." Cameron looked uncertain. "Shall I go with you? This man Ravenhurst looks competent enough to watch things here, if you'd like my company."

"Better not. Ravenhurst doesn't know this place as well as you do."

Cameron nodded grimly. "Just what I was hoping you'd say."

"You and Elizabeth haven't told her yet, I take it."

Cameron shook his head. "We've decided to wait until"—he looked grim—"until later."

Morland dressed quickly and slung several items into a leather satchel. At the door he turned. "See that the duchess and children stay out of this, too, won't you, Jamie? I've enlisted the aid of that plucky young fellow from London who has done errands for me on occasion. You can rely on him."

"I'll keep them all on a short rein, that you can be sure of."

Seeing Cameron's grin look, Morland recalled that Cameron was a tough campaigner in his own way. Instinct told Morland there was no one better to stay and keep an eye on things. He only hoped that his instinct was right. "Ravenhurst and I will be at the King's Arms in Dedham, should you need us. We ought to return by midday. If difficulties arise, we'll send a message."

Cameron caught him in the threshold, one hand to the earl's shoulder. "Don't worry, my boy. I'll keep her safe, I promise."

Somewhere between dreams and waking, he was there again. His hand stirred her cheek, and he shook her briskly.

"Chessy, wake up. It's important."

She opened her eyes. He was holding a candle that cast flecks of gold onto his bronze hair.

"T-Tony? What—"

"I need your help. Wake up, my dear."

She blinked as realization returned. "Help? What sort of—oh, no, it's not—"

His face was grave. "I'm afraid it's Elspeth. There's been an accident. She's been asking for you."

Chessy sat up, her face white. "Elspeth," she said softly. She came swiftly to her feet. "I'll be ready as soon as I can." She turned, already working at the buttons of her nightgown.

In her distraction she did not notice how the azure eyes followed her, avid and very chill.

Morland and Ravenhurst clattered over the wooden bridge across the sleepy Stour and thundered into Dedham. Through the town they flew, dodging coaches and carts, past the church with its pinnacled tower, past the mill and the old timber-framed inn.

Dust rose around them like smoke as Morland turned toward his friend. "There is it, just across the street. The magistrate said he would wait for me there."

Ravenhurst nodded as his friend slid from his horse. "You go on. I'll see to a groom for the horses."

Morland strode into the King's Arms, only to find the taproom empty. So were the entrance hall and the coffee room.

"Publican!" he shouted, tossing open the doors to several other rooms, all equally empty.

A door opened at the back of the establishment. A short, balding man with flour-strewn fingers came hurrying down the corridor. "It's myself as is publican, and Samuel Jones it is to you. What would yourself be wishing?"

"The magistrate—where is he?"

"Magistrate?"

"Hurry man, it's a matter of urgency!"

The publican scratched his gleaming pate, leaving white clumps in his wake. "Squire Buxted, d'you mean?"

"That's the one. Where is he?"

The publican looked bewildered. "Not to contradict you—er, your lordship." Belatedly the landlord had recognized the Earl of Morland. "But I fear it's a different magistrate you're seeking."

"What do you mean, man? Where is Buxted?"

The landlord shook his head in confusion. "Squire Buxted has been abed with the lung sickness for six months now. No, my lord, it's no urgent business he'll be tending to. Not for a long time."

Morland stiffened as he caught the first scent of betrayal. "And the blacksmith? You have no smithy with a cell for holding criminals?"

"Blacksmith? Why, Dedham's had no smith for five

years. Not since Thaxton and his two sons upped and hied themselves to America. But why—"

Morland did not wait for the questions to come. It had all been planned, he realized, all a careful trick so that he would be away from Sevenoaks when—

Cursing long and graphically, he ran back into the street.

But he had a terrible premonition that he was already too late.

They passed no one as they hurried out, for it was still some minutes before dawn.

"How did it happen?" Chessy asked urgently. "Was it another of her nightmares?"

The man beside her slanted her a sharp look. "So she's told you of those? You must be very high in her affections."

"She needed someone to talk to and I happened to be there, that's all."

"I see." A sharp sidelong frown. "Can't you manage to go any faster?"

Chessy bit her lips against the pain at her ankle. "Of course. But where is she?"

Her companion took her arm and helped her up over a steep incline. "She's in a shepherd's cottage across the valley. She's always loved the old mill and the tulip fields there. Apparently she was upset and tried to run away. Then she fell in the dark, and—" He sighed and patted her arm. "The doctor is already there, but—we had better hurry," he added tightly.

"Is Jeremy there too?"

"Jeremy? Of course. He was the one who found her, in fact."

"The poor child." Chessy winced as she stumbled on an exposed tree root.

Morland's grip tightened as he hurried her along. From the lower stretches of the lawn a groom appeared. Morland studied him for a moment, then jerked his head sharply, motioning the man up toward the house.

It hit Chessy then—some still, small voice that whispered something was wrong. It was many things and nothing at all. It was the way he had looked at her, sidelong and impassive. It was the way his hand gripped her elbow, hard and impersonal.

It was his lips, locked and unwavering.

And then, from the house behind her, she heard a shout.

"Chessy, no!"

She turned, frowning as she saw her father charging over the lawn. "Father? Why—"

Hard fingers bit into her arm. The next moment, she was jerked sharply forward.

"What are you doing? Why are we—"

Then she felt it, the cold point of steel nestled hard and lethal against her breast.

"You—you're not Tony." She swallowed as the puzzle pieces slid together with a snap. "Oh, God, you're the *other* one. You're his—"

"Twin," he finished for her. "Andrew Langford, Duke of Morwood." The bronze brow slanted up. "Congratulations, my dear. I was wondering when you would finally realize. I don't know whether to be flattered or offended that it took you so long. My brother and I are a great deal alike, of course, but—" He shrugged and hauled her roughly over the uneven ground.

They were nearly at the edge of the lawn now. Before them the woods stretched upward, dense and brooding. Behind her Chessy heard her father shout, heard the muffled tread of the groom, running fast.

Swiftly she studied the rise to her left, the stand of willows bowing low and thick to her right.

Yes, here was as good a place as any.

She was focusing her breath in preparation to strike when the man beside her laughed harshly. "Don't try it, my dear. Don't even think it. For Elspeth and Jeremy *are* up there in that shepherd's hut. They would follow dear *Tony* anywhere, you see. But one word from me, and they—" He shrugged. "Well, let's just say it won't be a pretty sight."

"You—you animal! You fiend! They are your own children!"

"Perhaps. Of course, with a wife such as I had, one could never be quite certain." And then his voice hardened. "Hurry up, damn you!"

Suddenly Chessy realized why he was rushing. "You're afraid, aren't you—afraid that he'll find us?" She tensed and tried to pull away. "Where is he? What have you done?"

"Your concern for Anthony is touching," her captor said coldly. "But at this moment my dear brother is combing the streets of Dedham in search of the two men who nearly murdered you yesterday as you rode to Sevenoaks." He laughed harshly. "Such a pity that he will not find them. Not in Dedham nor anywhere else. They were of no more use to me after they failed, you see."

Chessy felt cold fingers of fear tighten about her heart. What horror would such a monster plan next?

She fought to stay calm, to envision what this madman's next move would be.

She tried not to think of the two children held frightened and helpless somewhere up there in the hills.

Center, Midnight. The old teachings whispered in her head. Once more she saw Abbot Tang's round, wise face.

Sink deep. Hold all, and oppose nothing. Bend. Yield. In this yielding you will conquer all.

She did as her teacher had told her all those years before, casting her attention low, down to her navel, and then lower, past her knees into the very earth itself.

And as she did so, she felt the strength build.

By the time they reached the hut, Chessy knew she would be ready.

They came across James Cameron's inert body a few yards beyond the woods. His brow was streaked with blood, spilled recently enough that it was bright and flowing still.

"Oh, no . . ." Morland slid from Jupiter and felt for a pulse.

Ravenhurst leaped down beside him. "Good God, is he—"

"Alive, thank God. But just barely." Morland cradled Cameron's bloodstained head and bent close. "Can you hear me, Jamie? What happened here?"

The white-haired man stirred and gave a low groan. A moment later, his eyes opened. "You. Are you really—" His eyes sought out Ravenhurst. Satisfied by that sight, he swallowed and tried again. "*He* came—soon after you left. Must have tricked her."

Morland's heart lurched. He felt the fury rising within him. "Chessy?"

Cameron nodded. "I saw them—tried to call out— then that blasted groom took me from behind. He's got the others tied up in the house."

"Where was he taking her?" Morland's voice was as hard as the native Suffolk flint glinting dark on the hillside.

"Somewhere—up there." Cameron waved weakly to the north. "Couldn't see . . ."

Morland eased the man's head back against the grass. "Help him back to the house, will you, Dane? I'm going after them."

"After *whom*? Forgive me, Tony, but I'm all adrift. Exactly whom are you going after?"

"My brother. My bloody twin *brother*. Andrew is the one who has Chessy." He shoved to his feet just as Cameron's voice rose in anxious protest.

"What is it, Jamie?"

"Be—be careful, my boy. He's—" The old man swallowed.

"He's what?"

"*Them*. Not just Chessy. He's—he's got the children up there too."

45

They climbed ever upward through the woods, keeping to the hills where no paths ran. The pain in Chessy's ankle was constant now, sharp and stabbing, but she struggled to ignore it, her whole attention focused on the confrontation to come.

The forest thinned and then disappeared. Finally green gave way to red.

To a field of red, rising in every glorious shade—scarlet, pink, vermilion, and gleaming copper. Suddenly Chessy was surrounded by the tulip fields Morland had mentioned yesterday as they rode to Sevenoaks. Only his casual description hadn't given Chessy any sense of their vast size.

Row on row the flowers spread, like tiny dancers with their gaudy bonnets unfurled to sun and wind.

Beside her Andrew Morland stiffened. "Another of my dear brother's ideas. There were tulips in this area, already brought by Flemish settlers in the seventeenth century. It had been a hobby of our mother's, but Tony made it something more. It was his idea to expand the yield, improve the bulbs, and sell the flowers in London. Now Sevenoaks is the second-largest supplier outside Lincolnshire. Like everything else he touches, this, too, turned to gold."

Grimly, Andrew crushed a crimson bloom beneath the toe of his polished boot. "*These* will be the first things to go when he dies."

Chessy fought a wave of panic at that flat, cold-blooded vow. "But why? Why do you want to kill him? What has he done to you?"

"Done?" Her captor jerked her to a halt and glared down at her. "*Done?* He's ruined my life, that's what he's done. Have you any idea what it's like to grow up with a mirror image, to know that you can never do or say anything that *he* won't also do or say sometime in his life? That he'll outdo you in anything he attempts?"

A vein began to pound beneath Andrew's right eye. "To know that he'll always be there, dogging your every step, casting your every success into shadow by his own performance. Horses, gaming, and women—it was always the same. How I *hate* him for that!"

He shook his head sharply. His gaze refocused and came to rest on Chessy. "And you," he said mockingly. "How does it feel for you to know I touched you? And that you responded? Oh, yes, I felt it, my dear. And I mean to show my dear brother that this blade cuts both ways, that *he* can never be rid of *me* either."

Chessy was chilled by the fury in the man's voice. She had the sudden sense that he was perched on the knife-edge of reason, and that anything at all might send him plunging down into madness.

And right now, there were two children up the hill, two innocent children. At any moment they might fall victim to his wrath.

"So the coaching accident was a fake?"

Andrew's eyes narrowed. "He told you about that too? Really, I am flattered that my dear brother considers me so important."

Keep him talking, Chessy thought. *Keep his mind off what he's doing. That might just give Tony the time he needs.*

If he comes.

If he knows where to find us.

Andrew jerked her forward, through the waving field of flowers. "Yes, it was entirely a fake. I'd been draining funds from Sevenoaks for years, you see, and I had a tidy sum set by in Jamaica. So it was time to disappear, time to cut myself free of my mocking little shadow at last. And so it was that Andrew Morland had to die. A coaching accident seemed the best choice, as I—or at least the person dressed in *my* clothes—would be rendered utterly unrecognizable from the violence of the impact when the carriage plunged over the cliffs to the beach below."

As he tugged her forward, Chessy hazarded a surreptitious glance behind her into the valley. There was no sign of horses or pursuers, but surely Tony would try to keep his pursuit a secret.

"But how did 'dying' free you from your brother? *You* were the duke, after all, not he. With your death the holdings in Somerset and Sevenoaks became *his*, until Jeremy grows up at least. You were left with nothing but crumbs from the table." She was trying to provoke him, to goad him. Anything to throw him off balance and disrupt his carefully laid plans.

"Crumbs?" Andrew shook his fist in her face. "Do you call twenty thousand pounds *crumbs*?"

Chessy blinked. "But how—"

"By careful work, that's how. By selling off the paintings and the silver, then the jewelry. By letting go of a parcel of land here and a field or two there. All done slowly, so it would not be obvious. My father was clever, you see. He knew my vices well. Before he died, he put legal limits on how much property or art could be sold from the estate. He wanted Sevenoaks to pass intact to his grandson." Andrew sneered. "And then my brother came back from the Peninsula. I had hoped he would die there, but he has led a charmed life, curse him! And I knew I would have to disappear, before he discovered the losses."

They were almost at the top of the tulip field now. Before them stood a weathered windmill with wide white sails that stretched silent and unmoving in the rising sun.

So little time . . .

"Why did you come back? Surely you haven't run through twenty thousand pounds already."

He turned then, jerking Chessy to a halt against him. "Your little scheme is really quite pathetic, my dear. All these delays and distractions can change nothing. But I will be magnanimous and answer your question." His eyes blazed. "I came back for one reason and one reason only: to destroy my annoying little shadow once and for all."

"But Sevenoaks will never *be* yours. You're dead! If you come back, you'll have to explain how and why—"

"Oh, but *I* won't come back, my dear Francesca. Coming back was never part of my plan." He ran a finger across the pale skin that rose and fell above her lace-trimmed bodice. "No, I have a far better idea. I will simply take my brother's place. I will become Anthony Morland. The perfect revenge, is it not?"

"You'll never get away with it!"

"No? I rather think I shall, my beauty." His hands curved lower, cupping her full breasts. "In a week I'll have everything of his, right down to his passionate little wife, panting in my bed."

"Never!"

"Oh, yes, my dear Francesca. You'll place your slender hand on mine, and you'll smile tremulously when the parson pronounces us man and wife. And then you'll follow me upstairs dutifully and bare yourself before me, offering me every pleasure of your naked body." He jerked her face upward and stared down at her. "Because if you don't, if you resist me in *any* way, then those two sweet little children that you like so much will fare very, very badly indeed."

Chessy swayed, choked by horror. Staring into those flat, soulless eyes, she realized what Andrew said was true. Unless she was very careful, he would do everything he threatened.

"Impossible. You—you wouldn't!"

"Oh, but I would." He smiled coldly. "There is one more reason you will do everything I ask. One more thing that will keep you in line, my dear. Have you forgotten it so soon? It is the only thing that will placate your father's quite nasty friends.''

Chessy's eyes widened. ''The book? The pillow book? *You* have it?''

Andrew Langford threw back his head and laughed. ''Of course. It took a great deal of planning, but I finally managed it. The book was the final piece in my plan. As soon as I learned that my brother needed it, I set about to find it first. An art dealer in Macao located it for me. I paid him very well for his assistance, of course, but it seems the man had a lamentable penchant for drink. Afterward he fell from his roof to his death, I'm sorry to say. That left no witnesses, which is so much safer, don't you agree?''

They were almost at the top of the valley. Chessy blinked back tears of pain as her captor shoved her up the slope toward the old windmill.

The door opened. A woman appeared, her face faintly familiar.

''Ah, there you are, Louisa. Are the children behaving?'' Andrew asked lazily.

''Perfectly.'' She smiled as she saw Andrew's captive. ''So, you finally managed it. And now we shall have our own little reception for the bride and groom, shan't we?''

Halfway down the hill, just inside the forest, a dim figure knelt in the shadow of a giant yew tree.

The warrior known as Khan watched in taut silence as Chessy was shoved up the hill, watched as the woman appeared at the door of the windmill.

His body was tense, and his eyes were dark and hard with shadows. For it was a debt of honor now.

If he failed, he would die slowly, painfully.

And by his own hand.

46

Andrew Langford turned, surveying the valley.

"A perfect spot, isn't it? I can see everything and everyone from here, long in advance. And now I think it's time to let my brother know where we are, don't you agree, Louisa?"

She nodded and disappeared inside the windmill.

Without warning Andrew shoved Chessy inside. A moment later, the great white arms of the mill shuddered and then creaked to life, making their first laborious transit under the force of the wind.

Soon the whole structure hummed with the surge of the arms, white in the sunlight. Chessy knew they would be visible for miles.

Which was exactly what her crazed captor wanted.

"Now for the children. Remove their bindings, Louisa, so they can come forward and say their welcomes."

The scuffling of feet brought Chessy around sharply. Her heart twisted when she saw the two pale faces emerge from the adjoining storeroom at the rear of the windmill.

"Let me go, you witch!" Elspeth was jerking wildly

at Louisa's hand, while Jeremy looked frightened but mutinous.

There were ugly red marks at their mouths and wrists.

Chessy felt fury slam through her as she ran to catch them against her. She felt Elspeth give a convulsive shudder, then lapse into dry, racking sobs.

"It's all right, little love. Don't worry."

The girl's face rose, pale and bewildered. "He—he's *not* my father! It's all a trick, isn't it? All some kind of trick?"

Chessy caught her close and stroked her head. "Of course it is, Elspeth," she whispered. "Now you must be brave, and do everything they ask of you."

"But I don't want to—"

"Everything," Chessy said firmly. She studied Jeremy's defiant features and repeated the word. "Everything. Do you both understand?"

After a taut silence, the children nodded.

Andrew strolled closer. "A touching little scene, to be sure. But now I think the children need to rest. For we are soon to have visitors, I think."

At that announcement Jeremy's fists clenched. "You'll never touch him, do you hear? Never!"

Andrew's face hardened. "Take them away, Louisa. I shall have to teach them that children must be seen and not heard."

As Louisa shoved them into the adjoining room, Andrew strode to a dusty table near the door. "And now, I believe that this is what you were searching for all over London?"

He opened a box and lifted out a jewel-encrusted rectangle. Emeralds, rubies, and diamonds winked in the bar of light from the window.

He flicked the ivory closings free and then opened at random to a sheet. A pair of lovers laughed, sporting amid a garden of peonies. Idly he turned the pages, showing scene after scene of jewellike colors, with lovers caught in sensual dalliance.

"Inspiring, is it not, my dear?" Chill eyes scoured Chessy's face. "It almost makes me wish I had more time . . ." He ran his hand across her cheek, her full lower lip. "Ah, yes, I can see why my brother was intrigued with you. After we are through here, we will enjoy this book, you and I. It offers endless amusements." Again the chill smile. "Louisa can attest to that."

Chessy swallowed, fighting to stay calm. "How—how did you find it?"

The bronze brow arched, mocking her attempts at distraction. "Still being devious, are you? But never mind. It hardly matters. We still have some time before our visitors arrive."

He smiled thinly as he moved on through the pages. "Louisa has quite a collection of the books, by the way. This one was in the possession of a rather jaded Italian count who had just purchased it from an even more jaded Manchu prince. As I recall, Louisa was part of the purchase price in both cases." The thin lips curled upward. "She is really quite insatiable, that one. And Tony is the only man who has ever spurned her." He made a clucking nose. "But he would do better to mind his bard. 'Hell hath no fury,' you see. And Louisa is most determined to have her moment of revenge for that piece of public humiliation. But where were we? Oh, yes, she is by now quite an expert with this particular book. The price of its acquisition was her participation in the amusements of each page, you see." He smoothed a fold from his lace cuff. "Not that she found the job overly onerous."

Above them the great sails spun on, moving in quiet precision. They had been recently oiled, Chessy realized. No doubt Andrew had planned for this detail too.

She shivered, feeling as if she were locked in a nightmare, with no avenue of escape.

But there had to be *some* way.

And then her captor's white fingers closed upon her arm. "But I wonder . . ."

He jerked her against him, his turquoise eyes blazing with madness. His fingers locked in her bodice and wrenched downward.

And then his mouth came down, hard and grinding

against hers. Chessy twisted, locking her lips, but fear for the children kept her from clawing at him as she wished to do.

He swore, gripped her face, and jerked her immobile. "Open your mouth, damn it! Open it, if you want to see those damned children ever again."

Choking back nausea, Chessy complied. Instantly his tongue thrust against hers and his fingers probed greedily at her gaping bodice.

And then, suddenly, it was over.

He shoved her from him and stood back, surveying her.

"Yes, very nice." He gave her a cool smile. "And exactly the thing to provoke my dear brother."

Chessy caught her hands behind her, balling them to fists. She knew how she looked, flushed and disheveled, her lips red and swollen from the fury of his kiss.

And that was just how Andrew wanted his brother to see her, to inflame his anger.

For that, too, was part of this cruel plan.

And then every thought but one was driven from Chessy's mind. Boots hammered against the earth, outside the opened door.

She heard a voice, a familiar voice, raised hard with rage. And then the man she loved stepped before the door.

"Let her go, Andrew. *I'm* the one you want, not her! Let her go, and the children with her. Then, by God, you can have me!"

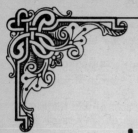

47

Instantly Andrew thrust Chessy back, into a recess beside the narrow half-shuttered window.

He stared out at Anthony, his eyes glittering with mad triumph. "So you came, my dear brother. I see you noticed my little beacon light."

"The mill is unsafe, you fool. I had it closed down months ago."

"Too bad. For your lovely Miss Cameron and the children, that is."

"Let them go, Andrew. Then come out and face me like a man."

Chessy's captor gave a cold laugh. "I think not, Anthony. You are not going to be free of me quite so easily this time."

He seized a squirming Chessy and shoved her in front of the open window. "She's a very tasty little mouthful, by the way. I can see why you were enticed by her."

A raw curse ripped the air.

"Do you want her? If so, you're going to have to work for her." His lips pulled back in a thin, bloodless smile. "Louisa must be paid, after all. And the wench

410

is wealthy enough that money holds no interest for her. She is determined upon a prize of a different sort, you see."

Chessy raised agonized eyes. Tony stood grim-faced, a pistol clutched in his hand. Behind him lay a leather satchel, half hidden among the tulips.

"Let Chessy and the children go. And then I shall— see to Louisa."

"First things first, my dear boy. Drop your pistol. Then kick that satchel over here where I can see it." Andrew's hand moved, leveling the muzzle of his own weapon against Chessy's breast.

After a low curse Morland obeyed.

His pistol hit the flowers. A moment later, the satchel went bumping over the ground.

"Very good. Now come closer, so I can be sure you have no other tricks up your sleeve."

Chessy stiffened as she heard a muffled sound behind her in the storeroom, but Andrew, his attention focused on his brother, did not seem to have noticed.

From the corner of her eye she saw the door inch open. Two childish faces beamed at her, and then another face, cast in shadow.

The face of a warrior she had not seen since her months at Shao-lin.

She saw his warning nod and his silent gesture at Louisa, whom Chessy saw lying bound and gagged against the far wall.

Hope surged inside her.

And then Chessy cried out as Andrew's fingers clenched on her arm and jerked her into the doorway. There he held her, braced before him.

"Very well. And now you may have one last kiss. Never say that I am not magnanimous. But I advise you to be very careful, Anthony. For the children's sake, you understand."

Chessy felt her heart lurch. Out of the corner of her eye she could see the children crawling out of the storeroom window. A few seconds more, and they would be safe.

She had to see that they got those few seconds.

"He—he has the book, Tony. He knew it would bring you exactly where he wanted you. Just as it brought me."

She saw Tony's look of surprise, which he quickly concealed. "My congratulations, Andrew. I never realized you were so resourceful."

"There are many things you do not know about me, Anthony. But I am afraid you are not going to have any time to discover them now."

Elspeth was out, and Jeremy was inching over the weathered sill. Chessy caught a breath.

"I'll give you Sevenoaks, you know," Tony said. "I'll see it's deeded to you free and clear. I'll even see if we can have those other limitations removed."

"Paltry, my dear brother. I'm after much more than Sevenoaks."

"Name it. If I can, I'll—"

Andrew Morland laughed. "Ah, but this is one thing you cannot share. For it is *you* I want, dear twin. Your name—your very identity."

He dug his pistol into Chessy's breast. "I've had enough of you dogging my every pleasure, haunting my every dream. It was always you, the one my mother preferred, the one our father secretly wished could be duke one day. You even had your first wench before I did, right up here in the hay of the storeroom." His eyes glittered. "Don't you remember? Mollie, the miller's lush little daughter?"

"Mollie had everyone in pants. By the time she was seventeen, she had had me and every other man on Sevenoaks land. *You* included."

"That's right, brother dear. But after she had *you*, it was never the same, damn you."

Chessy saw Tony frown, saw his eyes flicker off to his right.

She realized he had seen the children.

Morland inched closer. "Too bad, Andrew. I never knew about any of that. If I had, it might have changed things."

He took another step.

Instantly Chessy's captor stiffened. He drove his

pistol against her ribs until she winced. "Don't come any closer. Not unless you want the children to pay for your arrogance."

"The children?" Tony said silkily. "But they are quite safe, Andrew. Right now, they are standing over beside the windmill. In fact, it looks as if your schemes have failed again."

Cursing, his twin glanced back over his shoulder.

It was all the distraction Chessy needed. She wrenched sideways, drove the heel of her hand against his throat, then slammed her knee into his groin. Without stopping for breath she stumbled forward, gritting her teeth as she plunged down the wooden steps fronting the windmill. The great vanes were spinning fast now, and the air gusted wildly around her face.

She heard Andrew groan. Then came the crack of a pistol.

The ball struck Tony full in the leg, exactly where he had been wounded at Salamanca. With a wild cry Chessy plunged beneath the rising sail and caught him as he staggered.

Inside the windmill she heard his brother shoving himself upright, tugging at the rickety table for support.

"Get down, Chessy!" With a growl, Morland dove forward, knocking her to the ground as a second shot rang out.

She felt him flinch, felt the race of his heart. Something thick and wet struck her shoulder.

"Oh, Tony, did he—"

"As soon as I move, run for the side of the mill." Gritting his teeth, he rolled sideways and staggered to his feet. Here I am, Andrew!" he growled. "Or are you still afraid of me, just as you always were?"

Andrew staggered into the doorway with a curse. Bracing himself against the frame, he aimed again. This time the shot cracked wide, plowing through the crimson tulips.

"Come and get me!" Tony shouted. "Or are you going to bungle this plan too?" He was staggering now. His breeches were soaked with blood at his knee.

Numbly Chessy scrambled toward the side of the windmill, as he had ordered her to do. There she caught Elspeth close and tried to soothe her trembling. She did not question the presence of the tall man she had not seen for years, not since the day she had left Shaolin.

This must have been part of her father's plan.

And then she saw the half-dragon hanging from a silken cord around his neck.

Abbot Tang . . .

Her teacher's words came back to her: *When you need me, I will be there, Midnight.*

Chessy scrubbed the tears from her eyes. Help had come to her, had been with her all along. But now it was Tony who was in danger, and there was nothing she nor any one of them could do to help him.

Red-faced with rage, Andrew charged through the doorway and lunged beneath the white sails of the mill, pistol in hand. "No!"

"Face me with honor, Andrew." Tony jerked at the forgotten leather satchel and tugged out two gleaming rapiers. "Sword to sword. If you dare," he challenged coldly.

"Throw it, you bastard. And then prepare to die!"

A second later, the blade hissed through the air. Andrew's pistol fell unheeded to the ground as he caught the rapier close. Without a second's pause he drove forward, before Tony had even pulled his own weapon free.

His first thrust left a slash of scarlet at Morland's sleeve. Grimly Tony jerked the second rapier from the satchel and leaped backward.

On Andrew came, with skill and confidence that showed long practice. Again and again he thrust, always to the side, always where he could take advantage of Tony's weakened right leg.

Through the swaying fields of crimson they moved in a grim ballet, while Chessy and the children watched white-faced with horror.

Once Tony stumbled, and Andrew delivered a savage thrust to his chest. Chessy cried out as Tony staggered.

She started over the field, but the hard-faced warrior beside her caught her back.

"You cannot interfere, Midnight. It is *his* battle now, and his honor to be won."

"But he's hurt. He's—"

"*His* honor. Warrior to warrior. No matter the cost."

Chessy swallowed back her fear and her protest, knowing it was true. Morland would not thank her for her intervention. His pride was too great for that. All she could do was watch, hands clenched to fists, while Andrew closed in upon his prey.

Once more he thrust.

Elspeth's fingers closed hard around Chessy's.

Laughing, Andrew lunged again, and this time Tony did not move fast enough to escape the full force of the gleaming blade.

"That is for Mollie and for all the other joys you robbed me of. And this one is for the future—the future I'll finally be able to enjoy without you around to torment me."

The man was quite mad, Chessy realized, but even in his madness his skill did not waver. He dropped low and drove his blade forward with deadly speed.

Grimacing, Tony swung sideways and parried. Their blades crossed, rang out with a mortal keening.

And then Tony twisted sharply. His blade went spiraling down over Andrew's. A second later, his brother's rapier sailed free, twisting hilt over blade as it spun up in wild circles.

It struck the ground with a thud and then stood blade down, hissing softly as it rocked back and forth amid the bloodred blooms.

"No—not again!" Cursing, Andrew bent low, digging frantically at the ground.

Too late, Chessy realized his deadly intent.

With a wild cry of triumph he staggered upright, his pistol clutched in his outstretched hand.

He fired.

Tony flinched but did not fall. He just kept coming.

His brother cursed. His hand began to shake, and he gripped the pistol with both hands to steady it.

"It's over, Andrew. Give it up. We'll find some way to—"

"*Never!* I'll have it all or I'll have none of it! I'm tired of sharing my face and my life, of being forever second to *you!*"

He took a quick step back as Tony staggered forward. His arm straightened, the pistol gleaming in the sunlight.

Chessy froze, hearing the wind rush past her face, feeling the wild drumbeat of her heart.

And then Andrew fired. "No arrangements, damn you! No deals. No more promises. I've done it, once and for all! I've won!"

Laughing shrilly, he lurched backward as Tony swayed and fell to his knees, his hands locked to his side.

And then—

The rest would always remain a nightmare to Chessy. Long afterward, it haunted her in wisps and glimpses of memory.

It started with Andrew's hoarse laugh. His wild, staggering dance of triumph.

And then his surprise as his boot hit a hidden rock.

The tottering. The flapping hands. The sudden, blind descent backward.

And his fall, straight into the great white arms of the windmill.

Chessy jerked the children to her chest as the gleaming blades swung down, hurled relentlessly in their path by tons of weight and well-oiled machinery.

They struck with an awful, muffled thump.

A scream, and then a terrible silence.

In the field the tulips shook, their petals splashed red upon bloodred in the sunlight.

Releasing the children to her grim-faced friend, Chessy ran down the hill to Tony. His face was lined with pain as he caught her close.

"Damn him. I never thought, believe me I never imagined—" Chessy felt him shudder. "And I led you here, right into his trap. God, Cricket, can I ever make it up to you?"

Chessy ran her hand gently over his pale forehead and brushed back a strand of unruly golden hair. "Never. But I'm going to spend hour after hour seeing that you try." Her voice fell. "Night after sultry night. Oh, I promise you that."

Tony's fingers tensed on her waist. "I'll—I'll hold you to that promise, my love. Starting—"

He clutched at his knee. His eyes closed in pain. "Starting tomorrow . . ." he muttered. Then he collapsed in a sprawl against the swaying tulips.

48

"**Y**ou are without a doubt the most infuriating—the most *impossible* patient! Hold still while I—"

"I've had that ghastly mix before." The Earl of Morland's face was mutinous. One bronze brow rose in an arrogant slant.

"Don't give *me* that look, Tony Morland!"

The earl's arms locked atop his chest.

"It is far past time for your medicine." Chessy tried to avoid the dark pull of his gaze. "You'll have to—"

"Kiss me, harridan."

"Tony, stop this, or you'll—"

"*One kiss.* Freely bartered for one spoonful of that abominable brew you're intent on forcing down my throat."

Chessy glared at the earl. White bandages circled his ribs and shoulder as he lay upon a mountain of soft white pillows. After his collapse at the windmill he had slept on and off for two days.

Now in the sputtering light of the candle his eyes were full of determination.

"But this is treachery! This is blackmail. This is—"

"Love. Love at first sight." Tony's voice was low and

very soft. "Ten years ago, Cricket. Do you remember? Ah, God, but I do. The moon was casting nets of silver over the bay. We went swimming there by the boat, in water that felt like smooth black silk."

Chessy's throat constricted. Oh, yes, she remembered. Perhaps she remembered too well. It made her hands tremble, her knees go all weak and quivery.

"That was a long time ago." She made her voice crisp. He was weak from his wounds, after all. What kind of nurse would she be if she—

"You've forgotten?" Again the lazy challenge. "You don't remember that night when I came upon you swimming? Swimming without a stitch on?"

Chessy swallowed. Her hair fell in a dark curtain across her face as she fussed with a clean strip of gauze. She muttered something beneath her breath.

"What? I don't believe I heard that, Cricket."

"I said that perhaps I had a vague memory or two."

"Ah. A vague memory."

"Perhaps," she corrected scrupulously.

Tony's fingers slid around her wrists. He tugged her toward him.

"What are you—"

His hands tightened. A second later, she toppled onto the bed beside him, her silken peignoir flowing about her like a glistening pool of liquid amethyst. Instantly his fingers slid deep into her hair.

"Tony, stop! You can't!"

"*Ummmm.* Can't . . ."

"But—"

"Closer, Cricket."

"No! Your leg!"

"*What* leg?"

"The one that terrible man nearly shattered with his bullet. Now let me go before—"

His only answer was the deft loosening of her sash. Before Chessy knew it, the amethyst silk was sliding down her shoulders. "I won't do this, do you hear? It's crazy. It's irresponsible! It's—"

"Ah, Cricket, I love it when you talk to me that way."

"*What* way?"

"Sexy. Sultry. With unbridled passion."

"I did no such thing!" Chessy struggled upright. At her movement the dark silk pooled around the ivory swell of her breasts.

Morland groaned. "God, just look at you." His eyes darkened, all smoke and azure. They reminded Chessy of a chunk of Himalayan turquoise her father had once given her.

"Tony, no. We can't—"

He didn't seem to hear. "So full. So sweet. Just like you were that night in the moonlight. I watched a drop of water slide right down *here*, did you know that?"

Chessy shivered as his fingers traced a path across her naked breast.

"And I thought I would die if I couldn't touch you the same way." His voice was hoarse. "I mean to do it right now, Cricket."

"T-Tony. Oh, please . . ." Somehow Chessy never got around to that other word—the *no* she knew she should be saying. And then her breath fled as his long fingers found her swelling softness.

"*Ummmmm.*"

Silence. Small, suggestive wiggling movements. And then a soft sigh.

"Well, Cricket?"

"I—" Chessy shivered as he ran his nail gently over the pouting terminus of her breast. "You must—" She swallowed audibly. "You must s-stop." Her lashes fell, masking the sudden hunger in her eyes. "It—it cannot be good for you."

"If I stop, it will be even *worse*," he growled.

Chessy trembled at the gentle stroking of his fingers. Heat began to course through her. "Then—then perhaps you could do that again. Just once more. Surely that c-can't hurt you. . . ."

He did. Chessy sighed.

And this time her wriggling was most urgent. Then abruptly she frowned. "What about your mistress?"

"Germaine has sought comfort with a gray-haired

viscount. I never saw her again—not after that night, you know."

"I'm glad to hear it, you rake. But where did you learn—" Her eyes darkened. "Not from *her*. That wretched Louisa Landringham! Just the thought of you—you and her—"

"Hush, harridan! I never touched Louisa. That was the reason she hated me, if you must know."

Chessy went very still. "Oh." It was a small, wondering sound. "Not ever?"

"Not once, you intractable creature. And Louisa will not be tormenting anyone for quite a while, I think."

"Oh, Tony, what did you do to her? Nothing—terrible, I hope."

"I suppose it all depends on your point of view. I simply gave her a choice." His expression hardened. "Have you forgotten that she nearly had you killed?"

"She did not succeed."

"And that is the *only* reason she got off so lightly. Since you're dying to know, I'll tell you. I gave her a choice of being turned over to the magistrate or going off to Macao."

Chessy's eyes widened.

"To work on one of the pleasure boats," Morland added grimly.

"Oh, you didn't! But she—"

"My dear Chessy, the woman will probably find it a positive delight. She's had more than a little experience with the pillow book already, from what Andrew said. At least this will keep her out of *our* hair. And a lot of men in London will sleep safer tonight with her far, far away."

"Then you really didn't—you two weren't—"

Morland clicked his tongue. "Foolish, my dear. Unforgivably foolish."

Chessy's brow creased. "But everyone said—" She colored faintly.

Morland gave her a knowing look. "Ah, my sweet, don't tell me an intelligent woman like yourself believes everything she hears."

Chessy sniffed. "One would have to be *deaf* not to hear the stories about *you*, my lord."

"Intrigued you, did they?"

"Of course not!" But the faint flush that stained Chessy's cheeks belied her protest.

"Fascinating, were they? Shameful? Totally outrageous?"

"So they were. And you seem positively proud of it!"

Morland made her a lazy little bow. "I try my best. One has an image to maintain, after all." Then he caught her wrists with surprising strength and pressed them down against the silken coverlet.

"Stop that right now, Tony Langford! Otherwise I'll call my father in here to hold you down while I administer your next dose of medicinal tea!"

"Your father? I'm vastly sorry, love, but you'll find Jamie is unavailable right now. He and your mother are busy making up for all those lost years."

Chessy gave him a tremulous smile. "Are they really? Oh, Tony, I'm so glad. . . . My mother," she said slowly. Wonderingly. "I never thought I would have a chance to meet her. To know her . . ."

"You have accepted what has happened? Even though it hurt you deeply?"

Chessy stared off at the sunlit hills, remembering the encounter with her father and the white-faced woman she now knew was her mother. She had been stunned, left trembling and speechless at the news they had broken to her in the silence of Sevenoaks's sunny front parlor.

In the wake of Chessy's shock had come anger. How could Elizabeth have left her husband and child like that? And why had she never tried to repair the estrangement in the long years that followed?

Afterward Chessy realized her anger was for her father as much as for herself. She knew he had suffered deeply and in silence, and that he had remained true to his wife in his heart. It also explained why he had refused to remarry and grew adept at parrying the

matrimonial attempts of widows and sly-faced debu-
tantes alike.

But when Elizabeth began to cry, agreeing that all
was as Chessy charged, that she could never be forgiven
for her wickedness, Chessy felt her anger fade. Like
yellow sand carried before the seething currents of
China's Yellow River, her bitterness, too, was swept
away.

This was no time for bitterness or regrets. She had
found her mother again, the mother she'd thought long
dead. They would have years before them—long and
happy years to rebuild their past, and the rest of a
lifetime to share in laughter and understanding.

They'd embraced then, anger and remorse forgotten. They were only mother and daughter then, only
two people cruelly separated, and then reunited with
equally cavalier unpredictability.

And a beaming James Cameron had caught them
both close, pronouncing them the two most beautiful
creatures on the face of God's green earth.

Remembering that afternoon, Chessy smiled wistfully and looked at Tony. "I *have* accepted it. At least I
think I have." And as she spoke she knew it was true.
Why wallow in bitterness when the future was open for
them to start all over? "She's—she's lovely, isn't she?
My mother," she repeated softly. "I am very lucky to
have found her again."

"As she was lucky to find you. And she is no lovelier
than her daughter," the Earl of Morland said huskily,
wiping the single tear from her cheek.

At his movement the folds of Chessy's peignoir
drifted further apart, framing her ivory beauty from
knee to shoulder. Only her sash lay across her, gleaming at her slender waist.

"Ah, Cricket, I was wrong. You are not as beautiful
as you were ten years ago. You are *even more* beautiful."
And then his mouth skimmed her sweetly pouting
breast, at the same spot where the water droplet had
tormented him a decade before.

"N-no, Tony, you mustn't! You *cannot*. This will only
lead to—"

"Hush, woman! I'm busy maintaining my reputation." His lips curved against her, strong and suckling and utterly implacable.

"T-Tony! Oh, p-please . . ."

Only when she was taut beneath his lips did he release her. He smiled darkly as he surveyed his handiwork. "Nice. Yes, *very* nice, Miss Cameron. Now that that particular bit of business is settled, you can give me your foul liquid and be done with it." He sat back calmly against the pillows.

"Done?" Chessy could only stare. "B-business?"

"Quite. There will be no more of *that* until after our errant cleric finishes his work. I'll take no chance of further aspersions upon your reputation." He studied her darkly. "Especially not now, since I've satisfied myself that there is nothing between you and that stony-faced fellow you studied with at Shao-lin."

Chessy's fingers curved into the crisp sheets. She was growing angrier by the second.

"Of course, I had to be sure first. If there had been anything between the two of you, I would have had to do something drastic."

"Drastic?"

"To *him*. That great cave creature who never seems to smile." Tony's frown grew. "Except at you."

"Ah. You mean Conn."

"Oh, we're to first names, are we?"

Chessy gave Tony a confiding smile. "Well, it's really Jean-Luc Connor MacKinnon, but no one could pronounce that at Shao-lin, so we came up with Conn. Considering that he's part French, part Scot, and part Manchu prince, it seemed appropriate to give his name a Chinese intonation. 'Khan.' " She demonstrated. " 'Khaaaan.' You see?"

Tony's face was thunderous. "I rather think I do. A pity I can't boot the fellow out on his backside. But under the circumstances, considering the assistance he gave you and the children . . ."

"Oh, Tony, you're jealous!" Chessy gave a delighted laugh.

"I? Jealous?" One bronze brow arched skyward. "Don't be absurd, woman."

"You *are*, you great fraud! Right down to the tips of your arrogant toes."

"Nonsense," Morland said loftily.

"You are, you are!" Chessy clapped her hands.

"Well, perhaps an iota or two." The earl frowned. "After all, you and that brooding fellow *were* immured together, training day after day, week after week."

Chessy gave him a devilish smile. "Month after month," she purred.

In a trice she was on her back, with her arms caught firmly above her head. Tony's eyes were glittering. "You like to live dangerously, woman."

"Very dangerously, my lord." Her tongue slid suggestively across her full lower lip. "But what about your promise?" she asked innocently. "I distinctly remember your saying that there would be no more of *this*. Not until after we were married."

Again the dusky lashes swept down, veiling Chessy's eyes. "Can it be that you've changed your mind, my lord?"

Her expression was all innocence—considering that she was lying nearly naked beneath him. And her smile could have melted ice in December.

The earl muttered irritably beneath his breath.

"What did you say, my love?"

"I said, you stubborn creature, that you are going to be sorry for this. Very sorry, I promise you. I am going to work you like the very devil until you can write *every* word in *every* book in my whole library." His palm cupped the silky warmth of her breast and a shudder went through him.

"Indeed? I suppose that means a great deal of investigation." Chessy's eyes centered on Tony's lips. "All sorts of personal . . . scrutiny. To be sure I've learned everything you have to teach me—"

As she spoke, Chessy moved slightly, ensuring that the silk skirt of her peignoir slid the rest of the way from her creamy thighs.

Now the only scrap of clothing left was the dark length of her sash.

Trailing across her slender waist, across her creamy nakedness, the swath of amethyst was unspeakably erotic.

Morland closed his eyes and prayed for patience. And barring patience, at least some vestige of sanity.

"That *is* the only way you can be certain I've learned these, ah, lessons, is it not, my lord?"

Her look was guileless, but her voice was husky with need.

The combination stole Tony's breath away.

"Ah, God, woman, you'll be the very death of me! I was safer at Salamanca with Napoleon's *voltigeurs*, I think."

"I devoutly hope not." Chessy smiled slightly as she felt the hard thrust of his manhood against her thigh. "And I rather think you have the same thought in mind, my lord. Despite all your protestations."

"Chessy, one of these days, so help me—"

"Why not right now?"

"Are you *always* this stubborn, woman?"

Chessy slanted him a smile. "Is that a yes or a no, my love?"

"I'm not sure. I'm trying to decide whether to kiss you or throttle you."

"Kissing sounds much the nicer choice." Chessy's hip moved delicately against his thigh. She felt Morland's telltale quiver, followed by the awesome tensing of male muscle too long denied. "Besides, I've already begun my lessons." She gave him a proud smile. "Elspeth has been instructing me."

Morland rolled his eyes skyward. "Elspeth? May the good Lord preserve us."

"Just watch, you arrogant man." Biting her lip with concentration, Chessy leaned forward and begin tracing letters against Morland's thigh.

Somehow, despite the fire that blazed to life at her touch, the earl managed to keep from moving. He watched her face as she concentrated on her task.

It was the face of a fighter. The face of someone

determined, stubborn, and wonderfully alive. The sight made him offer a silent prayer of thanks to heaven for protecting her through the last dangerous weeks.

And then he swallowed as he realized exactly what her fingers were tracing upon his naked thigh.

I L-O-V-E Y-O-

He didn't wait for her to finish. The E was backward and the Y was crooked, but they were still the most beautiful letters Tony Morland had ever witnessed.

And Chessy was tight in his arms before she even knew what had happened.

"Did I get it right?" Her eyes glittered with sudden tears.

Tony heard the tremor in her voice and it made him bleed inside. He caught her hand to his lips. "Perfect, my love. I couldn't have done it any better myself. Of course, I'd be delighted to try. Perhaps in a slightly different spot, if you'd care to—"

"You're sure they were right?" She ran her fingers uncertainly across the bronze skin at his shoulder. "I've been so embarrassed—so ashamed. All this time, and I never learned to read. I've always been so afraid someone would find out." She looked up then. "Does it—do you still—"

"Love you? To distraction, I'm afraid. And something tells me you'll soon be reading far better than I."

"Then you don't care? It doesn't bother you that—"

With a groan, Tony pulled her closer.

And then he silenced her. Authoritatively. Autocratically. Completely unequivocally. His lips were hard and driving, but his hands were gentle, full of wonder at the tender discovery of her passion.

As he slid his leg to her side, Tony fought unsuccessfully to conceal a grimace of pain.

"Oh, no—is it your leg?"

He gave her a crooked smile. "I'm afraid so. It—it appears that I'm going to need a little help, Cricket."

Chessy pushed him back onto the bed. Her body eased atop his. "Like this?"

"Like—that." His eyes closed as Chessy continued her slow, melting conquest of his body. At that moment the hero of Salamanca had a sudden realization: Showing an occasional bit of weakness might not be such a bad idea after all.

Especially if *this* was the result.

Abruptly, he frowned. "Wait just a minute, hellion. Exactly who is seducing *whom* here?"

"I'd say it was just about equal, your lordship." Chessy inched lower, slowly, inexorably drawing him inside her velvet heat.

Morland went utterly still. Beads of sweat broke out upon his brow.

"Well?"

"*Ummmmm.*"

"Good?"

"Ahhhhhh, God."

"Tony, I asked you if—"

Morland fought for sanity and won—just barely. "Good? Sweet heaven above, woman! *Good* isn't *nearly* the word for how you feel against me. Your texture, your scent—yes, I think I'll have to get myself wounded more often."

Chessy released the breath she had been holding and gave him a roguish smile. "Ah, well, there's no need to thank me, you know. After all, that's what we women are for, isn't it? To rescue our men when they get in over their head."

Tony's eyes promised her a devastatingly sensual revenge for that particular comment. Then his breath caught as Chessy fitted herself with aching sweetness to his awesomely aroused manhood. "Lord, woman! Now I *know* I'm dying."

But Chessy paid no heed. At least he had given up fighting her calculated seduction. And there were so very many things she had yet to learn. . . .

"*Stubborn*—" A shudder worked through him as she sheathed him totally. "Yes, that's the only—ahhhhh—word for you, Cricket."

"Thank you very much, my lord." Chessy's eyes were shining as she felt him begin to move, deep and sure and powerful within her. "Coming from someone as stubborn as *you*, that's an exceptional compliment."

Without warning his fingers shifted.

Her eyes widened.

"Yes, my love. Give me the sounds of your pleasure. Take me deep. Take me to forever."

"Oh, Tony—oh, yes, I—"

And then the first tremor began. She held him close, flung blind to the edge of madness, blind to the edge of paradise. And there she found she had no need for *any* words at all.

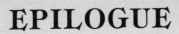

EPILOGUE

East
of Forever

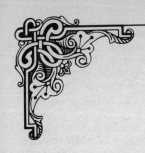

Sevenoaks
June 1819

"**I**t really is *most* amazing, isn't it?" The Duchess of Cranford stood surveying the guests thronging the broad green lawns of Sevenoaks. "I sometimes wonder if I know *half* these people."

"Of course you do." Beside the duchess a striking woman with amethyst eyes turned her head with a smile. "Besides, what does it matter? They certainly know *you*, my dear Amelia."

As if to prove the truth of this, a laughing couple hailed the duchess as they moved toward the buffet tables set up beneath a gaily striped tent of crimson and white.

The duchess harumphed. "I never saw *those* two in my life! Besides, the fellow's wearing stays. *Stays*, my dear Lizzie! I can hear the man creaking from here!"

Mrs. James Cameron patted her hand soothingly. "Well, my dear, not all of us are blessed with such a willowy figure as yours."

433

The duchess slanted her glowing companion a shrewd look. "I haven't see your husband showing any dissatisfaction with *your* figure, my dear. It was rather a nice idea to have Chessy wear your wedding gown, by the way. She looked quite lovely in the old style. So much more elegant than these bits of nothing women wear today."

"Yes, she was beautiful, wasn't she? All those yards of white satin, and those lovely flowing lace sleeves set with seed pearls. I designed that dress myself, you know." Her gaze wandered over the milling crowds on the lawn.

"Humph. Morland certainly thought it was beautiful. If you ask me, the man looked positively wolfish during the ceremony. So did that husband of *yours*, come to think of it!"

Lizzie's eyes crinkled. "He did, didn't he?" She sighed. "Did James tell you that we're going to repeat our vows next week? He even asked that I wear my old gown. He is really the most romantic man." She sighed again. "And did I mention that he—"

The duchess raised an imperious hand. "No, you didn't, and I don't wish to hear either. Not one more word about that man's Don Juan ways."

Chessy's mother barely heard. She was too busy searching the crowd for her distinguished husband.

The change that came over her when she finally saw him was electric. Her eyes grew bright and her cheeks took on a becoming blush.

"Why, Lizzie Granville, you're blushing like a chit fresh out of the schoolroom!" This bit of censure only made Mrs. Cameron's color rage higher.

At that moment James Cameron strode up, two crystal goblets in hand. The first he offered to the duchess, who accepted it grudgingly. The second was presented to his wife, with a most handsome bow.

"I'm afraid you're going to have to call her Mrs. Cameron from now on, Your Grace. It's been a long time since she was Miss Granville, you know."

His wife dimpled as he touched his goblet to hers, offering a silent toast.

"Humph! It's all moonbeams and magic with you two! Next thing you'll be telling me there's a child on the way." As James Cameron gave her an arrested look, the duchess held up a papery hand. "No, I don't want to hear about it! It's your daughter I'm looking for. And that scapegrace husband of hers."

Cameron hid a smile. "I believe they have left, Your Grace."

"Left! But I haven't had a chance to—" The white-haired duchess cleared her throat. "Ah well, I suppose it can wait." Her eyes narrowed on a crowd of women who were gathered at one end of the buffet, tittering loudly. "What in the world are those silly females making such a fuss about?"

At that moment the throng of gaudy parasols parted to reveal a lean-limbed man in crisp black worsted. His eyes were an arresting tone of gold-flecked amber, and his skin was exactly the shade of the dragon pendant of burnished bronze that hung at his neck.

"So that's Chessy's warrior. Even in English dress he looks exotic. And ferocious. Nearly as ruthless as that dragon he wears around his neck."

"I suppose he can be. Actually, no one knows very much about his past," Cameron added. "He says next to nothing about himself."

The duchess looked thoughtful. "He doesn't even notice, does he?"

"Notice what?"

"How the women fawn over him, following his every word and gesture. He actually seems oblivious. Chessy told me he's always been like that. Do you know, for a while I actually thought the man was in love with *her*."

"So he was," Cameron said softly. "Once." He shrugged. "But it appears he's gotten over it."

"Either that or he gives an impeccable performance." The duchess fingered a lace frill at her sleeve. "I wonder . . ."

"Now, Amelia." Lizzie Granville slanted a worried look at her friend. "You know it's not a good idea to interfere in other people's lives."

"Oh, posh! At my age, what else is there for me to do?"

"Any number of things! You just can't go around pulling people's strings and making secret plans for them. It only brings pain and—"

But the duchess was not listening. Her thoughts were already moving to her next scheme. And Lizzie Granville Cameron never finished her admonition anyway, because her husband began to tug her toward the maze that beckoned cool and green at the far side of the lawns.

"But James, we can't!"

"And why not, woman?"

"Because—because it's broad daylight. Because we have a wedding to celebrate. Our daughter's wedding!"

"I have my own way of celebrating."

"But Chessy—"

"Tony will keep our Chessy busy, my love, never you fear."

"Then—you know where they went?"

"Let's just say I have a fair idea. Now forget about those two children. They've plagued us quite enough. We've got business of our own to attend to."

"We do?"

"We do." He gave her a smoky look.

"Oh, James. I couldn't possibly—"

He cut her off by tugging her into the screening lanes of clipped yew. At the maze's first turning he caught her close and slid his fingers into her lustrous chestnut hair.

It was flecked with white now, but the effect was extraordinarily becoming, he decided. "I hate you in pins. Why do you wear the bloody things?" With one tug he sent the carved bits of tortoiseshell flying. "There, that's infinitely better."

"Really, James, one would think you were naught but a reckless boy of sixteen!"

He gave her a devilish smile as he inched her back against the wall of foliage. "Do you mean to tell me I'm not? Ah, but when I'm with *you*, Lizzie, I surely feel like one."

And then his hands circled her waist. His lips nibbled their way over hers.

"Oh, James—"

"Hush, wife."

This time she did. And the next sound to be heard in the yew maze came from him.

Groaning as she slid close and kissed him back—with what James Cameron decided was a most delightful want of propriety.

"That does it! Dash it, I don't see the boy anywhere!" Frowning, Sir Reginald Fortesque watched Chessy's mother and father slip off into the maze. "He's not with the countess's parents, for they've just snuck off into the greenery. Smelling of April and May themselves, I might add."

"Such an unusual family." Exquisite as always in sober black and pristine white linen, Lord Alvanley stood surveying the throng. "I had hoped to offer my felicitations in person, but it is only to be expected that the bride and groom would have, er, other things on their minds this day."

He smiled slightly as he watched the duchess descend upon the Duke of Wellington and detach him from the clutches of an encroaching female in puce satin.

Alvanley shuddered slightly. "Puce, my dear Reginald. *Puce!* One positively despairs. Since Brummell left us, the world has gone to the dogs!"

His companion stared owlishly at the gaudily dressed company. "Puce? Never liked the color much myself. Always reminded me of Louisa Landringham's eyes." He frowned suddenly. "By the way, where is that female? No one seems to have laid eyes on her since the night of the Duchess of Cranford's ball. Deuced havey-cavey, if you ask me!"

Impassive, Alvanley continued to survey the assemblage. "I might allow to possessing some information about that."

"You know? So where is the man-eater? I felt certain

she'd be here! After all, she's been lusting after Tony for years now."

"My dear Reginald, do try and moderate your speech."

"Well, it's true, by gad. You know it as well as I do!"

"Of course it's true. But that does not necessitate your trumpeting it about to half the *ton* as they stroll past."

The gaily dressed dandy toyed with an ormolu watch fob. "Demned stickler. That's what you are!"

"Why thank you, Reggie."

"Dash it, that was no compliment!"

"Indeed?" The exquisite figure studied him impassively. "I'm desolate to say it, Reggie, but you've had a very strange sort of upbringing." He smoothed a tiny wrinkle from his sleeve. "I shall, however, endeavor to see your shortcomings rectified."

Sir Reginald muttered something, then frowned. "Don't think you'll put me off the scent this time. Where *is* the woman?"

"Far away. In a place where she'll trouble you no more, my friend."

Sir Reginald heaved a sigh of relief. "Something deuced smoky about that female. And now I think of it, what about this talk I've been hearing? Something about that brother of Tony's—the one who died last year in a coaching accident."

"Ah, you mean Andrew." Alvanley's eyes hardened. "I'm afraid you don't know the half of it, dear boy." And then, as his friend began to frame another question, he started forward over the lawn. "Now I do believe I must offer my felicitations to the duchess. And as for our dear Wellington, I fear he must be given some gentle direction in his choice of cravats."

Behind him, Sir Reginald gave a long-suffering sigh and shrugged. It was clear that he would have no more questions answered this day.

"Lovely day. Yes, a most lovely day. And a charming ceremony. Nicest I can remember ever attending, in point of fact." The Duke of Wellington patted the duchess's arm and bent close. "By the way, thank you for rescuing me, Amelia. A positive shark, that female." He looked over the gaudy throng. "Ah, there are Viscount Ravenhurst and his lovely wife." He beckoned to the pair imperiously.

The viscountess was looking particularly luminous in a gown of emerald satin that set off the russet fire of her hair. Wellington made her a deep bow and then offered his arm. "Anytime you tire of that listless old navy dog, you let me know, my dear. We army men have a great deal more stamina, you understand."

Tess smiled. "Two of your officers have just been telling me the very same thing, Your Grace. Indeed, this rivalry with the navy seems to be of long standing." She sighed dramatically. "But it is part of our English character, I fear. If we fought our enemies with the same vigor that we fought each other, we would be unconquerable."

The duke gave a crack of laughter that sent heads around him bobbing. "Demned if you're not true to the mark, my dear!" He nodded at the viscount. "Keep her safe, Ravenhurst. Shouldn't want such a one as this to fall into enemy hands."

The lapis-eyed ex-naval officer smiled lazily. "I shall endeavor, Your Grace. I have reason to hope that the task may soon become less arduous."

"Oh? And why is that?"

The viscount gave his wife a rakish smile. "Because my blushing wife, who is right now shooting me such a furious look, is breeding."

"*Dane!*" Tess's cheeks flared crimson.

"Well, so you are, my dear, and I'm damned proud of the fact!"

"As well you should be, my boy." Wellington beamed upon the pair. "We need more stalwart sons to bear the English colors abroad."

Tess dimpled. "Forgive me, but what if this hypothetical son should decide to choose a career at sea? Or worse yet, what if this hypothetical *he* turns out to be a *she*?"

"I don't mean to deny that women do their part, my dear. Just as the navy does. But they must first learn their place, of course."

Tess's brow rose slightly. "And exactly who is it must learn their place, Your Grace—the women or the navy?"

"Why both, of course."

As he saw his wife's eyes begin to gleam, the viscount intervened smoothly. "I'm forever telling her she must rest more often now."

"Pooh! I'm as fit as I ever was." Tess looked at the duchess for support. "Surely you don't believe in such archaic notions, Your Grace."

Privately the duchess thought that the viscountess looked splendid and in no need of cossetting, but she chose the diplomatic course. "A little pampering never hurts, my dear. Make that husband of yours do some work for a change, that's my advice!"

At that moment the Duke of Hawkesworth strolled up, with his lovely wife on his arm. "What was that I just heard? Something about making us poor men work harder?"

The duchess snorted. "You're too pampered, the lot of you. I was just telling the viscountess that she needs to set that husband of hers to work. Especially now that she's breeding." As a clamor reached her ears, she turned. "What is creating all that commotion down on the lawn?"

"It is probably Rajah," Hawkesworth said dryly. "My wife's mongoose has yet to learn that the world does not fall prone at his arrival. I believe he was chasing a large brown frog with quite hideous spots."

"That would be Napoleon, no doubt." The duchess sighed. "I suppose I'd better go have a look. Unless I'm mistaken, two exceedingly silly females have just fainted dead away." With that withering comment the white-haired duchess moved off in search of new problems to solve.

Meanwhile Alexandra, the golden-haired Duchess of Hawkesworth, gave Tess a warm hug. "So you are to

have a child. How exciting!" The two women stepped a
little apart and began to talk animatedly.

Meanwhile, the three men did the same.

"Rest and plenty of quiet," the Duke of Hawkesworth was saying sagely. "Keep her still. *That's* what
she needs most right now."

Ravenhurst smiled. "That will be easier said than
done, I'm afraid."

Wellington looked thoughtful. "Send her to the
country. Let her redecorate the nursery, perhaps make
a few calls on the tenants. That should keep her nicely
occupied."

Meanwhile, the young Duchess of Hawkesworth was
offering her own brand of advice to Tess. "Plenty of
fresh air and sunshine. Good, vigorous exercise. Yes,
that's what you'll be needing now, my dear. Above all,
don't let him handle you like some fragile china doll.
Otherwise, you'll go demented with boredom within a
week." She gave Tess a mischievous smile. "As a matter
of fact, I've just had a capital idea. Perhaps we should
convince your husband to take us sailing to Greece on
that wonderful smuggling vessel of his."

"You mean the *Liberté*?" Tess nodded slowly, her
gray-green eyes gleaming. "It will be the perfect thing!"
With their heads together, the two women moved off,
already deep in plans for their seagoing adventure.

Meanwhile their husbands followed tranquilly. And
perhaps it was just as well that they were out of hearing
range.

This way they remained blissfully ignorant of the
escapades their wives had in store for them.

"We're going to have to run for it, my love." Tony
Morland was looking exceedingly handsome in crisp
black and fawn gray, with a single diamond winking at
his lapel.

He looked questioningly at his wife. "Unless you
care to endure more of these endless felicitations." He
fingered the long satin sleeve of her wedding gown,
brushing the tiny seed pearls clustered at her wrist.

"Although you deserve each and every encomium, my love. For you really are most extraordinary in that gown."

His bride of one hour offered him a deep curtsy. When she rose, her face was bright with mischief. "I'm sure your guests thought it was markedly eccentric of me." She slid her hand over the slim waist and full satin skirts. "But it felt right, somehow, to wear my mother's gown. Do you know what I mean? Considering that I had just found her again after so many years."

"I understand perfectly."

Tony brushed her cheek, and the sun glinted off Chessy's exquisitely worked filigree earrings of gold and precious stones. A matching bracelet gleamed at her wrist, the gift of the Duchess of Cranford, who had redeemed it from the jeweler on Curzon Street. He gave a quick glance over his shoulder. Two matrons in salmon-colored damask were bearing down on the gazebo where they were hiding. "Good Lord! Unless we hurry, we'll be captive here all afternoon."

Chessy gurgled. Lifting her skirts, she darted past him into the maze. Tony cornered her a few moments later. "Minx. Soon I'll have no reputation left."

"That's to repay you for tossing me over your shoulder and carrying me into the inn like a common—like a—well, you know."

Morland caught a glistening strand of blue-black hair and raised it to his lips. "Come now, my dear. I have said many things, but I have never called you common."

Chessy studied him suspiciously.

At that moment they heard soft laughter nearby. Chessy's head cocked. "But that was—"

The next second James Cameron and his wife rounded the corner.

Lizzie's hair was flowing loosely about her shoulders, and her cheeks were flushed most becomingly. "Chessy!" she gasped.

"Mother!"

"We were just—that is, James thought—"

Chessy's father laughed. "Chessy knows *exactly*

what I thought and has a fair notion of what we were doing, my dear. There's no need to explain to her."

His wife's flush increased. "But—"

"After all, she and Tony must have come here for precisely the same reason."

The Earl of Morland gave his old friend a roguish smile. "We had hoped to find a bit of privacy. I should have known you would map out every quiet corner in advance."

"Always pays to be prepared, my boy. I suggest you remember that." James looked at his wife. "Well, my dear? Shall we stroll about? Leave these two to their adventures?"

Lizzie was delighting in the sight of Chessy in her billowing white gown. Suddenly she looked down. James saw her brush away a tear.

Carefully he caught her chin and raised her face. "No tears, my dear. Not today."

"It's just—I'm so happy." She accepted the handkerchief he pressed into her hand, then turned to her daughter. "I—I know you still must be angry and hate me. I can't blame you for it. All those years wasted."

"*Hate* you? Impossible! I'm perfectly delighted to discover I have a mother after all this time." Chessy gave Lizzie a warm hug. "Besides, you look much too young to be my mother. Don't you agree, Father?"

James Cameron cleared his throat, preferring not to discuss his own opinions on the subject until he and his wife were in a more private place. "Come along, Lizzie," he said gruffly. "Let's let these children have some peace. And the sooner we've made *our* rounds, the sooner we can sneak away to our rooms."

"*James!* Whatever will Chessy and Tony think?"

"Think?" Cameron gave the couple a wry smile. "Why, the very same thing that we are, my dear."

"But they couldn't possibly!"

"No? If not then they'd better. Otherwise, how am I going to get that grandson I've been dying to dandle on my knee? And teach him all my new excavation techniques?"

Lizzie's chin rose defiantly. "Why, James Cameron,

you are without a doubt the *most* exasperating, the *most* rag-mannered man I have ever had the misfortune to meet! Just you come along right now. I have a few words to say to you, and I don't care for Chessy to hear me saying them."

James Cameron's brow rose. "Only a *few* words, my dear?" At his wife's look, he subsided meekly and allowed her to tug him off toward the gazebo. "You've got to show them who's boss, Tony," he called over his shoulder.

"Well, that's certainly showing *her*, Jamie." Morland was enjoying the sight of his friend's discomfiture greatly.

Meanwhile his wife dug her elbow into his ribs. "While we're at it, my lord, why don't you show *me*?" Her eyes glittered suspiciously. "Who's boss, that is."

"Oh, there was never the slightest doubt, my dear. *You* are, of course. You have been ever since that night you tossed me into the South China Sea for accusing you of having scrawny legs."

"Scrawny legs! I've never in my life had scrawny legs! Well, perhaps for a short while when I was eight. But—look here, I'll prove it to you." She lifted her skirts high, displaying calves encased in silk stockings and peach satin garters trimmed with rosettes of seed pearls. "You see," she said triumphantly.

"Indeed I do," the earl said hoarsely.

"And do you still say they're scrawny?"

"Not at all, my heart." Morland's eyes darkened. "Ah, Chessy." He moved closer. "That was really most unwise of you. I've been very patient, after all, but now that the ceremony is finally over, I don't think I can—"

He didn't finish. His wife had gathered her skirts and was making for the center of the maze. It seemed that she had spent her time profitably, too, for she moved unerringly to the only exit.

"Come back here, baggage!"

The sound of her laughter drifted to him on the wind.

Philosophically Morland flagged down a passing

servant and pocketed two etched crystal goblets and a bottle of chilled champagne.

His smile grew wolfish. As it happened, he knew a shortcut, too, one that even Chessy had not yet discovered. With thorough aplomb he walked right into a wall of greenery—

And chuckled as a hidden door opened, depositing him on the far side.

He caught his wife as she was just rounding the corner.

"Now, minx, you're going to pay and pay dearly!" He caught her wrist and began tugging her toward the trees beyond the maze.

"Tony? Where are you taking me?"

"You'll see."

"Tony, stop this second. I want to know where—"

Her husband pushed her back behind an ancient elm tree just as the duchess sailed over the hill, with the Duke of Wellington and two officers in tow. "I could have sworn I saw them here a second ago," the older woman said. "But why would Tony be avoiding me?"

Wellington took the duchess's arm firmly and steered her back toward the throng. "Perhaps, my dear Amelia, the young people wish to be alone. Newlyweds do occasionally desire that, you know."

As he steered her off, still protesting, the duke turned back and stared at the spot where Tony and Chessy were hiding. Tony poked his head out, and the duke gave him a conspiratorial wink.

"Now I see why the man was triumphant at Waterloo," Tony muttered. And then he caught Chessy's hand and tugged her over the smoothy clipped grass, where sunlight danced against dappled shadows.

Finally Tony stopped. Before him stood a vast oak tree with an elaborate spiral of wooden planks leading up to an elegant treehouse.

Chessy frowned at the lush foliage. Her amethyst eyes widened. "This isn't—"

Morland watched her face.

And then she began to smile. "Elspeth and Jeremy's treehouse?"

"They were most insistent, my love. Elspeth thought you wouldn't care to go far from home this first night. And she thought it would be the very best way for me to welcome you properly to Sevenoaks. At a place where we could be *very* private."

Chessy gasped. "Tony! Surely you didn't tell her that—well, about—"

"Of course I didn't. But sometimes I think that female is five years going on fifty! One would think so to see how she orders that urchin, Barnaby, about. And the boy positively dotes on her. I must remember to put Whitby on locating the lad's parents." He frowned. "But perhaps . . . that is, if you don't care for the treehouse—"

"It's a lovely idea! How clever of Elspeth to think of it."

"In that case, after you, my dearest love. I *would* carry you over the threshold, but this particular threshold is about thirty feet high." He gave her a crooked smile.

Chessy knew at that moment he was thinking of the knee that would always pain him. In his way he wanted to be sure that she realized he might always have this encumbrance.

She ran her hand gently across his cheek. "Unforgivably foolish, my love," she whispered, turning his own comment back upon him.

A muscle flashed at Tony's jaw. He caught her hand and brought it to his lips. "Someday I might figure out what I've done to merit such a woman as you, my heart. But until then . . ." Grinning rakishly, he reached into his pocket and displayed bottle and goblets.

"Quite prepared, aren't you, rogue!"

"Always, my dear!" He offered her an elegant bow. "After you."

Chessy caught up her voluminous satin skirts. Her husband's eyes darkened as he studied the expanse of creamy thigh and saucy peach-colored garters.

From over the hill came the sound of noisy laughter.

"Quick," Tony said urgently.

Up Chessy went, with her white skirts billowing and her long, lacy sleeves drifting in the sunlight.

Borne by a gust of wind, the white satin floated out, tickling Tony's cheek and dancing about his face. Struck with a devilish impulse, Morland bent slightly. "Good heavens, what are those lacy things you're wearing, wife?"

Chessy laughed down at him. "Those, my husband, are drawers."

"Never tell me you've taken up that outlandish bit of fashion. It's nothing short of scandalous!"

"Really?" Chessy's look was pure innocence. "Tess assured me it was all the rage. She brought them back for me from Paris. Did you know that she's a *smuggler*? In fact, she told me that if I promised to be very careful, she'd take me along with Dane when they—"

"Over my dead body!" Morland growled. "I can see I'm going to have to have a talk with Dane. That woman is too impulsive by half. And I won't have her enticing you into reckless escapades. As if you *needed* any encouragement!"

The white satin flew up once more, drifting about Morland's face.

He took another look beneath. "Drawers! By heaven, they're—they're nearly invisible, set with all that lace." His voice was growing hoarse.

"Tess tells me they drive men wild. And *she* should know, considering—" Chessy caught herself back with a groan.

"Considering *what*?"

"Oh, no! I wasn't supposed to tell."

"To tell what—that the woman is a hoyden? A minx?"

"No, that she's pregnant."

Morland froze. "Is she indeed? I was wondering how long it would be before—" He cleared his throat abruptly. "Well, at least that should keep her out of trouble for a while. Come to think of it, that should keep them *both* out of trouble." He moved up the steps, shaking his head. "Drawers, indeed."

And then he stopped. "What's that smell? If I

weren't sure it was impossible, I'd have sworn I smelled gardenias."

"So you did." Chessy smiled down at him. "That was the duchess's gift. She had it specially distilled from the blooms in her greenhouse." Chessy's eyelids fell. "She said that the flowers had worked once before, and she didn't see why they wouldn't work once again."

At that moment the wind gusted anew, giving Morland an unforgettable glimpse of peach satin and sheer white lace. His eyes closed and his fingers clenched upon the wooden slats. "May heaven preserve me."

Morland felt his blood begin to pound. Was this some kind of conspiracy? In a few more minutes he would go stark, raving mad! "Work?" His voice was smoky. "Work to do what, woman?"

"I have no idea. I was hoping you could tell me." Chessy's tongue moistened her lower lip delicately. "Or even better, I hoped you would show me."

He was doomed, Morland could feel it clearly. How was he to keep his head under this erotic onslaught? But confound it, this time he didn't want to be hurried! This time he wanted to be slow and masterful and exceedingly thorough, until Chessy was utterly wild for him.

And he'd do it too!

His hands tensed. "Go on, hoyden. And while you climb, you might as well tell me about any *other* surprises you have in store for me."

Laughing softly, Chessy swung her skirts up and slipped through the door to the tree house. Then she went absolutely still.

Inside, the wooden planks were covered with oriental rugs, which were strewn in turn with silken pillows. At the windows curtains of gold-shot crimson danced in the gentle wind.

"Oh, Tony!"

Morland shook his head in amazement. "Those two really are quite thorough. I must remember to congratulate them." His eyes turned smoky. "If I'm still able to talk when I climb down from here, that is."

"It's almost like our own little world up here, cut

off from everyone and yet close enough to hear and see. It's—it's lovely!" Wide-eyed, Chessy settled back against a pile of pillows.

Morland slid down next to her. "You're right. It *is* lovely." But he was looking at Chessy's cheeks, finely flushed from her climb. And at her hair, billowing out in an ebony cloud around her shoulders. "Impossibly lovely."

And then he spied the box in the corner. "More gifts?"

"The duchess must have had them brought up here. Alexandra has been ever so nice, you know. She said we're to go and visit at Hawkesworth whenever we like. Oh, and she promised me a baby mongoose too! Of course, I shall have to pass Rajah's test first. He's a very particular pet."

Morland did not look greatly thrilled by this offer.

"And *this* is her gift." Chessy held up a book.

"*The Female Instructor*? It sounds fascinating," he said dryly.

Chessy's nose wrinkled as she thumbed through the thick volume. I'm afraid it's not at all interesting." She opened to a page at random and began to read. " 'The general properties of the cold bath consist in its power of contracting the solid parts, and of dissipating the fluids. Any part of the body exposed to the sudden contact of cold water experiences at the same instant a degree of tension and contraction and becomes narrower and smaller.' " She sniffed. "Who would find that interesting?"

Morland, who had begun to think *he* needed a cold bath at that moment, gritted his teeth and concentrated on working the cork from the champagne bottle. Yet somehow all he could think of was lacy drawers and pearl-strewn garters.

And the silken thighs beneath.

His forehead was beaded with sweat by the time the cork finally exploded with a resounding crack and sailed out the treehouse window. Somewhere down below they heard a man curse in surprise.

Chessy began to giggle.

Morland's eyes gleamed. "Hard-hearted woman. Read me some more." Maybe that would help him keep his thoughts under control.

"Let's see. 'Irritability of the nerves may be mitigated by the cold bath. It overcomes their tendency to rigidity and other disagreeable sensations.' " Chessy looked up, frowning. "I wonder what sort of rigidity the book is talking about."

Morland filled her glass and pressed it into her hand. "I'm coming to have a fair idea," he muttered.

Chessy looked confused. "There are other chapters, you know. Cooking, for example. Here's a recipe for stewed ox-cheek. Another for pickled tongues. And one for lobster cakes."

Morland seized the book and tossed it in the corner. "I assure you, I have no need for lobster cakes, my dear," he said grimly. "I need nothing, in fact. Nothing but *you*."

"But—" Chessy wriggled free. "Oh, look. The Duke of Hawkesworth has given us a second book." She squinted down at the handwritten note. "It's called *The Per-fumed Gar-den*." She sounded out the words carefully. "It's never been translated, but he said—well, he told me not to open it until we—until you—"

Her face colored.

Tony began to smile. "Indeed. Then go ahead and open it, by all means. Because in a minute I am most certainly going to—"

Chessy looked down to hide her flush, quickly opening the book. "Lovely colors. And such a beautiful gold binding." And then her voice wavered. Her eyes widened. "But this is . . . I mean, they are . . ."

She flipped to the next page.

Tony smiled wolfishly. "You mean that it's rather like our pillow book, I think. Which is on its way to China right now. And good riddance, if you ask me. I only hope that our envoy will be able to keep it safe from the Triads. But enough of government problems!"

"What?" Chessy did not seem to hear. Frowning, she studied the couple on the page before her.

She turned the book sideways.

She turned the book upside down.

Finally, her head cocked to one side. "But Tony, how ever do they *do* that?"

"Very carefully, my love." Gently her husband removed the jewel-covered volume and tossed it onto the coverlet, then tugged Chessy down on top of him. "And with a great deal of practice, I suspect."

Chessy's amethyst eyes began to gleam. "Should you like to—practice, my lord? With me?"

Morland groaned. First erotic underclothes, then seductive perfume, and now an excruciatingly sensual pillow book. He shook his head. "Something tells me that life with you is going to be anything but boring, Cricket. Now be quiet, woman."

Chessy's head slanted back. "Why?"

"So I can kiss you, of course. And so that we can begin our *practicing*."

Chessy offered him her most alluring smile. Her dress slid slowly from her shoulder. "My dear forever friend," she said huskily. "I thought you would never ask."

Author's Note

Dear Reader:

I hope you have enjoyed *East of Forever*. (I also hope that Tony will stop bothering me now that I've given him his own story!)

I confess that it has been an unadulterated delight to bring you this headstrong but vulnerable pair of lovers. And of course I had the added pleasure of recalling four more of my favorite people: Alexandra, Hawke, Tess, and Dane.

As with my other books, *East of Forever* is based upon historical fact. After the Congress of Vienna in 1815, the British resolved to send a delegation to the Chinese court. Their purpose was to negotiate for free trade and an opening of more northern ports to British ships. The leader of the delegation, Lord Amherst, was the former governor of India.

The Chinese emperor, Chia-ch'ing, was singularly uninterested, however. China needed nothing that England had to offer. English woolens and manufactured goods were considered of no importance.

Upon his arrival in China, Lord Amherst made it clear that he refused to perform the correct Chinese ritual of respect to the emperor. Called the *kowtow*, this involved three kneelings and nine complete prostrations during which the head was knocked against the floor. As a result, Amherst was denied an audience with the emperor and sent on his way back to England.

The Amherst mission (like an earlier mission in 1793, which cost the English government a staggering seventy-eight thousand pounds) was a complete and very expensive failure. Other attempts at diplomacy also failed to convince the Chinese that they should welcome permanent diplomats or open their ports to trade. As an earlier Chinese emperor had written, "We possess all things. I set no value on objects strange or ingenious, and have no use for your country's manufactures." (Immanuel Hsu. *The Rise of Modern China*. New York: Oxford University Press, 1970, p. 206.) Of course, all of this was soon to change. As the eighteenth century ended, the amount of opium smuggled from India to China rose dramatically. Between 1817–1834 smuggled opium amounted to three quarters of Britain's total China trade. There, too, hangs a tale, but that one will have to wait for a future book!

Suffice it to say that when the Amherst mission failed, diplomatic contact between England and China nearly ceased. The British soon adopted harsher measures. Military strength and gunboat diplomacy became the rule. Tony Morland was correct in seeing the importance of resolving the problem peaceably as soon as possible.

Of course, I like to believe that English attempts at diplomacy failed because the Triads finally managed to find Chessy's pillow book and then used it in their *own* negotiations with the emperor. If so, we will never know. What respectable historian—Chinese or British—would have recorded such a thing?

After Waterloo, Wellington continued to occupy an important position in British government. Unfortunately, his personal life was marked by unhappiness. An austere man with an abrupt manner, he completely overshadowed his timid, retiring wife. He had little tolerance for indecision or error and he began to regret his marriage almost immediately. As he remarked to his longtime confidante Mrs. Arbuthnot, "In short, I was a fool." Divorce was out of the question, however, and the two lived separately until his wife's death in 1831.

Puffer, or blowfish, which figured in Tony's attack, contains one of the most toxic poisons known to man. Known as tetrodotoxin, it is twenty-five times more potent than curare. Every year a small number of diners die from eating improperly prepared *fugu*, as this delicacy is known in Japan. As one Japanese poet put it, "Last night he and I ate *fugu* together; today I carry his coffin."

Yet the fascination with the fish continues. Although avidly sought after by gourmets, *fugu* should never be consumed except in restaurants where trained chefs are licensed to prepare it. (And even then, I suspect, only after some careful consideration. . . .)

The warrior-monks of Shao-lin have been famous in China for centuries. Legend has it that the martial arts were originated by no less than the Buddhist patriarch Bodhidharma (A.D. 448–527), the founder of Ch'an Buddhism. Over the centuries the Shao-lin Temple in China's Henan Province has been built and destroyed many times. In the late eighteenth century the Manchu rulers of China finally ordered the building razed, since they believed it was a source of plots to overthrow the government. (They were right; it was.)

But monks continued to train and practice in secrecy, and today many famous schools of martial arts trace their parentage back to Shao-lin. For an interesting account of a Western student of martial arts who has developed his own principles of training and awareness, readers might enjoy *Cheng Hsin: The Principles of Effortless Power*, by Peter Ralston (Berkeley: North Atlantic Books, 1989).

Last, but not least, literacy continues to be an issue of serious concern today. A recent U.S. study revealed, for example, that 80 percent of sampled adults could not read a bus schedule, 63 percent couldn't follow written map instructions, and 73 percent could not understand a newspaper story. It is estimated that 15 million adults holding jobs in the U.S. today are functionally illiterate. This figure grows by 2.2 million a year (44,000 per week). It is further estimated that the cost of illiteracy to businesses and taxpayers is $20 billion per year.

In Philadelphia, the Mayor's Commission on Literacy is working to develop resources and coordinate citywide efforts to help adults learners. (For more information about the national Gateway program, you are invited to call [800] 766-2828.)

For referral nationwide to literacy programs in your local community, call (800) 228-8813—the National Literacy Hotline.

Finally, I want to thank all of you who have sent such enthusiastic and inspiring letters about *Defiant Captive*, *The Black Rose*, and *The Ruby*. I am glad my books have brightened a rainy day or helped you hyperventilate through a midnight hour or two. If you would like to receive a signed bookmark and my current newsletter with information about past characters, upcoming books, and odd research tidbits, please send a stamped, self-addressed envelope (legal-size works best) to me at:

> 111 East Fourteenth Street, #277-E
> New York, New York 10003

I would love to hear from you.

In the meantime, I hope you'll turn the page for an excerpt from my next Dell historical. A clue? I've always had a soft spot for a highwayman! A very *dashing* highwayman, that is.

Set in the Regency period, *Come the Night* is the poignant story of two volatile, intensely stubborn, and very passionate people on a collision course. I hope you'll watch for it in the summer of 1994.

With warmest regards,

Christina Skye

Christina Skye

◇

Be sure to watch for Christina Skye's exciting new historical romance, *Come the Night*, appearing in the summer of 1994. We hope you enjoy the following excerpt from the first chapter of
COME THE NIGHT.

◇

The moon was full. The wind was high. All in all, it was a perfect night for revenge.

He sat his horse easily, reins clasped loosely in gloved fingers as he watched the distant ribbon of silver where the road curved east toward the Norfolk coast.

He knew every rock and shrub of that road, every twist and every spot that offered concealment. He had walked it, studied, dreamed over it. And now he was ready.

Grim-faced, the rider slid a mask of black silk down over his chiseled features, down over the single scar that gleamed cold at his full lower lip.

He had no more time for dreams and regrets. Not tonight.

For it was midnight and the heath was trapped in shadow.

It was time for the Lord of Blackwood to ride again.

The small inn room was crowded, thick with drifting smoke and the pungency of cheap spirits.

"What price do I hear for the wench?"

Half-drunken mumbling met this challenge.

"Come, my friend. Are you men or beardless boys to

refuse such a chance to sample female beauty? Look you there. The wench is flawless, her skin as smooth as damask."

The five men clustered around the smoke-ringed table sat forward. Their bloodshot eyes narrowed as they tried to make out the image of the woman revealed through the hole in the inn room wall.

The concealing curtain was sheer, but they could see little more than a luscious silhouette.

"Who's to say she's all you claim, Milbanke? You fleeced us grand last time, so you did. I paid three hundred pounds to sleep with an untouched virgin and instead I found a poxed doxy fresh up from Falmouth!"

"Gentlemen, gentlemen." The man at the head of the table waved an airy hand. His florid features eased into a practiced smile. "A slight miscalculation, I assure you. My, shall we say, *supplier* did not understand the exactness of our club's requirements. 'Only a female of flawless form. And only a virgin untouched and unblemished.' That *is* our motto, after all." He moved to the wall and slid the shielding silk from the viewing hole. "And *that* is exactly what you find before you."

The woman went on combing her long golden hair around shoulders covered by the sheerest of peignoirs.

"She will be submissive?" A balding squire with whiskey on his waistcoat studied Sir Charles Milbanke uneasily. "Won't do to have her screaming down the house when she finds what's to happen to her."

"She will be well prepared, never fear."

"Then you've drugged her?" The question came from the squire's son, a raw-boned youth of nineteen. "Not too much, I hope. A wench without fight is never good sport."

The squire snorted at his son. "As if you'd have any chance of winning the bid. You've no money to speak of, young fool."

"I've enough to top any stingy bid of yours!"

Sir Charles intervened as the pair seemed ready to come to cuffs. "Gentlemen, a little decorum, please. The rules of our confederation demand strict order at our meetings. Now what price do I hear for the delectable piece of womanhood in the neighboring room? Three hundred pounds? Four hundred?"

"What about Silver?" The squire's son sat forward. Lust gleamed in his muddy eyes. "It's her as what you've been promising us this six months and more!"

The other men began to mutter. The word "Silver" ran from one man's lips to the next.

"Aye, what about Silver?" The squire slammed his tankard down upon the rough-hewn table. "To taste her, I'd pay twice four hundred pounds and more!"

Sir Charles Milbanke scowled at the mention of his beautiful sister-in-law. Once again she thwarted him!

But he was careful to keep all traces of anger from his face. "The Lady Silver St. Clair is being readied. When the time is opportune she will be offered for bidding, just as promised. But until that time . . ." He snapped the peephole closed and turned, glaring at the assembled men. "Of course, if you do not care to bid now, you will not be informed when my sweet little sister-in-law goes up for auction. And that is something you will regret dearly, gentlemen, I assure you."

A harsh silence gripped the room. Every man's breath caught as he envisioned the silken beauty of Silver St. Clair's skin, the husky timbre of her voice, and the glory of her sandy-colored hair.

"By God, I'll stand for two hundred." The squire's son leaped to his feet and tossed down a purse full of gold guineas.

"Three hundred." His father followed, not to be outdone.

As the bidding leaped to a furious pitch, Sir Charles sat back in his chair. Smiling thinly, he steepled his thick fingers.

Yes, his beautiful, despised sister-in-law was going to bring him a great deal of money this night. And if he was very clever, she would bring him even more than money. . . .

Across the heath, where the yews coiled thick and the rooks cried shrilly against the rising wind, a mounted rider plunged over the rocky ground that bordered the fens. Patches of fog rose in strange, swirling spirals. Pale and cold, they lapped at horse and rider, but the lonely traveler spurred desperately forward.

The Lady Silver St. Clair was abroad late this night, far too late for safety or peace of mind, and she meant to make up for lost time by taking a shortcut through Worrington's Wood.

Or the Devil's Wood, as it was known hereabouts.

Her fingers were not quite steady as she touched the ivory cameo pinned to the lace at her throat.

Never mind that the forest was said to be haunted.

Never mind that a carriage was said to have disappeared in its shadowed depths just a week before.

The treasure she carried this night demanded bold measures. And if her odious brother-in-law Sir Charles got home before she did and discovered her plans, all would be lost.

But what if you meet the Lord of Blackwood? This is his domain, after all.

Silver could almost hear the mocking question. In answer, she tossed her hair over her shoulder and slid her silver-handled pistol closer within reach inside her cuff.

"If so, I shall simply dispatch the notorious highwayman, as someone should have done long ago!"

But the wind seemed to catch her words and toss them back in her face, shrill and cold.

Silver shivered, hugging her black cape closer about her shoulders. It was chilly for May, chilly for a Norfolk spring. She frowned, wondering if she should cover her newly sprouted lavender beds with the sheets of fine linen she kept for times of unseasonable cold.

She had spent too many days of backbreaking work to lose her beloved lavender crop to the vagaries of a cold Channel wind now. . . .

She was just calculating how to drape the fabric about the young plants when slashing hooves hammered out of the darkness behind her. She had no time to prepare, no moment to turn aside.

And there was no hope of escape.

For only one man dared to ride this unhallowed stretch of heath, only one man whose eyes gleamed like the brimstone of Hell itself.

The Black Lord. A lace-clad highwayman who spoke with the elegance of a gentleman—and killed with the precision of a hardened assassin.

And it was he who bore down upon Silver now.

Wildly, she spurred her mare, aiming for the dense forest to her left. At the same time she wrenched her pistol from her sleeve.

Behind her, hooves rang harsh like metal upon metal. Black horse, black rider thundered closer in the black night.

Biting back a cry, Silver hunched forward, urging her mare to go faster.

But no horse was a match for the black stallion that raced behind her, a horse said to be sired of the legions of Hell itself.

Only ten yards until the tree line. If only she could . . .

But her wild hope was crushed in the next instant. The black stallion pulled alongside her, eyes straining, sparks cast like hellfire from his great hooves.

And then Silver was flying upward, caught in iron fingers while her terrified mount dashed away into the forest.

"Oooh!" She collided with a velvet-clad chest pungent with the smell of brandy and tobacco. Clawing wildly, she fought the hands that slung her up before the saddle.

"Ho, Diablo." A man's voice cut through the taut silence. Harsh and deep, it carried just a hint of foreignness. "We've company now, so mind your manners."

Somehow Silver found her legs trapped beneath a male thigh and her wrists secured in one large and very powerful male palm.

Suddenly Silver remembered her nanny's oft-repeated warnings over the years. *Don't look at his eyes! Aye, one look into those demon eyes of glowing amber and ye'll be lost, my girl, for he's as fair as he is foul, that devil's son!*

But that was superstitious claptrap, Silver told herself fiercely. It was flesh and blood that held her now.

And flesh and blood could be tamed—or at least made to bleed.

She shoved free of his hand. The next minute her pistol was aimed at his black mask. "Put me down, you fiend, or you'll taste my powder between your t-teeth!"

His lips eased back in a slow smile. "So I've caught

myself a spitfire, have I?'' His voice caressed her like the smoking peat fires that burned here on cold autumn nights. Rough-soft, it was. Dark, like finest whiskey. ''Who dares to breach my domain by night?''

Silver locked her lips.

''Come, tell me what name graces such beauty?''

''No name that *you* may claim the right to!''

''So the Black Lord's reputation outpaces him, does it!'' The rider threw back his head and laughed. The sound seemed to work through the very fabric of Silver's cloak and caress her trembling skin.

''Your reputation is known all too well, you fiend. Now unhand me or I'll send a ball through your grinning face.''

The highwayman reined his mount to a trot. Smiling still, he eased back in his saddle until Silver was pulled down atop him in the most wanton sort of sprawl. ''Unhand me, you brute! I vow I shall sh-shoot you otherwise!''

''And where do you plan to aim first, my beauty? Atop my nose? Between my brows? Or is it to be through the eye itself? I'm told that way is most effective, although you might find it a trifle hard on that elegant lace of yours. Bloodstains prove so tedious to remove, after all.''

The villain was laughing at her! Silver's blood burned as she watched his eyes move lazily over her heaving chest. She tightened her fingers and moved the pistol to his neck. ''*Here* will do perfectly, I think. And never doubt that I shall do it!''

His voice came low and silken. ''By all means, my sweet. Go ahead and pull the trigger. I've tasted all the delights of a life misspent. I might as well see what death has to offer.''

The coldness of his voice made her shiver. ''But surely—that is, you cannot *wish* to die. No one does.''

Her captor gave a shrug. ''There is so little spice left, my beauty. You can have no idea how trying life becomes when one has tasted every vice and gratified every whim.''

''In that, you are right,'' Silver said stiffly. ''I have no idea of such wantonness.''

But her breast was shoved against his arm while she

spoke, and this robbed her disapproving speech of its sting. Flushing, she tried to squirm away from him, only to feel her hip lodge against the saddle of his thighs.

None of which escaped the notorious highwayman's notice.

He shifted beneath her, bringing her lower still, until she came into full and heated contact with his exceedingly aroused male anatomy.

Silver gasped. She tried to struggle to a seated posture but found it rather like trying to fight upright against a Channel wind. "L-let me go, you—you brute!"

"I think not, my beauty." Amber eyes blazed through the slitted silk. "Not until I have your name. And perhaps more than that . . ."

"You shall have neither my name, nor anything else from me this night!" Closing her eyes, Silver shoved her pistol downward, somewhere in the vicinity of his shoulder. "I warn you, I know how to fire this weapon. And I shall most certainly use it! Any—any second, in f-fact."

"By all means, fire away, my dear."

Her eyes snapped open. "You—you damnable creature! I *will* fire, I warn you!"

"Of course you will," the highwayman observed calmly. "As soon as your fingers stop shaking. After all, it would hardly be good form to leave me lying bloody and only half dead out here upon the heath."

"I could hardly miss at this distance!"

"Ah, but your aim seems rather in question, my dear. Never done this sort of thing before, have you?" His tone was utterly sympathetic.

Silver looked down, furious when she saw that her hand was shaking violently. "Oh, bloody Jupiter!"

But the rakish highwayman who had faced death with utter equanimity suddenly froze. His fingers tightened on her waist. "Be still."

"Why should I even consider—"

"Silence, I said!"

The flat violence of his command left her breathless.

The Black Lord slid back into the shadows, turning his mount to face the glimmering strip of road visible in the dim moonlight to the north.

And then Silver heard it, the quick clip-clop of hooves, coming fast.

Her pistol was wrested from her trembling fingers. Sputtering furiously, she tried to regain it, only to feel a hard hand clamped across her mouth.

"Quiet now, little love. It appears that my domain is to be breached a second time this night." The highwayman stared down at her. "I'd advise you not to move. You are very delectable, you see, and you might not care for the consequences."

Silver gasped as she felt taut muscle drive against her hip. Her face flooded crimson.

"Exactly," her captor said grimly.

Don't listen to him, Silver told herself wildly. *Above all, don't look into his eyes!*

But it was too late. She stared deep into the amber fires gleaming behind his mask and shuddered. Heat swept her cheeks. The night became a thing of heat and storm and fury.

His full lips curved in a mocking smile. "A grave mistake, little one. You have looked into my eyes and that makes you mine. For 'tis all true, my beauty, every grim tale and black deed that legend assigns me. The Lord of Blackwood has done them all, I assure you. So do not think to trifle with me." As if to strengthen this warning, his fingers tightened on her waist.

A moment later three riders broke from the wooded vale. Their faces were muffled in dark wool and their pistols gleamed chill in the moonlight.

"Damn it, where'd the wench go? I could have sworn—"

"Her horse! It's over there!"

"But where's the bloody female?"

Silver felt a knot of fear block her throat. She watched in horror as the riders pulled her mare to a halt and jumped down to claw at her saddlebags. But she had nothing of value there. Nothing except . . .

He face paled. She felt the highwayman's fingers tighten.

It had to be a mistake, of course. They could not really be looking for *her*!

"Aye, she's a bold piece, that St. Clair bitch. But even *she'd* not venture into the Devil's Wood at night.

She must be farther down the hill. Maybe her horse threw her."

His companions laughed roughly. "That'd be a sight, lads. Let's go enjoy it!"

The trio wheeled about and disappeared, but Silver's horror only grew. They knew her name. And they had followed her here. There could be no more doubt that they had come for *her* and her alone.

"Friends of yours?"

She twisted her head, trying to avoid the harsh probe of those unnatural eyes. "I h-have no idea who they are."

"But it appears they knew exactly what they were looking for, my dear. What treasure do you carry that escaped my eye?"

With a quick thrust he lifted his leg over the saddle and slid to the ground, with Silver still locked tight against his chest.

They landed upon the heath with a thump. She was up and struggling even before her breath was restored. Thrusting her russet curls from her face, she scrambled toward the road.

And then she felt a prick, the slightest of pricks, at her shoulder.

She turned slowly—and stared down the gleaming length of a polished silver blade.

The rapier rose and gently lifted a strand of hair from her shoulder. Silver shivered, feeling the man's control as he brushed the lace at her neck and skimmed the cameo pinned there.

"A nice enough bobble, but hardly worth the interest of those ruffians. You see, I know all the men who work these roads. That particular trio will perform any task for a fee, but they are singularly expensive. Which means that someone thought the job worth doing well."

His eyes narrowed. His rapier slid lower, into the lace clustered at her bodice.

The next second his steel sliced off two buttons, leaving her riding jacket and underbodice to fall open over creamy skin.

"Stop that! You cannot—"

He ignored her, moving with lightning skill and a

grace that left her feeling only the barest kiss of wind upon her skin.

This time her chemise was slit. And then the velvet ribbon beneath.

With one quick twist he found the small linen bag she wore and captured it on his blade.

"Noooo! Give it back. It's all I have to—"

The highwayman's eyes narrowed. "Do continue, my dear. You interest me vastly. What is all you have? And why is it so valuable as to provoke this heated outburst?"

"N-nothing." Her lips clenched. "It's . . . nothing at all."

He fingered the small and rather unimpressive piece of linen.

His nose curled. Frowning, he brought the bag close and sniffed. "Lavender? A very elegant scent, of course, but hardly worth—"

"Give it back to me!" Silver launched out, her fingers flying wildly for his masked face. "It's *mine!* Those seeds are all I—"

In her fury she knocked the bag from his fingers. Her face bled white as the precious seeds, the result of five years of planting, scattered over the forest floor. "Oh, no! They cannot—"

Silver bit back a sob. It was all gone. With the loss of those seeds she had surrendered any hope of independence from her hated brother-in-law!

A single tear spilled from her silver-green eyes.

"It was of such value then?" Her captor frowned. "A token from a lover perhaps? Or some family memento?"

Silver rounded on him, her pale face flushed with two bright spots of color at her cheeks. "What do *you* know about such things? What would a villain like yourself know of hard work? Of backbreaking days spent in blazing sun or a chill Norfolk drizzle? And now it's gone, all gone. I can never hope to—" She caught herself with a sob and swung her head down, away from that piercing amber gaze that refused to let her go.

"Come, my sweet. It can hardly be so bad as that."

Oh, but it was. *It was all that bad and more,* Silver

thought wildly. But there was no point in telling this ruffian that.

Breathlessly, she turned away, wiping a line of tears from her cheek.

But his fingers slid over her chin and forced her to look up at him. She closed her eyes, avoiding his strange, amber stare.

And then she gasped as he seized her small hands and raised them, palms up. "Yet again, you astound me, little beauty," he whispered. He frowned, running his fingers over her callused skin. "So you actually have done all those things you spoke of." Slowly he drew one work-rough finger to his mouth.

Silver shuddered as his lips brushed her palm. Heat seemed to flow wherever he touched.

"So you are in service to Lady St. Clair. She must work you hard that you wear such calluses. Did you borrow her riding costume tonight? Is that why you were hurrying home so rashly? Did you mean to return it before she discovers your theft?"

"It was no theft!"

"Of course not." The man's full lips curved slightly. "Merely a loan." His mouth curved around the base of one finger and his teeth tugged at the sensitive curve of skin.

Silver shuddered. What was *wrong* with her? Why were her knees shaking so strangely?

Her captor drew her slowly closer. His hand slid deep into her wild auburn hair.

She had to get away! She had to get home before—

"Give me your name," the highwayman demanded hoarsely. "I must know to whom I've lost my heart." He spoke softly, but there was an edge of darkness, a hint of hunger in his voice that made Silver's heart do odd little flip-flops in her chest.

"Silver."

"Pardon?"

Her eyes widened. "You are French?"

The scar gleamed at his full lips. "I am . . . many things, little one. But why this word?"

Once again something kept Silver from correcting the story he had proposed. Yes, it would be far safer if he believed her only a lowly servant and not the Lady St. Clair.

"Because it is my name."

"Silver." He repeated the name slowly, measuringly. "It suits you. I should have expected nothing less. For you appear quite exceptional, my dear. And something tells me you've eyes to match your name, if only this damnable light were better."

He sounded genuinely angry that the gloom hid her face. For a moment Lady Susannah St. Clair forgot about her vicious brother-in-law, forgot about her dogging poverty, forgot even about the precious lavender seeds that now lay scattered upon the damp earth.

Such was the power of the man's charm. She understood now how the Lord of Blackwood had acquired his vast reputation as a seducer of women. And in spite of that, though she knew she should be fighting to escape, she felt oddly reluctant to pull away from the warm brush of his lips against her hand.

Not that she could have escaped him anyway. At that moment her legs possessed all the strength of mounded blancmange, she guessed.

"And what if I restore those lavender seeds you place such value on?"

Her eyes widened. Hope surged through her. "Could you? Oh, w-would you?"

"I might be persuaded. For a small token."

"What manner of . . . t-token?" Her voice, usually low, now fell even lower. She knew the risk she took in opening any sort of negotiation with a hardened criminal such as this.

The catch in her voice made her captor's eyes glitter strangely. It made his fingers tighten, sheathed deep in her warm, brandy hair. It made his body go tense and made him yearn to tug that silly little riding hat from her head, then push her down beneath him while he bared her silken skin.

But he did not. He told himself that he had not yet stooped so low as that. "Token? Not your brooch, for you can ill afford to lose that, since it, too, must belong to your mistress." His lips curled. "Not that it's worth much except as an inferior copy." He saw her tense and gnaw at her lower lip. "No, not your virtue either, little fool. Acquit me of the offense of ravishing virgins."

Her eyes widened. "But everyone says—"

"My crimes are legion, sweet, but they do not run to *that,*" her captor growled.

"Oh." And then a second realization came to Silver. "But how did you know . . ." Again her cheeks flamed.

"That you're a virgin?" The highwayman known as Blackwood smiled darkly. "Oh, any number of reasons, my dear." His rapier toyed with a dark curl that had strayed across her cheek. "Because of the pulse that beats there at your neck. Because of the flush that stains your satin cheeks. They make incontrovertible evidence, little one. To experienced eyes like mine, that is."

There was bitterness and something else in his voice. Something hard. Something that sounded almost like regret.

It made Silver frown. "It must be a great trial to you, this life you lead. Dashing about the heath courting death. Dogged everywhere by languishing females just waiting to be seduced. It cannot be very . . . well, *pleasant.*"

The highwayman broke into a startled laugh. "And so it is rather a trial. Alas, there is such riffraff upon the High Road these days, and all of them claim their felonies in my name." Abruptly he sheathed his rapier, then frowned down into her shadowed face. "But what would a slip of a thing like *you* know about seduction and languishing females?"

Silver shrugged. "Oh, not so very much. We live very quietly here." There was regret in her voice for a moment. Then she drew herself up to her full five and one-quarter feet. "But I am not *totally* without contact with the world, I assure you."

The amber eyes gleamed lazily. "Somehow I did not expect you were, my sweet."

Silver blinked at the softness that crept into his voice. Suddenly she felt excessively dizzy, hot and cold at once. It was not precisely uncomfortable, this feeling—but it was not entirely pleasant either.

Certainly it was unusual. Silver had never before

felt this way in the presence of any man. Perhaps it was sheer shock that held her still.

She saw his eyes darken and realized his intention. Yet even then she did not move or cry out as she should have.

"You . . . cannot," she whispered. "I should not even think of—"

His eyes glittered. "All too true, little one. But it's too late for running. And though my dark domain has many roads leading into it, not one of them leads out again."

His lips curled. The movement made the scar at his mouth gleam. "Besides, you have looked into my eyes. Now you are mine forever . . ."

And then his mouth swept down, hot and hard atop hers. Silver closed her eyes, shivering, knowing what he said was true.

She was lost, well and truly lost, just as her old nanny had warned.

And as his full lips opened over hers, Silver decided she didn't even care. . . .